I0717293

THE NIGHT BAZAAR LONDON

TEN TALES OF FORBIDDEN WISHES AND DANGEROUS DESIRES

EDITED BY LENORE HART

NORTHAMPTON HOUSE PRESS

THE NIGHT BAZAAR
LONDON

. . . London was drab and grey; was exploding in colour; was a raucous din, bursting with life; was eerily quiet, haunted by ghosts and graveyards.

—R.F. Kuang,
*Babel, or the Necessity of Violence:
An Arcane History of the Oxford
Translators' Revolution*

I wants to make your flesh creep.

—Charles Dickens,
The Pickwick Papers

TABLE OF CONTENTS

WELCOME, GENTLE STRANGER.
The Night Bazaar is once again open . . . to you.

It goes without saying that those allowed into our secret gathering must be Invited in some way. . . by an elaborate, handwritten note which later vanishes, perhaps. Or an oddly-worded message on a mobile phone. A tap on the shoulder in a crowd, or the furtive beckoning of a pale hand thrust from some darkened alleyway.

So—congratulations! You, Dear Reader, have been admitted, having only received a singular Invitation, which is seldom repeated. Thus, if this is *not* your first sojourn with us, you're indeed among the fortunate few; those souls for whom Fate has granted access to our fantastical fairgrounds more than once in a lifetime. And I, Madame Vera, shall be your guide.

Of course we know what you must be wondering now: *To what secret places will the peripatetic denizens of the Bazaar take me this time?*

To you alone shall we reveal our current destination: London of the 1880s. We'll wend our way down its cobbled lanes, pale tendrils of fog curling about our shins like the tails of hungry, inquisitive cats. Strolling to corners of that rapidly-industrializing City where, when one inhales, they're greeted by mingled notes of coal smoke, wood fires, cheap gin, over-brewed tea . . . and sometimes, the coppery tang of blood.

Dirty Old London, as it's often called in this era, may be the seat of power for the largest empire the world's ever known, but it's also infamously filthy. Wood-smoke, grime, sooty fog, horse-dung and piss-spattered mud, slimy dark alleys, and penny-a-visit public toilets . . . though mostly only for men. And the Thames . . . well, better to drink (and perhaps even bathe in) only ale and beer, or thrice-boiled tea. For the waters of that historic river are also a popular repository for London's garbage, dead livestock, human corpses, and all the flushings of domestic waste and acrid factory runoff. Frankly, this aspect of the City does indeed make one shudder. As sometimes does the menu, so heavily dependent on mutton, glutinous fish, bacon, brown sauces, and overcooked potatoes. Not to mention steamed "puddings" with such unsettling names as "spotted dick."

In any case, amid crumbling mews and dank basements, tottering tenements and millionaires' mansions, our accompaniment will be the cries of costermongers pushing barrows of shellfish, the rumble of fashionable carriage-wheels over cobblestones, the cheeky jibes of grimy-faced newsboys, and the shrill entreaties of consumptive violet-sellers.

Of course, our Bazaar is unconstrained by such pedestrian concepts as Time and Space. Thus, gentle Guest, be forewarned: there may also be the occasional temporal judder backward or forward. One moment you're browsing the Victorian mercantile shops near Kensington, and the next reading texts in a luxurious hotel suite in present-day London, only to find yourself suddenly trudging through a muddy, raucous medieval marketplace. Expect the odd detour from 1880s Baker Street, to 1960s Carnaby Street, to the 1530s Tower of London, to contemporary Park Lane, and beyond—and do try and keep your wits about you.

Now, should the Invited wish to dress for the occasion, feel free to ascend to the attic and plunder steamer trunks and chests, pulling out those old miniskirts and Nehru jackets . . . or slashed doublets and gartered hose, if you prefer. The Night Bazaar shuns the very notion of a dress code, though we understand one does like to feel appropriately attired for an adventure.

Oh, and regarding the sudden appearance of this (no doubt unexpected) Invitation, as well as the vague nature of your destination: We assure you, there's nothing to fear. Well, *almost* nothing . . . for one should never feel *too* comfortable while in the midst of a gathering which knows no limits, save those of the human imagination . . . and sometimes, perhaps not even those.

But I digress. For here, from midnight to dawn, amongst the oddities, antiques, forbidden entertainments, unusual services, and hauntingly exotic wares, you'll see a host of strange faces along with a few familiar ones. The ubiquitous ghosts, witches, Fae, and Hidden Folk, as well as modern (and not at all modern) denizens; human, beastly, mechanical, conjured, and otherwise. Rest assured my loyal staff of money-changers, jongleurs, dancers, tumblers, fortune tellers, mountebanks, accountants, players, and masked purveyors of oddities are always at your service. Whatever is strange, questionable, and averse to the light of day can be discovered here; you need only browse our endless aisles.

The Bazaar, however, cannot simply be stumbled upon and found. For our tents and stalls are pitched each night in a different secret locale, for seven evenings in a row—to move on at the end of the week and never return to that city again. So please bear in mind that, throughout your visit, one simple rule universally applies. You, the Invited, will enjoy our offerings for what at least *seems* to be a single night only.

Ah, but what a night it will be! We guarantee an unforgettable outcome, and have never yet been wrong about that . . .

Two aisles over, inside this tall tent resides a shop called The Doll Hospital, whose proprietor maintains shelves of artfully-mended stuffed toys, toy soldiers, puppets and marionettes, and of course dolls. For example, see this delicate porcelain-faced lady, so beautifully dressed in hand-stitched green velvet? Her real human hair is swept up in an elegant chignon, her dainty feet clad in satin slippers. She appears new, but is actually a very old plaything just refurbished by the skilled hands of the shop's toy-mender. Who nevertheless intentionally did not repair one highly-visible flaw: A stain like a port-wine birthmark that mars one side of the doll's otherwise smooth porcelain face. Why, you wonder? The reasons will become quite clear, once you know her story . . .

Broken Little Hand Me Downs
by Corinne Alice Nulton

To say that Little Ben had mixed feelings about staying at his grandmother's house was an understatement. Of course he had to go. His parents were always off somewhere: touring the Continent, or at the next high-society London cocktail party befitting their station. And it seemed to him Mummy and Papa were always happy to abandon him to his forgetful grandmother and addled great-aunt. The first of whom kept endlessly asking about relatives that, as far as he knew, didn't exist. The second of whom called him Benjamin Bear, though his name was simply Ben.

Grandmama Guinevere was kind. She baked him rich, sticky-sweet treats and taught him how to read from her bedtime storybooks of kings and castles. She spoiled him with fancy new toys. Brutus the wooden horse had been one such a gift. Yes, *she* did the things Grandmamas were supposed to do.

About Great Aunt Loretta he felt less sure. She had a bedroom in the Tower and came downstairs mostly just for meals. Sometimes she drifted into Little Ben's nursery and sat and watched him play. Cooing at the make-believe scenes he created, or shrieking with laughter. Once, to his horror, she'd even wept. But he hated being watched, as if he was on a stage.

Grandmama Gwen had told him, "My sister is merely remembering, and reliving something from our past."

What, though? Neither would say. And then, as if her spying wasn't creepy enough, sometimes as he played at soldiers or with his barnyard set, Etta would hold out an old broken doll with a smashed face, or a toy knight with a missing leg. And ask in an oddly childish voice, "Might we join you?"

If Ben said no to her, Grandmama scolded him. So every other time he'd simply say, "Sorry, but I'm finished playing today." And then go read a book or take a walk in the garden. Somewhere Aunt Loretta's nearsighted gaze couldn't find him.

When not lurking, she was whispering to herself up in the Tower, in her circular attic bedroom with floor to ceiling shelves of toys. She collected them. Not normal kinds, though—only broken ones. Cracked, limbless, grimy, and somewhat scary antiques she must've pulled from somebody's trash pile. He knew their names from overhearing those nightly monologues. On the few occasions he'd entered her bedroom he felt the toys watching him, too. He almost expected them to speak.

That, at least, would've been interesting. Sometimes at night he thought he did hear voices speaking back to crazy old Aunt Etta. He'd cried in fear, the first time. None of *his* toys talked! His parents had assured him they weren't supposed to.

But now Aunt Etta was very ill. She didn't leave her bedroom anymore. Grandmama Guinevere was up there a lot, too. She still baked treats, but not so often. One morning when he came upstairs looking for her, she was perched on the end of Ella's bed, watching her.

"Will she get better soon?" he asked, trying to decide if it would be rude right now to tell his gran he'd like a lemon tart for tea.

She shook her head. "Afraid not, Benjamin Bear." She'd lately begun to call him that, too.

"Is she . . ." He swallowed hard and plowed on. "Um . . . going to . . . *die*?"

His grandmother wiped her eyes on a lace-edged old-lady hankie and nodded. "I wish you'd known her when we were children. You remind me of Etta. Brave and strong."

This astonished Ben so, he forgot to feel insulted. "Why was she brave?" Then he gasped, for Auntie Etta had opened her eyes and was looking right at him.

"We were both brave," she whispered. But now Etta was looking at her sister, not at him. "We had to suddenly be . . . adults."

And then, with a lot of pauses in which to catch her breath, or sip from a cup Guinevere held to her lips, Aunt Etta finally did tell him why.

●◖◗○◐○◑◗●

Etta had learned, quite early, the cost of clumsy hands. She knew how easily a porcelain face could crack, leaving a cobweb of scars that made teatime conversations awkward. She saw, too, how spilt milk could spoil her handkerchief-made baby doll, for now she gagged on the rotten-cheese stink every time she rocked her little darling to sleep. Worse, her beloved stuffed bear, Benjamin, grew thinner and more frail with each hug, as little bits of stuffing bled from his seams. His limbs loosened at the slightest tug. She was mindful of every touch, because every touch had a cost.

Clumsiness was carelessness, in her opinion. A spilt cup of tea could ruin just about anything, from her mother's exquisite ribbons and decadent lace to her father's imported Asian rugs and Corinthian leather boots. Even God sometimes spilled a little. That's what her parents had told her: He had overindulged on the night of her birth and accidently splashed a little red wine onto Etta's forehead. A stain the size of her hand veiled the left side of her face, running up into her hairline and down to her left cheek. Such divine branding could not be washed away no matter how hard she was scrubbed at bath time. Her mother had tried lye soap and even dabs of laundry bleach over the past ten years.

No use. Etta had been stained before she was even born. How careless of God to ruin her like that.

So she treated her toys with great delicacy, wrapping them in blankets against harsh winter drafts, gently picking them up and setting them down as if the smallest thump would shatter them. Even though none were made of glass, and all had passed through the hands of several older relatives before reaching her. Still, she certainly could not have her favorite doll get a bruise! Poor Jenny was already missing a hank of hair, making it hard for her to join the more fashionable societies of the porcelain dolls who sat on the top shelf of Etta's bookcase. How would Jenny ever find a good husband? What would Etta do if she could not marry Jenny off to a rich Duke? Who'd pay the family debts, or support the lifestyle Etta now enjoyed?

It was all very stressful in the nursery. The wind-up mechanical clown laughed at Jenny's fears of becoming a spinster. He laughed so hard his rusted gears scraped and tinged. Meanwhile, Captain Lewis, the painted wooden soldier with a chipped red coat, the most handsome toy in the household, refused to ask Jenny to dance at nursery balls, no matter how Etta pleaded. In fact, none of the toys would speak to the poor, deformed doll.

Jenny the near-hairless, with a slightly cracked porcelain face on a fabric body, and Etta the stained girl, had much in common. In the midst of so many toys, they were lonely together. For Jenny was the sister Etta'd always wanted. But Guinevere was the sister she was actually stuck with.

"LOR-ETT-A!" Guinevere bellowed from down the hall just then, as she posed before a large ornate mirror. Adjusting her ruffles, as if just the right amount of fluffing would hide the pudgy belly that poked out farther than her chest, no matter how tightly the corset was laced. Likewise, she poked and prodded at her chubby neck, as if she could somehow fold it more neatly under her chin. Guinevere was twelve, but already as doomed to be a spinster as poor Jenny. For she looked like a suckling pig in every single outfit.

"It's night time." Etta glanced out the window, cocking her head to take in the dark landscape beyond the panes. She'd just bathed. Usually at this time of evening she'd throw a ball for her dollies in the dying firelight, before agonizing over which toys would share the bed with her that night. Usually, she couldn't decide. Usually, she'd throw them all in, even the mean porcelain aristocrats, because she couldn't bear the thought of anyone languishing on the dark shelves alone. Still, it made sleeping terribly uncomfortable. Too often she'd roll onto the hard metal bike of the mechanical clown, or whack her face on the flat unyielding tin of the Captain's puffed-out chest. Yet there was something so warm about having them all with her, late at night.

"No toys!" Guinevere shouted when Etta peeked out of the nursery door, Jenny cradled in both arms, head resting just under her chin. Her sister gave the balding doll a disgusted glare. "Must you show everyone just how poor we are with that motley bunch you play with! Aren't you getting too old for such things? Pathetic!"

Etta took a step back into the safety of nursery and slammed the door, hoping the heavy oak panels would muffle her mean older sister's words.

"But where could we possibly be going in the dark, anyhow?" Etta whispered to her room full of toys.

All she got in response was shrugs and equally perplexed expressions. Even Patrick Bunny, the wisest of the toys, simply had no clue.

Of course the closed door did not keep Guinevere out. Nothing ever did. She cracked it open just enough to shriek one more time. "No toys!"

"Not even one?" Etta begged. "Oh please! I'll keep Jenny hidden."

"LORETTA!" A new voice shouted.

The sisters cringed at their mother's raspy, shrill tones. A woman who'd cried three months nonstop since the demise of her husband. All the sobbing and heaving gave her words the same tone as rusted nails scratching glass.

Etta nervously yanked her old wool pelisse out of the closet and then sighed, looking at the room of toys facing her. "Don't worry about the dark, my dears. I won't be long."

"You *are* crazy! They aren't real. They *can't hear you*!" Guinevere insisted before disappearing down the hallway towards their mother's voice.

Etta had told a lie, of course. Who really knew how long she'd be gone. She scurried to the far side of her bedroom to kiss her handkerchief baby goodnight and to tuck Benjamin Bear into his place: the summit of pillows at the head of the bed. Finally, she gave the Captain a little curtsey, before scooping Jenny from the floor and slipping her beneath the folds of her pelisse. Where she could wrap one hand around the doll's feet to gently keep her upright and concealed.

Etta left, then doubled back to the doorway of her room. She stuck her tongue out at the mechanical clown, whose gears tinged as if to say, *Uh-oh, this can't be good!*

At the bottom of the stairs, a shell of a woman waited, still in the same black mourning dress from the funeral. Hadn't ever changed it. Hadn't even washed it. Her mother's complexion would have made her a twin to Etta's porcelain dolls, except they, at least, had rosy painted cheeks and cheery expressions. Mama was dull white and blank as a page; a loose sheet blowing in the wind. Hair tangled and unkept. Dress seams ripped. Arms begrimed with dirt. At her feet sat a mouldy grey box—damp, reeking of dirt, and something much more foul.

"What *is* that, Mama?" Guinevere asked.

Their father had been put into a box, then lowered into the earth and sent back to God. But this one was smaller. It could possibly hold one of Etta's larger toys. Perhaps Benjamin Bear. Perhaps even a much younger Etta.

She waved around what looked like a small square of parchment; the elegant writing on it had been done in India black. "The key," Mother rasped. Her eyes grew wide. Sounding almost giddy, she added, "The key to a secret place. A magical place."

Jenny the doll knew otherwise. She'd been around for generations in that household. Her warning was pitched so low Etta almost couldn't hear it in her mind. *It's your baby brother, Etta. You remember . . . he didn't make it, poor tyke.*

Etta whimpered. Poor little Benny. Had he not died, perhaps Mother would not now be so obsessed with marrying off her two girls. Perhaps she wouldn't have had to sell every piece of movable furniture, all the artwork that'd once lined the halls, and all their finest dresses. In the past three months, from the threshold of her room Etta had seen the rapid deterioration of her life. She, once a little lady with fine clothes in a fine house with a fine family, now wore ratty too-tight gowns she'd long outgrown. Her home had emptied of lovely things until, like her mother, it was just an empty shell. A rotten relic of a gilded age.

"This . . . is the key . . . to all of our problems." Mother went on heaving and sighing as she lifted a small carpetbag—clearly every remaining coin and trinket had been stuffed inside.

"You mean Baby Ben is the. . . ." Etta started to ask, but Guinevere stepped on her foot, her favorite way to tell her younger sister *Shut up*.

Outside, a hired carriage rumbled to a halt. Mother went out onto the front portico, still cradling the moldering coffin, still gripping her overstuffed carpetbag. She looked back over one shoulder when the girls didn't immediately follow. "Come, my soon-to-be beautiful little darlings."

When neither one moved, she gritted out, voice shaking with anger, *"Climb into that carriage. Now!"*

Guinevere and Etta exchanged startled glances. They rarely looked into each other's eyes. They never really connected on any sentiment, usually, but were tonight shaking with fear in unison. Feeling such dual terror of the woman with the dead baby, Etta actually reached out her free hand. And Guinevere, shockingly, wrapped her plump fingers tightly around it.

They did not let go for several hours, throughout the crazed carriage ride that took them off the main road and down narrow trails through the woods at a break-neck pace. Tossing the girls all over the compartment, bruising their arms and legs as they tried to brace themselves.

Even after they departed the black carriage, still they held onto each other. Standing trembling, watching their mother barter her way into an odd marketplace by waving the parchment invitation about and offering goods from her stuffed purse. Finally she beckoned and they left the carriage behind, entering beneath a fanciful archway woven of bramble roses, colourful scarves, and . . . were those small animal bones?

The aisles that lay beyond it were lined with booths and tall canvas tents which so overlapped often Etta couldn't see the slightest patch of night sky. Each vendor was selling a good or service odder than the previous one. Decadent crystal bottles of acid-coloured potions, tiers of black dominoes and painted masquerade masks, walls of photographs of sleeping . . . or perhaps dead people. Some men sat around a table with a Ouija board before them, beside a rack of jointed metal monsters made of pewter. Next to this was mounted an exhibit of oddly taxidermized animal heads: a bunny with antlers, a lion with a human face . . .

Such strange things! Etta flung her head every which-way, trying to catch a glimpse of something normal. Something safe. Something familiar. All the while clinging to Guinevere's hand.

Next was a tent which offered artful sculptures. Bones—from animals, she hoped—had been carved or somehow melted together to make flower bouquets, wedding rings, linked necklaces, elaborate hair clips. From that point on the displays only got stranger. Weirder. Soft music lured Etta's gaze to a vibrantly painted caravan at the end of the widest lane. The covered wagon had a built-in wooden stage. Lifelike marionettes danced away there, but while their bodies moved gracefully to the music, their faces and glass eyes seemed fixed on Etta.

She cringed and looked away.

This a bad place, said the imaginary voice of her doll, Jenny, who occasionally poked her balding head from Etta's woolen cloak to look around. *You won't be found if you lose yourself here. Hold tight to your sister and don't lose sight of your mother!*

The vendors seemed as uncommon as the trinkets they sold. Once she saw a feeble old man vanish into his own voluminous black cape and emerge as a scantily-dressed woman coyly fanning her half-naked breasts with a bunch of feathers. One short gentlemen had small horns protruding from his balding head. A child with greenish-blond hair was eerily beautiful, despite the mermaid scales covering her arms.

Poor Etta was gaining inspiration for a lifetime of new nightmares.

She finally stopped looking around and buried her face in Guinevere's shoulder. Ahead, their mother kept stopping at nearly every tent, hoisting the coffin higher, asking the same questions: *What will make my daughters beautiful? What will make them marriageable? What will make my dead son live again?*

The venders all shrugged and pointed in another direction. Etta suspected they were simply sending the obviously-mad lady away from their wares in order not to put off less-insane customers. At least until Mama approached a black-velvet tent embroidered with golden stars, whose tall shopkeeper nodded and beckoned her in at the end of the questions.

As their mother dragged Guinevere inside, Etta let go. Because at that moment Jenny commanded, *No, sweetheart. You wait out here! That is a very bad place indeed!*

Desperate to hold on to someone after letting Guinevere slip away, Etta took the dolly out of the pelisse and buried her face in its cloth stomach. Perhaps if she hid her eyes the strange people couldn't see her, either. Perhaps then they couldn't hurt her. She stood alone amongst the nightmares, outside the black velvet tent, clinging to Jenny, while a throng of strangers surged past. Sometimes bumping into her, like the tide that pulled you to and fro at the seashore.

Etta, dear, it's not safe to stay alone out here, Jenny said. *Open your eyes. Be a brave girl for me!*

At last Etta did, slowly. One lid at a time. When she took a step forward, toward the black tent, she heard an inhuman voice chanting some sort of incantation. None of the sounds made words she could recognize. She quickly stepped back again.

No, don't go in there, Jenny agreed.

Etta turned in a slow circle to take in the neighboring tents instead. One held glass jars and fine net cages full of insects. Those in the jars lay still, while the caged ones still fluttered and scurried. The next tent's booth had no objects laid out for sale, save for a humble wooden doll house. *The Doll Hospital,* a small sign said.

Etta, listen to that song! You know it! Jenny said.

She could imagine her doll's cloth arms reaching up to point at the tent. Someone was humming a lullaby, within. The same song Etta sang to her handkerchief baby before bed. How strange! She'd thought she invented the tune, just as she invented the voices of her toys. But this singer was clearly real.

She followed the melody inside, holding Jenny loosely at her side as she stepped in. Rows and rows of dolls, clowns, and tin soldiers looked down from the shelves. Fat stuffed velvet animals were piled high in the corners. Four small wicker carriages held three baby dolls a piece, sleeping soundly. Ah, a toy store, Etta thought. How delightful! She'd never been to one before, nor had she ever owned a new toy.

But then she noticed all their lace dresses were stained, the knitted caps and booties pilled and stuck with fluff. All the wear and tear and scars of use and previous owners. These were old toys, like hers at home.

The person singing was a little old lady in a dark gown with a high neck. She was leaning over, fixing the cracked window of a wooden doll house that sat in the very center of the tent. As she peered up at Etta from her chair, half-moon spectacles slid to the end of her nose. "Why hello, girls. Welcome!"

Etta looked behind her to see who the other girl was, before realizing the woman was also addressing Jenny. She pulled the doll close to her chest, afraid the toy-mender might snatch and add her to this collection of broken things.

"Why do you have . . . so many dolls?" Etta asked hesitantly.

"Why, they are my dear friends." The lady smiled, a toothy jack-o-lantern grin. "They tell me things. Keep me company."

"But you *sell* them." Etta made her free hand into a fist and propped it on her waist in outrage. "That's not what friends do!"

The old woman laughed at Etta's fierce conviction. "Is it wrong to give them a home with a deserving child? Or some desperate adult?"

Adults don't need toys! Jenny hissed in Etta's ear. *What a strange thing to say!*

"But adults *do* need toys," the lady said. "They keep away the bad things, Miss Jenny."

This old woman could hear her beloved doll's voice! Etta flinched in shock and dropped Jenny's fragile little body on the hard, cold ground. She gasped and quickly scooped her up again, inspecting for cracks or broken pieces. Legs? Check. Arms? Check. And head?

"Aaaahhh!" Etta screamed. For Jenny's head was no longer attached; it was rolling around on the floor by her slippers. "Oh, no! What've I done! No one will want her now! The captain will never love her! Jenny, are you well? Say something!"

The doll was silent—her voice no longer in Etta's head. Dear Lord, had she killed her?

"There, there," The old lady drew close, patting Etta's back. "She's a hardy thing. She'll be fine!"

"Then why won't she speak to me?"

"I wouldn't, either, if you'd just dropped me." The woman chuckled. "She has no head so she can't talk right now. But she's in there still. I can feel her."

Etta caught her breath; hugging Jenny's body tightly under her chin as she closely observed the toys surrounding her. Each had stitches and scars, some only the stumps of broken limbs. Wounds were caked with a white liquid pus of dried glue and mismatched paint. Some pairs of eyes didn't match. Some limbs were longer or shorter than their mates.

One brown bunny with a rather large head had mismatched ears and the white fuzzy body of a different rabbit. What was this old lady . . . an amateur toy surgeon? Or a murderer of toys, a nursery-room Spring-Heeled Jack?

"Aren't you going to ask me to make Miss Jenny beautiful again?" The woman fished a ball of red yarn from her apron pocket. A vibrant red—perhaps the same shade originally stitched onto Jenny's scalp. "I have the perfect match for her hair!"

Etta gave Jenny a squeeze. What should she do? She couldn't ask the doll, who'd fallen silent. But the old hag might further mutilate her best friend. Or sell her to some foolish adult who wouldn't appreciate her.

And yet . . . what if Jenny was made beautiful again? She and the Captain could marry. Etta's future might hold all sorts of horrors and deprivations, but at least she could escape into her favorite doll's happy ending.

"Ask the toys, if you are afraid, deary," the toy-mender instructed.

Etta held her breath and tried to listen. Only silence, and the cloth rustle of skirts, the muffled boot-thuds of passersby beyond the canvas tent.

And then, all at once—a chorus.

She fixed us.

She is an angel.

We love her.

She will make Jenny the best she's ever been!

Better than new!

She understands us.

With each comment, Etta's grasp on her doll loosened until she was holding her only by one arm.

The old woman snatched the doll up then and carried her to the worktable where the dollhouse sat. She laid Jenny's little body across its roof, drew a shining silver needle from the sleeve of her dress and began stitching the severed head onto its cloth neck. In minutes Jenny was not only un-decapitated; the balding doll once again had luscious, thick red hair.

"I can give her an updo, like a princess. How about a new dress, too?" the woman asked.

"No thank you," Etta said firmly. After all, if Jenny was too pretty, might she not also no longer treasure the friendship of her poor, deformed human friend?

The old woman looked puzzled. "You've been parading her around in these rags for so many years. Doesn't she deserve nice things, too?'

Etta rolled her eyes. Finally, unwillingly, she muttered, "I suppose."

The toy mender went to a rack hung with rolls of fabric and stood there, waiting for Etta to choose a colour and pattern.

"Blue, I think. It'll match her eyes."

Etta pulled up a crate alongside the old woman's chair and watched her transform Jenny—polishing the scratched porcelain face, touching up her painted lips and eyelashes with a tiny brush, fluffing up her insides and restitching the cloth torso, and sanding down some of the splinters on her wooden limbs.

"What sorts of bad things do toys keep away?" Etta asked thoughtfully. She was still trying to decide whether she was totally delighted or horrified by the new, evolving Jenny. "Mine must be lazy, because we've had terrible things happen the past few months."

"Shame." The old woman tsked. "Beloved toys hold a very particular kind of magic that can satisfy the hunger of bad things. There's not an exact word for the bad ones in this language. Nightmares, yes—but I'm speaking of the real, waking ones. Unpleasant oddities. Hauntings that are not ever mentioned in polite conversations. Daemons is the word that comes closest, I suppose."

"Really? But there's no such thing." Etta snickered, recalling Sunday-school lessons.

"Only those who've never experienced the worst can say that. And you, little one, should be especially careful. I saw which tent your mother and sister entered."

"But toys can't really be magic," Etta insisted, thinking back to all the times Mama and Guinevere had mocked her obsession with the nursery denizens.

"What! Of course they are. Else how do you explain their voices?" The old woman laughed. "Every time you play with a toy like Jenny, you leave a little bit of your soul behind. And before you, several others played with her, leaving bits of themselves behind, too. Jenny has a soul stitched of patches from every child who's ever loved her. So do all your toys. That's why each has a unique voice and wants and personality. So you can't just command the Captain to marry Jenny, or will the porcelain dolls to let her into their high societies."

"Oh." Etta tilted her head. That all sounded reasonable. "But Mother says it's merely my imagination, and they can't speak. She says I'm getting too old for it. That no man will marry a girl who still sleeps with her toys in the household nursery."

"Hmm," the lady mused. "Love makes them alive, in a way. But only people who truly love toys get to hear their voices." She ended the sentiment with a wink.

Etta smiled. Finally, someone who understood and could explain why she loved her toys so much. Not because they were fine, or because they were her possessions, but because when she played with them, she was also playing with the children who'd held them before her.

The toys had gradually become the family she'd always wanted. Giving her nothing but love. Letting her sleep with them and cry into their soft bellies when her father had died. So, if she continued to love them like this woman did, surely she'd never have to outgrow them? She could still hear their voices until she was as old and frail as the lady before her.

Etta, look how new and splendid I am! Jenny's voice was suddenly back.

Etta's eyes filled with tears. Her sister of porcelain, wood, and fabric was alive and well!

Oh, my dress, my hair! The Captain will surely marry me now. And you can come, Etta. Come live with us in the fine doll house with Benjamin Bear. We will have the biggest, most fashionable wedding celebration!

"Pftt . . the Captain!" The old woman scoffed. "Jenny, you're a very special doll, and Etta here is a very special little girl. You both deserve a real Prince! Forget that rascally captain fellow!"

The woman turned around and stood on tip-toe, sliding one wrinkly old hand behind a group of marionettes. She grabbed an exquisite Parian marble-made man with painted blond curls. He had a blue coat with gold buttons that matched his golden crown.

"For you both." She held the doll out to Etta.

Etta gasped and shook her head. "But we have no money."

"Jenny told me about your great loss. I'm so sorry, little ones. You both deserve much better."

We deserve a King for all we've endured. But a Prince is nice, too, Jenny conceded. *And we'll need him. For I have a feeling worse is coming.*

Jenny was usually right about those sorts of things.

Etta held a doll in each hand, looking happily down at her new and beautifully restored family members. So what if Mama married her and her sister off to some mean, aristocratic tyrants? No matter where she was sent, she could still escape into Jenny's world.

"*Loretta!*" Her mother's shrill voice sliced through the night air, rising above the rustle and bustle of the crowd outside.

Oh no! She'd almost forgotten about her real family—was Mama still in that black tent with Guinevere? Etta hesitantly lifted a corner of the Doll Hospital's canvas flap, wondering whether she should answer. Her mother stood in the centre of the aisle, twisting and turning, gazing in every direction. She no longer held the mouldy box. Instead, she had a wicker carryall, handle hung over one arm, the basket cradling glass vials of various sizes which held an array of glowing black, green, and brown liquids. Her mother's other hand clutched Guinevere's fiercely, as if she feared she might escape the way her younger daughter had.

"Go on now." The old woman gave Etta a gentle little push to propel her out the doorway. Etta quickly tucked the two dolls into her pelisse, then cautiously approached her mother.

"There's my soon-to-be beautiful girl!" Mama grinned.

Etta bowed her head, expecting the usual scolding as the cost of wandering off. She tensed, preparing her body for the usual quick, sharp slap on the back of the head, followed by an even more painful tongue-lashing, and a week of no dessert or playtime.

Her mother merely continued smiling, looking for once eerily calm. She held up the basket. "Did you see all the wonderful spells we got, my dear?"

She bent to explain each bottle, voice giddy with excitement. "One for that birth mark of yours, one for your sister's puppy fat, one for your baby brother. . . oh, and a few for me!"

Etta gasped. She hoped her spell was some sort of beauty cream, but she couldn't imagine tasting that thick, black sludge. She glanced at Guinevere's petrified face. Her sister appeared frightened beyond speaking. Or maybe her spell had already been forced down her throat, scalding the usually ceaselessly-wagging tongue.

As Etta's mother dragged them towards the carriage, Etta glanced back at the black-velvet tent with gold embroidery. She could swear a darkness moved out of its shadows and followed them, skulking through the dense crowds. Though perhaps that was merely the trick of blurry vision from her exhausted eyes.

●◗◗○○○◖◑●

For seven nights after that terrifying night-time journey, Mama dosed them both with the noxious-tasting tisanes and potions for which she had traded away all that was left of Baby Ben. But as far as Etta could see in the mirror each morning, nothing had changed. And Guinevere still looked the same, as well.

She sighed. Well, perhaps beauty took longer to show itself in mended people than it did in mended dolls.

On the eighth night, she threw the most extravagant wedding for Jenny and the Prince. She'd spent the whole week making paper chains and bouquets of crepe-paper flowers, draping her best bedsheets into a make-believe cathedral. She'd found fabric scraps in a trunk, and sewed bridesmaid dresses for the French porcelain ladies. They were very eager to befriend Jenny and her betrothed Prince now. She'd also made sashes and bows for all the stuffed animals and a bonnet for her handkerchief baby. She'd filched a few apples from the overgrown, neglected garden behind the house and pocketed her biscuits each morning. She'd even purloined tea and honey and chocolate from the pantry, saving it all for the wedding feast.

Jenny's nuptials were indeed beautiful. The ceremony was Etta's new favorite make-believe memory. Patrick Bunny stood behind a biscuit-tin pulpit to marry them. Benjamin Bear walked Jenny down the aisle to her new, beautiful prince while the tin solders filling the pasteboard pews surreptitiously played cards. The creepy clown carried the train of Jenny's very long, perfectly white dress, which Etta had sewn from a guest-room bedsheet. The Captain stood fuming in one corner all through the "I do's", the wedding toasts, and a night full of dancing.

Etta imagined she was in the ballroom wearing her best lace and pearl-trimmed gown, dancing with Jenny and Benjamin. It was the first time in her life she'd felt beautiful.

She fell asleep, exhausted, encircled by the wedding decorations and party guests just as the sun started to peek through the east window. They all lay on the threadbare nursery rug in a ring of fading candlelight.

Sometime later she woke abruptly; someone had called her name.

Etta.

The Captain's voice. Deep and serious as a perpetually-annoyed father's. The tone of a military man who'd never known laughter.

On your feet, Etta! Something lurks in your sister's room!

Etta bolted upright, heart beating like a toy drum.

The wedding had been such a beautiful distraction from a horrid week. Yes, her mother had finally left the mouldy, stinking box behind in the black-velvet tent. And it had seemed she'd carried nothing else home save the bottles of vile potions and the dubious promise their lives would change. That baby Ben would return anew. That the girls would become beautiful and marriageable.

But something else *had* accompanied her and it was not little Ben. Rather, something as dark and liquid-like as the black potion she'd poured down Ella's throat the next morning. Something perhaps tucked in her reticule or hidden in her shadow. A thing that now lived in the hallway mirror and roamed the mostly-empty house at night. For Etta had seen it creak her bedroom door open an inch or so and peer in. Not a person, but rather . . . the absence of one. A dark void. A shadow that had long ago lost its humanity. The creature seemed to gaze around at all the toys surrounding Etta, lick its lips and perhaps drool a little, then move on to the next room.

And now it was back.

Etta, hurry! Get my sword! the Captain shouted.

She groped wildly over the floor, seeking the little needle-like rapier the Captain had laid down so he could dance with her. Her scrabbling fingers found it, and she shoved the tiny blade into his hand. Then grabbed him up and ran down the hallway to her sister's room.

She halted outside the door, panting. Being just a child, after all, what could she actually do? The only adult in the house was mad. Their mother thought this beast was here to help them.

Cautiously, Etta opened the bedroom door an inch or so.

Guinevere lay snoring on the bed, mouth agape as the daemon hovered over her. Slowly morphing into a spider, it used long, hairy front legs to widen Guinevere's mouth so it could crawl down her throat.

"No!" Etta screamed. She flung the Captain at the floating spider.

And missed.

Even so, the demon hissed like a wounded cat, and morphed back into a sort-of person double Etta's size. It took several steps towards her before a groggy Guinevere rolled over and opened her eyes. Etta scooped up the limp Captain from the counterpane, and threw him again. This time right into the maw of the black beast.

"What *is* that horrid thing?" Guinevere screamed. "What was it *doing* to me?"

Etta cried out as the Captain disappeared into the demon's belly. The entity shoved her back over the threshold, morphed into a wild boar and trotted off down the hallway. It leapt back into the ornate gold-framed mirror, the Captain's little steel and wooden sword poking from its mouth like a horrible toothpick.

Etta heard the Captain's voice screaming in her mind . . . or was that her own scream? Sometimes it was hard to tell where she ended and her toys began.

"What shall we do?" Guinevere wailed. She gripped her little sister's hand, watching the dark spot in the hallway mirror glare out at them. It slowly took the shape of a toy soldier with the Captain's features and waved at Etta, as if daring her to come get him.

Etta sobbed. She hadn't really liked the Captain much. Still, he'd died to protect them.

Guinevere embraced her tightly. "I'll buy you a new one, I promise."

Her sister still didn't understand. A new toy wouldn't have the same voice, or the same soul. And it was that soul the daemon now feasted upon in the mirror, especially relishing the tin bits. It bit off the Captain's head first, then each limb, and finally swallowed the torso whole.

Then it spat his needle-like sword down the hallway, right at the girls.

Apparently the meal didn't agree, though. For the monster gripped its gut, fell out of the glass, and took a fit on the floor, foaming at the mouth and shrieking.

Etta stared, horrified. The Captain's soul, traded for Guinevere's. Was that what had just happened?

Maybe they were safe for tonight, at least. Or . . . was it dead? Oh, please, let it be dead!

Hand in hand they ran to the opposite end of the hallway, to the master bedroom. Guinevere burst through the door first, shrieking, "Mama, Mama, there's a monster! A monster in the mirror!"

The woman before them did not stir, or even turn her head to face her tear-smeared, screaming daughters. She sat in the rocking chair, moving rhythmically, never missing a beat. All the while chanting so softly her lips barely moved. "My life should've been so much better than it was. . ."

She listed an incantation of all that should've been, the words coming furiously fast and intense, like a witch's spell. Etta only caught bits. Something about a dead baby. . . dead husband. . . dead parents. . . ugly daughters. . . beauty lost to age . . . money lost to debts . . . every regret, no matter how small, was woven in. Every mean word that spiteful, more fortunate ladies had hissed. Every complaint of disappointment from their mother's mother. Every slight from her former mother-in-law. Every tear shed by her dead son. Her dead husband. Every single little regret linked like a dark string of beads chanted in a loop, in perfect rhythm with the rocker's movement.

Once the whole of it had cycled through again, Guinevere ran to their mother and tried to yank her from the chair. Pushing her face right up close, screaming, "MAMA! MAMA, STOP! STOP IT! IT'LL KILL US ALL!"

She desperately yanked the unmoved woman's long greying hair. But their mother was in a trance so deep that, despite curses and blows, she never missed a mumbled regret nor lost time with the creaking rocker.

Something dark flickered in the corner of Etta's eyes. A black spot in the hall mirror. If the Captain's last stand had weakened the daemon at all, their mother's spell seemed to be reviving him. She watched the darkness swell like stagnant pond water in a rainstorm, until it overflowed from the mirror. The darkness Etta had never entirely believed in, before now. Her mother was fanning its flame with a flood listing all she'd hated about her life. Too busy to notice she'd left her girls to drown.

There wasn't time to explain the correlation between spell and beast to Guinevere. So Etta grabbed her sister's hand and pulled her back out into the hallway, where the monster swelled in synch with their mother's rhythmic chanting.

"We need to run!" Guinevere tried to drag her sister over to the staircase in the grand foyer.

Etta didn't budge. "Run where?"

They had no family. No friends. All the servants had been let go, their rooms vacated months ago. There were no neighbours for miles. Even if the children started running now and didn't stop, they wouldn't reach the nearest town before nightfall.

And monsters hunted quite easily in the dark.

"The only place to run to is the light," Etta explained. She pulled her sister in the opposite direction, toward a patch of dawn flickering through the nearest window.

The darkness continued to fill the hallway like a raging river. But it split and flowed around the little square of light where the girls fell to their knees embracing each other, sobbing. Still, whether the worst happened today, tomorrow, or the next day. . . there was no doubt the dark shape-shifter would slurp up their souls. The sun wouldn't stay around forever to save them.

●◑◐○◐○◐◑●

The following evening Guinevere pushed her mattress through the doorway of Etta's room, her pillows, blankets, and books piled high atop it.

Uproar ensued. Etta thought her head would burst from the bombardment of angry voices rising from every toy in the room.

What is she doing here?

We can't stand her!

Etta, tell her to leave!

Get out, Guinevere! No one wants you here!

Many of the toys had belonged to Guinevere before they came to Etta, though her sister had never heard their voices. But she'd also never hugged them tight or let them sleep with her in the big canopy bed. She hadn't given them special names or acted out little scenes with them. They were just decorations that made the nursery look girlish and quaint, before Etta came along.

Guinevere had sometimes abused the toys, kicking or stepping on them when she entered the nursery. Taking pleasure in slamming the door so hard the porcelain ladies rattled and sometimes tumbled down and cracked. She'd picked up Jenny by the hair once, just to rip out a lock or two in front of Etta, chanting, "They're not real, see? When will you grow up?"

She's a monster! The handkerchief baby wailed.

Panting, Guinevere arranged the two mattresses alongside each other under the imaginary wedding cathedral tent. She helped Etta carefully move the toys to one side, then piled up her books in a stack, in the order she planned to read them: top to bottom.

Etta, the entire nursery is in revolt. You cannot let your wicked sister sleep here tonight! Benjamin Bear shouted.

Guinevere set him gingerly on Etta's mattress. "I know how much *you* love to sleep with toys." Then she frowned. "I thought I heard that bear say something just now." Guinevere glanced at Etta. "Or was it you who spoke?"

"Not me," Etta said quickly, then shook her head at Benjamin behind her sister's back, to shush him.

"I used to hate these toys so." Guinevere admitted, folding up all the blankets on the floor, making a quaint little sanctuary within the tent. "Then, when I saw how happy they made you—Pftt. Why? Nothing ever made me that happy. It was so unfair how easily you could leave the endless family problems, just by picking up some hairless old doll. Always abandoning me for make-believe high-society dramas."

Was that all Guinevere had really wanted—a sibling present with whom to face each day? To talk with, to be grown-up with, since their parents were often not around? Etta felt like she understood her sister for the first time.

"I'll be right back," Guinevere instructed. "Just going to get more food from the pantry. And some books I want from the library, for research, before the sun sets."

"No, stay!" Etta's gaze skittered to the window. Only a few minutes of daylight left, at best. Then the illumination that kept the monster inside the mirror would be gone.

Guinevere hugged her. "Someone must take care of us. Don't leave. I'll be right back!"

Etta frowned. Did she mean, *Don't escape into the fantasy world of your toys*, or simply, *Do not leave the room*? Perhaps both. She watched Guinevere tip-toe out into the hallway, sidling past the darkness that was already pooling at the lower edge of the mirror's frame.

I can't believe you're letting her sleep in here with us, Jenny sniped.

"Just for a little bit," Etta cajoled. "Until the real monster leaves. The one who actually devours toys."

Where is the captain? The clown asked.

Yeah, what happened to him? Benjamin echoed.

Etta gazed sadly at the shelf where the Captain usually stood at attention during the day. Without answering them, she wove together some paper flowers left over from the wedding and made a funeral wreath.

The baby cried. The clown stopped laughing and sobbed. The Captain's empty spot was a grave now. And though she said nothing, the toys seemed to understand, growing sad and quiet alongside her.

"I'm back!" Guinevere announced.

A tablecloth full of food was slung over her back like a tramp's rucksack. More books were tucked under her armpits. She slammed the door shut and pulled the baby stroller and miniature tea table in front to barricade it. "That should keep it out tonight!"

Etta wasn't so sure. "It can change shape."

Guinevere frowned, then stuffed a sheet into the crack beneath the door.

"Maybe you were right. Maybe we should run away," said Etta.

"The closest town is too far—we'll never make it before dark, even if we start very early in the morning. And what if the . . . thing . . . follows us?"

True. There'd be even less light in the woods. No candles. No fireplaces. No beds or toys. Just strangers and beasts their mother used to warn about.

"And then, well . . . Mama . . ." Guinevere trailed off to silence.

In the nursery, daylight had disappeared quickly; the sun was already setting. At dusk it would be harder to see the shadow-like being if it entered the room. Both girls jumped onto the mattress with the toys and closed the tent flaps.

"What a terrible night this will be," Guinevere whined.

"It doesn't have to be," Etta whispered in a low voice so the toys couldn't hear. Her sister had never wanted to play before, so this was probably a terrible idea. But huddling in fear and staring at the door all night would only make everyone more afraid.

"What do you mean?" Guinevere frowned.

Etta smiled. "It's Jenny's royal coronation tonight. Would you like to attend?" She held out Jenny and her husband.

With a slight smile, Guinevere took the prince.

Soon, trumpets rang out. Tin soldiers lined the royal red velvet carpet, and Benjamin Bear took his place beside a decadent new throne constructed of stacks of Guinevere's books.

The sisters stood in the front row, hand in hand, waving streamers in the vast cathedral of toys. Suddenly Guinevere looked startled, and turned to Etta. "I . . . I can hear them!"

"Then you know they really are people. The very best sort," said Etta.

Afterward they attended a ball so beautiful it put Jenny's wedding celebration to shame. The sisters danced and laughed until they passed out from exhaustion inside their bed-linens tent, still clinging to each other and to their dolls.

Only to wake after dawn to find several of their dance partners from the night before had been dismembered and strewn about: Patrick Bunny, Rodger Rocking Horse, and a handful of tin soldiers. The monster had clearly drawn close as they slept and feasted on the toys instead of the girls.

This time.

●◗◖○◖○◗◖●

That became the daily pattern. After the sun rose the girls hid and took turns sleeping, barricading themselves and the remaining toys into a new room each time—basement, attic, pantry—hoping the demon wouldn't find them. They drank tea and nibbled dwindling rations of cheese, crackers, and apples. They read about ancient monsters in Guinevere's books . . . and came no closer to discovering how to kill the one hunting them.

At night, when the house was darkest and most terrifying, they'd play. A day in real life encompassed a whole year in their make-believe kingdom. One full of tea parties, yuletide balls, weekends in the country, and great hunts that ended with the fox being invited to dine with them. Jenny and the Prince lived a lovely life with three handkerchief-made children. Plus Guinevere and Etta, their adopted daughters and future queens of the nursery. The sisters passed the evenings tending to the new cloth babies, and other needs of the kingdom. All the while knowing there'd be more dead toys in the morning. But they dared not talk of that. Or think about who may be next. Or what would happen when they ran out of toys altogether.

Next to go was the remaining tin soldiers, bravely standing watch in a circle around the sleeping girls. The second night the porcelain French dolls were shattered. Two nights later Etta's handkerchief baby was shredded into tiny frayed scraps. All that was left of the mechanical clown at the end of that week was a few broken gears. And one morning Etta thought she'd woken to new-fallen snow. But it was Benjamin's cotton stuffing . . . the bear's only remains.

She'd cried for all her toys, but was inconsolable after the loss of Ben and her Baby. No imaginary story could quell that grief. Guinevere held her close the following night after they barricaded themselves in the garden shed with the royal family. All that was left now. One night soon would be their last together. Both toys and humans cried and hugged each other, before finally passing out from fear and exhaustion.

The third week, the demon finally returned.

Etta heard the prince's bloodcurdling scream. She bolted up to see a big black shadow, hunched like a gigantic rat, feasting upon the doll's marble face.

Guinevere woke up and whacked the monster with her pillow. It dropped the royal marble fragments and turned to Etta's sister, wrapping large claws around her waist. Baring huge yellow fangs, about to pierce her.

"No!" Etta screamed.

The daemonic rat turned back into that spider-like creature and, when Guinevere screamed at the hideous sight, leapt into her open mouth and crawled down her throat.

"No, no," sobbed Etta. She understood now. It wanted to *be* Guinevere. To eat her soul in order to possess her.

Desperate, Etta flung the royal fabric babies at the beast. It crawled out of Guinevere's throat just far enough to eat them, still clutching her sister.

Etta looked at Guinevere, weeping and helpless in the beast's grasp. She looked down at Jenny, beautiful sweet Jenny, cradled in her arms.

How could she betray either sister?

Throw me, Jenny said. *You can't let him possess her. It's fine, dear Etta. I'm only a toy. You'll have others.*

"They won't be you! Or have your soul, or souls of the children before you—" Etta sobbed. But she stopped short, remembering the words of the toy surgeon at the Bazaar.

That was why it ate so many toys—to also consume the souls of their former owners, the children who'd come before.

She knew then what she must do. Hugging Jenny close, she scooped up pieces of the prince from the shed floor and threw them at the demon's horrible black-olive eyes.

The creature shrieked and dropped Guinevere. It morphed into a flock of fanged bats.

"Still hungry?" Etta dangled Jenny just out of reach of the flapping throng.

They swooped at Etta, biting her, pulling out clumps of hair, ripping her nightgown. She kept running, Jenny clutched to her chest. She ran and ran through the dead, neglected gardens all the way to the main house. Then raced up the grand foyer staircase and down the hall to her mother's room.

Three weeks had passed. Yet there sat Mama, still chanting out all her wounds. Still frozen in her rocker.

And soulless! As Etta now realized. The reason she would not, could not wake.

"Mama," Etta panted, slamming the door on the cloud of pursuing bats. She ran to her mother and set Jenny on her lap.

Jenny, the nickname for Guinevere. A name Etta's mother had given the doll back when it was hers. She'd told them how she used to act out elaborate stories in which Jenny was her beautiful daughter. "Long before the real Guinevere was born, of course," she'd say, and smile.

If Etta's mother had truly loved the doll, some bit of her soul still lived inside Jenny.

The bats kept slamming into the closed door. *Bang! Bang! Bang!* Soon they would break through.

Etta cried, "Please, please, Jenny! Give my mother a bit of her soul back."

But I don't know how! Jenny sobbed.

The creak of the rocker halted. Mother sat upright, looking down at the doll in her lap.

"Jenny used to be yours, Mama," Etta cajoled. "Remember? A piece of you is still inside her!"

The woman smiled gently and stroked the doll's hair. " My Jenny," she whispered.

With a great crash, the daemon burst through the door in form of a great wild boar, snorting, trotting straight for them. But its hooves stumbled on a fold of carpet, and it staggered. Without the everlasting Chant of Regrets, it seemed, the monster quickly grew weak. With a great groan it rolled onto its back and gave a thin shriek. It morphed into a belly-up possum, then a coiled snake.

"Guinevere is the name of your real daughter! And I, Etta, am your beautiful, darling girl, too!" Etta insisted. "See? You have the daughters you always wanted as a child. You got your dream, Mama."

Her mother held Jenny, staring as if fascinated by her restored look.

"You can't stay only sad and angry. It's feeding the monster. Remember when you used to be happy with your ugly broken children, like your ugly broken doll?"

Her mother rose and took a step forward, towards the floundering daemon on the floor.

But it had enough strength left for a final lunge. The monster swallowed woman and doll whole, feasting on whatever bits of soul remained in them. Jenny's head tore loose again. It fell off and rolled across the floor as the monster crunched her up. Then, no sadness and regret left to feast upon, the fiend disintegrated into a puff of black smoke.

That night, when the sun set, no terrible darkness moved about the house. But there was also no Mother.

No Jenny. No Prince. No Benjamin or Captain or Clown.

The girls were truly alone. They had no choice but to be the grown-ups they both desperately needed. Thank goodness Guinevere'd already had years of practice.

Hand in hand they left their childhood home and ventured through the woods toward the nearest town. What future awaits us there, Etta wondered. Obscure distant relatives? Unhappy marriages? The poorhouse? The orphanage? Who knew. Whatever fate they received, she feared it would be cold, difficult, and messy. With even more loss and pain, perhaps. But she did know that, together, it absolutely could not be worse than the darkness that lay behind them.

Finally the house disappeared from view. When nothing but dense forest surrounded them, Etta squeezed her sister's hand. They'd gone far beyond their mother's expansive garden and even their father's favorite old walking trails. Everything familiar was gone.

"We'll get you a new doll as soon as we're settled." Guinevere forced a smile at Etta. Perhaps she thought her little sister was still afraid of the dark.

But she was not. Instead, Etta feared in that moment she might've finally grown too old for toys. That she might no longer need playthings in which to immerse herself. For now she had a living, breathing someone who loved and needed her. Hand-in-hand, they could conquer any monster that might lurk on the road ahead.

And they had, it seemed, for decades and decades. But one can't cheat death forever.

And so, three days after ailing Aunt Etta told Little Ben their story, the servants carefully carried her on a stretcher all the way down the Tower steps and into the foyer. An ambulance was waiting outside on the gravel drive, its two bay horses blowing and stamping. Grandmama Guinevere had insisted on calling for it, even though Etta protested.

Little Ben pressed his lips tightly together, because he couldn't tell how he felt now. Happy? Sad? Relieved?

His gran gave him a little push towards the stretcher. "Benjamin Bear, it's time to say goodbye."

He couldn't let the first thought that rose in his mind escape, though. Instead, he forced his lips upward into a false smile. For the bad word still trying to get out was *Yay!*

He still had Grandmama, and surely would sleep much better without his witchy old auntie tinkering away upstairs all night . . . her creaky whisper carrying down to his bedroom through cracks in the floorboards. Not to mention those other, fainter voices . . .

Then why did his eyes sting, now? Etta would never again tousle his curls until they tangled. Or awkwardly cradle his beloved wooden horse, Brutus, dropping voracious kisses on his real horsehair mane as if she wanted, well . . . to eat him.

"Goodbye, Auntie Etta," he finally whispered, stepping up beside her. She opened her eyes, then closed them again slowly, much the way the barn cat did to say it liked you. Now that she was leaving—dying, he supposed—he'd sleep peacefully here for the first time in his life.

But then, just as he was turning away, with one withered, trembling arm Etta drew something from the blankets tucked around her: a porcelain princess doll.

But I'm a boy, he thought, feeling insulted. One sharp look from Grandmama silenced his rising protest, though. "T-Thank you," he muttered. When he turned the doll over he saw it had a port-wine stain on its face, just like Etta's.

"Listen to her," said his aunt, voice frail and dry as desiccated leaves blowing along a sidewalk.

"OK," he whispered. And then he heard it; a woman's voice faintly whispering, *"Benjamin Bear."*

"Just Ben," he said automatically. But when he looked up, Aunt Etta was gone. They were already sliding her stretcher into the back of the waiting ambulance.

That night he did not sleep well, after all. Somehow the voices from the attic above still came to him. Through the floorboards he could hear them carrying on lengthy conversations. Most strange of all, he thought he recognized his dead Aunt Loretta's voice among them.

When he looked over fearfully for the princess doll, though, she was still propped in her chair. Watching over him, as Grandmama had said she would.

In the dim light her stained porcelain face looked not just kind but beautiful.

He did cry then, because he finally understood he really would never, ever see Crazy Aunt Etta again.

Years later, after Grandma Gwen was long gone, too, and he'd inherited the house, Ben's new wife wanted to redecorate the Tower bedroom. She asked so many times he finally reluctantly gave in.

"We'll donate all those old toys to the local orphanage," she said, and kissed him before rushing off to look at drapery fabrics and hand-painted wallpaper.

For days servants went in and out of the attic bedroom, carefully packing up Loretta's toys. Those poor kids, Ben thought. Life has surely been hard enough, already, at the orphanage. Now they'll be living with broken little hand me downs that talk. And no one to even tell them why.

As the servants carried more boxes down the stairs, a red-haired doll fell out and rolled across the marble tiles.

"Hey! You forgot one!" Ben yelled after the man, but he mustn't have heard, for he didn't turn back. Ben scooped it up and ran after the servant, calling, "Stop! Wait!"

Wait, Ben! another voice said.

He gasped and halted abruptly. "What?"

You've no more old toys like me left now to talk and look after you. Don't you want to play?

That was the day Ben decided he really was far too old for toys. He did not want to follow in dear old Aunt Etta's footsteps, so he even added battered, beloved old Brutus the horse to the Oxfam donation box.

Many more years later, when he thought about this day again, he decided: Every toy must be a little possessed. Mere children's playthings, perhaps, but clearly each holds inside a bit of all the children who came before . . . as they would one day all hold a part of all the children who came after.

This next booth is the traveling version of a famous old London establishment which carries only the finest of tools for the writing set: sleek handcrafted pens, pencils carved of exotics woods, thick, crisp sheets of creamy linen paper, artfully tooled leather-bound journals, and pots and pots of exquisitely-tinted inks made of rare ingredients procured from around the world . . . like this set of three crystal bottles with coloured glass stoppers. But they and the accompanying, matching fountain pens are not for sale, at any price. These objets d'art are associated with a strange, unsolved case that has yet to happen. They've been set out here now only for display, lest a similar fate befall some incautious shopper in this era . . .

The Shopkeeper's Tale

By D Ferrara

Alicia Ann Abercrombie needed to kill someone.

Not just anyone. Someone loathsome. Someone whose loss would not evoke a moment's grief in the world—only celebration.

And not just in any old way. No. It must be done in a manner that would cause gasps of horror. A shudder of dread. And, finally, a hastily suppressed smirk. Better yet—giggles.

Murder was how Alicia Ann Abercrombie ("Triple A" to her legions of online fans) enticed readers. Her victims perished not by mere stabbing, but lanced by a medieval knight charging on a modern racetrack. Not ordinary drowning, but from boiling alive in a nice Bordeaux wine sauce. She'd once crushed a creep into an asphalt driveway, after sending a slattern in full Gilded Age regalia off a cliff without her parasail.

Yet this morning, as she, wrapped in the fluffiest of Egyptian cotton hotel bathrobes, stared at the glossy screen of her tablet (the best, the latest, the fastest), nothing uniquely lethal came to mind. Everything she considered had already been done. Or was too gruesome even for her base of (mostly) females of a certain age. By now, they would be pandemic-crazy, starving for a new AAA novel—a mystery about a murder that had nothing to do with masks, vaccines, social distancing, hydroxychloroquine, aquarium supplies, or horse pills. After all, her books had to *seem* realistic, while not actually *being* realistic.

Not even coming to her favorite hideout, the swank Alerton Hotel overlooking London's Park Lane, had generated the appropriate level of fictional mayhem. Yes, of course they had the Prince's Lair Suite decked out for her with all the usual tasteful frippery. A Regency China tea set awaiting her whim. Biscotti from that tiny bakery whose name she could never remember, stashed in Waterford biscuit barrels in every room. The double-felted slippers she preferred to the terry cloth ones. Two bathrobes in each of the three bathrooms—even the one without a tub. The French and Italian newspapers they thought she could read. Roger, the floor butler, had seen them in her suite once and decided Miss A wanted to stay *au courant* in multiple languages. She had actually only picked them up by accident in the lounge.

As it lent a pleasing cachet to her image, though, Alicia chose not to correct the misunderstanding. Now, foreign papers must be a regular feature of her writing escapes. Like the massive portraits, painted by her most faithful followers, that dwarfed the enormous flatscreen television serving as an easel for the triptych. There, her three faces—one, in the style of a medieval religious painting, one Cubist, and, the third, Super-Realistic— normally evoked the warm gush of inspired mayhem that heralded yet another bestseller. She took them everywhere. Carefully wrapped and packed as if en route to a museum, the paintings had preceded her to the Alerton, and the staff of Mayfair's best gallery had hung them as if the suite were the National Portrait Gallery. As always.

Today, however, the faces seemed different, a bit more more…menacing, perhaps? The white outfit worn in the Cubist portrait appeared starker, harsher, almost like plastic. The Della Robbia blue scarf on the medieval Alicia's throat seemed tighter. And had that lumpy brown background figure always been there? As for Super-Realistic Alicia—she just looked lost.

Grimly, she picked at the afternoon high tea. Presented, just for her, at ten-thirty in the morning by a liveried butler, who also wore a matching black domino mask. A stack of faxes (by now, her agent and publisher knew that their emails were too easy to ignore) printed out by the hotel, demanded in ascending levels of irritation, *When will the new manuscript be ready?* Her agent had dangled promises of exotic book tours. The publisher reminded her snippily that the seven-figure advance had been a record amount. Her licensing manager moaned that no one seemed to want the facial product line AAA had lent her name to.

And then some nonsense about a retweet on her author account deemed insensitive to…well, someone. AAA neither recalled, nor cared. Her Twitter feed was carefully curated by a personal assistant. Or had been until AAA had fired the . . . hmm. *Oh yes, the red-headed one.* She hadn't yet broken in the new guy. Though, come to think of it, thanks to the N-95 mask, androgynous clothes, and wafer-thin body, one could not be certain of the preferred pronouns.

She hadn't even allowed the new assistant to delete the latest mound of unsolicited outlines, chapters, stories, and utterly rancid fan fiction. The stuff followed her everywhere. In desperation, she'd even flicked through *that* stack for an idea, a theme, even a unique setting that might spark a new story. Generally, fans were thrilled when one of their ideas wormed into her work, even though their only compensation was to have a minor character named after them.

Her agent had tried to dissuade her from the London trip. "It's insane to travel now! The pandemic—you'll get sick."

AAA had simply grabbed a seat on a fan's private jet.

The agent had also whined about a rash of bizarre criminal happenings, which continued, even in posh Mayfair—reports of muggings in which the thief stole only a scarf or a single earring. Lightning striking post boxes, incinerating the contents without even scorching the exterior paint. Unearthly music flowing from storm drains. Underground trains that left a stop on the Northern Line, and arrived at one on the Central Line, all in the blink of an eye.

That one, in particular, had caught her attention: No official explanation had sufficed, and the only one that fit—the train had transported itself through miles of packed earth, burrowing up to the tracks—was "simply ridiculous," as she had scoffed.

Probably some kind of, what do they call it? Flash mob thing.

No, odd occurrences be damned: London was her muse. Her new story would be born here.

And she'd tried the usual methods. Strolls on Regent Street. Riding in Hyde Park. Endless cups of tea at Fortnum and Mason, Tea and Tattle, the Savoy. A new designer outfit, tailored to accent her best features and disguise the less than perfect. A brutal two-hour Pilates session, followed by an Aperol spritz.

Such tactics had pulled best-sellers from her before, time and again.

Not today. Not yesterday. Not the whole past week.

She was unable to conjure a device, let alone a plot. Tapping her keyboard only resulted in paragraphs of nonsense in perfect Helvetica. Not a potential killer in any of it. Without a murder, there'd be no new manuscript, no new book tour, no more royalties, no new fans.

She gritted her teeth and slammed the still-full cup onto its saucer. But not even the shattering of porcelain sparked an idea. Scowling at the tea stains on her robe, she stormed into the main bedroom to choose a smart trouser suit. Kicking off the robe, she carried three outfits (all carefully curated by her stylist, every piece—underwear, garments, jewelry, and hair suggestions—colour-coordinated and tagged) into the brighter light of the living room. Satin bags with the correctly-hued make-up for each outfit were also clipped to the hangers.

Still, AAA found fault with the selections, re-arranging the pieces into something at least tolerable. Then she examined herself in one of the many, many mirrors, almost satisfied. Draping a clean robe over her shoulders, she began applying make-up in short, stabbing motions, flinging each of the supplies in the general direction of the trash can after it had served its purpose. A particularly vivid eye shadow compact hit the Cubist portrait squarely on the chin.

She glanced at the shallow dent it left in the canvas, then froze. *Are those damn paintings sneering?* The three faces seemed to form a virtual wall of…what? Recriminations?

"Dammit!" Yanking off the new robe, she swept it across the pile of newspapers and telegrams on the polished table, plush terrycloth creating a paper tornado that swirled to rest on the antique Turkish rug. Leaving, as tornadoes sometimes did in the wild, a single item untouched and exactly centred on the table.

This seemed to be an advertisement, a facsimile of an old handbill. GENTLE FOLKE, it read in elegant Copperplate, BE YE WELCOME TO THE MOST FASHIONABLE AND PRAISE WORTHY EMPORIUM OF TOOLS AND ACCESSORIES FOR SCRIBES WHO WRITE WITH ONLY THE FINEST IMPLEMENTS. ALL SUCH NEEDS WILL BE MET AT PEN PARTNERS.

No street address, mobile number, or website. Not even a Facebook page. The only directions, in smaller script below, referred to *the elegant array of shoppes and sellers, newly erected adjacent to the home of Lord Devon of Cavendish.*

Something about that name prickled. She scrabbled through the papers on the floor, finding a Pepto-Bismol-pink fan fiction manuscript titled "Lord Devon's Portal."

According to the helpful synopsis, Lord Devon of Cavendish had purchased Burlington House, an 18th-century mansion, and, not wanting to travel far for retail therapy, installed plenty of artisans and craftsman nearby. The "shoppes" must be Burlington Arcade, the Regency version of a strip mall.

For a moment, she vacillated. The tablet, the laptop, the reference books all regarded her in mute accusation. The portraits' sunny smiles had soured into glares.

"Oh, screw it," she advised them.

To justify the escape, she could enjoy her Long Walk—another ritual that had never failed to produce a murder, arson, mayhem, or at least treason. Down Park Lane towards Wellington's Arch, around Wellington circle to Grosvenor, then Lower Grosvenor. Wander towards Buckingham Palace and the Birdcage Walk. Through the Gardens toward Piccadilly. A stop at Fortnum and Mason if the mood hit, or that tiny, amazing chemist, floor to ceiling, bowed glass-fronted oak cabinets, piled high with boxes, bottles, and jars. Hardly bigger than a phone booth, but never had they failed to produce anything she wanted, no matter how distant or exotic.

Grabbing her enormous Hermes messenger bag, she threw in phone, key card, and water bottle, then headed out.

The day appeared fine, at least on Park Lane. Yet as she walked she caught a flash of something racing from behind her, along the sidewalk, headed to some distant point ahead. The brightness momentarily blinded her. She reached out to steady herself on a stone wall. *Lightning? No…a fireball? Ridiculous. It had to be lightning.* Blinking, she checked the sky. All clear. *So where had that flash come from?*

As she paused there an enamel-black carriage, windows curtained, pulled by four perfectly matched black Frisians, hurtled down Park Lane. It passed a few feet from where she stood, yet neither the wheels nor the horses' hooves made a sound. Alicia flattened against the wall, staring after the carriage as it careered down Park Lane and out of sight. If not for the slipstream that buffeted her hair, she might've believed it was a hologram or a hallucination.

This impression was heightened by the complete lack of reaction from anyone else. Actually, the major thoroughfare was almost deserted. The shops proffering fine rugs, imported furniture, and handmade jewelry all appeared to be closed. The usual hordes of Burberry-clad Asian tourists were nowhere in evidence. *Bank holiday?* The few pedestrians in sight were uniformly dull, clad in browns and grays almost head to toe, despite the mild weather. Nowhere— not on the main roads or the dim mews—did she see more than two people together, and those, only at a distance.

Rattled, Alicia turned in a circle, trying to orient herself. And saw . . . no, *felt* a familiar upscale alley appear in her peripheral vision. Burlington Arcade!

At the same moment, the dark clouds released a deluge.

Holding the Hermes bag over her head, she dashed into The Arcade. A lovely corridor of shops with bowed-glass fronts, it was also deserted. No one else out to enjoy the peaceful sanctuary, bathed in soft light, still looking as it must have in the 19th century. She shook herself, remembering her mission. Maybe something here would rouse the sleeping muse.

The space felt not so much ancient as timeless. She touched the mullioned window-glass of the first shop, an antique store. It displayed a tasteful array of Restoration silver jugs, Victorian jewelry; bits and bobs from here and there in the Kingdom. Alicia had purchased a salver there years ago; a silver tray meant to hold calling cards, though no one used such cards now. Across the arcade, a smaller shop displayed cashmere sweaters, jackets, and scarves, though the colours appeared oddly muted, the glass almost frosted over, as if it were midwinter. This recalled a January sale, years ago, when she'd found a vibrantly plaid pair of gloves in the same shop. Then she'd wandered into the next place, one stuffed with antique (or antique-adjacent) prints and books, searching for a gift or something, but in the end had bought the gloves instead.

As she (mused, recalled, puzzled over this lapse) she saw, slightly askew from the other shops, a sign indicating the one that held (she felt sure) the cure for her ailment.

Pen Partners.

It looked as if it had always been there, the name clinging to the glass door by a few gold flakes. As if shrugging off such a common idea as attracting walk-in business, the display cabinets backed right to the windows, requiring anyone interested to enter to see the wares. The few tastefully-inked signs visible through the glass touted names that had been on offer since the 19th century: Waterman. Schaeffer. Conway.

The last time Alicia had used a pen, she'd been a different person. Before Roger. Before Stan. Even before… well, anyone of note. Sometime in the 1980s, when she'd still practiced law. Had still tried to fit in with Ivy Leaguers, still forced herself to behave like a good Reagan Republican. Back then, she'd used only fountain pens. Elegant, gorgeous ones, with gold nibs, enamel bodies, rich colours. Some spun delicate webs of words, finer than spider thread. Others slashed darkly across cream vellum in broad streaks of insistent black. Others bled words, creating songs she could never sing.

Beauty begets beauty. Hadn't someone once said that?

Probably me, she decided.

Through the window, past glass cases and midnight-dark cabinets hung a metal sign for Conway Dinky, seemingly held together with mildew. A cardboard advertisement for Pelikan ink in German leaned precariously against a standing vitrine.

Oh, why not?

The door opened inward. Inside a short foyer, a single step abruptly rose as if intent on tripping browsers. Just catching herself, she stumbled further and braced herself on the cabinet to her right. "Hello?"

No one answered. *Odd.* Less tentatively, she stepped into the centre of the room.

The space appeared precisely as a shop that sold some elegant, barely-relevant commodity like telegraph keys or bustles should look. The glass cases were well-stocked with pens in colourful enamel and somber Bakelite. Brushed, polished, and etched metal stylii lay like dead soldiers in well-worn felt-lined cases. Smaller signs discreetly suggested Waterman, Elysse, Monteverde, Lamy, and even more obscure brands. Tidy stacks of thick, creamy linen paper awaited the scratch of a nib. Along the walls, glass-fronted cabinets held ink, organized by brand. Almost as an afterthought, a few journals, pads, and desk blotters were relegated to a small display case.

Also odd, she thought. *Wouldn't those be the most popular items? Well, maybe not the blotters…*

The air smelled papery. Dry and expensively aged. Not dusty, exactly, but as if the room had been closed up for a very long time, and her entrance had done nothing to refresh it. Despite the broad glass facade, the interior was dim.

Blinking, she looked around. (In her craft book on writing, she'd advised would-be authors to closely examine every new space, observing and cataloging the features for use in future work. After inventing that advice, she occasionally tried to follow it.)

"Hello?" she asked again. Again, no reply.

Well, screw them! She turned to leave.

The door was gone.

Moments before there'd been a glass-paned exit leading outside to the arcade. Now a person of substantial height and weight stood against a solid plaster wall. He—or she?—wore the plain gray cotton smock that had designated 19th century London shop assistants, and could still be seen in smaller, older, stuffier establishments. The smock's matching belt and ample pockets barely circumnavigated the wearer's considerable bulk. Beneath the straining fabric, the person wore faded jeans and a sweatshirt whose hood—its colour a perfect match for the smock's—covered the assistant's head. A face mask, sewn from the same gray fabric, completed the look.

Ah, the shopkeeper, she thought.

Perhaps it was the dim lighting, but the size of the figure—well over six feet—and its unexpected androgyny sent a shock through her.

"H-hello." She took a step back.

The figure nodded. There came a whispery sound Alicia mistook for the rustle of cloth until she realized it was a faint greeting. Then the shopkeeper simply waited.

"Er, good morning . . . ." She finally decided the proprietor of such a place would most likely be male. ". . . sir. I'm looking for, uh, a fountain pen." *Oh, genius! What else, in a pen shop?*

The proprietor nodded again.

"I'm a writer." She almost added *You may have heard of me*—but even she realized that would sound ridiculous. Instead, she blurted out, "I used to have fountain pens, a lot of them—really nice ones. I wrote my first book with one. They're, well, you know,... almost magical. So I...er, I..."

The masked figure gave an infinitesimal shrug, or twitch.

Alicia soldiered on. "My publisher's getting nasty. They want something, actually they've demanded a new manuscript for a long while, but the story just isn't coming. I mean, I've tried, everything that usually works, and—nothing! I'm ..."

She paused. *Desperate?* Too hysterical. *Anxious?* Too whiny. "...at the end of my rope."

No response to this cry for help.

"I would do anything..." She stopped. *Anything? Really? Am I really that desperate?* The knot in her stomach tightened, grew, threatened to vomit itself up, which would have rendered her humiliation complete. Clearly, she was *that* desperate.

The shopkeeper leaned back slightly as if alarmed.

Regretting her admission, she tried to walk it back. "It's just, I must get started on...before... I've always.... it's never...."

He, or they, leaned forward again as if to catch her words in that masked mouth.

"Anything," she repeated. And in this moment she meant it.

Another faint whisper. The shopkeeper inclined his head and motioned for her to follow along to the front counter. A skeleton key simply appeared in one hand, and he slipped it into a drawer-lock beneath the cabinet of inks. The drawer made no sound as he pulled it out, although a faint wisp of ethereal music seemed to sigh from its depths.

The Shopkeeper carefully laid out a sheet of dark-green blotter paper on the countertop. He weighted one edge with three crystal inkwells, each barely the size of an apricot. Then drew out a stool she hadn't noticed before.

She sat across from him. For the first time, the Shopkeeper raised his eyes to meet hers. Deep, intense orbs of green, ringed in black, they seemed to demand knowledge of her intentions, and willingness to pay.

"Yes. Anything," she confirmed.

As she leaned on the stone counter *(Wait. Hadn't it been glass, before?)* the shopkeeper produced a sheet of fine, nubby paper, woven with linen strands. The three crystal pots were each stoppered with a different coloured gemstone. Garnet red. Peacock Blue. Onyx. These exquisite, tiny, faceted treasures were filled with ink to match the stones. Next to each inkwell, the shopkeeper laid a long, thin, velvet bag, each dyed to match the inkwell lids.

Well, that was hardly practical. *How much ink could such tiny pots hold? Must be for testing a pen. Samples only.*

The shopkeeper picked up the bag next to the black ink and pulled out a pen, of sorts: a long wand of dark silken wood gripping a needle-fine nib. It glowed a brilliant lacquered black, like the careering carriage on Park Lane.

"Oh. No. I, er, wanted a fountain pen."

He still held it out.

"No, sorry. Not a dip pen… that won't work for me."

The hand remained unwavering.

"Really. Are you sure?"

A slight nod of encouragement.

"Well, all right then."

With undisguised ill humor, she snatched the pen. Immediately, it rolled and settled into position between fingers and thumb, ready to imbibe. As if it had a mind and locomotion of its own. As if it was, well . . . alive, even. The wood felt like satin: warm, sensuous, not stiff at all. The finely honed nib glowed with a rosy hue.

"Oh, my…" she breathed, feeling a sensual warmth. The pen felt liquid and solid and everything in between. But most of all, like a part of her, and vice versa.

She darted the nib at the inkwell, and the India black seemed to grow deeper, no—denser. Rather than a mere puddle in the crystal, the nib drew in ink as if sucking liquid from a bottomless well. Alarmed, Alicia yanked the pen out, spraying an ebony crescent across the paper.

"Oh! Sorry, I… sorry."

The figure calmly gestured toward the stained paper. Encouragement? Instruction? Censure? She couldn't tell.

"I really don't know how to… I mean, I haven't used even a fountain pen in decades."

Still, she touched nib to paper. Instantly, a blot. She jerked it back, face flaming. *Acting like a rube who's never written a word.*

More gently, she laid the nib on the paper and wrote:

Anno Dominus

She froze. *But I don't know Latin.*

After a moment, she began again. **In the name of our Lord, the just and the good, blessed be He, forever.**

She blinked at the words, not quite believing she'd written them. Yet, the next line came even more easily:

Oh, sorrowful year, of plague and death, we humbly beseech You, oh Lord, to guide our hands, our hearts and our swords. Today, in the field of clay, favored by those who make pots and vessels, a great faire has arisen. No man or woman in this shire dared to venture into the field, yet those within made merry, loud with lute, bright as in daylight, though it be past evensong.

"What in God's name….?" she whispered.

The pen tugged slightly, straining thirstily for more ink. Helplessly, she steered it into the pot, then back to the paper.

On this day of the feast of John the Baptist, we await your judgment, Lord. As your servant John was murdered by the evil king, we accept our fate, as those who trill and laugh must be made to accept theirs. Yet, we beseech you, Lord: did John escape? Was he spared?

The pen raced across the paper, line after line, without hesitation. A story unfolded, written in archaic language, yes . . . but intense, driven, complex, layered. The *true* story of John the Baptist. How, far from spurning the temptress Salome, he was seduced by her. They fell in love, insanely, deeply. Plotting their escape, the two beautiful sinners risked everything to be together.

Then Herod demanded that Salome dance. And dance she did, weaving a fantasy in veils, colour, and movement. The king was bewitched, drawn into that fantasy, falling headlong into visions. Entranced, he begged her, "What do you want? I will grant anything! Anything at all!"

Salome spun away, trailing gossamer veils, cooing, "Give me the head of John the Baptist." Slavering, Herod promised it. In a shockingly short time, a hooded figure appeared, carrying a hairy lump that he tossed before the now-horrified Herod.

No one in the court noticed the hooded figure melt from the room, or that Salome followed him. No one recognized the figure as John, disguised, freed by his lover. The head had belonged to one of John's most faithful, most gullible followers, willingly murdered to save the Baptist's life. The lovers fled the palace, Herod, and the throngs of John's betrayed supporters. Under new identities they reached Egypt, where they lived out their days, making love in the shadow of the Great Sphinx. Freed from the tyranny of religious fame and grasping despots. And with no mention of deserts, locusts, baptisms, or Jesus.

Alicia sat up as the pen scratched dry. The story was amazing. Lyrical. No gimmicks, no cynical "hooks." Just elegant prose and a gripping, timeless story. Better (she reluctantly admitted) than anything she'd ever written. There was a murder, of course, but woven with shades of poetry. Too short for a novel, but she could envision a longer framework—a proper cushion on which to cradle this jewel. Warmth and joy came with the realization: *This will sell!* She imagined the ripple of ecstasy that would spread through all the editors, agents, lawyers, and fans who constituted the empire of AAA.

The shopkeeper had said nothing as she wrote. If he'd even breathed, she could not tell. Now she wanted to say "Thank you," but that sounded stupid. After all, he hadn't given her the idea. And had she even reached for another sheet of paper? The one she'd used simply seemed to grow longer as she wrote, then end, just as the story did.

"I….I must get back to my hotel." She dropped the pen, and clutched the long scroll of story to her chest.

The shopkeeper reared back.

Jumping to her feet, Alicia sprinted for the door which—thank goodness—was there again. But oddly, no longer made of glass but rough wood. She gripped its crude iron handle, heaving the heavy thing creakingly open, stumbling through it to…

To where?

Burlington Arcade was gone.

Instead of the familiar Regency Shoppes, a gathering that vaguely resembled a low-rent Renaissance fair occupied the courtyard (or alley?) Tents, tables, billowing cloth shelters tied to crude wooden poles. A few wood-slatted stalls leaned against painted wagons. Instead of a quiet, elegant, cobblestoned galleria, there was a long stretch of mud, full of bleating, clucking, and mooing livestock, the cries of vendors, and bursts of ancient-sounding songs. People who resembled peasants in History Channel documentary clomped past, clad in rough-woven, shapeless clothing and crude leather boots. One middle-aged woman, swathed in black from collar to ankles, lounged on a nearby tree stump, eyeing Alicia with mild curiosity. The air was thick with horse droppings and cow dung, overlaid with stale sweat, bonfire smoke, and pungent spices…

Alicia clapped a hand to her nose, gagging. Then noticed her sleeve.

Instead of the stylish Tory Burch jacket, she wore coarse brown wool. The fringed tails of a headscarf hung down its front, woven in a beautiful shade of blue that seemed familiar, although she couldn't place where she'd seen it before. Gasping, she slid her hands down thighs, expecting to feel her smooth, silky microfiber slacks . . . and discovered a rough, heavy skirt, the hem of which dragged the ground in a dusty cloud. At least the Hermes bag was still slung over one shoulder, but instead of wallet, phone, and cosmetics, it held only dried bread crumbs and a bit of dust.

Even odder, the sunny day was turning dark—a deep, infinite blackness above, speckled with stars so bright that she wondered, for a moment, if she were witnessing a nova in some far-off galaxy. *But . . . it was only morning when I left the hotel. Where has the time gone?*

A few torches and a raised pot—a brazier?—set on an iron tripod over an open fire, barely frayed the night's shroud. *What….where….* Words formed in her throat but died on her tongue. She spun, seeking the sight of something familiar, and nearly smacked a man with her bag. He wore a long robe belted with a thick chain that suspended a leather pouch.

He spewed a guttural riff of angry-sounding words. The lounging woman sprang to her feet, waving him off. She addressed Alicia, soothingly, in words that sounded almost like English, but not quite. *Middle English? Old English? Middling Old…?*

The man growled a final curse and spat in the dirt before stomping away, into a tent.

"I . . . sorry, I don't understand," Alicia stammered.

The woman's brow creased. Slowly, deliberately, she laid both hands on her chest. "Hell Ayn Ah," she pronounced. "Hell Ayn Ah."

Alicia blinked. "Hell Ayn Ah?" She considered. "Oh, Helena!"

The woman smiled. "Aye." Somewhere between forty and death, her face creased more deeply, expectantly, awaiting a reply.

"Oh." Alicia pointed to herself. "Alicia."

That was the whole of their conversation. Helena was staring with frank curiosity at the paper clutched in Alicia's fist.

At last she waved at a nearby tent as if inviting Alicia in, rattling off something in the guttural language.

Alicia merely stared, uncomprehendingly.

Helena threw up her hands and ducked through a flap in another tent.

Alicia considered following but a sign propped before the canvas shelter brought her up short. A rough plank, whitewashed sloppily, was painted with a crude soot-black cauldron. Glancing around, she noticed most of the tents had similar pictographic signs. A bloody ram, impaled on a lance. A turtle holding a candle. A bonfire. A jug or cup, maybe earthenware, maybe metal. And over the tent where the menacing man had disappeared, a bolt of lightning.

That drew her interest. Patting the rough canvas, she sought an opening. The same man, face contorted with fury, sprang through the front flap waving a stout piece of firewood. Though barely her height, he was powerfully built.

Alicia stumbled back, raising both hands to shield herself. As she did, the crumpled story from the pen shop brushed his cheek. He grabbed for it, almost pulling the paper from her hand. She yanked it back, surprised it didn't rip in two.

The man muttered something threatening. She caught only "chap-woman" and "writ." He seemed offended by her and the paper.

Clutching it to her chest, she stumbled backward, then rushed off into the night. *Where was Helena? At least she wasn't hostile. But still, where am I?* In the distance rose the spire of a church, maybe a cathedral. Vaguely familiar, as if she'd glimpsed it before, in a different time. *Canterbury? Oxford? Salisbury? Nuts!* No matter where she was now, she had to get back.

She looked along the rows for the sign with the cauldron. *Wasn't it right… there? Or, no, the next row…*

This farmer's market, or Renn Faire, or whatever it was, was coming to life. More people appeared, all clad in dull, heavy clothing which covered them almost completely. A few stretched out a hand to beg, or to sell her goods in shockingly worn condition. Each time she broke away, fixated on finding the one friendly face she'd encountered. She staggered along, glimpsing shelves and counters within and outside the structures, laden with earthenware pots, wooden boxes, draped cloth . . . although, oddly, not a single description or price, except the vague wooden signs hung overhead.

She did not so much find Helena as fall into her. Gripping the woman's arm, she blurted, "Help me. Please!"

Murmuring comfortingly, Helena steered Alicia to a wooden bench, seat worn unevenly smooth, under the cauldron sign that decorated her tent. She was more slender than she'd appeared in the voluminous, shapeless dress. Thin, almost fragile. She gently pressed Alicia down onto the bench and sat beside her.

"He wanted this." Alicia held out the story to Helena, who jerked back sharply as if she had a phobia about paper. Though she studied it, frowning.

Can she read? Is my handwriting that bad? Or is it the language?

As if hearing her thoughts, Helena pulled a cloth bag from the folds of her voluminous skirts. Slowly, she drew from it a slender object, about a hand's breadth long.

Alicia tensed. *Was it a knife?*

Helena held it out on her open palm, for Alicia to inspect. With the other hand she pulled from a worn leather sheath a metal rod, probably bronze, about the size and shape of a crochet hook, notched on one end. Then she slid the object between her fingers, and mimed writing.

"Yes! The pen store!" Alicia cried. "I must get back there!"

Helena rose and stepped inside her tent. A lantern or candle flared, and for a moment, Alicia could dimly see rough shelving, laden with crocks, cups, and boxes. *Is she a witch? Maybe getting a potion, or working a spell?*

Helena returned, wrapped in a dark cloak, carrying a stout walking stick. No potions in sight. Gently, she pulled Alicia to her feet, and steered her down the bustling rows of stalls and tents, moving with certainty to the far end of the market. The rank smell of the place was, if anything, even more oppressive there. The laughter and complaints of humans and animals seemed to rise to a crescendo as they passed.

A few feet from the last tent, Helena raised her stick like a javelin and pushed Alicia forward with her other hand. In one swift movement, Helena flung the stick and shoved Alicia hard into the outer darkness.

She lurched forward, falling to hands and knees. Stunned for a moment, she finally levered herself up again.

She was back in the pen shop. The shopkeeper stood, arms folded, as if he'd never moved. The shop again had glass cabinets, clear windows, and shelves of pens, ink, and paper. Alicia staggered over to slump onto the stool. The counter—glass again—held only two inkwells and two pens.

The shopkeeper thrust out a hand. *Did he want the story back?*

Alicia looked at the paper wadded in her fist.

"No. I need this. I...I want to keep it."

He shook his head.

"But it's good! The best—I can work this into a great book. It will sell!"

The Shopkeeper pointed to the shop windows, to the Arcade, with its pricey stores, and electric lights, then, to the counter. He laid one palm flat on the glass as if to say, *Leave it here.*

Well, I can remember it, can't I? I don't really need the paper…

Sighing, she laid it on the counter.

The Shopkeeper picked it up. Instantly, the page burst into flame, disappearing before she could even protest. He (as far as Alicia could discern behind the mask) did not wince or flinch as the page vanished, leaving not even a smudge of ash.

Screwing her eyes shut, she tried to remember the opening sentences. Nothing. *What about that section in the middle, the dance, the head? What was the last line? It was so good!*

The Shopkeeper gazed at her steadily. At least, she thought he did. His head had retreated even further into the hood.

"So the paper has to stay here?"

He moved his shoulders in a close approximation of a shrug.

"And does…the pen?" She needn't have asked. It was gone.

"But, I still need a story. If I write another, must it stay here, in the shop?"

Again, a sort of shrug.

Alicia had not become a People's Choice Book Award winner without knowing how to persevere. Steeling herself, she straightened and reached for the pen in a peacock blue velvet bag.

Unlike the first, this was made of brushed metal. Dark gray, surprisingly light. While cool to the touch, it quickly warmed in her hand. The nib seemed an extension of the pen's body; seamless, elegant.

The pen immediately quivered (the sensation hardly seemed to be Alicia's doing) toward the inkwell topped with the peacock blue stone. As if waiting, the lid rose on its own. Again, the pen sank into the depths of colour, green-blue, iridescent, gleaming. As the nib descended, the ink shimmered. Smoothly, the pen drank and drank, then aimed for the paper.

She struggled to remember the first lines of the lost story.

The pen would have none of it. Instead, it shaped a different tale.

NXXY 52 did not recognize the humanoid, despite the 5,399,800,453 records it searched before the figure had stepped on the communication pad. Had the AI been human, it might have experienced pique that the figure had defeated its massive database and impressive processing power. As a superior mechanism, however, NXXY 52 wasted no energy on anything so utterly useless as emotion. Instead, it began the exchange."Greetings, Unit. Your request?"

The figure, identifiable as Homo Sapiens, full double XX, shriveled Y, K 15, might once have been classified as female. Such crude distinctions had been long abandoned, however. While some HS XX chose clothing of particular styles and colours, this one had merely draped itself in protective layers of the standard 7009 hue (NXXY 52 had once heard standard 7009 referred to as "beige" but as the word was unnecessary, it was dropped into the archive folder).

In response to NXXY 52's query, a small part of the figure's top section processor creased. "My request is that you solve a murder."

NXXY 52 hesitated, although so briefly the human organoid could not possibly sense that pause. "Murder is a criminal offence for which notification of enforcement authority is appropriate—"

The figure waved an upper appendage. "The murder has not yet been committed, so it requires your special talent to solve it."

NXXY 52 considered this for a particle of a nanosecond, while a dozen queries whipped through its circuits. "Who is the putative victim?"

Folding its upper limbs, the figure again creased its top part. "You. You will be the victim."

Alicia lifted the pen from the paper. *What the hell?*

The pen protested the interruption, straining toward the paper. She lowered it again.

But I don't do sci-fi, she thought, as the story continued unabated, full of "Proto-sentients" and "humanoid units" (clearly lesser beings). The humans were mostly happy blobs of flesh who led useless lives of decadence. The Proto-sentients ran everything. Perfectly.

She didn't understand how she knew all of this, though, as she'd barely written the first two hundred words. It struck her then that she needn't sit here, uncomfortably scribbling away. She could leave, go back to her hotel.

She swept up the pen and paper, barely glancing at the shopkeeper, who seemed to be slowly, slightly, shaking his head.

The shop's door was glass again, although now when she approached it slid aside automatically as a stage curtain. She stepped outside. The storefronts that lined the Arcade were still there, still fronted with curved glass.

Except...

These were not the same shops she'd passed on her way into Pen Partners. Gone were the pricey cashmere sweaters, the fusty antiques, the retro print shop. In their stead, stood—no—*floated* large bulbous containers, glowing softly. Within them moved figures clothed in what looked like the white Ty-vek bunny suits CSI techs wore on detective series. The colour, a harsh, cold white, reminded her of something, some outfit she had worn or seen….somewhere.

Looking down, she saw she was clothed in just such a suit as well.

What the actual….? Alicia whirled around; all breath sucked from her chest. She staggered slightly, then found her footing. *Wherever…WHENever this is, there has to be a way out!*

Plucking up the plasticky white legs of her jumpsuit, she headed for what should've been Burlington House. Instead of the elegant palace, a particularly huge, particularly bright globe rippled softly as she stared at it. Soft dinging like the alarm on a dryer or dishwasher emitted from nowhere, growing louder. She jumped as a sleek metal machine sailed past so closely its wake ruffled her hair. Shaped like a giant steel capsule, it had no windows or markings.

The dinging faded. The machine approached the globe and penetrated its skin silently. The surface of the glowing orb sealed itself behind the vehicle, leaving no sign of the breach.

It took her a moment to realize the vehicle possessed no wheels. It had, in a word, flown. In another moment, she saw that all the globes—and the buildings within—sat not on the smooth, pristine pavement, but hovered slightly above it.

Tentatively, she walked up to the large globe and touched it. The surface's warm, satiny feel yielded slightly to her touch. Instantly, two icons appeared on its surface. One shaped like an old-fashioned theatre ticket, the other a simple five-pointed star. On a whim, she tapped the star. Her hand slid through the thing's skin as if it were less substantial than a breeze. Jerking her arm back, she saw the star had been replaced by a slot a little wider than her palm. She stuck her hand into the slot, feeling a slight tingle. It glowed around her wrist for a moment, then turned an angry red. Her hand was pushed out as forcefully as if a tiny, highly focused hurricane had bloomed inside the slot.

Maybe it wants money. She rummaged through her bag, but, again, her wallet was gone, this time replaced by a collection of slick cards of varying shapes and sizes.

As she stared at the globe, another silent floating vessel sailed up, discharging eight small figures in matching white jumpsuits, with mesh faceplates like fencers' masks. Chattering happily in what might've been English, but cluttered with words she did not recognize, the figures—giggling and crowding as children do everywhere—tapped the globe at seemingly random spots. Too quickly for her to quite grasp, they slid their hands into slots that appeared after they touched an icon. The slots glowed green.

The children passed through. *School trip? eTickets?*

Alicia tried again, but the bubble would not admit her.

She made her way around the globe towards what she hoped was Piccadilly Street. Instead of the familiar crowded, smoggy boulevard of shops and restaurants, however, she found a gleaming slash of colour, light, and movement. Instead of buildings, more faceless bubbles. Although the ancient Fortnum and Mason clock protruded from one, providing at least that familiar landmark.

There were few pedestrians. Traffic raced through the air above her; layers of metallic bands spinning like the rings of Saturn. Here and there, a vehicle sank to the surface, discharging passengers, who then entered various glowing orbs.

"Entered"? Or were absorbed like a shrimp by a jellyfish? She shuddered.

Closer to the orbs, she saw signs glowing softly on their surfaces. Much like the London she knew, this street appeared to still house brisk commercial activity.

Just as at the ancient fair, the signs displayed symbols, not words. More artful ones, though. Glowing pictographs informing those who passed that shoes or food or entertainment could be found within. A few, like Fortnum and Mason, had a colourful scroll of picnic baskets, clothing icons, bottles, and fruit. There were numbers on the orbs, as well. Perhaps addresses? Apparently people found whatever it was they wanted.

But . . . where are the words, here? And the smells?

Unlike, well, anyplace she had been, but especially the Middle Ages, the air was curiously anonymous. Neutral, even sterile. Every identifying component—tactile, visual, aural, or olfactory—was missing. The weather was neither hot nor cold. No breeze, except from passing vehicles, and that barely a breath. Though she saw people, vehicles, stores, and movement, there were no smells of any sort. No petrol fumes. Not even the normal urban chemical wafts of disinfectant, or perfumes, or greasy fast food.

The placid, bland *sameness* of the street was disorienting. Instead of the limestone Regency facades, the colonnades, the plate glass exhibitions of every conceivable item, there were only globes, coolly glowing, with monochrome icons. The vibrant, colourful, overheated frenzy of London had been drained away, replaced by homogenized uniformity. Every globe was a mystery. Their icons, a test of her comprehension.

But was it the same? As she gaped at a particularly bright orb, two people, clad in the ubiquitous white jumpsuits, brushed by. As they passed through the membrane of the orb, their jumpsuits faded away like a cheap special effect.

The couple was suddenly clad in swaths of brilliant red and orange that were not so much *worn* as floating over the wearers, as they traveled into the orb.

What the actual....? She stared as their last remnant disappeared from view. Another silent vehicle stopped behind her, dinging madly. *Hell!* She was blocking the sidewalk, bumping into people. Irritated, she realized she'd devolved into the kind of gawking, stumbling tourist who'd always driven her mad.

Finally, she approached an orb markedly different from the others, being a fraction of their size. The light within was not as bright, nor its surface as cool. It felt . . . familiar. She pressed on the skin which instantly gave way, and peeked inside. This room she recognized instantly: a tiny chemist shop. The same chemist's shop that had always produced exactly what she needed, when larger stores did not.

Hesitantly, she poked one foot through the bubble, finding an astonishingly solid floor within. When she swung her weight onto that foot, she discovered she could pass through the surface with the merest sensation of movement, a faint brushing against her cheeks. Her clothing had transfigured as it passed through the membrane, although only to an even more drab, plasticky version of a jumpsuit.

The shop, however, was the same: Floor to ceiling cabinets, oak with glass doors, holding neat stacks of colourful cardboard boxes, metal tubes, and brown glass bottles. She realized for the first time there was nothing plastic here. Nothing except her glaringly bright white jumpsuit, that is. Again, it seemed vaguely familiar: the colour, the texture, even the impossibly sharp edges that made it seem like…*who was that geometric artist guy? Mondrian, maybe…*

The counter was of some clear material, possibly glass, but no one stood behind it. She approached and laid the paper she clutched atop it. The pen, still in her other hand, quivered again, as if longing to write on. She allowed it to descend onto the paper, and take up where it'd left off, as if she had just re-dipped the nib.

The story quickly shaped itself: beautiful beings wafted through corridors lined with softly lit alcoves. As they passed, the human beings—no, better than human; more perfect—examined shelves lined with glowing jars. As they touched these they appeared to feel an array of emotions. Joy, yes, though apparently nonstop joy gets boring in short order. Deep, sexual pleasure. A few prickles of sorrow—nothing too terrible. In the story, one being reached into a jar that glowed a seductive pale blue. Then screamed in horror, laughed hysterically, wept, raged—as if a tsunami of emotions was being forced all at once through their very soul. Finally, the being dropped, puddling into a glowing blob on the floor. In the next scene, Artificial Intelligence Unit NXXY 52 was framed for the crime and marked for termination.

A murder? Yes! But a crime such as she had never written or even imagined, swiftly committed to paper by the indefatigable pen. *Murder by infused, synthesized emotions.*

Despite the torrent of words spilling onto it, the page never ended. It grew longer and longer, accommodating the flood until the final, surprising end.

At last Alicia straightened, grinning. *This is it. My next blockbuster.*

Of course she'd expand it to the required sixty-thousand-word minimum, but that wouldn't be hard. She could flesh out scenes with descriptions of the streets, the flying vehicles, the rows of glowing orbs. A little backstory.

Carefully, she raised her hands above the page. It remained; the writing did as well. No flames, no vanishing. *Maybe if I keep pen AND paper together, the story can stay with me?* She set the pen down on the page. It quivered slightly, then lay still.

But how to get back to the right time and place? Surely it was possible, but how? Perhaps she could find the pen store again, but she dreaded returning. *What if he takes my story away again?*

Still, where else could she go?

She left the chemist and, after a few wrong turns, found Pen Partners. At least the future version. It, too, levitated just above ground level in its own bubble. She poked the toe of her white boots through the skin, found the floor, and entered again as if mounting an actual step. Again, the merest sense of motion brushed her cheeks.

Inside, the shop looked much the same, although the case stacked with journals, diaries, and papers held small glowing items as well. The proprietor was still dressed in brown, but his garment lacked texture, as if it had been sprayed into being, rather than woven.

She clutched pen and paper more tightly to her chest. "I… I must keep this story."

Was that sadness in those shadowed eyes? He pointed to the counter. The blotter held two ink pots but only one velvet bag. Slowly, she laid the pen on the blotter. To her surprise it rolled towards the shopkeeper, who stopped it with one thick finger. Then, as in a magician's cheesy stage trick, the pen vanished into his huge hand.

"I need this story. I mean it! this time I must keep it."

The shopkeeper slowly shook his head.

In her real life, Alicia never begged. But nothing about this day seemed like real life. "Please. I want it so badly."

He pointed towards the Arcade. Reluctantly, she turned to look. The space was lined with glowing bubbles, where figures were vaguely moving as if floating on a buoyant mist. Wherever, whenever this was, it wasn't her own here and now.

"Can I take it with me? May I? If I need to…" *Go home? Return?* She was unsure of the right verb. "Well . . . leave."

Was that a shrug? Reluctantly, she handed the story over. It'd barely left her fingers when it folded itself into a sharp-cornered rectangle, then disappeared with a barely audible pop.

Not really surprised, she gulped, "I still need . . . a story. Some story." She moved to her next tactic, usually foolproof. "And I can pay."

The shopkeeper did not even blink, but only pointed to the last velvet bag and inkwell. Taking this as a positive sign, she slid a new pen from the bag. Compared to the others, this one was modest, almost a disappointment. Wine red, like the inkwell's lid, it seemed to be made of plain, heavy-duty plastic or . . . what was that old-fashioned stuff called? Oh yes—Bakelite. It fit her hand reasonably well, but didn't generate the warmth of the other pens.

A clean sheet awaited. This, too, lacked the finer attributes of previous pages. It was simply paper, the copy bond type. Not luxurious linen with a nubby quality like the first. No warm sheen, like the second. The pen did not pull, eager to reach for the paper or the inkwell.

Still, this felt like the last chance. Thoughts whirred desperately through her head: what had she done or *not* done properly? Why, when, how did she fail to… to *own* the stories she'd written? Each time, she had started them in the shop…

Was that the key? If she started the story in the shop, did it have to stay in the shop?

But how could she use a story if she were stuck with it in some fusty store in a different time altogether? Besides, she had written most of the second one someplace else. So the creating did not have to occur here. *Right?*

What about the pen…and the inkwell? Maybe they must stay together. Maybe where I write isn't important, but that *is…*

She fingered the paper, then snatched and crumpled it up, and flung it at the shopkeeper.

He stepped back with a faint gasp.

Alicia grabbed pen and inkwell, the latter of which did not seem quite as heavy as the previous one. Cramming them into her bag, she dashed for the door. And it *was* a door now, not a bubble or a blank wall. It had to be pulled open on the wrong side in that infuriating, wrong-headed, European way, but then she was out.

She glanced briefly behind her. The Shopkeeper had not moved except to gently shake his head. She kept going, clocking briefly that her outfit had returned to its own proper time period, in the right colours, coordinated with the right shoes. She was herself again.

Burlington Arcade, too, had reformed into its 21st-century image. The shops again had bowed glass fronts, doors with handles, and ordinary cashmere sweaters, leatherbound books, pricey antiques, and expensive perfumes lining their shelves.

As she ran for the street, toward Park Lane, and her hotel, she was again struck by the odd lack of pedestrians and traffic. Slowing, she sucked in a few deep breaths. Unlike the sterile atmosphere of the bubble world, the air now had an odd quality and smell. Faintly…*what? electric? chemical?*

Whatever it is, she thought, *it feels . . . right.*

Sooner than expected, she spotted the hotel and dashed inside. But the lobby was deserted as well. Where was the doorman? The desk clerks? Had there been a bomb scare or a terrorist threat, and they'd all fled? But nothing looked amiss. No alarms shrilled, no police sirens wailed.

She called the elevator down and entered the car, then sagged against its mahogany-paneled wall. Relieved to discover her bag once more held room key card, wallet, cosmetics, all the usual detritus. And, most importantly, the pen and inkwell.

Once inside her suite, she carefully took out those last two items, set them on the desk, and looked around for paper.

The floor was still littered with everything she'd swept off the table earlier. Kicking through the detritus, she found an ornately bound journal, gift from a fan. Hideous, yes, but it undeniably shouted NOW. She settled with it at the desk.

Taking a deep breath, she smoothed the journal open, flipped up the inkwell lid, and dipped the pen. Without even a single quiver of enthusiasm, the pen sank into the ink. It tolerated being picked up, but dripped onto the desktop. Grabbing a tissue from a carved box, she mopped the spill carelessly and tossed the soiled scrap to the floor. As she did, the three portraits caught her eye. Were those normally somber faces smiling more than usual? Actually showing… teeth? Had the medieval one always had that blue headpiece pulled so low over the forehead? The Cubist portrait seemed to have developed even more sharp angles, and the white outfit in the picture was now unmistakably…*a jumpsuit.*

"Don't be stupid," she admonished herself, almost flinching at the strain in her voice. Those pictures were merely what they'd always been.

She began writing. A story formed, though slowly. Far more tortuously than in the pen shop or the chemist's. Still, it came. A murder. In a pen shop. The protagonist, a woman of a certain age, stylish and determined, stubbornly risked herself to investigate and solve the crime.

Faster and faster, she scribbled, gushing words as if possessed.

Gradually the old feeling returned. That rush of excitement that came with hitting on the Right Idea, the Perfect Execution, the Beguiling Details. Swept up in the excitement, she continued on to The End.

She knew it was, because the pen suddenly ran dry. The inkwell, too, held not a drop more.

Tossing the pen onto the desk, she snapped the journal shut and threw herself back against the chair. "Yes!"

She threw her head back to laugh, then noticed the three portraits were laughing, too. Silently, but still . . .

The laughter died in her throat.

The portraits' mirth continued.

Before Alicia could react, the closed journal flung its covers open, flipping pages in the still air as if waving goodbye. The pen and inkwell shimmered like a mirage in the desert, and disappeared with a faint pop.

She'd scarcely taken all this in when she was dragged forward uncontrollably by some invisible force. An insistent tugging. The came a pull, drawing her up, up, out of her chair. She rose, feeling oddly lighter, impossibly weightless, as if growing less…solid. Less *real* with every breath.

What the actual…? The pull became an irresistible force. Not just dragging her along but slowly, painlessly, *unpeeling* her physical being, discarding her bodily existence.

Until she simply wasn't there at all.

Sometime later (weeks? months?) Alicia Ann Abercrombie opened her eyes and bleakly observed her surroundings. At least it was an improvement over the wooden packing crates full of plastic peanuts that had been all she could make out since . . . the incident.

If she could, she would've laughed. For she was back at the Alerton, in the Prince's Lair Suite. Only now it was called the AAA Suite, dedicated to the famous writer of crime fiction who had disappeared so mysteriously from this very room three years ago.

Now that the pandemic was over, London in general and this hotel in particular were wildly popular with foreign tourists. She knew this because they kept CNN or the BBC on almost constantly, on the room's ever-more-massive television.

In one of those endless news loops, she'd watched the story of how Alicia Ann Abercrombie had mysteriously vanished from London, leaving behind a handwritten journal with most of an unfinished book, and three paintings.

Once it was apparent Alicia was never returning, the Alerton had turned the suite into a shrine. Thanks to donations from the estate and fans, the hotel had hit on a very profitable concept. For a mere prince's ransom, AAA fans could come to London and stay in the AAA suite, surrounded by bits and pieces of their favorite author. In a glass case, the journal lay open to the first murder scene. A few particularly nice outfits had been embalmed in plastic and hung in wall frames. Tucked here and there, her tech toys, cosmetics, contracts and other relics were available for inspection. Guests could eat exactly what AAA had ordered from room service on her final day in London.

The triptych of paintings had pride of place, of course. Everyone agreed on how well the writer had been lovingly "captured" in them. Some guests (and Alicia found this vaguely disturbing) even lit candles in front of her portraits.

The medieval icon.

The Cubist rendering.

And the Super Realistic portrait.

A few fans remarked on how the third painting seemed to subtly change as they viewed it.

Which was ridiculous, Alicia thought. A portrait is forever; it can't change.

Not even after it was taken away for cleaning, and then returned. A large figure in a grey shop-assistant smock had arrived, carefully unpacked the crate, and dusted it reverently, before hanging it up again between the others.

Not even when Alicia, captured in the portrait, forever frozen in oil paints, silently screamed, over and over, to be released.

Hear that faint jingling, as if tiny bells are ringing nearby? It issues from the booth in this alcove, where Hayward the Hierophant's Mercantile purveys all the homely domestic items needed in any Fae household . . . and more. As one overly-ambitious human shopkeeper discovers when he trespasses on the realm of the Hidden Folk. See that dusty glass-fronted display box, and its cubbyholes with tiny figurines? Some standing upright, others slumped or folded sideways as if asleep. Each has a carved, painted face and wears denim trousers, or red flannel shirts, or faded morning-gowns. The box's rusty latch rattles occasionally, and those high-pitched tinkling notes issue from within. But do take care! Don't touch the display box, or reach inside, for the occupants have been known to bite. Come now, let's not linger; the rest of the Bazaar still awaits!

Mickle's Oddities

by Rebecca Lane

The top half of a small capuchin monkey lay on the worktable in front of Alistair. There were no eyes in its head, only sunken pits with sewn-up lids. The skin was brown and tight, shrunken tightly as a glove to the torso. Yellowed cotton tufts poked out below the creature's stitched waist. It'd been taxidermized, clearly. Maybe even been done properly, many years ago.

Alistair had bought the specimen from a wandering junk seller who'd stopped his wagon in town one afternoon. He hadn't cared if the thing had once been 'museum quality,' as the peddler kept insisting. He'd simply paid the man two quid and carried the specimen to his shop, Mickle's Oddities. There, in the back room, he'd chopped it in half with a meat cleaver so forcefully the spindly legs and tail shot off the table. He hadn't bent to look for them amid the dust and cobwebs. Why bother? He only needed its torso and head.

Bringing an oil lamp to the table, he put on wire-rimmed spectacles and drew a long silver chain from within his shirt. With the small pair of crane-shaped scissors attached to it he carefully trimmed all the fur off the animal's pelt. Once finished, he murmured, "There, that's better."

His predecessor had always used a straight razor for this chore, but Alistair liked the scissors. With them he had more control over the outcome. A wrong move with a pair of small, narrow blades wasn't enough to ruin an oddity, usually. But one ill-placed swipe of a straight razor could destroy everything. Why take the risk, for when would he find another specimen like this? It'd been ages since he'd seen anything close.

A China doll lay nearby on the work table, next to a leathery, dried headless carp. With a wooden crochet hook, Alistair opened the fish's body and slid it partway over the monkey's truncated waist. With a curved needle and dark thread, he stitched them together, fusing two halves into one new creature. Then he cut some of the doll's brown hair from its porcelain scalp, spread a thin layer of glue over the back of the monkey's head, and carefully arranged the borrowed locks in place.

Now it was time for the project to rest a while. The glue must dry well; the stitches needed to settle. Tomorrow he'd move the new oddity to pride of place in the shop, under one of the smudged glass display boxes. All that was left to do was write out its identification card, and set a price.

The paper he selected for this purpose was heavy and precut, a rich cream linen stock. Fine paper always implied no expense had been spared. More money spent meant people would be more likely to believe the charade.

He dipped his pen into the inkwell and wrote:

Mermaid. Source: India.

Discovered 1807 by Captain A. Alcott of the 75th Regiment.

Price Supplied Upon Request.

He set the card aside to dry, rose and surveyed the shop. Each table, each cabinet top, was covered in skeletons and clay or cloth models. The glass cases were veiled in dust and a fine layer of coal soot. The thin carpet of road-dust stretched across the wooden floor revealed the paw prints of mice, which wove and swirled in fantastical patterns like a decorative border.

Mickle's Curiosity Shop, it had been called, when he'd taken over from his predecessor, a confidence man also fortuitously named Mickle. The old fellow had apprenticed him and gradually revealed the tricks he'd learned working circuses and side shows, and how one must rummage through dustbins of trash patiently in order to uncover castoff treasures. When the old man finally drank himself to death on cheap gin, Alistair had simply stepped into his place and never left. For wasn't it by then ordained? He hadn't even needed to change the name on the shingle.

The shop was a reliable spectacle for bored toffs and upper-class slummers.

A haven for curious outcasts; a treasure-trove for the gullible. The 'newly-discovered' mermaid would join his current popular favorite: a unicorn which was actually a sheared adolescent ram with a single spike of horn. Alistair had sawed both its own off, then carefully reattached one in the centre of its forehead. In a nearby case a two-headed snake's corpse was artfully arranged in striking position. Tiny straight pins held up its heads and propped open both mouths from which long, narrow forked tongues poked flaccidly.

Work done for the moment, Alistair stretched his arms overhead, then folded double towards the plank floor, groaning at a twinge in his lower back. He'd been leaning over the worktable far too long.

He went into the main shop area, opened the front door, and stepped out into the cacophony of a London street on a weekday morning: the rattle of wagon wheels on cobbles, the neighs and snorts of carthorses, the eye-watering coal-fire smoke, and snatches of conversation and laughter from men, women, and children headed to work at the factories.

On the sidewalk, a few feet from his door, a half-dozen grubby urchins sat circled on the pavement, hands behind their backs.

A boy stood in the middle. "Button, button. Who's got the button?" he called. His patched trousers may have been blue once, but were now a sooty grey, like the rest of the neighborhood.

The children squealed as they passed the object around. A deft squeeze as two hands met, trying the best young children could do to move the button almost invisibly, from one to the next.

Suddenly, the boy in the centre pounced, grabbing at two of the girls' thin shoulders. "Gotcha!"

They giggled and opened their clenched fingers, revealing a narrow box of wood slightly larger than their small hands. Not the usual button at all.

What *was* that thing? Alistair leaned forward to see.

The boy in the centre picked it up and held it close to his face, eyes narrowed. "Oi. What's this, then?"

Alistair squinted too. The wooden object was narrow at the top, curved outward slightly at the middle, then narrowed again at the bottom. A tiny glint of gold or brass flashed, capturing his undivided attention. *What've you got there,* he wondered. *And where'd you find it?*

"What's this bloody thing? What's it s'posed to be, like?" shouted the boy. He shook the box and it rattled faintly, as if something delicate inside was being jostled.

Alistair suppressed a groan. Whatever was in there was sure to be broken by these brats.

A little blond girl got up to face the boy. "Found it in the garden where we was diggin' weeds. I showed it to my nan and she scarpered off, screamin' the 'ole way. Sayin' not to touch it, or else they'd come after me."

"Who, Hannah?"

"I dunno. The Hidden Folk, I guess."

"So you stole it, then?"

"What else was I to do? Anyway, it looked dead interestin' . . . and fit nice in my dolly's house."

Alistair went inside the shop, picked up a delicate pair of tweezers from a table, and stepped back out onto the street. He approached the circle nonchalantly, as if he had no interest in their childish games. But he was prepared to steal the box straight out of their hands, if need be.

"You reckon it opens?" The boy tapped the tiny gold latch.

"Maybe." Hannah shrugged. "Looks like a lid, don't it? Let's find a rock."

"Try this instead," said Alistair.

The children jumped at his comment, apparently unaware he'd been standing nearby.

He was just handing the boy the tweezers when the girl grabbed the box and threw it onto the cobbled street. The fragile thing exploded into splinters, broken twigs, and bits of dried moss.

"No!" He smacked the back of her head. "What the bloody hell'd you do that for!"

"What's it to you?" She rubbed the spot where he'd struck her. "Anyhow, it's just ungodly rubbish. My nan said—"

"Where *exactly* did you find it?" he snarled. "Tell me!"

"Out on Hampstead Heath, near the tall crag. There's a faerie fort."

He gaped at her. The sheer nerve—or stupidity—it would take to disturb a faerie fort was astonishing. Most locals from Notting Hill's Pottery Lane would never go near the grassy mounds that stood untouched above the ground there. The lush, grassy hillocks where cattle balked at grazing. Valleys between them where sheep refused to be driven through. Yes, all superstition, he knew. And he would happily dig something up there, as well, if it meant a pretty coin or two.

"The Heath. Really? I thought you said it came from your back garden."

Hannah glared, lower lip outthrust. "Heath t'aint far from my nan's cottage. Whole place be like our back garden."

"Stupid girl," he muttered.

She hissed like a feral cat and kicked his shin.

"Ahh!" Pain exploded up his calf.

"That was fer callin' me stupid, so." Then she stamped on his boot. "And *that's* for the smack to the head." She laughed, scuffing bare feet over bits and pieces of the destroyed box, and dashed off.

"Cheeky baggage." Alistair knelt and gathered up the remaining bits. He lifted a pair of gossamer insect wings and frowned. "Who'd save a dragonfly in a box?"

"Where's the bells comin' from? Thought I heard somethin' chiming." It was the boy, who hadn't run off with the others. He bent to help Alistair gather the remains of the box.

"What's your name?"

"Noel." He didn't look up as he scooped bits of twig. "Hannah's a bloody brat. You'd just best ignore her."

"Good to know. I'm Alistair Mickle. I keep yonder shop and, er . . . *specialize* in certain kinds of antique oddities."

"I know. I like looking in your display window." The boy paused, head tilted. "Hmm. The ringing just stopped. Mebbe the church bells is broken. Oh hey—look." Noel tweezed up a scrap of fabric sewn to look like a tiny dress. "Somebody's toy. Like Hannah said, for a dollhouse."

"From a faerie fort? That won't be any toy," muttered Alistair. "Mind where you step, now!"

"Like puzzle pieces, innit?" Noel said, seeming unperturbed. "This one goes here, that piece goes there…" He sat back for a second on dirty bare heels, admiring his handiwork. "Looks kinda like a coffin now, don't it? Just needs a gravestone."

He'd managed to piece together from the splinters what appeared to be a tiny wooden casket. Which, oddly, now held together.

"A coffin?" Alistair frowned.

The boy was right. The tiny box was a perfectly-crafted miniature casket. Tiny gold hinges and a latch glinted in the sunlight.

An idea was forming, one that could provide some badly-needed cash. "Help me get it all back together, then. Ought to be given a proper reburial."

"Right, gov." With one finger Noel gently moved the rest of the fragments around until what appeared to be a whole, very tiny doll lay before them. Legs, arms, wings. All except . . .

Alistair's gaze caught on something like a pale marble next to Noel's bare foot. "The head!"

He snatched up the small round object and set it down at the top of the figure. The marble indeed was a head, with perfectly formed face, sky-blue eyes wide open, small rosebud mouth closed tight. Golden hair tangled with leaf mulch and dirt, worked into delicate braids, topped it.

"It's a dead faerie an' her coffin," Noel said matter of factly. "I ain't never seen one a'fore."

"Nor I," said Alistair. *Thinking, There're no doubt more of them out on the Heath.*

Back inside his shop, he grabbed a garden trowel and an empty satchel. He locked the door behind him and leapt back down the steps. He approached Noel again, and drew a copper penny from his pocket. "For your trouble, and your silence. I'll be taking this back up to the heath, to return it to the fort. Hopefully," he whispered, looking around as if afraid of being overheard, "they'll not have noticed it's gone."

"But—" Noel began.

Alistair pressed the coin into his hand. "Thanks for your help. Remember, you don't know a thing. Come by the shop sometime and I'll show you around."

"I know not a thing," the boy assured him, nodding solemnly. "Not about anythin'."

"Good on you." Alistair carefully tucked the reformed casket and body into a small burlap sack and tucked that into the satchel.

A faerie coffin, he mused. An honest to goodness, bloody faerie coffin. And he'd be the first to find its original resting place . . . where surely there'd be more. He slung the bag over one shoulder and headed out; past Spaniards Inn, Highgate Cemetery, and the Wells Tavern, as he made the long walk to Hampstead Heath.

●◑◐○◐○◑◐●

The heath ran from Hampstead to Highgate. Hundreds of grassy acres atop a high sandy ridge, all rambling and hilly. Cradled by ancient woodlands, it lay near the grounds of stately Kenwood House. The wild southeast end was called Parliament Hill, and its eastern border was a chain of ponds, reservoirs for London's drinking water.

The main road through was a glorified cow path, frequented by the painted caravans of Travelers, the horse vans of itinerant merchants, and the wagons of farmers bringing stock and produce to market. Geographically, Hampstead Heath was a cluster of large hills; about as much of a mountain as most folk in London would ever see. The forests, ponds, and moor reminded them what it was like to be around the green things of this world. So of course it was also the place where, if someone *did* believe in faeries, or witches, or goblins, they would naturally go, hoping for an introduction.

The spot rumored to be most haunted by the Hidden Folk was Hampstead Crag, the rock the girl had mentioned. That monolithic boulder appeared to have burst violently from the earth, long ago. Taller than any man, wider than a full grown bull, and clothed in patches of blue-green lichen.

Once he reached it, Alistair stepped off the path and walked around the boulder. "Now, where would you be lying?" He ran his hands over the cold, mossy stone, feeling for crevices or hollows. The shadows around the rock stretched in odd, contradictory directions, as they seemed to always do near the Crag. He kicked at its base, hoping to uncover something. But there were no loose stones, no telltale hollows, holes, or divots in the sod.

After three full circuits, he knelt and started feeling around for loose soil or rocks, for any soft or sunken spots. Halfway round again, his fingers encountered a depression. He shoved the trowel into the earth and dug carefully. Soon a tiny wooden coffin lay uncovered in the loosened soil. He lifted it out and set it next to the trowel, then pulled a rolled-up piece of leather from the satchel. He unfurled it on the ground, revealing rows of small, delicate tools lined up like a piano's keyboard. He withdrew a thin German steel pick and cleaned dirt from the tiny latch. When he lifted the lid, in the fading light a tiny face looked back. The skin pearly in colour and shape, the eyes closed, it was dressed much like a tin soldier in a toy shop. Alistair lifted the miniature corpse and gently rolled it over in one palm, revealing two long, gauzy folded wings on its back. He pushed on one gently to separate it from the other. It snapped off, and fluttered to the ground like a tiny autumn leaf.

"Ah, bugger," he grunted.

No matter; he could glue it back on. People wouldn't pay as well for damaged goods, but if mended with a light touch no one need know it'd been broken. He'd keep this one near the back, where the light was dim enough to hide flaws, and shadows would keep the colours from fading.

He set the corpse back in the coffin and continued to dig. Another coffin, and another, and then another he found: seven unearthed graves in all. The bottom of his satchel was nearly full of little boxes with their tiny occupants.

At last, satisfied, he stood and dusted flakes of dried mud off his trousers. Then he looked around for his tools. "Dammit," he muttered. "Now, where's the trowel gone?"

Someone tapped his shoulder.

Alistair yelped and flinched away. When he turned to look, he stood face to chest with another man.

"You mean this one?" The stranger held up the trowel. His voice was so deep, it was if the Crag itself were speaking. Not a growl, nor a whisper, nor a holler, but a rumble.

Alistair's stomach tightened. His heartbeat shuddered. "Y-yes. Th-thank you," he stammered. "Now I'll be on my way."

Make a run for it, he thought. He still had plenty of skeletons and coffins to puzzle together.

The other fellow stood as high as the Crag, fully two heads taller than Alistair. The skin on his face resembled a melting candle: long drooping cheeks and deep-set eyes that seemed to glow blue beneath thin red brows. Celtic tattoos crawled up his neck and behind his ears, like knotted snakes.

"Odd time to be diggin' up ramps, innit?" rumbled the stranger. "Which by the by don't usually grow in this spot."

"Oh, well . . . just an old tradition my gran taught me. You know, harvesting by moonlight," Alistair said hastily.

"But it's not full." The stranger looked around. "And wild onions dinna grow here. Like I said. Only such as these." And then he reeled off a list of flowers and herbs Alistair had never heard of. "So your gran must not know her stuff. Those are the ones you dig by moonlight."

"She was confused, I suppo—"

"Or else you was diggin' up something else," huffed the giant.

Alistair backed away. "What business is it of yours?"

The other's face changed then. His skin faded to pale blue, his ears grew pointed, his teeth jagged. The knotted tattoos swirled over his skin, slithering around his neck and face like a nest of poked snakes. Alistair thought he even heard a faint hissing. "It matters when it be my kin whose rest you're disturbing, *mortal.*"

He spat the last word with such vicious contempt, Alistair flinched. He grew lightheaded, and then toppled, crashing to the ground like a felled tree before all the things around him went black.

●◖◗○○○◖◗●

He woke later, feeling jostled and turned upside down. He'd come to whilst being carried over the shoulder of the tattooed man. If indeed he was a man at all.

"Put me down!"

"Ah! Welcome back, mortal." The stranger chuckled. "This is how it shall be. We'll go get what we need to properly rebury my family, which you so rudely dug up, or I'll snap your neck and bury you with them. Your choice."

"Let go of me!" Alistair punched and kicked at his captor. He might as well have attacked the trunk of a giant oak.

"Not until you choose."

"Fine! I'll help you."

"I figured as much." The mountain man leaned his head back and loudly whispered in Alistair's direction, "It's the wise thing, really." He stopped abruptly in the middle of the path and shrugged hard.

Alistair slid off his shoulder, landing on his feet so hard his ankles stung. "Ouch!"

"There you go. Come with me, and we'll get along fine. But no funny business, Alistair."

"How'd you know my name? What's yours?"

"Call me Puck. It don't matter how I know. The fact is, I do, and if your dear old granny taught you right, then you know what power I've got over you."

Dammit. He was in thrall to a faerie. "I-I didn't think you Hidden Folk were real." Alistair's hands were sweating. " The Seelie Court, Unseelie Court . . . it isn't just made up? My gran—"

"Now, your gran we *liked*. She did right by us," Puck rumbled. "We were always happy to pay her a visit. *She* had proper manners. But you, Alistair Mickle. . . ."

At the mention of his full true name Alistair's body went rigid. His mind turned fuzzy and soft, like he had nothing in this world to worry about. His left arm rose, and that hand balled into a fist, though he hadn't willed it. Then he landed a powerful punch on his own face, again and again. Pain exploded in his nose, his cheeks, his jaw. He tasted coppery blood. But his bewitched hand, possessed by someone else, did not relent.

"*You know better.* Yet you go on digging us up for a few shiny coins. So play nice now, or I'll make you do any number of unseelie things. The least of which would be drowning yourself in that bog over there."

Puck snapped his fingers.

Alistair's personal assault on himself ceased. "Please let's just return to the Heath." He reeled on his feet, dizzy and nauseated. "I'll put them all back."

"What? We can't, you eejit! We need a few things first. Come along. I know where I'm going." Puck turned quickly and headed down the winding cow path, back toward the city.

But when they arrived it was a part of London Alistair didn't recognize. His old street no longer looked shabby and soot-stained, with broken gas lamps and missing cobblestones. It wasn't even the same long narrow lane. Now colourful tents and wooden booths lined the sidewalks and alleys. As they made their way through this sudden, exotic marketplace, Alistair's mouth hung open wide enough to catch fish.

"Is this still Pottery Lane? But . . . how is it I've never seen any of these things before?"

It must still be his neighborhood, for he could hear familiar hawkers' calls and see some of the older storefronts from around the corner. But the rest . . .

The women—or at least some gorgeous, otherworldly creatures in feminine shape—strolled the aisles or danced clad in nothing but silken scarves. There were animals he'd never glimpsed in his life, as well: two-headed goats, winged cats, horses that walked on two legs clad in human dress. Down one alley a vendor was calling, "Fresh-boiled newt eyes! Deep-fried lizard tails!"

One booth had performing birds on perches: talking parrots and ravens, nightingales singing whole operas. And more exotic avian species he'd never seen before, even in books.

"What is this place? Surely I don't live here. I'd stay forever, if I could . . ." Alistair's voice trailed off as he looked about him.

"*You* were never meant to see this. It's for the likes of me and my kind, alone."

True, the purveyors of these wares looked somehow less . . . or rather, *more* than human. Taller, handsomer, more beautiful, more perfectly formed. And yet the goods for sale were sometimes ghastly. One set of tables displayed severed hands wearing silver cuff bracelets above the cauterized wrists. The metal there etched in runes and almost unreadable phrases. *Inescapable hands,* the carefully inked signs read. *Able to handle all your shadow business. Low maintenance. Clever.*

Alistair stepped closer to the table and reached out to inspect one particularly large specimen. "Why, look at—"

Puck yanked him backward. "Don't! Touch a Digger, and it's yours. No one can break the bond. But if you don't give 'em work to do, they'll find mischief instead. See the word 'clever' there? These are meant for treasure hunting. But if you ain't careful they'll dig your eyes right out of your head while you're sleeping."

"What?" Alistair gasped. "Impossible!"

Puck gestured at the stall keeper. "Does everyone who works here still possess two eyes? Maybe even missing something else, as well. The bracelets must be put on' em whilst wearing gloves so the hands don't get imprinted. Not 'til they been bought . . . or stolen." Puck turned and walked on. "Come along now. And touch *nothing*."

Alistair shoved his hands deep in his pockets and trotted to keep up.

"You asked, is it always like this," said Puck. "More or less, yeah. There's the showy part that the Invited get to see. While we comes in through the back door, where Fae like me—or the help, or family—goes in and out. We don't need front-door stuff. We need the bits and bobs, the nuts and bolts. This is where we restock our own cabinets. Divination shop's over there. Got your tarot cards, crystal balls, pendulums, scrying bowls, that sorta thing. Ahead's the apothecary. Potions and herbs, spells and curses. Heal or hex."

They ducked down an alley, stopping at a stall where a dusty glass-fronted display box with little cubbyholes was propped up. Carved wooden figurines were stuck into these any old way. Some were standing upright, others had slumped over, or were folded sideways as if in sleep. Each had a tiny carved face, though the features were rudimentary. Various faded outfits adorned the tiny dolls, if that was what they were: worn denim blue trousers, red flannel shirts faded almost to pink, worn calico gowns. A faint jingling emanated from the case, and the rusty latch that secured the lid rattled occasionally.

"In here." Puck gestured for Alistair to enter the makeshift shed that served as a shop.

The step up to the threshold was high. When he put his weight on it, the plank gave the deep, hollow groan of a ship's foghorn at sea. Inside it smelled of dust, mold, and the sweet-sour tang of dead mouse. It was a bit like his own shop, though he suspected these displays weren't just sewn together from dead monkeys and dried fish.

"Do you work here?" whispered Alistair.

Puck shook his head. "Nah. But I know so much about the contents, might as well." He looked around, then called, "Hayward, you here?"

Alistair's hands were getting itchy. He longed to pick up things and inspect them more closely. Perhaps even to slip a few into his pockets.

A short man with a face as pointed as a mole's popped up from behind a long counter. His ears were close to his head, his nose long and narrowed at the tip. He held a flannel rag so thin and worn, light shone through the threads.

"What c'n I do for ye, Puck?" Hayward stepped behind a wooden desk piled high with books, inkwells, cigar boxes, and various less-recognizable objects, the jumbled towers leaning precariously.

"I needs a shovel. Silver, not iron. Some dried marigold and lavender, and…."

As Puck's list droned on, Alistair turned away, fuming. How hard could it be, he thought, to just dig some bloody holes, and stick the little corpses in? It wasn't as if they needed a priest and mourners, or tea and cake after.

He walked his fingers over a table where crystals, polished stones, and geodes were on display. In the centre sat a blue carbuncle the size of a large chicken egg. Alistair scooped it up and balanced it on two fingers, then let it roll down into a basket that held at least a dozen similar gems. He flipped a nugget of golden yellow engraved with a dragonfly across his knuckles, into the palm of his hand, and then into his pocket . . . just a little souvenir. When Puck brought the bag back, he'd swap it for something good, a nice addition to his own shop.

He wandered back over to the counter where Hayward was slipping items into a linen sack. He nearly dropped the bag into Alistair's outstretched hand, but Puck grabbed it first.

"I'll carry that, Hay. You know how it goes with the punters."

Hayward smirked. "Take whatever tools ye need. Just bring 'em back."

"Thanks. I'll return shortly." Puck headed for door.

Alistair felt a queer tugging sensation, as if an invisible rope linked him to Puck. One that pulled him along so quickly his feet were tripping over each other.

"No dawdling, mortal," his captor muttered.

And they walked on. It wasn't late, but in autumn night fell early. They'd have to hurry.

Alistair looked up at the sky where clouds were building, a sky-wall of gray thunderheads. The two of them finally crested the main peak of the Heath, and hiked over to the Crag. As they climbed, Alistair glanced back over one shoulder at the dim orange pinpricks of lantern and gaslights in London proper. He looked left, then right—every which way, in fact. Squinting in the dusk, trying to spot those colourful tents and the many lights of the place they'd just been. But nothing out of the ordinary remained to betray their presence.

Piles of soil marked the spot where Alistair had been digging earlier. Puck stopped there and held out a short, silver-bladed spade. "Delve!"

Alistair knelt on the ground and forced the blade-end into the turf, overturning clods of peaty black soil.

"How many did you dig up in all?" Puck asked.

He paused and thought a moment. "I don't believe I actually counted."

"You didn't *bother* to count how many of the graves of my people you robbed?"

"I-I was interrupted!"

"They're all in there, though?" Puck gestured at the satchel.

Alistair nodded sullenly.

Puck crouched and gently poured the contents of the leather bag out onto the grass. His fingers shone with dew as he pieced each tiny skeleton together, precisely, respectful in his movements. Each time he completed an assemblage of bones, a tiny flash green as a firefly's lantern blinked, then winked out. Gradually all the skeletons were whole and clothed, faces still and composed, eyes closed.

They could be sleeping, thought Alistair. He leaned closer to see what Puck would do next.

"What're you staring at?" the faerie growled. He waved a hand over the corpses, and they shifted into a single line, straight as soldiers at inspection. "You need seven new graves," he added. "Keep digging!"

"How deep?"

"Enough so they won't be disturbed again, by some other eejit."

"Two hand depths should do it," muttered Alistair.

Puck frowned and coughed.

"Three, then!"

The faerie nodded and bent over the first figure. It had dark hair, and lips as red as if stained by cherry juice. "Elderflower, old friend." Puck gently touched a finger to the tiny face.

Alistair raised an eyebrow. "Was that really his name?"

"As if I'd use their true names around such as you," hissed Puck.

"I suppose not." Alistair toiled on until the last grave was dug, then wiped his soiled hands on his trousers. Seven small rectangles, side by side, a foot and a half deep. "What else should I do?"

Puck ignored the question. Carefully lowering each figure into a grave, bowing his head, murmuring words Alistair couldn't make out. He seemed like a mother tenderly tucking in her children, one by one, with prayers and kisses to each. Once the seven had all been unhurriedly settled, he stood again and glared at Alistair. "So? You can apologize for disturbing them in the first place." Looking as stony and immovable as the crag itself, he folded his arms over that massive chest.

Alistair bit his lip and shoved his hands into his pockets uneasily. How could he apologize to some silly, dried-out dolls?

Puck's expression turned darker, more threatening. Alistair got the impression that if he didn't do as he was told, he might not be leaving the Heath in one piece.

"Umm . . . I'd like to say I'm very sorry for what I did. I was only . . . well, thinking of making a quick coin or two. And I didn't know that…that you were all real."

Puck growled, "And?"

"And now that I do know, I'll not be disturbing you ever again."

Puck nodded. "Now, does anything else need returning? Anything at all you stole from them . . . or from someone else?"

Alistair shuffled his feet and didn't meet Puck's eyes. "So we'll be going back to the shop?"

"Aye. To return the tools."

He felt Puck's gaze on him. The stolen gold nugget seemed to heat up his pocket. But he only nodded. "All right, then: No. Nothing else."

"Very well." Puck waved his hands, crossing them over and over again before him. To Alistair's astonishment, a wave of soil rose from the ground and fell again, perfectly covering each of the tiny graves. Grass grew upon them in a trice, as if the ground had never been disturbed. Flowers rose, budded, and bloomed all around the perimeter of the fairy cemetery.

Then why, thought Alistair resentfully, did he make me do all that digging? In any case, now he was glad he'd taken the engraved nugget. "Those flowers only grow by the far slope—" he began.

"And you will *not* visit there. Because if I ever come across the thief you are scavenging here again . . ."

"All right! I heard you the first time." Thoughts of filling his purse with more hidden treasures flitted away like the butterflies swooping among the graveyard flowers.

"Come on, then." Puck tossed the borrowed tools back into the satchel and started off. Alistair felt the unpleasant tug of that invisible rope pulling at his waist again, dragging him along behind Puck. Soon he had to run to keep up.

After about an hour, Alistair noticed something on the air and inhaled deeply. "Smell that? The cooking fires." He sighed. "Wonder what they're roasting? Mutton, mayhap." His mouth watered, his stomach rumbled. It'd been a long day with no supper. His breakfast of tea and toasted bread had worn off hours ago. He inhaled deeply again, trying to identify the roasting meats. So many strange and delicious scents . . . though one did stand out oddly.

"What's that?" he asked. "The strange smell. It's like . . ." he inhaled again. "Like burning fabric?"

Puck stopped and pointed at Alistair's coat. "You lied," he snarled.

The heat in his pocket grew even more intense. He looked down and saw flames licking the cloth there. His skin prickled and stung. "Bloody hell!" Alistair wrenched off the coat and stomped on the flames. The dragonfly-engraved nugget he'd pinched from the shop glowed like a red ember in a fireplace. It burned straight through the pocket, and rolled a few feet away, toward Puck.

Who leaned over, picked it up, and slipped it into his own pocket. "You lied, mortal," he repeated. And when he looked up again his eyes seemed to glow as well.

"I'm so sorry, I-I don't know why I did that." He cowered under Puck's glare. "Please don't hurt me!"

Puck swore. "We liked your old Gran very well. But *you* are a thieving bugger. Still, because of her . . . out of respect for that fine old beldame . . . I'll not kill you. Instead, I'm going to grant you a wish." He smiled, sharp teeth shining between red lips. The knotted snake tattoos squirmed and writhe around his neck and shoulders again. "Seem to recall you saying, *I wish I could stay here forever.* Well, guess what? Today's your lucky day."

Puck grinned and snapped his fingers.

The breath fled Alistair's lungs. His limbs tightened and pulled up short. Bolts of pain shot through his legs and feet. He tried to scream, but could not summon words, or any voice at all. Instead, a faint jingling noise erupted from his mouth.

He toppled to the grass, and now somehow its blades were tall as trees. His body stiffened like a tin soldier's. His eyes, however . . . he could still move them to look around. And what he saw at that moment was Puck, a true giant now, reaching down, down towards him. The huge fingers pinching at, lifting, and then dropping him into a shirt pocket. The mingled scents of cotton, dirt, and sweat cocooned around him, warm and stifling.

He tried to scream, but again only that faint tinkle of bells emerged from his mouth.

Puck patted his pocket. "Come along, then, Alistair. I won't make you walk the whole way this time."

Jostled, breathless, unable to see, Alistair feared he knew their destination.

◕ ◑ ◑ ◐ ○ ◐ ◑ ◑ ◕

"You in, Hayward? Puck called sometime later, voice booming in the confines of the tiny shop like cannon-fire. Shuffling footsteps drew near as the mole-man appeared from the back. A faint, metallic clinking rose as Puck handed over the bag of tools.

"Thanks for the loan." He dug into his trouser pocket and retrieved the gold nugget. "Think you'll find you're missing this."

Hayward waved a hand across the table. The bowl where the yellow stone had once been rattled and glowed.

Puck dropped it in with the others and the ruckus died down. "Thank you, again, my friend. I'll leave this 'un in the front case. With the others."

"Aye." Hayward walked Puck back to the door. "Never learn, do they?"

"Seems not."

Night had fallen at last. In the alley torches and lamps were being lit, casting the shops and tents in a net woven of shadows and light. Puck stepped out, pausing at the stall with the rickety table and wooden display case. He flipped its metal latch and lifted the lid.

A cacophony of chimes and tinkling of bells rang out.

He felt around in the display case for an empty cubby. The first spot he poked was occupied. He cursed, jerking back a bleeding finger for his trouble.

"Little arsehole," he muttered.

Reaching back inside again, he pulled out the offending doll, snapped one arm off, then poked it back in place.

The next cubby was empty. Puck withdrew the new little wooden man from his shirt pocket and popped him inside it. "Enjoy the view, Alistair."

He closed the lid and snapped the latch shut with a faint click.

The chimes grew muted then, beneath the muffling glass lid. The wooden rattling inside the case gradually quieted, too, as Puck walked away.

●◑◐○◐○◑◐●

Something was pounding inside Alistair's chest as if it meant to get out, too. His heart? He wanted to beat his fists on the clouded, grimy glass of the box's lid. The thumping grew louder and louder, until he thought his head would burst. He screamed and cursed. Yet his body was so stiff, no matter how he struggled to move his limbs, neither arms nor legs so much as twitched. Other screams rose close by, echoing in the confines of the collection box.

He wasn't alone, then. But like the rest, he was trapped.

Someone will miss me, he thought frantically. *They'll notice the shop isn't open. My customers, or . . .*

He recalled the dirty little street urchins from that morning—had it really only been just half a day ago? But yes, they always hung about the shop, sometimes peering in the front display window. They'd surely realize he was gone, and—

And then what?

And then, nothing. Nothing at all. Alistair had seen to that, himself. *I paid the boy, and ordered him not to tell a soul.*

Little Noel wasn't going to peach, thanks to the coin in his pocket.

Alistair screamed out against the glass lid, against the wooden walls that surrounded and contained him. Maybe his shop would be sold. Perhaps one day a grown-up Noel would run it and keep collecting oddities. He'd seemed quite keen on them. But how long would Alistair have to wait to be discovered?

Forever. For no one will miss me. No one else knows I went to the Crag on the Heath.

His screams went on and on, shattering and falling like shards, like dust, inside the display case. So far . . . much too far away from where anyone would ever even think to look for the missing proprietor of Mickle's Oddities.

Had you attended the Bazaar last night, dear visitor, you might not have noticed my absence. Even though it was the first time I hadn't personally presided over the Night Bazaar in many, many years. No matter in the end, but . . . here, I shall explain. As you've doubtless realized by now, the Bazaar exists outside of what most know as Time and Space. Even outside of Causality, and the principles of quantum uncertainly, for it inhabits quite a different realm. And being beyond all physical laws means it is normally operates outside the jurisdiction of mortal laws, as well. Yet we denizens of the Bazaar may from time to time become vulnerable to certain illicit threats or coercions from human (or daemonic) enemies, cabals, or conspiracies. Even from The Old Adversary himself. So: how to respond when, for understandable reasons, the mundane forces of constabulary and prosecutor cannot be resorted to, or even be effective? How else but by turning to the world's foremost practitioner of the craft of investigative ratiocination . . .

The Adventure of the Abducted Sorceress

by David Poyer

I believe I require little introduction as the narrator of this singular tale, though readers may wonder why its recounting comes so late. In fact, over a hundred years after the passing of the protagonist. In explanation, I can only quote Holmes himself: "Some facts should be suppressed, or, at least, a just sense of proportion should be observed in treating them."

Thus this adventure, withheld so long.

You shall soon see why.

"A blood moon to-morrow," my companion observed, shaking out the pages of the *Daily Telegraph*. "Or so the almanac predicts. We might catch a glimpse, if this fog permits."

I turned a skeptical eye across the breakfast-table. "I thought you had no interest in astronomical observations. That if it had nothing to do with criminal investigation, you didn't care whether the sun revolved around the earth, or vice versa."

A second rattle of the pages. "Really, Watson. I was perfectly in earnest that the theoretical motions of the more distant sidereal bodies were no concern of mine. But the moon? Its periods of illumination directly affect the incidence of crime. Especially in areas where modern gas-light has not yet reached."

Holmes read aloud about how, during the eclipse, the refraction of the atmosphere would lend the tint of blood to our companion satellite. I half-listened, contemplating the memory of the evening before, spent with Miss Mary Morstan. Unwillingly, my hand sought the ugly furrow in my lower leg.

"Women have a way of looking past such things, once they've made their decision," Holmes said.

I started from my reverie. "What?"

"You were thinking of Miss Morstan. Wondering whether she could accept the proposal of a half-crippled, nearly penniless Army surgeon. How did your call upon her go, last night?"

"Once more you seem to have listened to my thoughts. How'd you do it this time?"

"Quite elementary, to the close observer. Your hand sought the place where the Afghan bullet took half your muscle. Those mooncalf sighs, and the way you tormented your boiled egg, earlier, invited the logical conclusion." He folded the paper and reached for his tea. "It's the minutiae that tell, Watson— the tiny oddities one's eye so easily looks past. But you are coming along quite well, I think. Yes, quite well indeed."

◑ ◐ ◑ ◯ ◖ ◯ ◑ ◐ ●

By then Holmes and I had resided at 221b Baker Street, three upstairs chambers in a Georgian mansion on Portman Square, for several years. Our modest sitting-room was adequate to bachelor demands, with fireplace and coal-scuttle. The mantel held a slipper of Holmes's black shag pipe-tobacco, a half-packet of my Gold Flakes, a magnifying-glass, and an empty brown-glass bottle that'd once contained a stimulant solution. The rest of the shelf was cluttered with some skeleton keys, a pocket-knife, and several red-taped files of recent cases.

A table with one chair sat beneath the window which looked down upon the street. Just now it held a carefully-wrought case of wood and glass. Inside was a cube of polished copper, several thermometers, and a dead mouse.

Over the past week, with much muttering and tinkering, Holmes had carried this cube back and forth from the fireplace; consulting the thermometers, making calculations. The unfortunate mouse had intruded of its own accord. The other doorway led to Holmes's bedroom. Another table was visible through it, strewn with experimental apparatus. My own room was no larger, but I'd made it a practice since the days of my military service to keep everything tidy.

This sitting-room, as I have mentioned in previous pieces, also served from time to time as Holmes's consultation-room. Of late clients had been scarce, leading to more stinks and minor explosions from the chemistry. At times I feared my friend was sinking into one of his black moods, the consequence of being unable to whet his restless brain upon some conundrum of crime.

"Most interesting, the results I've obtained." He gestured at the case. "You have no doubt wondered what I was about."

"It hadn't crossed my mind."

"An Irishman named Tyndall argues before the Royal Society that the advance and retreat of glaciers upon the northern reaches of Europe were due to variations of certain gases in the atmosphere."

"Surely the presence of a trifle more or less of this or that could have little effect on the weather of those boreal lands."

Holmes spread long pallid hands. "I tended to agree, but decided to subject the question to investigation. I heated that cube of solid copper to a temperature of three hundred degrees. Then drew a graph of its cooling rate.

"I next introduced one hundred percent of carbonic acid gas into the box, generated by the reaction of sulphuric acid with a solution of bicarbonate of soda. The gas is an interesting substance, by the way. When compressed, it liquifies. Sprayed into an evacuated vessel, it turns into a solid compound resembling ice."

"And?" I prompted, to get this latest lecture over with.

"The cooling rate of the cube slowed markedly."

"Which proves?"

"Tyndall speculates that the burning of coal by British industry may one day result in a disastrous rise in the mean temperature of these isles, if not of the globe itself."

He sat with chin in hands, contemplating the cube. "But if that were so, Mankind would obviously cease such burning long before it became dangerous."

I snorted, eyeing the swirling yellow fog outside the window. "Do you truly believe that, Holmes?"

He nodded, looking serious. "Yes, my dear Watson. With all my heart, I do. In that distant future, Mankind will no longer be guided by ignorance and fear. Only by the cool, clear light of reason."

He sat up abruptly when, some minutes later, Mrs. Hudson appeared in our doorway, smoothing her apron and looking anxious. "Beg your pardon, sirs. There's a . . . sort of omnium-gatherum downstairs. They look rather . . . well, disreputable."

Holmes nodded. "My Irregulars? Show Wiggins up please, if it is he."

"No, sir. These folk I do not recognize." She frowned. "They seem to be foreigners."

A few moments later, the party was ushered over our threshold. Our housekeeper twitched her skirts back to allow their passage, turning a wondering gaze upon me. My smile faltered as I examined their dress, lineaments, and comportment. They crowded in, each person bowing upon coming face to face with us.

"I fear we haven't chairs for so many," Holmes said gravely, rising. "Shall we hear you out standing?"

"If I may sit, sir," said the oldest, to judge from the long white beard nearly covering his breast. Holmes pulled out the chair by the window for him, then stood back, studying them.

I did so as well, hands clasped behind me, observing the three men, and a diminutive female in voluminous skirts. Dressed like mountebanks, or perhaps poverty-stricken courtiers from a bygone era. The bearded elder wore a dull-brown robe lined with tatty fur. The tallest was in a kaftan such as might've adorned inhabitants of the Mongol steppes, and a flap-eared leather cap. The third man styled himself as an Elizabethan courtier, with slashed doublet, short-sword, a large, floppy green cap pierced with a pheasant feather, and a too-prominent satin codpiece. The woman was laced into a corset and stuffed into many colourful petticoats; her head bore a turban fastened with a green gem far too large to be aught but paste. All were splashed with the mud of our London streets.

Suppressing a smile, I looked to Holmes. Surely in a moment he'd essay the sort of insight I'd come to expect. Our visitors' origins, occupations, and most recent destinations, perhaps, gleaned from the traces upon their shoe-soles. For my part, I supposed them a troupe of actors snatched from mid-performance; the type who played Shakespeare or Jonson in our smaller hamlets. Or revelers from a costume-party, interrupted by some troubling event.

Imagine my surprise when Holmes said nothing. His obvious puzzlement was novel.

As the room warmed an unholy mélange of smells arose: patchouli, tamarind, and sage, along with the decidedly less-pleasant odors of ancient flesh and tooth decay. It reminded me of Afghanistan, the markets and soukhs of that faraway place in which I'd left my youth—and much of my health.

Holmes said, "How may I be of service, my friends?"

The three looked to the eldest, who'd arranged himself in his seat, a hand resting upon the knob of a twisted cane that resembled narwhal ivory. Those clouded orbs indicated one troubled by cataract.

He turned toward the window's grey light. "I am yclept Doctor John Dee. I beg thee indulge us, sir, as we needs must throw ourselves upon thy mercy without further introduction."

Or so I understood, for his speech carried the timbre not just of age but of accents long vanished from our island. English, yes, but not the tongue spoken under Queen Victoria.

"Feel free to explain yourselves." Holmes cast me a glance which read plainly: *This interests me.* But the glitter in his eye had already revealed that.

"In sooth, sir, we arrive here from a lodging scarce easy to tell of, to those who hast yet not witnessed it. To begin, we be all what thou might calleth magi . . . er, scryers . . . or p'rhaps sorc'rers—"

"Magicians?" Holmes supplied.

The old man frowned, working the word around inside his beard as one might test a loose tooth. "If that term please thee, aye. We visit thy city for the space of a single week."

"I see you originate from different places." Holmes squinted. "From the variety of textiles and footgear. And you are not all English."

The old man bobbed his head. "Thou perceiveth rightly. Aside from mineself, we hail from diff'rent lands." He indicated his friends with a trembling finger. "Italia—Egypt—Sarmatia." Once more they bowed. From within their voluminous habiliments came sundry clinks and jinglings and creakings, as if they were elderly marionettes moved not by tendons and muscles but strings and springs.

"And you yourself, sir? Wales, I gather?"

"Many long years ago, aye, I were a-born of yon rocky hills. Thou'rt possessed of a canny ear, s'truth!"

The fellow with the floppy hat grimaced, I was not sure at what. His fingers moved furtively within his cloak.

"And you've sought me out in hopes of—?"

With many gesticulations, the old man imparted that he and his friends had only recently arrived in the City. Here he waxed obscure, but I gathered they were a sort of committee appointed to help organize a traveling exhibition or perhaps a midway sideshow. Holmes nodded along, reaching for his briar pipe with a questioning glance. Dee waved assent, and drew a clay pipe from his robe. Holmes was bending to strike a match when, in some way not visible to me, the old man produced a flame first.

"Proceed, if you please," my roommate said, puffing away.

Doctor Dee glanced at the gentleman in the fur robe and snapped his fingers. The fellow presented two empty hands, front and back. Then, an elaborate flourish, and a live serpent appeared between them, writhing and hissing, one malevolent orange eye casting between Holmes and myself.

I flinched back, recollecting the Roylott case, and felt shamed by a chuckle from Holmes. "Relax your guard, Watson. It's no swamp-adder but a harmless smooth-snake. The eye-stripe and crownlike markings give it away. And the magic trick? Our friend has a tube or reed concealed under his wrist. No doubt spring-loaded, to urge the reptile forth."

Apparently having understood his objection, the steppe-dweller hiked his sleeves, displaying bare forearms. But Holmes only patted his palms in mock applause.

"Vadoma," said the old man. "*Ukážte mužovi, co dokážete.*"

The petite woman stepped forward. From under her shawl she drew forth a transparent sphere perhaps six inches in diameter. Lifting it in both hands to just above eye level, she released it, drawing her fingers apart. The ball remained suspended, unsupported, vibrating slightly as it floated before us.

Holmes narrowed his eyes, leaning closer.

The ball began to hum, a note just above the lowest the ear could detect. Then it glowed. Shifting clouds or mists seethed within. The woman, hands still apart, advanced a pace. With a jerk of the chin, she invited Holmes to look closer.

As he squinted into the sphere its note rose to a higher pitch. From my place to the side, I could only make out a portion of what transpired within. First, darkness. Next, tiny running figures following what seemed to be a bullseye lantern floating though mist and shrubs . . . or a moor? And then abruptly from the dark loomed the glowing jaws and eyes of some gigantic beast. A bear, perhaps, or an enormous hound.

Holmes reached out—intending, I suppose, to check the space around the ball for wires or strings. The woman spat and drew back. With a spasmodic gesture she snatched it from the air. A moment later the orb was once again hidden in her bosom. The hum faded to silence.

"My God," I breathed. "Did you see? Within the sphere, those figures—"

My friend rolled his eyes. "Quite easily explained. It is suspended by a black thread, which blends with the hue of her cloak. The sound emanates from a hidden tuning-fork. The images, drawn upon coloured cards, are suspended within the ball, magnified by the curve of the glass."

"But they *moved.*"

"A riffling of the cards tricks the eye. The same principle as the zoetrope or *stroboscopische scheiben.*" He smiled. "Also, there exists no such dog of that size, let alone with glowing jaws."

He turned to Dee, who'd sat calmly smoking. "If your performers can do no better, sir, perhaps you should seek an easier audience. Is this the purpose of your visit? To demonstrate your . . . magical arts?" He cast me an amused glance, clearly having smoked the fellow out as a mountebank. Or, more charitably, a character actor of some talent.

The old man smiled grimly and held out his left hand, which until now had been concealed within his robe. The fingers thereof were a dead, reflectionless black, as if dipped in India ink. Upon the index glowed a gigantic ruby set in gold, engraved with a mystic rune.

Dee glanced out the window, as if to ascertain the weather. Struggling up with the aid of the cane, he staggered in a circle around Holmes.

My friend sighed, folding his arms.

Stepping back a pace, Dee lifted both hands, crying out a chant or incantation. I recognized certain Latin phrases, but so decayed or alloyed with another tongue that I could not follow with my schoolboy Cicero.

Holmes still stood smiling. And then, he disappeared.

My startled expostulations proved useless, as did frantic searches about the room. My friend was gone without a trace. The old magician leaned on his cane, frowning into the distance as if counting out a given span. Now and again he muttered a few words. The old woman squatted on the rug and tucked a pinch of snuff into one cheek. The Italian lit a cheroot, while the Mongolian perched on the window-sill, fanning himself as if he found the room overheated.

The mantel-clock ticked round a quarter hour before Holmes reappeared, just as suddenly and silently. He stood a moment transfixed, then staggered to the chair by his desk. Collapsing into it, he looked bewildered. "I seem to have returned wherein I went," he murmured at last.

"For God's sake, Holmes! Whatever happened?"

"As to that, I am uncertain." He passed a hand over his brow, which shone with perspiration. "I recall what I *think* happened . . . but the difficulty is, that would be quite impossible." He stared at me. "Was I not physically in this room the whole time? Was I actually . . . elsewhere?"

"You were not here for a long span; that much I can attest. What do *you* think happened?"

He blinked as if groping after a dream. "I . . . the room grew dim. A group of . . . phantasms . . . appeared above me. These were succeeded by four horses. Commanded by a voice I didn't recognize, I seized the bridle of a stallion with red trappings. When I mounted, a scepter and a sword appeared in my hands. The voice warned me to commit no evil while I was caught up, or else my safety could no longer be guaranteed.

"We vaulted into the air. The earth fell away beneath me. Over many leagues I was transported in a flash. Until at last, descending, my mount came to a halt.

"I stood in the forecourt of the Agia Sophia, in Istanbul. Entering, I was importuned by a bevy of veiled houris. Obeying the same voice, I turned from them and for some minutes strolled about the edifice. Then my unseen interlocutor instructed me to remount. In a flash, I was rushing through the clouds once more. Until our familiar green isle loomed below.

"I cannot say how, but I then found myself *here* once more." He gazed imploringly at me. "But—surely I was present the entire time? And my experience merely the effect of some powerful drug, a derivative of hashish or the zombie cucumber of Hayti?"

I shook my head. He slumped, but after a moment he looked up at the old man. "I confess, sir, you've bewildered me with this latest legerdemain."

Dee wagged his head so violently a white curl shook loose. "The purpose of our fair 'tis neither to puzzle nor mystify. But to tender those we invite an opportunity to change their fate."

"Indeed." Holmes seemed to still be struggling for self-possession. He touched a match to the pipe, which, apparently to his surprise, he still held. "Their *fate*. Which is predestined, no doubt?"

"*È nella natura del destino essere predestinati,*" observed the gentleman in the floppy hat, fingering his sword. He seemed follow the conversation, if not perfectly.

"*Co hovoří?*" muttered the small woman, and was promptly hushed by the Mongolian.

"Very well." Holmes exhaled a shaky stream of smoke. "I cannot explain your last trick, sir. Therefore, when one excludes every other explanation . . . the investigator may allow a certain breadth of view. At least, for the present. You say you are magi, sorcerers—wizards, if you will. But why the devil—pardon me—why come to us?"

The old man leaned forward. "A cousin of ours hath gone missing. We cannot supplicate to the police, for reasons thou shalt und'rstand shortly. Thus, after sev'ral inquiries, we vowed to partake of thy services. Thou'rt reputed a most cunning fellow, well acquainted with the thieves and felons of today's London. "

I said, "You believe someone is missing?"

Dee turned to me. "She who maketh sure all is well arranged for our compliment extern, and our stay. Who contacts those we wish to entertain, and maketh certain nay invitations wend astray."

"Vale a dire, la nostra guida e padrona, " the Italian added fervently.

"Any idea who might've taken her?"

"Here be the only mark we possess." Dee drew a slip of paper from one voluminous sleeve.

Holding it by the corners, Holmes carried it to the window-table. He held the missive to the fading light of sunset, looking not at, but through the paper. Then smoothed the half-sheet out upon the tabletop and fetched his glass from the mantel. As he bent, examining it minutely, I peered over his shoulder.

"What do you make of it, Watson?"

"Appears to have been written using a machine of some sort," I said. Unlike handwriting, the letters were regular, exactly spaced, impressed into the weave of the buff-coloured paper almost as neatly if set in a line of book-type.

"Indeed. Done upon one of the new typing-machines. And?"

By now I'd learnt something of his methods. Which were, first of all, to see exactly what was in front of one, much as a skilled draughtsman observes the scene he's about to limn. "The paper is of a fine make. Perhaps linen. There's a watermark I cannot make out. A small spot of a brownish material present on the obverse."

"Good. As to the message?"

"It demands aluminium and sapphires. More specifically, four solidly-cast bars of twenty pounds each, and two hundred carats of perfect star sapphires. Otherwise, it warns, this shall be the final appearance of the Night Bazaar, as the Great Witch will meet her doom in a fiery midnight spectacle. Her eclipse will astound all London. It ends: *Rationalitas de ignorantia triumphare debet.* And is signed with the initials S.C."

"Reason must vanquish ignorance," Holmes translated. "An epigraph with which I can hardly disagree." He turned to the others. "Indeed, a stimulating case. Who, precisely, is this so-called Great Witch?"

"Per spiegarlo, dobbiamo portarlo al Bazaar," said the gentleman of the pierced doublet.

"F'r yond, we shall escort thee to our lodging of demonstration," the old man supplied.

As he stood, hoisting himself upon the twisted ivory cane, I wondered why a true sorcerer could not furnish himself sturdy legs. Or if, indeed, he might heal mine . . . but obviously not.

Holmes rose, glanced outside, and reached for his overcoat. "Coming along, Watson?"

"I would not miss it for the world," I said.

● ◐ ◑ ○ ○ ○ ◐ ◑ ●

We went in two hansoms. Myself, Holmes, and Dee squeezed rather tightly into the lead, the others following. Night was falling; gas-lamps flickering on. No need, these days, for lamp-lighters. As Holmes had once explained, a rare element in the mantles automatically ignited the combustible gases. But their glow barely pierced the dark.

By my watch it was not yet six, yet the swirling yellow vapors of London's famous fog had settled hard. Its acidic nature rasped the throat and teared the eyes. The streets were empty, save for a few forlorn creatures crouched in recesses or wandering the ways. Pale faces flashed past as the clop-clop of hooves echoed from grimy facades. Lights were winking out in the shop-windows. Men in dark suits and slim-waisted shopgirls in overskirts and shawls hurried home.

We wheeled onto Waterloo Bridge. The river spread to either side below; grey, steaming, rippled by an evening wind. Over it too hovered the sulphurous haze that vomited from the thousand chimneys of the City. All was suffused in a gloom that spoke of an even darker future. When perhaps the flourishing of our Empire, exhausted by long struggles in distant lands and challenged by younger, more virile powers, should sink—and rise no more.

As our carriages rattled on our mysterious guide explained the history of what we were about to witness. After first warning us that, should we ever commit it to print, he could not be responsible for the consequences. I will not attempt to reproduce his archaic turn of phrase, to which, however, my ear grew more accustomed as he spoke.

What he termed 'The Night Bazaar' had originated in the year the Great Plague arrived in Europe. Held for the first time in St. Mark's Square, in

Venice, the festival had been convened at intervals since by a Dark Lady of uncertain origin.

"None knoweth whence the Lady cometh, 'r what her antecedents be. De Monte Ulmi"—he indicated the Italian—"has been with her nearly from those early days That gent perhaps knoweth a dram more than I, but not much. The Lady is an expert horsewoman, with a deep knowledge of the mystic arts. But more than yond nay one kens, save she be our duenna and headmistress."

Holmes looked abstracted again. "You say this event has been celebrated since the fourteenth century . . . though in different cities?"

"Not each year, sir, no. But since then, aye."

"I take it you descend from those original celebrants? As, no doubt, this Lady numbers the original Dark Lady among her ancestors. You said she arrives in advance of each performance?"

"Indeed aye. The Lady selects the locale. Gen'rally 'tis a deserted, remote location. Oft a lodging frequented during the day, and masterless by night."

"You only open at night?"

"Precisely so. The Lady arrangeth for rental-payment, oft in gold. At other times, a barter in the form of an invitation."

"Tell us more about these invitations," Holmes said, peering out. We were leaving the City behind. New, cheaply thrown up homes lay to our right, dark woods and the occasional open field were lightless gaps to the east. Soon we'd be in Sydenham. "To whom are they issued? And how?"

"Some art handed over p'rsonally, from a dark corner of the street. Other times, other conveyances be used. Somehow the Lady knoweth those at a crux, and presenteth them a choice. Usually, an offer to obtain the most secret desire of a heart . . . if one be willing to bear the toll thereof."

"A test of character, then?"

"Oft times, perhaps, sir . . . but truly, all 'tis retained firmly in her hands. We did suggest, from time to time, others be involv'd. This she refuseth. Except, on occasion, to employ one of us as a messeng'r." Dee looked uneasy. "You may well be the first mortals to visit without her invitation. But we couldst not see a way oth'rwise. "

I noted his curious use of 'mortal', but did not remark on it. Our cabriolet rocked and clattered. Were we now rattling over cobblestones rather than brick? Certainly it was darker; we'd left the gaslit areas of the City behind.

Holmes said, "Tell me more of your Lady."

"She is et'rnal. Ageless. Seeth the future and knoweth the past. And manipulates the present, to accord with her own secret designs."

Holmes whispered aside to me, "We are gaining a picture. A dominating *prima donna,* of extraordinary will. She has convinced these simpletons she possesses mystic powers. And like other cult-masters, she exercises that influence for her own benefit. Perhaps too firmly for some of her subordinates."

I murmured, "You think there may be a conniver within the organization."

"It's not impossible. If we should—"

Dee suddenly hammered the roof with his cane. A whistle from our jarvey, and the conveyance rumbled to a reluctant halt.

●◑◐○○○◐◑●

As soon as I stepped down I knew the place. In my boyhood this had been Sydenham Hill. We were some miles south of the Thames, upon a rising ridge. Night-time London spread below us, softened by fog and coal-smoke, but glowing with the golden radiance of innumerable windows, coal-fires, and the soft yellow of street-lamps. Here and there rose church-steeples; the Thames was a silver serpent in the distance. A cool breeze bore the smells of sulphur and ash and stewing cabbage: the scents of the teeming masses inhabiting the greatest city on earth.

I turned and gazed up at a massive structure, ominous in its bulk, yet familiar to every Londoner. Those vast curves of glass. The cast-iron decorations over the portals.

"The Crystal Palace," Holmes murmured. "This is unexpected."

The enormous building of iron and glass had been erected for the Great Exhibition of 1851. Now it housed schools of architecture, art, and engineering. A railway station served it, and the nearby park.

Holmes stood still for a moment, gazing about, then trailed our party in.

When I'd toured the Exhibition as a child it had been a paean to Progress and Civilization. But what now occupied the vast acreage under the glass dome and long barrel-vaults seemed less bazaar than a half-assembled jumble sale. Booths and tables were stocked with merchandise, true. Threading the narrow aisles, I noted antique costumes, ancient armor, and heaps of jewelry, along with medical curiosities, antiquated weapons, and medical instruments. Also curious offerings that seemed imaginative if warped *objets d'art,* perhaps the products of disordered minds. Stall after stall also offered aged, crumbling tomes, ragged scrolls and manuscripts, foxed and torn prints, and stacks of incunabulae. Shabby painted fronts offered services: alchemical treatments, palmistry, Tarot or tea leaf-reading, and other benighted practises.

I averted my gaze as a veiled houri, tattoos writhing over smooth, bare shoulders, beckoned me to step into a shadowed alcove. *Was* she a woman or something else? I could not be sure. The scents of burnt opium, musky perfumes, rough-cut tobacco, theatre grease paint, spilled brandy, and spicy patchouli reeled the senses. Yet despite this excess the place felt somehow abeyant. Bereft, as if poised above a yawning chasm. Strange, crouched creatures prowling within the darkened tents plucked at their wares as if arranging them for sale, yet their furtive glances at us betrayed one overwhelming emotion.

Fear.

These jongleurs, charlatans, mountebanks, harlots, the denizens of this nocturnal underworld were one and all deeply frightened.

"They appear terrified," Holmes whispered.

"I sensed it as well. But surely not of us?"

"Perhaps it's simply that their guiding hand has been lifted, and they are uncertain whether it will return. Or be supplanted by another . . . we must gather data. Without that, it's useless to theorize."

"So you have often said."

Dee and his party had hobbled a few paces ahead; they now turned and gestured us forward. Beneath the great central dome was parked a sort of gypsy caravan, two dozen or so wheeled vehicles painted in garish, glaring colours. Curiously, I noted no traces or harness for draught animals. Ushered up the steps of one waggon by the small woman, Vadoma, and through a beaded curtain-hanging, we entered a cabin not unlike that of a modest pleasure-launch. Here the same musky perfume lingered. The cabin held a single, neatly-made bunk with a piecework coverlet in many once-bright, now faded colours, a cabinet for clothing, and a desk inlaid with mother-of-pearl. Atop the latter lay an account book bound in cracked green morocco and a peacock-feather pen stuck into a blue glass inkpot.

Holmes looked about. "This would be her abode? The Lady's."

Vadoma spoke rapidly, with darting gestures. She pointed to a line in the accounts, then flipped pages to point out another.

"We assumed the lib'rty of examining her books," the aged magi translated. "And found a recurring fee, a payment of one thousand golden ducats per annum. T'was due just before this latest convocation."

"But not paid," Holmes ventured.

With more questions, my companion elicited that revenue from the Night Bazaar's previous appearance had been disappointing. He examined the accounts, flipping page after page. "They're kept in an antique hand . . . a script I'm not familiar with . . . it is perhaps Greek?"

"Madame Vera knoweth many scripts."

"So her proper name is Vera." He flipped another page, frowning. "I confess, it is not clear how your festival's income is derived . . . she also writes in other languages?"

"Sooth. Many of those folk, east'rn tongues. Even that of far Cathay."

"I see these accounts go back centuries. No doubt by succeeding generations of recorders? All trained in precisely the same school of penmanship."

Neither of our hosts responded, merely exchanged glances.

Holmes turned another page. "Aha," he muttered.

I recognized the half-sheet of buff paper he held up. "An earlier note!"

"Indeed. Typed, it seems, upon the same machine." Again he held it to the light, close to his eyes, then sniffed it. Closed his eyes, and sniffed again.

"What does it say?"

"This one is addressed to Signora Vera Fortunato. 'You have failed to render that which is due. This is your final warning. If we do not receive our funds before the reappearance, you will suffer the consequences.' It also is signed, S.C."

Dee and the woman looked somber. Holmes, though, appeared elated. He fanned himself with the paper; it *was* rather close, with four of us crowded in there.

"Very well, an avenue of investigation appears," he said. "Over a period of time, monies have been demanded by this 'S.C.' Since no receipt is registered, we may assume the payments were in the nature of what the criminal element calls 'protection,' 'squeeze,' or the 'shake down,' but which the law terms extortion. With such demands, officers of the law often cannot be resorted to, for whatever reason.

"When the Lady missed a remittance, he first imparted a threat, then made good on it. Kidnapping your impresario, and demanding payment from you, her adjuncts in this . . . carnival of the occult."

The old man made as if to object. Holmes waved him to silence. "Though now the demand is for a different specie. Not gold, but an even rarer metal. In fact, twice as valuable, per troy ounce." He glanced at me. "What thoughts does that trigger, friend Watson? As well as the fact that the note was not written by hand?"

"Typewritten because its author was known to her?" I ventured.

"Perhaps, perhaps not. And the request for payment in a different form?"

"That someone new is making the demand?"

"Again, perhaps. Or the original extortioner recognized, if belatedly, that ducats haven't been minted since Napoleon's suppression of the Venetian republic in 1797." Holmes produced the original note, and laid the two side by side. "The paper is identical. The printing, the same. Yet, do you note any difference?"

I bent close to scrutinize both. Then seized a half-sphere of glass from the desk and scanned them again, utilizing the hemisphere's magnifying properties.

"I do not make out one."

"Well, perhaps there is none." He straightened, facing our interlocutors. "I believe we've finished here, my friends. You may with confidence leave further investigation in our hands."

On the ride back Holmes remained silent, parrying my attempts at conversation. He retired at once when we reached our rooms, after asking me to be ready for an errand at dawn.

◕ ◑ ◐ ○ ◯ ○ ◑ ◐ ◕

After a hasty breakfast of tea, bread, and French marmalade, Holmes outlined a series of errands that would take me to several locations around the City. Then asked Mrs. Hudson to send for a pound of black shag tobacco, and to make another pot of strong Lapsang Souchong. I inferred from this that he wished to be left alone, to engage in one of those episodes of solitary ratiocination in which he traced effects back to their causes by analysis alone. Combined, of course, with his expert knowledge of chemistry, soils, textiles, and the history of crime.

My first visit was to the office of the Remington company, on Threadneedle Street. Holmes thought identifying the machine which had produced the notes might prove a fruitful line of inquiry. Type-writing machines cost fully as much as a new carriage; there could only be a few score used in the entire city.

A drawling American agent heard me out and examined the first note, which I'd brought along. At last he shook his head. "You sayin' this yere is a inquiry from Mr. Sherlock Holmes? Yeah, we heard 'a him. Sure."

"I'm glad to know it. Was this written upon one of your machines?"

"I can tell ya it was not. The type-face's different. An' the register. There's a number o' other writing-machines, though none offers the speed an' convenience of the Remington Perfected. Over ten thousand sold."

"I assure you, sir, I'm not in the market. My own penmanship quite satisfies me."

"OK, then. I kin direct you to the Hammond offices." He glanced at the note again. "But this yere's not from a Hammond. Nor a Caligraph. Nor any other machine I ever heard tell of."

Over the next few hours it appeared he was correct. I viewed machines, and samples of their product, from half-a-dozen manufacturers. After exhausting these, I tried printing establishments. At last my search was rewarded. A sharp young jobbing-printer with a Teutonic accent examined the note for a long time. Finally, he looked up. "I belief, sir, this vas produced by a Malling-Hansen."

"That's a typing-machine?"

"*Ja.* A Danish *schreibemachinen*. Made by hand. Expensive, light, and portable. If you could find the owner of a Hansen in London, I believe you vill haf the author of this note."

"Are such machines sold here?"

"Unfortunately you vill haf to search upon the Continent. The market in England is almost exclusively served by the American product."

But he'd convinced me of one essential point. The note's author was unlikely to be an Englishman. This also accorded with the illegible watermark, which I assumed now was foreign.

But if neither the writer, nor the person to whom it was addressed, were English, why was the note itself not in a language they shared?

I pondered this while walking back through the City. For as Holmes has often said, it is the unexpected that presents the possibility of new insights.

◐ ◑ ◐ ○ ○ ○ ◑ ◐ ●

In the late afternoon I climbed the stairs to our rooms, and found the smoke swirling within as dank and choking as the fog without. I dimly made out my cohabitant. Holmes lay wrapped in his mouse-coloured dressing-gown, slouching by a smouldering fire. His violin reclined against the wall. Several books, the uppermost Tilden's *Practical Chemistry,* were stacked at his feet, interleaved with slips of yellow paper.

"You haven't stirred from here, I see. I hope at least you've not resorted to a drug."

He looked annoyed. "As I've told you, Watson, when my brain is challenged, I have no need of artificial stimulants." He stretched until the ligaments of his thin, sinewy arms snapped audibly. "Actually, I've made a bit of progress, I believe."

"So have I." I recounted my travels and conclusions. Holmes's tilted head implied he was listening, but one slipper tapped impatiently. I added, "And have *you* arrived at any insights?"

The sleuth tented his fingers. "Well . . . I began with the question, *cui bono?* Who would benefit from attacking a rather shabby carnival of legerdemain to the point of extortion, kidnapping, and the threat of murder? What would he gain?"

"Aluminium and sapphires. Or so he hopes."

"Yes, but such a striking demand! Why not ask to continue the payment in some other gold coins, which seems to have been satisfactory before? Or a more modern medium—bills of exchange, Bank of England notes, even silver bullion? All readily negotiable."

"Aluminium is more valuable than gold."

"But nearly impossible to obtain! Indeed, the fabled tableware collection of the Emperor Louis-Napoleon would not, melted down, equal forty pounds of the light, lustrous metal." He bit the pipe-stem so violently I feared it might break. "So, I had to think more deeply. And eventually realized no reasonable blackmailer demands what cannot be had. Therefore?"

"Therefore . . . this S.C. believes Madame Vera has a source for what he desires."

Holmes nodded. He nudged *Practical Chemistry* with the toe of one slipper. "Aluminium is rare and valuable. *To us.* It can be reduced, by chemical means, but only with great effort. *By us.* But it is actually one of the most common elements of the earth's crust."

He studied the ceiling. Its brownish stains from past smoking-sprees; the holes pocked there by his occasional pistol-practice. "The answer is obvious. Sometime in the future, we may expect Mankind to be able to produce precious metals and gems very cheaply, by artificial means. Thus, this S.C. must believe Vera, or her Bazaar, can *travel through time. "*

I mused on that for a moment. "Or that they can produce the metal magically. Through alchemy, perhaps."

"Yes, another possibility. Though both expectations are obviously preposterous."

"Patently."

"Yet it provides a clue to his motivation."

I nodded. "And his credulity."

"These people can be quite convincing." Holmes grimaced, sliding a finger round the inside of his collar. "I confess, I was nearly hoodwinked." He swung his legs down and reached for his boots. "Perhaps together we've made some progress. And may expect more.

"Now, I've made arrangements for us to pay an afternoon call."

I raised an eyebrow. "Don't tell me you've already located the author of our threats."

"Not yet, no." Holmes stood, shucking his dressing-gown, glancing at the mantelpiece-clock. He tapped the pipe out into the fireplace; a little shower of sparks hissed and glowed redly. "We're due in a little less than an hour. I suppose I must get dressed."

"On whom are we calling?"

He said, "We've an audience with the most esteemed spiritualist, medium, and clairvoyant currently resident in Great Britain. We're going to consult with Mrs. Helena Petrovna Blavatsky."

●◐◑○◐○◐◑●

"They call it the Theosophical Society," Holmes said quietly as we looked up at a three-story building set back from Lansdowne Road. "But it has a darker side, or at least that's the rumor. Have you read *Lucifer* magazine?"

"I've never even heard of such a periodical."

"Well, it does not appear on the common street news-stand. There are corners of England even I do not know as well as I might. The esoteric. The cabalistic. That which shies, for whatever reason, from the light of day."

I gazed about uneasily. "I did not expect this aspect of our search."

"Nor did I, Watson. But the hound must follow where the scent leads."

As dusk fell, fog crept up from the river. I flicked open my watch. If this was the Lady's fated night, little time remained. For should S.C. intend to make good on his threat, her life lay in our hands.

A number of well-dressed but rather furtive-looking gentlemen and ladies were issuing from a hall to the right of the lobby as we entered. Apparently a lecture had just concluded. Holmes sent in his calling card. We waited, hats in hand, until a slight young woman in black, a secretary or assistant, ushered us back through several small, badly lit, inadequately heated rooms. Only to arrive at an even more poorly lit and worse heated chamber in the rear.

Here sat ensconced a large, rather stout grande dame enwrapped in Calcutta fabrics, worn beneath a soft-looking, gold-embroidered cloak. Her greying hair was piled atop her head, secured by a tortoise-shell comb. The only light came from a solar-lamp in the corner. It was draped with a scarlet pashmina, casting a roseate glow. A cigarette smoldered in a brass dish, permeating the chill air with the scent of cloves.

The first thing that struck me about Blavatsky was her eyes. Set within a flabby, lethargic visage and deep-set above swollen, wrinkled cheeks, they exercised a mesmeric influence. After but a moment, I had to drop my gaze. At the same I time I felt . . . not intimidated, but rather accepted. Enfolded. Welcomed, in an intimate way I could not quite explain.

The second thing I noted was the unhealthy yellowish tone of her skin.

Without rising, the famous medium extended a small, ring-bedecked hand. Holmes bent over it in the Continental manner. Then introduced me, and I too saluted her in the way she seemed to expect. Noting, as I did so, the enlarged joints and crooked fingers of a serious arthritical condition.

"I understand you are a consulting-detective." A faint smile accompanied her husky voice. A fat white Persian cat at her feet blinked lazily up at us. "Pray tell me, what is that? Are you associated with the Metropolitans?"

"Countess, I'm a mere amateur. Not a police-detective, nor do I report to them. I pursue occasional cases more or less—*ahem*—as the spirit takes me."

Another faint smile acknowledged the jest. "Yet you've earned some credit in your trade. As Miss Cracknell tells me. You will forgive my ignorance. I've spent many years abroad, in America, Tibet, and In-di-ya. And I no longer answer to any title of nobility." Her Russian intonation combined with the American accent was something I'd not heard before. "I've only a moment to spare," she added. "I must meet with students."

"I would not intrude, save that a Lady is in mortal danger."

"Now you interest me." She waved at a small divan covered with an embroidered throw. Sipped at her cigarette, then reached for a dish. The cat rose to nibble a treat from her palm. "Present your queries, *Shri* detective. If I cannot answer, I will say so."

"It is related to the Night Bazaar."

Those spellbinding eyes widened above their pouchy underlids, then narrowed. "Ah. The *Bazaar Nocturnalis*. Then . . . it truly exists?"

Holmes nodded. "And is present in this very city."

"Astonishing news! Yet, that is consistent with The Wisdom. You have seen it?"

"I have strolled its aisles, and met its denizens. Such as they are. Yes."

The cat leapt to her lap. One puffy, bejeweled hand stroked it. "You fascinate me more and more, sir. What is it you wish to know?"

Holmes held out the notes. When she'd conned them over, he asked,

"Would you, as the foremost seer in England, be able to advise us as to whom this S. C. might be?" His tone betrayed no hint of derision.

She stroked the Persian. "The One has no conditions. But the Absolute is masked. She veils her beauty to tempt the lover's gaze. Likewise, the Mulaprakriti is hidden beneath the material."

Holmes merely waited. Finally she whispered, as if fearing to be overheard, "Like everything else above and below, knowledge comes at a price."

I reached for my purse, but she waved me off with a peremptory gesture. "I do not refer to base coin. I'd rather starve in the gutter than take one penny for that which all men should know."

Holmes inclined his head gravely, as if in respect. "Then what may we offer, Madame?"

"It's said one requires an invitation to attend the Night Bazaar. You shall obtain one for me."

We exchanged glances. My friend looked even more grave. "I can make no promise, but it might be possible. If we can rescue the lady in question. She is in some sense the inheritor, or perhaps ringleader, of—"

"You refer to Madame Vera Fortunato," Blavatsky interrupted. "A high adept of the Hermetic mysteries. Perhaps even an unascended Master. Her name resounds through many realms. She is threatened, you say?"

Holmes nodded. "Then we have a bargain?"

She lifted her chin and tapped ash from her cigarette. "You do not seek a *person*. It is a cabal, formed to combat what they call The Dark Arts. Founded by a renegade monk in times long past, and called Sursum Corda."

"S.C.," I said, just as Holmes said, "'Lift up your hearts'. A phrase from the Latin Mass, I believe."

"Calling the faithful to participation in the mysteries. As above, so below."

"You say it was founded to combat these so-called dark arts. In whose service does it act?"

"Accounts vary. Some say it began as an Order charged with the persecution of Catharism and witchcraft. But its most zealous members went farther. Claiming, even after their Order was suppressed, that the Inquisition had not probed deeply enough in burning out heresy. It may receive funds from the Lords of the Dark Face. Others assert it is a Masonic creature, or directed by the Anarchic Council." She frowned; one small foot twitched in its silken slipper. "Those who teach the Ageless Wisdom arouse many enemies and slanderers. I too have experienced malice, hatred, and persecution."

She reached again for the cigarette. "I can tell you nothing more, sirs. I sense, *Shri* Holmes, that you're a skeptic in these matters."

"I believe in what I can comprehend," my friend said.

"I see. And in nothing else?"

Holmes smiled sardonically. "What else is there? I must be honest with you."

"Well, that is a beginning. Will you admit that perhaps you might come, one day, to comprehend things you do not at present?"

He hesitated for only a moment. "Well . . . certainly."

"Then you are already on The Path. You strive to uncover The Truth. You seek justice; you uncover that which is hidden. Thus you serve the Good, in your way. Perhaps Life will bring you more wisdom as it unfolds."

I sat riveted, engrossed in this joust of two supremely powerful wills. Holmes nodded thoughtfully, and made as if to rise. Her index finger shot out. "You won't forget our bargain!"

"I will not, Madame. If we can rescue the victim, I will relay your request."

"On any night, at any time," Blavatsky said, and I detected a note in her voice of yearning. "It's rumored one's innermost wish may be granted there."

"But there's always a cost," I told her. "Or so we've been informed."

"As for all knowledge, above and below," she murmured, lifting a little bell to summon her assistant. "Which I have already told you. And I'm ready to pay it, to obtain what I desire."

◑ ◕ ◑ ○ ◐ ◑ ◐ ◑ ◑

A telegram awaited us in the hallway of Baker Street. As Holmes perused it, I took out my watch once more: nine o'clock. One hundred and eighty minutes until the witching hour.

"Your typewriter was purchased for the Imperial Count Ladomer Breuner-Szécsényi, and shipped to Buda-Pesth," Holmes said, waving the flimsy. "The only Hansen machine ever manufactured with the double-acute accent used in Hungarian. The note was in English, yes, but the second strike of the letter 'o' in 'doom' included the double acute. A momentary and understandable oversight. But one that stands out glaringly to the investigator who's made a study of such things."

"I didn't notice any accent marks."

"Then once again you failed to observe closely enough. Thus, we gather in the final threads leading to the solution of our puzzle. An organization. A name. Though not yet a motive. Unless destroying this occult marketplace is the reason for his act, in and of itself."

"I'm glad my sleuthing yielded something useful." I confess to feeling a bit resentful that my contributions were not always appreciated.

"We should ready ourselves," Holmes said. I followed him up the stairs, and he unlocked our door. "Perhaps you should drop your service revolver in your pocket, my dear doctor."

As was his wont, he had not revealed all to me. To mystify, to dramatize, or perhaps simply out of impatience at my so-called wooden-headedness. A hint of anger crept into my voice. "Where *are* we going, Holmes? Readying ourselves for what?"

He called back from his bedroom, "Forgive me; I should've explained. Remember the words of the note? 'A blaze of light.' Where else should we seek this spider and his intended victim, but at the very source of light itself?"

I frowned. Why must he persist, even delight, in being recondite? "The sun?"

"By night, Watson, by night. Where does our light come from then?"

I rubbed my jaw. "The moon?"

Holmes sighed. "Once more, my dear Watson."

"The, er . . . lamps?"

"Which draw their luminosity from. . . . ?"

When I still stood wordless, he prompted again. "Or rather, draw their fuel from . . . ?"

I grasped his point at last. "Beckton!"

"Precisely. The largest gas-works in the world. Supplying the greatest city in the Empire."

Every Londoner knew Beckton. Having amalgamated earlier gas-works throughout the city into one sprawling establishment, its storage tanks loomed over the Docks. Its flares lit the east at night as if dawn had come. Each and every day those piers received shipload after shipload of hard coal from the mines of the north-east. Fed into the furnaces and ovens of the Gas Light and Coke Company, they supplied illuminating-gas for most of the city north of the river.

Holmes emerged from his bedroom carrying a black leather valise, much like a doctor's. "The coal is baked in the absence of air until it yields up flammable vapors. Other products include coke, coal-tar, and coal-oil—also a valuable illuminant, though it's being supplanted by Mr. Rockefeller's patent 'Kerosene.'

"Thus, 'The Great Witch will meet her doom in a fiery midnight spectacle. Her eclipse will astound all London.' There it is, plain as day. At midnight tonight—the night, mark you, of a lunar eclipse—our mysterious opponent will carry out his hideous crime."

"Unless we stop him." Going into my own room, I took my revolver and a handful of cartridges from the bedside drawer.

In the hallway Holmes seized a card from the table and scribbled upon it. Stepping outside, he hailed a passing urchin and pressed a shilling into the lad's grimy paw. Then called over one shoulder, "Are you quite ready, Watson? The game is afoot."

But before that, it seemed, we had one more stop to make.

The railway deposited us at the lower level platform of the Crystal Palace. But its vast aisles, to my astonishment, lay empty. Holmes turned in a circle beneath the arches of iron and glass. "They have decamped, it seems," he muttered.

"Nay, not at all," a voice echoed, as a cane clicked upon the tiles. The old man was alone this time. "Hast thou found where she be?"

"Not only where, but with whom. Though not yet for what purpose," Holmes told him. "Has your Bazaar folded its tents and stolen away? I'd understood it will be here for four more days."

"Oh, it be here." Dee swept an arm outward and for the merest fraction, as if through the flickering shutter of a detective-camera, I seemed to see it all again: the aisles, the booths, the peculiar vendors. Yet . . . not quite. A trick of the light, no doubt.

"Tell me you've brought the ransom," Holmes said.

Dee grimaced. "I cannot, valorous sir. For though some 'mongst us can conjure gold from lead, or concoct elixirs to heal and prolong life, none can produce this unnatural metal."

Holmes nodded grimly. "I thought as much. And the sapphires?"

"Nor those," Dee said. "Or rather not perfect ones, as the villain doth specify."

"Then we must make the best of it." Holmes hefted the Gladstone. "With this."

Dee gave the bag a curious glance, but enquired no further.

Holmes strolled a few feet away and bent to my ear. "Shall we take him with us?"

"Why? In a struggle he'll be of little use."

"Perhaps those illusions of his may serve as a diversion."

I couldn't hide a smile. "But you thought them mere play-actors."

Holmes said quietly, "Doctor John Dee died in 1609. Astrologer, mathematician, advisor to Queen Mary. This fellow cannot possibly be him. Therefore, he's an impostor."

My companion could stubbornly maintain his opinion even in the face of contradictory evidence. "And Blavatsky?"

"A charlatan. Nothing more."

"You're committing a tautology, my dear Holmes," I pointed out.

"How so?"

"By saying it's impossible they may be what they say, on the basis it is impossible they could be what they say."

"I also said they might be mad."

I bristled. "If that is so, then would we not also have to—"

But he'd already turned away.

●◐◑○◖○◗○◐●

The moon had risen; full, lambent, pallid as a chalk cliff. As we descended the hill, though, it waned. We sank like mariners buried at sea into the city's pestilential vapors. Once we emerged from the Underground at the Docks, and Holmes had hailed a hackney, the orb was hidden by miasmas ever-shifting above, a grey vapourous veil between us and the heavens. For a moment I recalled his outlandish prediction: that at some future eon the atmosphere itself, choked with the waste of human industry, would seal in the heat of the sun, and bring an end to all life.

Despite myself, I shuddered. I place no credence in superstition, yet it seemed we were penetrating into shadows deeper than those of night alone. Into realms of forbidden knowledge, and of monstrous villainy. Who was the mysterious Hungarian who'd pursued the mystic marketplace across Europe? Who seemed both to set his will against the uncanny, yet be willing to harness it to profit himself, or others behind his plot?

Perhaps we would find out tonight.

The Works loomed ahead, high towers capped with vertical tongues of flame. Their reddish light cast a hellish glaze over the maze of pipes and valves and railways sprawling for many acres across formerly empty moorland. Gigantic tanks of riveted iron, their crown of lacy gridwork showing they aimed to grow loftier still, towered far above the masts and cranes of the waterfront.

We descended, paid the driver, and passed an untenanted guard-station. Then threaded between enormous sloping piles of wet-looking black sea-coal as the ruddy light flickered in a disorienting play: now brilliant, now obscure. A muffled clinking and chuffing thudded from the buildings we walked between. Ahead, emerging from the smoke and steam that streamed like fog across the muddy ground, rose three immense cylinders, built on such a titanic scale I had to crane my neck upward as we neared.

"The gasometers," Holmes said, as much to himself as to Dee and me. "The illuminating fluid is stored in those immense containers, before being piped into the City."

"I confess, I still don't grasp the connexion between this Bohemian noble and a modern industrial site," I said. "How is it you made that leap?"

"All proceeding from a chain of logic, my dear fellow. It only remained to reconstruct it. We know Szécsényi sent the notes. We also know the Szécsényi Works is the largest producer of illuminating gas in Buda-Pesth. In fact, one of the largest in Europe. The gentleman is literally in the business of manufacturing light. The only thing we do not yet know is why he's declared war upon magic. Perhaps his family's been part of this secret society from the beginning. It's useless to speculate upon the hobby-horses of the immensely wealthy."

A few steps behind us Dee wheezed, "If thou wouldst slow thy steps, good sirs—I being an old fellow, and the air so damp."

Holmes flicked open his watch, then glanced at the sky. The moon was still obscured, though a luminous patch low to the west hinted at its presence. "Apologies, but we must go quickly. Only ten minutes remain to the eclipse."

I shaded my eyes against the glare from an immense torch of flame. "Over there!" I pointed.

Atop the highest tank two figures stood. The slighter one with both arms raised, as if to signal us, or to embrace the night.

"Hurry!" Holmes rushed ahead to a spiral staircase wound about the immense tank. The clamour of our hard leather soles on iron steps echoed amidst the hissing of steam, or gas, through the multitude of pipes over which we clambered. I reached the stairs a few steps behind, and took them more rapidly than the weak leg liked, drawing my revolver as I climbed. Dee labored along as well, but far behind.

We stepped out upon the top of the gigantic construction, a circular plate of heavy iron wider than a tennis-court. This massive disc floated upon the gas as it was produced during the day, compressing it so that when called upon in the evenings it flowed out into the City. The iron surface drummed as I lurched across, cursing as the old leg-wound stabbed me.

As Holmes rushed ahead, I saw the smaller figure was that of a woman. Lithe and slim, nearly as tall as Holmes, wrapped in a flowing gown or robe of some diaphanous fabric. A dark purple or perhaps blue—it was difficult to tell in the ruddy light. Her arms were not lifted, as I'd thought, but lashed above her to the framework of the gasometer. Long dark-auburn hair stirred in the wind. I caught a glimpse of large dark eyes, a prominent nose, cheeks of dusky rose, and full lips that parted slightly at our appearance. Attractive, yes. In fact, surpassingly lovely. Yet there was a hardness as well about her features. They spoke of determination, perhaps even suppressed, inhuman cruelty. But of softness or kindness, the meekness and tenderness that are the highest attributes of Womanhood, I gleaned not the slightest indication.

And . . . eternal, ageless? This woman could not have been far above thirty. But if Miss Morstan's blue eyes were limpid pools, the Lady's were a dark abyss. And like one hesitating at a precipice's edge, I was drawn down, down into them, whether I willed it so or not. Even though I clearly would be lost forever, to take that fatal stride.

"Signora Vera Fortunato?" Holmes shouted. I pointed my weapon at the man who stood a few paces from his captive, holding fast to a complicated assemblage of pipes and valves that led in her direction.

"Stand back, *bolond*, whoever you might be." The gentleman's accent spoke of Eastern Europe; the tone guttural, as if he labored under some terrific strain. His jowls sagged, though he seemed no more than five-and-forty. His out-thrust, grotesquely swollen jaw resembled that of a Habsburg. A thunderous brow and tightly-drawn lips betrayed the resolution of an unhesitating fanatic. His black frock-coat and trousers were cut in the European style. The pipe-assembly he stood beside led down into the gasometer itself. With his free hand he trained on us a long-barreled dueling-pistol of a dated but no doubt still-effective make.

It was plain what he intended. To wrench the relief-gauge open, and plunge some source of ignition into the instantaneous, unimaginably violent rush of escaping gas. Which would envelope his captive in a gigantic sheathe of living flame. Visible, if I guessed aright, for many miles over the dark city.

Just as his missive had promised, the Great Witch would meet her doom in a spectacle that would astound all London.

Vera's lips parted again. "Good evening, *Signor* Holmes. And *Dottore* Watson. I'd foreseen you would appear. But rather earlier than this."

Her gaze still locked with mine. Her voice struck me as both foreign and incredibly intimate. As if we'd known each other for years, even shared nights of romance. As if she knew all, and understood the deepest secrets of my heart.

"Holmes!" The Count said, then pointed the weapon at me. "And Watson. I am honored to meet the very apostle of English rationalism. The gentleman who most perfectly embodies our philosophy. I had hoped, perhaps—"

"That I would be approached for the case? Which explains why you wrote your notes in English, rather than a language more conducive to secrecy," Holmes stated. "And you, sir, will be the Imperial Count Breuner-Szécsényi, of Buda-Pesth, Kingdom of Hungary."

The other nodded, and my friend advanced a pace. "May as well give yourself up, milord. I've dispatched a note; the Metropolitan Police are en route. All that remains is to explain yourself."

Breuner-Szécsényi turned to the city below, to the west. Behind him, I noted, mists were rising. A reddish light growing as the sky cleared. And just in time: above his head, a darkness was gnawing at the pale orb of the moon.

"I owe no one an explanation," he said. "My actions alone will speak for those whom I represent."

"You mean Sursum Corda. Who are they? Whose interests do they serve? Not Moriarty?"

"My interests are my own," the Count said, then hesitated, as if loath to finish this exchange. "Our order is dedicated to the liberty of Man's mind. But I have personal reasons for revenge, as well. This *witch*"—he glared at Vera, who twisted her wrists within the bindings, though seemingly without much effort —"Cast a spell over my ancestor, Baron Topat Szécsényi. Sheared him of his honour, his fortune, his title. Casting our family into the depths. Yet I rebuilt our fortune, and regained the esteem of the Emperor."

Holmes said, tone ironical, "It seems you've already achieved your revenge, then."

The Hungarian gave a rictus-like grin. "Not at all! For centuries her evil saturnalia has snatched innocent men and women from their safe and comfortable existences. Its prizes are curses, scourges, torments. Leaving wrecked lives and weeping in its wake. This is why I am come! To put a stake in the heart of the monster, and end the career of its cursed Witch-mistress forever."

Above us the moon had darkened, a good half already bitten away by the black shadow of the circular earth. The remainder was shading deeper and deeper into the hue of ancient blood.

Holmes took another step forward, and the Hungarian twisted a valve. A hiss rose, as if from a massive adder. Backing away to a safe distance, he held the pistol steady on my friend. I realized then what he intended: with one depression of the trigger, he would both destroy Holmes, and ignite the impending pyre.

The woman spoke again then. Casually, as if musing on a pleasant evening. In a musical accent, but in perfectly clear English. "Doctor, if you will," she called.

For a moment I thought she addressed me. But Dee stepped past us, still wheezing from his climb.

Extending that sooty claw from his sleeve, the old man lifted both arms and began to chant. His ruby ring caught the bloody glow of the moon. With a quivering stir, the stars above us whirled slowly into motion, like silver coins stirred in a vat of black tar.

No. Not stars. But rather… *beings* … which took gradual shape from the night.

Phantasms. Demons. Each visage more horrible than the next. I gaped in horror as the creatures gathered speed, whirling in a dizzying Sarabande. With each rotation they gained form, gathered shape, became *real,* and circled inward. At another gesture from Dee they swerved, converging and battening upon the man opposite us like an unkindness of ravening ravens.

With a hoarse, agonized scream, the Count flicked up his pistol and fired. And with frightening suddenness, ignited by the burning wad from his gun, the gush of gas burst into a vertical torrent of lambent, roaring flame.

Within it, limned by that fearsome blaze, glowed for a single yet endless moment the lithe form of Madame Vera. Her silken garments shrank and blackened in the terrific heat. Yet her skin, white and smooth as the finest Wedgwood jasperware, remained unblemished.

Holmes was already reaching into his valise. With a heave worthy of a stone-slinging David he threw something which landed at her feet. Glass shattered on iron, and the flame quenched. Cut off at its root, even as its upper edge, many yards overhead, remained afire.

He hurled a second projectile, which I saw now was one of his chemistry-flasks. That final remnant of flame too snuffed out, leaving only the vibrating gush of escaping gas. But it vented harmlessly now, unignited, streaming off toward the declining moon with a hoarse unearthly roar.

I leapt forward. Gripping the valve, though it scorched my palm, I twisted it shut. The bellow tapered … whispered … and ceased.

While the Count still screamed, gripping his face as he staggered toward the edge of the gigantic disc. Howling as if tormented by all the Furies, raking the skin from his cheeks with his own fingernails.

Dee gestured again, and the howling Count vanished.

Holmes and I stared for the space of a drawn breath at the spot where he'd stood. Then the sleuth rushed to the captive, flicked open his pocket-knife, and began cutting her free.

I fought to avert my eyes. With all her clothing burned away, her naked figure stood invitingly revealed. That momentary glimpse burned the sight into my memory so deeply that closing my eyes, I can see her yet. But she did not seem to mind this imposition on her womanly modesty. Rather, she stared at her bare, slender, graceful feet, where white flakes were deliquescing upon the iron surface like snow. Some detached part of my mind noted her splayed toes, like those of the women I'd seen in Afghanistan. Wherever she'd grown up, she had not worn our tight, confining European shoes.

She murmured, "So you too, *Signore* Holmes, practise the Craft."

He smiled, loosening the last bond. "Simple chemistry, Madame. A solid precipitate of carbonic acid gas, or carbon dioxide. It possesses the useful property of dousing a flame."

The Lady stepped free, graceful as Eve, seductive as Aphrodite. Shattered glass crunched beneath those white feet, but she expressed no pain. Merely massaged her wrists, glancing from Holmes to myself, and smiled deep into my eyes.

Then she too made a complex gesture, like those of the old magus. And suddenly both the Lady and Dee, with neither sound nor fuss, simply . . . *were no longer there.*

Leaving us standing alone atop the cylinder, astonished and nonplused, as the shouts of the arriving Metropolitans echoed amid the iron jungle.

●◗◑○◗○◑◖●

We explained as much as we could to Inspector Lestrade when he arrived at the works. As far as the police were concerned, the Count had most likely fallen into the Thames, never to emerge.

●◗◑○○◑◗●

Some days later, with both of us snug again in our humble abode, Mrs. Hudson came up to announce visitors. "Them same queer folk, Mister Holmes. Doctor. But only two as is come this time."

I started up eagerly. "Please show them in. Would one be a Madame Vera?" Yet I felt all too certain I'd never meet her cryptic gaze again. Nor was I exactly sorry.

Our guests turned out to be Dee, complete with beard and cane, and the Romany woman, Vadoma. Concealing disappointment and relief, I showed the old man again to his place by the window. Again, though Holmes set a chair for her, the short woman spread her voluminous skirts to squat upon our figured carpet. Dee took out his pipe, and again in a way I could not make out, lit it and puffed a few times.

"You know, I've come to some conclusions," Holmes said, resuming his seat and stretching out his slippers to the fire. "On sober reconsideration, I believe there was more to your, and the Lady's, participation in this matter than originally met the eye."

Dee puffed silently. The woman glanced around curiously at every object in the room.

"It's obvious Madame Fortunato could've slipped the clutches of the Count at any time. Therefore, I believe she cooperated in her abduction—or at least did not resist." Holmes filled his pipe and lit it with a taper from the fire. "And why? Weary of paying her extortionists, she saw in his threat an opportunity. Submit to capture, and perhaps root out the S.C."

"So they had no need of us?" I said angrily. "We were their dupes?"

"By no means! Madame Vera had no idea who Breuner-Szécsényi was, or how connected to the Corda. I doubt he told her his name. We laid him by the heels, and ended his threat to the Bazaar. No doubt the cabal will continue to plot. But I'll send Dr. Dee back with my notes on the case. With what I've told her there, she is assured of holding them at arms-length. At least for a time."

He turned back to that old gentleman. "You will no doubt enquire as to my fee. Rest assured on that score. I am happy to bury this episode, and the disquieting thoughts to which it gives rise. So I bid you farewell, Doctor. May you and your confreres continue with . . . whatever your curious purpose may be."

Dee nodded, puffed again, and coughed. Then rumbled, "The Lady sendeth her respects, and extendeth this offer to ye. Be it known, though, tonight is the last we shall rest in London-Town. Our week is ended, and we must away."

He reached into his musty black robe.

Holmes accepted the slips Dee held out. Examined them; then tendered his own back to the old man, and the other to me.

I cast my eye over the Gothic lettering, the ancient parchment, crisped at the edges, as if it too had been touched by flame. The innermost wish of one's heart? I hesitated, conscious of Holmes's eye upon me. But why should I feel obliged to do as he had? Avoiding his gaze, I slipped the document into an inner pocket, intending to decide later.

He said quietly, "And Madame Blavatsky's?"

Dee nodded, fingering his pipe. "Delivered. And accepted."

"Then our business is at an end."

The old mountebank grunted, hoisting himself with the aid of the narwhal-cane. "Aye. But I wit show thee one marvel further."

"I'm at your service," Holmes said. "As long as it involves no more hasheesh-induced air-voyages." He flashed a sardonic glance my way.

Dee gestured, and the old woman rose. She reached into her capacious bosom, and came forth with the same crystal orb demonstrated previously. Again she drew her hands apart. Once more the sphere hummed, floating in the air.

Holmes smiled, glancing at me again. Shrugging, as if to say, Will they never cease with their tricks?

He rose and stepped forward. I shifted a bit, the better to see over his shoulder.

Within the sphere a tiny manikin all in black raged, and raged, and raged, pounding with tiny fists against the interior of its transparent prison. Its minute mouth gaped in a scream, but no sound emerged beyond the high-pitched hum of whatever power pinned it there.

The Imperial Count himself, sealed helplessly and forever within the crystal globe.

Holmes backed away, paling. "Merely the flicker of a coloured card," he muttered. "An illusion. A parlour-trick. Like all they have shown us."

Yet he looked shaken to the core.

● ◐ ◑ ○ ○ ◐ ◑ ●

As they saw themselves out Holmes stood staring into the fire, hands clasped behind him.

"I wonder if he believes now," I remarked.

"If who does?" Homes said sharply.

"Why, our Hungarian. He professed himself a rationalist, to the point of murder. Does he credit her powers now?"

I hadn't meant it as a reproach, but Holmes' narrowed gaze said he'd taken it as such. "You *will not* write of this case, Watson," he told me. "If you've made any notes, destroy them."

I agreed, of course. But over the years I was unable to shake such a remarkable series of events from memory. And wrote, at last, such an accounting as I could recall, placing it in a surety-box at the Bank of England. Along with instructions to my heirs for its eventual publication in some obscure journal of

Gothic fantasy, where it would never be credited as veracious. Which is how you, reader, have come upon it now.

I still do not grasp its lesson, though. Was Holmes correct? Was all simply prestidigitation, trickery, sleight-of-hand, some form of mesmerism? Or had Blavatsky been right, and there exists, beyond what we can perceive, another realm entirely?

Perhaps I would've found out, had I acted on my Invitation. The one I distinctly recalled slipping into my pocket. But later, when I finally searched for the aged bit of parchment, it had vanished. As if it'd never existed, or been merely the figment of a dream.

Yet even without it, I still attained my dearest wish. I sit now in our garden beside the former Miss Mary Morstan, who became my beloved wife. Both of us are aging now, with not many years left to us.

Yet still I cannot hazard a conclusion. Very well then! Let the rest, as the Bard says, be Silence.

This lovely old tinker's handcart is painted with wildflowers and charming forest creatures. In its pine-planked bed lies a heap of pocket watches crafted of various metals, in a wide variety of hand-carved designs. Do you carry a timepiece, that fashionable must-have accessory for any gentleman or lady of means? And of course one always wishes to avoid being late for an engagement, lest there be consequences, whether social or . . . even more severe. Do you see the gold watch in that far corner, with black-painted roman numerals and silver flourishes? Well made, though its overall appearance is rather mundane. Yet this timepiece is anything but ordinary. As more than one person gifted with it for a span has discovered— albeit, sometimes, too late . . .

Beautiful Lie

by Dana Miller

The midnight stillness of Hull Manor was shattered as screams echoed through the second floor's ornate ivory archways and galleries, all the way down to the Great Hall. The eternal fiery rage that lay banked within Lord Henry Richmond had burst forth yet again. An intense inner blaze touched off by frustrated desires and unfulfilled needs, it smoldered like a subterranean coal fire that finally must break free to the surface. Starting in his legs, traveling up past the heart to the ears, and eventually all but blowing off the crown of his head.

Gripping the gold brocade curtains over the floor to ceiling windows of his chamber, Henry tore them from the brass rods. The fabric fell to slump corpse-like at his feet. Swiping a sterling paper knife from the desk, he darted toward his four-poster bed, sank the blade into the fine silk coverlet, and slashed until goosedown flew like an out-of-season blizzard.

Should the servants awaken during one of these not-infrequent fits, there was an unspoken rule: They would remain tucked away until the following morning, after the chaos had abated and their master departed to go riding, or to visit his club in London. Only then did they dare enter his chamber to carefully erase all evidence of the previous night's outburst.

For most gentlemen of means, losing a game of cards was a mere trifle. But for Henry, losing at anything was torture. He *must* be known as the finest whist player of his circle. His home *had* to be the most grand. He craved a reputation as the most handsome man in London and environs. And a reputation for throwing the most elegant and popular balls at his country estate.

So when such triumphs did not materialize, the staff knew all too well the telltale signs of discontent. Should he return home later than usual after an evening of gambling, it meant he'd played poorly and would spend the wee hours punishing the bedroom furniture. Or, should he return at a reasonable hour but speak not a word, simply retreat upstairs and softly close the door behind him . . . the night would be just as unpleasant.

These violent fits first manifested during his childhood. Henry had always wanted what he wanted, at once. And he became used to getting his way, as the son and only child of Lord Percival Richmond and Lady Phillipa Richmond. His late parents had coddled him, doing all they could to keep him happy, providing anything he desired to keep that abominable temper from clawing to the surface. They'd wished to keep this flaw hidden, lest gossip sully the Richmond name. For Henry eventually must marry, and a scandal could scotch a good match. He was to inherit everything, after all.

◐ ◑ ◑ ◑ ○ ◑ ◑ ◑ ●

There was a masked ball the following night, at Lord Benjamin Blackpool's enormous, fashionable London townhouse. His county estate's formal rose and boxwood gardens were famous throughout England, but it was the Season now, and he'd moved back to London.

Henry Richmond entered Blackpool's ballroom wearing a royal blue and gold Venetian domino. Before him ebbed and flowed a tide of ladies in silk and lace dresses, most with gentleman already dancing attendance. They whirled to an eloquent Austrian waltz played by a full orchestra, and everyone wore Carnivale masks. One silver half-lune sported multicoloured jewels. Another full-face number was ivory satin with radiant gold-flecked swirls; so well-fitted it gave the appearance the design had been painted directly onto the lady's face.

Of all the town and county balls, those thrown by Benjamin Blackpool were the most diverting; all the nobility could speak of for weeks on end. This fact maddened Henry. He hoped no one would expect him to agree on how splendid was this current bash. And that it had even managed to surpass the excellence of the last. As it most clearly had.

His hope was in vain.

"Not to say *your* soirees aren't wonderful, Lord Richmond." The Countess of Cornwall tapped his arm with her folded fan. "But one simply understands Lord Blackpool's are undeniably superior. Exceeding comparison with any other social affair."

"Of course." Henry endeavored to make his gritted teeth pass for a smile.

He'd tried on numerous occasions to outdo Benjamin, but always fell short of that one special element that amazed invitees, whether a newly-invented aperitif or an hour-long fireworks display. At Blackpool's, the imported champagne flowed until well until after sunrise. The midnight supper was cooked by the most talented chefs in London. Blackpool always concocted a unique theme for each ball, too: medieval costumes, or a certain colour of gown all the ladies must wear. Once, guests were required to attend in the most outlandish hats they could find. A prize was given to the most unique.

For this latest soiree, attendees wore elaborate masks to match their extravagant costumes, *a la Venezia*. Henry felt his own outfit—inspired by Louis Quatorze—showed his legs off to great advantage. He was sure he was far more handsome than other men of his acquaintance—including Blackpool, who was also not nearly as cunning at cards.

But there *was* something about his old friend Benjamin that Henry bitterly envied. The man never seemed unhappy. Always smiling, always a positive fellow, never displeased by any possessions or friends he couldn't acquire. He was, as far as Henry could tell, content with his world. Whereas Henry always needed more.

They'd both been popular at Eton and then at Oxford. Henry had been known for daring outbursts during class, and a cocky demeanor. Blackpool, for being an all-around genuine good fellow. They'd first met when paired to work on a project for Greek studies.

"Just so you know, Rigby has it out for me. No matter how well-done our translation work is, he shall find some reason to fail us," Henry had told Blackpool after class, as they'd crossed the green.

"Well, the professor likes me. Perhaps it'll help your marks for us to be matched," Benjamin replied, patting his shoulder.

But, just as Henry'd predicted, Professor Rigby failed them both and refused to reconsider, no matter how Blackpool flattered and begged. So the two friends had decided to pull a prank.

"I'm sneaking a hedge-creeper into Rigby's office," Henry told Ben, grinning. He explained his plan. "Are you with me?"

Blackpool had gaped. "Are you mad?" he'd whispered. "We'll both be expelled for bringing a streetwalker here. I feel wronged, too, but is this really the proper way to address it?"

"No one will know it was us. I'll pay the jade extra to not breathe our names to anyone."

And it had been a delightful joke, seeing Rigby's scarlet face as the heavily-painted woman had followed him out of his office, caressing and hanging on him for all to see, right there on Balliol's Ashmolean quad.

From that moment, the two young lords remained inseparable—despite Henry's increasing jealousy over the years.

Now he spotted Blackpool immediately, despite his scarlet and silver mask that boasted an exaggerated, pointed nose. A young lady stood at his side, her visage obscured by an elegant black domino studded with paste diamonds. Still, she was clearly a rare beauty. Caramel-hued ringlets framed a perfect oval face. Beneath the half-lune mask, rosy bow-shaped lips curved in a faint smile. One delicate pale hand held the mask's stick.

"Henry!" Blackpool shouted. They bowed, then gripped each other's arms. "So glad you could come."

"Benjamin, this may be your best ball yet." Henry strained to sound genuine. "Everyone will talk of it for months."

"Oh, I do hope so." Ben laughed, then turned to the young woman. "My dear, may I present Lord Henry Richmond? Henry, I'd like to introduce you to Lady Emmeline Crane. My fiancée." He peered back at Henry, his hopeful look suggesting he sought approval and praise.

The lady dipped her head and curtseyed, then flashed what seemed a flirtatious smile.

"Fiancée!" Henry raised his voice to be heard above the swelling strains of Strauss's 'On the Beautiful Blue Danube.' "Aren't you the dark horse, old chum. I wish you both the very best!"

He turned to Lady Emmeline, lifted her hand, and kissed it. She raised her mask to reveal a petite nose and sea-blue eyes, a fetching beauty mark beneath the right one.

Henry was mesmerized. "My lady, I . . . I hope we shall . . . all be seeing a lot of each other."

She replied warmly, "Lord Richmond, how marvelous to finally make your acquaintance. Benjamin speaks not half so well of anyone else."

"My dear," Blackpool laid a hand on her slender forearm, "might Hal and I have a moment?"

"Of course." She headed off toward the other side of the ballroom, where a group of giggling young ladies had congregated near the musicians.

"Good gracious, man! How'd you bag such a magnificent beauty, and get her to agree to marry the beast?" Henry teased.

Blackpool laughed and rubbed his chin. "It blindsided me. Absolute perfection, is she not? Just the sweetest, most innocent, kindest soul I've ever met."

"And she chose you," Henry replied flatly. "So . . . very . . . quickly."

Blackpool shot him a chagrined look. "Sorry I didn't tell you sooner, old boy. You're my dearest friend. But I've hardly had a moment to come up for air."

"Not to worry, old thing." Henry punched his shoulder. "When's the big day?"

"Two weeks. We do hope you'll come." Blackpool smiled.

Henry whistled. "So soon." He took a deep breath. "Certainly I'll be there."

"As my best man, of course."

"Me?" Henry scoffed. "Are you bloody well certain?"

Blackpool chuckled. "As long as none of your infamous pranks are forthcoming. Who else would I want by my side?"

Henry looked around awkwardly, wishing he didn't have to answer. "It's all been decided, so how could I refuse? I wish you both every happiness." He bit his bottom lip to stem the trickle of envy seeping within. He *wished* to feel happiness for his friend. He'd also never been more jealous.

Just then Giles Chandler, a close family friend of the Blackpools, approached. A short, stocky fellow whose greying hair and thick black moustache gave him an imposing air. "Sorry to intrude," he murmured. "Might I have a word with Benjamin?"

Henry threw back the dregs of his flute. "I'll take a turn about the room."

"Lord Richmond." Mr. Chandler nodded. "Shall I see you at the card tables later on?"

Henry flashed a grin. "Wild horses couldn't keep me from it." He walked off, hoping to appear nonchalant. For the luscious Emmeline now stood alone, sipping champagne.

A few steps from her a waiter held a tray of filled flutes. Henry set his empty glass on it and took a fresh one. Emmeline smiled at him.

He quickly covered the last few steps to her side. "Wonderful ball, is it not? Old Ben has outdone himself. Yet again."

Her lashes fluttered as she gazed up. "Indeed, all so very lovely. The music, the décor, the masks."

"Tell me, milady…" He leaned in closer. "How do you occupy your time? What is it you like to do?"

"I greatly enjoy riding. And please, call me Emmeline."

"How is it we've never met before during the Season?" He adjusted his mask.

She lifted one shoulder charmingly. "My family's only just moved to London."

"Yet you're already to be married."

"Yes." She gave a mirthless little laugh. "Papa was most impatient to see me settled."

"Surely you could've had your choice of any eligible gentleman."

The muscles in her jaw tightened. "It was a . . . for convenience's sake, I suppose. I've five sisters . . . and well, no doubt we were all becoming a bit of a burden. Papa desires peace and quiet at home."

"I see. Well, every woman longs for marriage, no?"

"Most dream of love." She sighed. "But dreams and reality rarely coincide."

He swirled his champagne. "Do you not love Ben?"

"I did *not* say—" she snapped, then schooled her tone. "It's only that…I hardly know him. He certainly seems a good man." She blushed. "Really, we shouldn't speak of such things, having only just met."

Henry ignored this objection. Just standing near her made him feel somehow different. Oddly calm. Almost . . . happy. It was the damnedest thing.

"Benjamin's a safe choice. Surely you'd be happy for a time. Comfortable. But I wonder, will that be enough?"

"The choice has been made. But if we are speaking truthfully now, behind these masks . . . I always longed for passion. Excitement. Adventure."

Henry nodded. "I see." He could sit and listen to her melodious voice all night, and never grow bored or irritated. If only—

"Ah! There you are, my dear." Blackpool strolled up. "Might I have the next dance?" He held a hand out and led Emmeline away.

Henry watched the couple romp to a lively Schottische. And, even though he normally loathed dancing, wished he was out on the floor with her. Emmeline was fascinating. Kind. Calming. And very beautiful. Pure perfection.

He simply had to have her.

●◖○◗○◖○◗●

The carriage returned Henry to Hull Manor as the sun was rising. He felt the familiar pride, taking in its formal gardens; the Georgian red-brick façade trimmed with pink-brick accents. Past double iron gates, the long pebbled drive was lined with well-pruned hornbeam trees. In the distance stood an immense yew hedge walling in beds of hydrangea paniculata, blue irises, and roses. What a lovely setting for a jewel like Emmeline, he thought. But of course Ben had already won her.

He stomped in past the massive front double doors, to be greeted by Mrs. Dean, the housekeeper. "Good evening, milord. I was just about to—"

"Not now!" he snapped. "The hour is late. Whatever it is must wait. And see to it I'm not disturbed the rest of the night. Is that clear?"

"Yes, milord," she choked out. Dread twisted her face as she hurried from the hall.

Henry did not care. He stormed up the stairs and slammed the heavy mahogany door to his chamber. As he undressed he thought about Emmeline. Might he somehow steal her away? But the engagement was now public knowledge. Such a thing would cause scandal, and sever his friendship with Benjamin. Something drastic would have to arise, or else . . .

"Curse the sodding luck," he growled. Why'd Blackpool find her first? He grabbed a nightstand and flipped it over. Flung a desk chair into one wall; it shattered into kindling. His ears rang. His head thumped. Henry clenched his fists and howled in rage, then proceeded to destroy what was left of the room.

● ◑ ◐ ◔ ◯ ◔ ◑ ◑ ●

He slept amid the wreckage until midafternoon, then rose and headed to the stables, where Evans was grooming Banner, an Arabian from the same bloodline as Queen Victoria's favorite, Comus.

"Ready the horse at once. I'm going riding."

"Right away, milord." The groom set down the currycomb and headed for the tack room.

But no amount of exercise or fresh air could blow Emmeline from Henry's mind. At last he wheeled Banner about and galloped five miles to the Cranes' country home. He'd speak with her father; perhaps a new arrangement could be made. At the very least, he might catch a glimpse of the lady.

The Cranes had acquired a large wooded estate overlooking a tranquil lake. An elderly butler answered Henry's knock, and informed him in a monotone, "Lord Crane is away at present. The family's in London. Care to leave a note, milord?"

Henry sighed. "Not necessary." If he left anything in writing, Blackpool might get word he'd stopped there.

● ◐ ◑ ◯ ◯ ◯ ◑ ◐ ●

That night he was unable to sleep despite quantities of brandy. Recalling Emmeline's voice, her rare beauty, the singular peace he'd felt in her presence . . . it drove him mad. At last he threw back the coverlet and went outside, into a pouring rain. The air was chill but he didn't care. The bitter cold made him feel alive and numb all at once. He walked down the long, winding drive, toward the front gates.

Just as he was about to turn and come back, to try for sleep again, a voice called, "Lord Richmond!"

He sluiced water from his face. Behind the wrought-iron bars stood a woman as drenched as he, hair the dark red of river clay. Her dress was simple brown wool, but a fanciful shawl embroidered with strange symbols draped soddenly across her shoulders.

"Who are you? What's your business here?" he demanded.

"Call me Lady Vera, Lord Henry Richmond." She smiled mysteriously, as if she saw into his mind.

He frowned. "Have we been introduced?"

"We have not. But I know a great deal about you, and your desires."

Outrageous. He took a step forward, fists clenched. "My *desires* are none of your concern!"

She slipped a slender arm through the wrought iron-work of the gate. In her outstretched palm lay a rolled-up parchment; its edges appeared scorched. "Take this, Henry."

He hesitated, then snatched the thing up; somehow it was still dry. When he unrolled it, the sheet was blank. He scowled. "Is this some feeble joke? Did Blackpool tell you to—"

"No." She shook her head. "Hold it up to the sky at the next blood moon. And follow the directions writ there."

"Balderdash!" He looked down, about to crumple and toss it away, but his curiosity was piqued. "What happens then?"

No reply. He lifted his head; the woman was gone. "What the bloody Devil?" He flung open the gates and stepped out onto the lane, expecting to at least see the back of her, hurrying away.

There was no one on the lane in either direction. And the rain was quickening to a deluge. He stuffed the parchment in the pocket of his dressing gown and hurried back to the house.

● ◑ ◐ ○ ○ ◐ ◑ ◑ ●

The next morning, Henry could do nothing but think of Emmeline. That perfect creature, spending her life with Blackpool. Entwined at night, waking in each other's arms each morning. "A travesty," he muttered. "Unthinkable." She should be his, instead.

Then he recalled the visitor of the night before. The parchment pressed upon him. He fumbled in the pocket of his still-damp dressing gown.

"Found you," he muttered. And wasn't the next blood moon in two nights? Of course only a credulous fool would hold a blank scrap to the night sky and think to receive answers. But at the moment he'd try any remedy, even one provided by a roving madwoman.

● ◑ ◐ ○ ○ ◐ ◑ ◑ ●

Two days later, just before midnight, Henry grabbed a lantern and slipped out to the front gate. He hoped the outcome of this errand would not merely leave him standing in the cold, gaping up like a gullible moon-calf.

The fiercely-hued blood moon was still rising. He set the lantern on the gravel and fished out the scroll. Then lifted it overhead, aligned with the flaming orb.

He gasped as hair-fine letters appeared on the parchment, glowing red.

"Impossible," he muttered, then bent and held the paper over the lantern's flame. No words were visible. Again he lifted it to the sky.

Now he could read the words:

Invitation to the Night Bazaar, for you alone.
Search no longer. The forbidden one
you seek is in reach. At London Bridge
Catacombs, tomorrow after midnight.

Henry took the brougham the following afternoon, driven by Tarrants the coachman. His lacquered black and crimson carriage was a point of pride, too: its wheel-rims were painted red, with gold flourishes. It had fashionable glazed windows and padded, dyed red-leather upholstery. He rode all the way to London's financial district, the heart of the City, in comfort.

On arrival at 19 Old Broad Street, he stepped out and said, "It'll be too late to drive home when I'm through for the evening. Find a room at Furnival's

Inn, Tarrants."

The coachman nodded. "Very good, milord." And he drove off.

Henry climbed the steps to The City of London Club, his home away from home. He had dinner, then passed the time with games, tossing bales in the large drawing room. Later he had fine luck at many hands of Primero against Lord Mackay, Lord Baldwin, and Lord Balfour, all well-known for their pasteboard skills. Mackay, stout and boisterous, was the most popular player. Baldwin, the newcomer, was tall and reedy with a moustache too broad for his narrow visage. Lord Balfour, admired by the ladies for his confident manner and fashion sense, was not nearly as cunning at cards. But Henry feared he might be considered more attractive, and thus detested him.

While wagering, Henry indulged in the Club's finest port and cigars, and was soon utterly sozzled. Still, he consistently held the lucky hand, winning all but two games.

"You've bested me again, Richmond. I dare say I haven't lost so much in a single night before, my entire life." Mackay made a face and threw down his hand.

"Nor I," Lord Baldwin agreed, shuffling the deck.

Henry smirked. "What can I tell you, gentlemen. Must be the drink." He glanced at his pocket watch: the hour grew late. He'd better cut his intake or risk inebriation, and possibly be swindled—or worse—by the mysterious witch from this so-called Bazaar.

The night was bitterly cold when he finally left the Club, breath preceding him in a ghostly gas-lit haze down Old Broad Street. He traversed Cornhill, taking in London's fine nightlife. Aristocrats strolling in and out of the many gentleman's clubs on Old Broad and Threadneedle. Chatting, laughing, bellies warm with drink, dressed up to the nines in black wool cutaway coats, top hats, and fine silk waistcoats and cravats. The sweet strains of private orchestras trickled from within. Carriages still drove slowly up and down the cobbles, despite the late hour.

The gas lamps stood a good distance apart, so he passed repeatedly from light to dark, and back again. As he neared London Bridge, though, the scenery shifted to less pleasant, less savory views. Countless grimy street urchins. Beggars trolling for pennies. Bold doxies in scanty attire. Some left him alone, others begged doggedly for "A spare coin, gov! Anything a'tall."

Prostitutes lurked in alleyways, displaying a bare bosom or leg to entice Henry to have a brush. They wore corsets and grimy shifts, often covered only by thin shawls. Before, he might've stopped for some sport. . . but not now. Not with Emmeline in reach.

An older prostitute with frizzled red hair hiked up her skirts, displaying a scrawny calf draped in a ripped black stocking. Open sores pocked that pale, unwashed flesh. Henry shuddered, lowered his head, and hurried past.

A gaunt old hump-backed beggar in tattered rags rose from his spot against a brick wall and began following Henry. Every street he turned down, so did the scrounger. A raised, jagged scar ran from the bugger's chin to the outer corner of one eye — probably earned in some back-alley scuffle. Henry hastened his steps, turning right at the next corner. But when he glanced back, the beggar was gaining.

He wheeled to confront him. "Why do you follow me?"

"Good sir, a shilling for food? I'm so hungry!" the man begged.

"Why should I spend good money when you've done nothing to earn it? Your misfortunes have naught to do with me! Brought about by carelessness, I'd wager."

"Milord, I beseech you," the beggar implored. "Take pity. I only wanted to warn you—"

He was so close now, Henry's nose wrinkled at the stench of stale urine, sweat, and filth radiating from that no-doubt feverish body. Repelled, he flinched away. "Bugger off, you infuriating git! You'll have no help from me." He walked off, huffing, "Filthy degenerate."

The encounter made him wonder whether the invitation to this mysterious Night Bazaar could likewise be a trap. A ruse to separate him from his money. Yet he was curious to see what such a thing was, and what it might offer.

At London Bridge, though, he hesitated. The street lamps on Tooley weren't lit; the foot of the bridge was a wall of darkness. He contemplated turning back when faint sounds of revelry and song came to him, along with the mouth-watering aromas of baking pies and roasting meats. His stomach growled appreciatively.

He followed the scents beneath the bridge, to a set of wrought-iron doors that stood open just wide enough for him to slip through into a narrow corridor. He trod on, heart clenching at each rustle and rodent-squeak. His head said turn back. His feet tramped on as if ensorcelled.

Around a bend he came up against an oaken table lit with a motley assortment of lamps. A boy of fifteen or so stood behind it. Lank, greasy hair obscured his eyes. He handed a battered oil lamp to Henry. "Cheers, gov. Carry on."

"But . . . how far?" Henry croaked.

"Past a line o' wooden caskets, then veer left. Follow that 'un all the way down 'til ya reaches the Bazaar."

Henry traversed the damp, brick-walled corridor according to instructions and finally entered a cavernous chamber full of colourful tents and wooden stalls. The subterranean market seemed to stretch on forever into the dark. Torches and hundreds of oil lamps flared and flickered, illuminating various sections.

The first aisle he wandered featured hand-dipped candles, strangely-designed clocks, ornate silver and gold rings, enormous hunks of crystal, astronomical devices, and ancient, unsettling medical implements. The sign on one tent read *White Lotus Apothecary*. Past an open door-flap, the proprietor, a Chinese fellow, was grinding a red powder with mortar and pestle. Other potions, some of which seemed to change colours, were stored in glass decanters. As the apothecary vigorously plied the pestle, the powdery concoction emitted puffs of smoke and green sparks.

Henry moved on, looking for the Lady Vera amidst the motley throng. Barefoot urchins ambled about, gawking, next to well-dressed matrons who appeared to have just arrived from a ball, clad in gold silk and crimson taffeta. Beyond them Henry spotted a gentleman he was acquainted with at his Club. The Earl of Falkland was soft-spoken and very well-heeled. What need could *he* have for visiting the Bazaar?

Henry ducked down the next aisle to avoid him, stopping occasionally to view the wares or services on offer. Some alcoves had illusionists; one gentleman shuffled cards so fluidly they appeared to be connected. Henry scowled, annoyed at the man's superior skill.

Another fellow held out a gemstone in one palm. A flick of the wrist; it vanished. Some other alcoves hosted fortunetellers and mesmerists, while in one a gentleman in striped silken trousers calmly levitated. The tenth or twelfth aisle on—he'd lost count—was devoted to handcarts and braziers of smoked meats with pungent foreign seasonings. His mouth watered. He could actually taste the food without consuming a bite.

As he was purchasing a skewer of grilled chicken golden with saffron and curry, tendrils of a dense fog swirled about the crowd's ankles. Henry frowned, staring down. No one else seemed to notice it.

"May I assist you in finding something, milord?" asked a voice behind him.

When he turned to see who'd spoken, a man in a colourful silk patchwork vest stood in the alcove across, watching him. He seemed to be the proprietor of a tinker's painted handcart. In its bed lay a large heap of watches. The fellow gave Henry an assessing up-and-down look, then rummaged through the pile and pulled a timepiece out. "This one is for you."

"I've more watches than any gentleman needs, already."

"But this, milord, is an unusual specimen with magical properties."

Henry snorted. "Poppycock. You simply wish to open my purse."

The man chuckled. "Not at all. It's free of charge. For this timepiece was meant for you, and you alone."

"Hmm." Henry took it to inspect more closely. The gold watch had no cover, chain, or fobs. Its ivory face was painted with black Roman numerals and silver floral embellishments. Rather ordinary, except . . it felt oddly warm cradled in his palm. Weightier than a thing that size ought. The crystal was deeply scratched; it appeared very old indeed.

"It has the ability to change one's history," the vendor added. "Pull the stem out, twist it counter-clockwise. You'll be transported back to any time of your choosing, simply by focusing on a particular moment from it. You may travel thus once, then must give the watch away to someone else you deem deserving. To fail on that score earns . . . repercussions. So my advice is, be smart with your time, milord. Consider carefully what you truly want and what you wish to change. For either can be a blessing—or a curse."

Henry laughed. "What events could *I* possibly change? Anyhow, I don't believe in witchcraft."

The man smiled. "What *you* do during that past event decides whether a better, alternate world will present itself. And you must vow to pass the timepiece on after one use. Do you swear?"

Henry huffed, still skeptical. But the thing was free of charge, so what would he be risking? "Very well. I swear."

◉◑◐○○◐◑◉

In his room back at the Club the fireplace had already been laid. Henry paced before the flames, watching the minutes tick by on the watch. As the sky lightened from black to grey to rose, he imagined an altered life. One spent with Emmeline. She, his wife, waking next to him each morning. Sitting by the fire, evenings. Riding or shooting during the day. The most beautiful woman in London on his arm as she accompanied him to races and balls. The other women all green at her unparalleled beauty; the men wishing they were him: lucky in life, and in love.

But acquiring this future meant stealing her away from Blackpool. Only dark scenarios made such a thing possible, each ending with his old friend's demise or estrangement. Even if Benjamin saw reason, and ended his engagement, Henry would lose his best, his only friend. For why would Blackpool agree to simply step aside? Henry wouldn't, in his place. And if it came to a duel, would he not regret taking the life of his friend?

He vigorously shook his head, not wanting to consider such an outcome. But nothing must diminish his nerve. He pulled and twisted the watch-stem, holding his breath. Envisioning the night he'd spoken to Emmeline, alone at the ball. And then . . .

Nothing happened.

"Flim-flammery!" he shouted.

No sooner had he shouted those words than the walls spun, familiar furnishings blurring like watercolours on a damp page. Henry grew dizzy, then ill. He clutched the watch, bracing himself on a bedpost. Squeezing his eyes shut, holding his breath, hoping the world would stop churning.

Until at last all colours died to black.

●◑◐○○◐◑●

Henry's eyelids were still pinched shut. But now he heard orchestra music. The tinkle of crystal. Laughter and lively chatter. His lids flew open. He was indeed back at Blackpool's ball. And before him . . . Emmeline stood holding a champagne flute. Even more glorious than he'd remembered.

"I did *not* say—" She paused, frowning. "It's only that…I hardly know him. He seems a good man." She tore her gaze away. "Really, we shouldn't speak of such things, having only just met."

"Ben would be a safe choice. And yes, you'd be happy, for a time. Comfortable. But would that be enough?"

"The choice has been made. But if we are speaking truthfully now, behind these masks . . . I always longed for passion. Excitement. Adventure."

Blackpool would be approaching soon, to whisk her off for a dance. Henry had to stop him.

"Ah! There you are, my dear," his friend called, wending through the crush.

"Benjamin, old man!" Henry exclaimed. "Might I steal your lovely fiancée for one dance?"

Blackpool halted, looking surprised. "Oh. Well, of course."

Henry extended a hand. Emmeline took it and he whisked her away.

"Why ask me to dance?" She looked baffled. "There are many young ladies here far more interesting. And unattached."

Henry smirked. "You're mistaken about that. If I could steal you away for the whole evening, I would."

Her cheeks flushed a lovely rose. "Don't. I'm to be married to your oldest friend."

"What if there was someone else, offering all you desired and more?" Henry stared intently down, resisting the impulse to lean forward and kiss her.

She looked startled. "And where might I find such a one?"

"You needn't look far."

She drew back, eyes wide. "Lord Richmond, what're you saying?"

"Asking for your hand, of course." He grinned. "You feel the attraction, do you not?"

She bit her lip, as if considering. "Tell me, then," she said at last. "Who has the larger fortune, Benjamin or you?"

He cocked an eyebrow. "I do, of course."

"The grandest house? The most horses and carriages?"

"Again, me."

She pursed her lips. "Oh, but it is impossible . . . Papa would be livid. The betrayal . . . he'd quite possibly die of embarrassment." Again she looked thoughtful. "And yet . . . all that money! The largest manor house. Everything he said I should have." She paused briefly. "What a scandal it would be. I love it!"

Henry blinked, surprised. "You don't mind that part? The shame."

She gave a low, wicked laugh. "No. Why should I care? I've no friends in London. My father all but sold me away."

"Your reputation, ruined. Does that not bother you?"

"Truthfully, after such a dull life, I'd prefer a bit of excitement."

"You accept my offer, then?" They stopped dancing and stood staring at each other as other pairs whirled around them.

"I do."

"And Blackpool? Do you worry about wounding him?"

"All I shall wound is his pride. I leave the rest of the injury to you."

The instant the waltz ceased, Henry rushed off. He found Benjamin conversing again with old Mr. Chandler. He grabbed his friend's arm, leaned in, whispered, "We must speak, urgently."

"Of course, come with me." Ben led the way to a drawing room and closed the doors behind them. "Is something amiss?"

"Regarding Lady Emmeline—"

Benjamin smiled. "Unlike any other, is she not?"

"Indeed, a rare one." Henry nodded. "Which is why you must call off the engagement."

"What?" Blackpool stiffened. "Call it *off*? Are you mad, old chum?"

"I've made her a counter-offer and she's accepted. She wants adventure and passion, as do I. Our attraction and desires are mutual. My fortune and home, larger. We're far better suited."

"You scoundrel! Jealous I've found a beautiful woman to marry. Can't stand to be shown up. You never could."

Henry shrugged. "She's already agreed to marry me."

Blackpool's face went scarlet. "And you think I'll simply give up? The engagement was arranged weeks ago."

"Yet you will consent, and break it."

"Never!" Blackpool shouted.

Henry sighed, long and deep. "How unfortunate. I'd hoped to work this out civilly."

Blackpool clenched his fists. *"You can't just take everything you want in life that doesn't belong to you!"*

"Yet I know what I want, and *will* have her," Henry replied.

Blackpool gritted his teeth. "Then honor demands satisfaction. Pistols at dawn. And I will reluctantly kill you then, old friend."

●◕◑○○◐○◑●

Bunhill Fields burial ground was the agreed-upon location. The morning dawned gray and overcast. The cemetery preternaturally silent, as if every bird and woodland creature knew something terrible was to occur, and had already fled.

Henry's cousin, the Viscount of Annandale, accompanied him. It'd taken some persuasion to get him to agree to stand in as second. Henry had to promise to make it worthwhile. "I'll give you the ancient mantel clock of Great Grandpapa's, since you've often admired it." He'd been reluctant to part with the lovely heirloom before. But for Emmeline, he did so without hesitation.

Blackpool's second, the Earl of Conway, was a mutual friend from Oxford. An athletic chap with thick dark hair and mutton-chop sideburns. The seconds walked up to the duelists and handed each a pistol. The men saluted each other, turned back to back, walked a dozen paces apart, then pivoted to face each other. For several seconds they silently stood there, staring.

"It needn't be this way," Blackpool said at last. "Only give up your insane claim to my fiancée, and all will be forgotten."

"Unfortunately, I cannot," Henry replied grimly. "I don't want to kill you, old friend. But to have her, I'll do whatever I must."

"Why 'must' you, Richmond?" Blackpool shook his head. "Friends all our lives. Does that mean nothing?"

"A friend might call his engagement off for me. It's you who pushed things to this point."

Blackpool jeered, "Oh, no. That would never be enough for you. Always wanting what others have. Always thinking to simply take it. Well, if I die, you shall live with the knowledge you killed your best friend simply to steal his bride. It will hang like a curse, to wear forever on your shoulders. And if she's so easily swayed, do you think she'll never be swayed again, by another?"

Henry snarled. "She's meant to be with *me*, forever. I'll do what I must to ensure that."

Blackpool shook his head. "Is she truly so wonderful as either of us believe? The loveliest of ladies, yes. But something here begins to seem… unnatural. Her father was all too eager to be rid of her, though as yet I have not discovered why."

"Be silent!" Henry growled.

"Hal, why can't you admit to error here? Losing your only friend to satisfy a lust for a woman who isn't—"

"I said stop speaking!" Henry lifted his pistol.

"No!" cried the seconds, together.

Blackpool jerked his pistol up too. But Henry was already closing his eyes, pulling the trigger. When he dared look again, the lifeless, bloodied body of his oldest friend lay still and silent on the grass.

Night after night he relived that horror: his friend lying dead, blood soaking the white linen of his shirt. That death-pale visage, the eyes halfway open, accusing him . . .

Instead of tearing his chamber apart, now he trembled and cowered on the bed, unable to erase the terrible moment from his mind.

Desperate to believe he'd not made a terrible mistake, he rushed to arrange the wedding. Such an event normally meant a lavish celebration, but Henry was now a pariah to society. He wondered whether those who cut him on the street were more upset over Blackpool's demise, or that his death meant the end of those extravagant, popular balls.

He and Emmeline agreed a small ceremony would be most fitting. But as the wedding drew nearer, his nights grew sleepless. He again heard Blackpool's voice calling him a scoundrel. Saying something was wrong with Emmeline. That his gain would be a curse. He dreamed of Lady Vera at his gates; of the Bazaar vendor ordering him to pass on the watch to someone deserving or else. Even of the wretched beggar who'd dogged his steps in London, pleading for coins.

"But the watch is mine now," he muttered, "I *won't* give it up."

On his wedding day he consigned every doubt to the farthest attic-corner of his mind. The moment he saw Emmeline, radiant as the rising sun in a yellow silk brocade gown shot with silver and gold threads, it was easy. The only attendees at the church were her parents and five sisters, so he needn't worry about public opprobrium. Still, as he said "I do," before God, the priest, Emmeline, and her family, the touch of a cold finger ran slowly down his spine. He moaned.

"Are you well, my love?" Emmeline whispered, glancing with concern.

"Perfectly so," he managed to whisper back. Nothing must ruin the happiest day of his life.

Still he had to remind himself to look joyful. Emmeline's father, at least, couldn't seem to stop smiling. Such a look of relief, almost ecstasy on the man's face, once the vows had been exchanged.

That night, a breathtaking bout of connubial relations made Henry forget all concerns for a span. But once Emmeline slept, he lay tossing and turning, dozing off briefly only to wake again.

A floorboard creaked somewhere in the room. He shot up from the pillow. "Who's there?"

No answer. He lay back down again and reached out to his new bride for reassurance. She wasn't in the bed. "Emmeline? Is that you, my darling?"

His hand trembled as he lit the brass oil lamp beside their bed. Now he saw her, pacing the room, hair tangled, staring as if entranced. "Emmeline. Are you all right?"

"Like a curse. Just like a curse. A curse. Wear it like a curse," she chanted, a horrible off-key song in the darkness.

The hair rose at his nape. "My dearest, come lie down." When she did not, he sprang to her side, took her hands and led her back to bed. "You had a bad dream."

She gazed around blankly, but lay back and settled into sleep again. Rest evaded him the remainder of the night, though.

◉ ◑ ◐ ◯ ◯ ◯ ◐ ◑ ◉

The following morning at breakfast, he could not take his eyes off Emmeline. It was odd. She appeared quite rested, and spoke to him sweetly and pleasantly. Her hair was perfectly coiffed; not a line or crease indicated she'd passed a difficult night.

"My darling," he began, "the strangest thing. I found you pacing the bedroom in the wee hours, and uttering…well, very strange words." He held his breath, awaiting her response.

Her brow furrowed. "Oh dear. Truly? Nothing like that's ever happened before. At least, not that *I* know of." Yet her tone held a false note. She gave a charming little shrug, then took a bite of egg.

"Oh, Mr. Hitchens!" she called abruptly.

"Milady?" The butler came attentively to her side.

"I'll need a new breakfast. The eggs and tomato were touching. Tell Cook: no foods on my plate must touch."

The poker-faced butler lifted it from the table. "Of course, milady. I shall tell Mrs. Walker at once."

"And be quick about it. I'm famished," she huffed. Then, to Henry, "How very odd to sleepwalk yet recall nothing of it! I hope I didn't give you a fright, my darling." She laughed merrily. "I want to order new gowns today. Lots of them."

"No, I wasn't frightened." Henry felt cold again. "And, er, call the seamstress, by all means."

Who *was* this woman across from him, really?

"Well, if it was done, it was *unknowingly* done. Surely never to be repeated." She reached for his hand.

"Yes. Of course." He gave her slender fingers a gentle squeeze. "The excitement of the wedding, and all…"

Yes, surely a mere aberration.

◉ ◑ ◐ ◯ ◯ ◯ ◐ ◑ ◉

That evening was marked by a torrential thunderstorm. An unseasonal chill permeated the manor's rooms, despite all the fireplaces. After supper, Henry and Emmeline retreated to the drawing room to sit by the fire and read. They were discussing a honeymoon trip to Paris when a knock sounded at the door.

"Come," Henry called.

No one entered. After a moment he said, louder, "Come in, please!"

Emmeline looked at him oddly. "My dear, what is it?"

"Someone knocked."

She frowned as if puzzled. "I heard nothing."

The pounding resumed. Closing his book, he rose from the couch. Opened the door, then gasped and drew back.

The same beggar from London, gaunt and soaked with rain, stood dripping on the threshold, a hand outthrust. "I beg you, please," he whispered through blackened, chattering teeth. "I must warn—"

Astounded, Henry whirled to look at Emmeline.

Bewilderment paled her rosy cheeks. "Was there truly someone there, dear?"

"Yes! There is still. Don't you see him?" He turned back to gesture at the beggar, but he was gone. "What the deuce?" Henry sprinted down the stairs and toward the front doors, which stood ajar. Outside, rain fell like a dark waterfall cascading down a mountain.

"Hello!" Henry shouted into the roaring night. "Who's there?"

"I beg you, please!" shouted the same voice, from somewhere out in the grounds.

How had the filthy wretch discovered where he lived? Indeed, how had he even reached the estate, so far from the city? And worse, slipped inside undetected.

Through the downpour Henry chased the voice, here, then there. At last he stopped, bent over, hands on knees, panting and cursing. Unable to spot the damned creature.

"Henry!" Emmeline called from the portico. "Come inside. You'll catch your death!"

"I beg you, please!" the beggar called, louder than before.

Why has he come to torment me? Henry wondered. What've I done wrong? Then he recalled the watch-vendor's words: *You may travel thus once, then must give the watch away to someone deserving. To fail on that score earns . . . repercussions.*

"No! It's mine!" he screamed into the night.

The only response was Blackpool's voice, as clear as if his old friend were still alive and standing beside him. *"You will wear this on your shoulders like a curse, never to leave you."*

"No, no, no," Henry moaned. The world spun. Faint shouts rose from the house, and the thud of running feet, before he collapsed onto the gravel drive.

●◐◑○○○◑◐●

After that night all Henry desperately wished for was to talk to Blackpool about this ongoing horror. But the one person he'd ever confided in was gone forever. He relived Benjamin's death night after night, for a week. On the eighth night, a noise startled him awake. The gas lamps still flickered on the bedroom walls, though he'd turned them down himself before retiring. In their bluish glow he saw he was alone in bed again. Outside the windows thunder boomed and cracked. Lightning flashed, illuminating the room in eerie bursts.

"Emmeline?" he called. "Emmie, where are you?"

She came staggering suddenly from a dark corner, dragging her feet, again in a stupor.

Henry gaped. "My darling, what on earth—?"

She lurched toward the bed. Something long and shiny caught the light: a butcher's blade clutched in one upraised hand.

Henry pressed against the headboard. "Dearest, put that down! *Emmeline.* Can you hear me?"

No response. He lunged and seized that wrist. She freed it with a vicious yank, her sheer animal strength astonishing. Henry threw himself sideways, but the blade-tip still slashed one cheek.

"Help! Someone, help!" he shouted.

But why would the servants respond? He'd so often yelled and cursed and broken things late at night, and ordered them to always stay away.

Panicked, he knocked Emmeline down. Racing up the hall to one of the guest bedrooms, he slammed its heavy door and turned the lock. Crumpling to the floor, he crouched there, holding his breath. Listening for footsteps. A warm trickle of blood threaded down his face; he touched the wound and winced. He shifted, and something hard scraped away, a short distance over the floorboards. He glanced down. The enchanted timepiece lay beside him.

What on earth? How could it have ended up here? As he stared, dumbfounded, he thought he heard the Bazaar vendor's voice again, whispering, "*. . . give the watch away to someone deserving. To fail on that score earns . . . repercussions.*"

"Stop tormenting me!" he cried.

God, he'd made a dreadful mistake. This life he was now living was not at all what he'd envisioned. His best friend, dead. Voices haunting his mind, intent on driving him to madness. A bride who was mad and seemingly bent on murdering him.

But he could return. Go back in time, once more. To the ball where he'd betrayed Blackpool, who'd then challenged him to give satisfaction. He need merely arrive earlier than that moment, and undo all the evil it had evoked. He didn't want this life anymore. Not any of it!

And if the timepiece didn't work a second time?

Well, he had no better options at the moment.

There came a low scraping just then, as if someone on the other side of the door was dragging a metal blade down its mahogany panels.

Henry gasped. He twisted and pulled the watch-stem, squeezed his eyes shut, and envisioned Blackpool's ball at the moment he'd met Emmeline.

This time, the room did not spin, but rather *buzzed* around him as if the air swarmed with wasps. His skin felt hot. A wild murmur of voices filled his overheated brain. His bare feet stung as if cut by a thousand shards of glass.

Moments later, the voices fell silent. The pain receded. In its place came the sort of chill evoked by icy winds nipping at bare skin. The surface he sat on was frigid. His clothing felt dirty, sodden.

Henry opened his eyes.

He sat propped against a brick building on Farringdon Road in London. The sky was grey and hazy, as if it would soon be dawn. A recent storm had left puddles in the cobbled street. He pushed up and staggered a few steps, then caught a reflection in a nearby shop window. All the breath whooshed from his lungs. Staring back was the same beggar who'd been haunting him.

"What the devil?" Henry raised a hand to touch his face. So did the reflected tramp. A jagged scar on the specter's cheek stretched from chin to the outer corner of that eye. The wound *Emmeline* had just inflicted, yet . . . somehow, already long healed.

He wanted to scream, but had no breath left to summon.

Hunger pangs dug at his belly: a bleak emptiness he'd never known before. Starvation. He slapped at his clothing, but the watch was gone. Shivering violently, he slunk beneath an awning near a narrow alleyway. Now and then people passed, and he thought to approach someone, to explain who he was. To ask for help. But who would believe such a wild tale? They'd just call him mad.

Henry lay miserably atop a pile of rags and newspapers. He had no one now. No wife. No fortune. No manor house. No servants. He owned nothing. He was not the best in the world at anything, and perhaps never had been.

But now he at least understood one certain, bitter truth: that he richly deserved this fate.

Take care, gentle Guest, not to lean too heavily on the lid of this elaborate glass coffin in the Odds and Bitter Ends Shop. As you can see, it is beautifully crafted: the glass panes expertly leaded, the interior well-padded and upholstered in fine blue velvet. And that it currently lacks an occupant. Though large, it is a rather delicate antique, much written of all over the world. This one is of course the original *model, brought here straight from the Black Forest by a mysterious troupe of rather diminutive bearded men. It is a unique piece currently for display only; not for sale at any price. But I can give you something else, gratis: a peek into the future. Where it one day will serve as the inspiration for a slew of imitations. Including at the very time period to which this next story will deftly whisk us . . .*

The Middle Man, the Worker, the Error

by A.A. Balaskovits

An Interview with a Man Whose Office is in Middle Management

Harvard Stone's desk was neat, tidy, and held no personal effects save for the latest 3-D handphone. There were no framed photos of a beloved spouse, of children with cake smashed in their faces, or even a print of a dog, to imply the man loved anything other than the work he did. His office was sandwiched between upper management, those suites with leather couches and private bathrooms—a place he one day dreamed of occupying—and all the dregs beneath him, where bathrooms were shared by many and the toilet paper plied only once.

He was important enough to have a receptionist. A brunette hired for the quickness with which she answered the phone and neatness with which she stacked papers on his desk. The current neat pile consisted of resumes with her notes; she seemed to think the majority of applicants were qualified for the position, and they were. But one stood out in particular, a Dale Volk. Who now sat outside Stone's office, facing the brunette, no doubt wondering whether or not he should attempt the wishy-washy way the small talked.

Volk's resume was littered with errors—mechanical ones, mostly. Commas where there should be periods, present tense when he should've used past, even an unfortunate misspelling of his address: 19th Boolevard. As though his street was haunted, or he only had a minor grasp of the intricacies of phonics. This was a man who did not care for details, who did his work without the despair of the second-guess. The brunette had written "trash" at the top in her neat cursive.

As soon as Stone was done chuckling, he pressed the intercom. "Call Volk in for a chat."

The man did not disappoint. Volk had arrived twenty-three minutes early for the interview, exactly five minutes too early to hide his nerves. Those five minutes would have been better spent ironing his shirt, or at least tucking it in. A little taller than average, and wiry, he had the most unfortunate haircut. Bangs slashed across his forehead like a razor-line, and the hairs were a few millimeters too short to be fashionable, giving him the appearance of a military enthusiast gone to seed. When he was finally called in and sat across from Stone, back as straight as pinewood, he did not make direct eye contact. He looked just to the left of Stone's shoulder and kept his gaze steady, a sure sign of diligent practice in front of a mirror. Or he had been on several failed previous interviews. In this economy, the business could afford to be picky.

In other words, he was exactly what Stone was looking for.

"What's your relationship like with your father?" Stone asked.

"Sir?" Volk blinked.

"Was he a tough man? Or was he soft-bellied and came to all your tee-ball games, cheering you on even when you failed to connect bat to ball?"

"I don't—" Volk stammered and glanced around. "I never played tee-ball."

"Doesn't really answer my question," Stone said, though it did. "You don't meet the minimum qualifications for this role. We're looking for a college degree."

"Yes, sir," Volk said. "I can lift a hundred pounds, though. I can lift even more. It said in the ad—"

"You've got good arms," Stone interjected. "The work is mostly manual labor."

Volk nodded with three jerks of his head, one too many. "I've got experience lifting and pushing things, just like you asked for." He pointed to the resume Stone held carelessly between thumb and middle finger.

Stone balled up the paper and tossed it over his shoulder. It hit the glass of his broad floor-to-ceiling office window. "I don't need words to tell me what I can see, Volk. Your musculature speaks for itself." He leaned back in his chair. "Do you take direction well? Do as you're told?"

"I learn quickly."

"Not what I asked. Here, stand up. Come on now, do you take directions or not?"

Volk stood, nearly knocking his chair over.

"Very good. Now, walk to the corner there. Back straight." Stone was pleased to see the man do exactly as ordered. He had potential, this one. "Now, take one step forward. Take another one. Lift your knees, yes, that's a good man. Put your right foot forward."

Volk did as he was told.

"Put your right foot back."

Volk did as he was told.

"Put your left foot forward."

Volk's stare wobbled, but he did as he was told.

"Now, shake it all about."

Volk shook his left foot vigorously, nearly losing his balance.

"Put your left back. Now, do the hokey pokey."

Volk found his voice. "Sir?"

"You know, the hokey pokey. Turn yourself around. That's what it's all about, my good man."

Stone led Volk through several dances: the Grapevine, a waltz, and one robust take on Cotton Eye Joe. He'd never realized how depressing these moves looked without music, but the feeling could be tempered by remembering it was not *his* legs kicking madly without a beat.

Stone was looking for a particular kind of worker, and with each awkward gesture, Volk better fit the order. The kind of man who crafted a resume but didn't know what one looked like. The kind who said 'good communicator' under Skills, with nothing to justify it. The sort who did not pay attention to details and did not ask questions. The man who didn't know how to do a Tango but took direction as best he could.

The job was not technically illegal, but what was allowed changed so quickly it was difficult for authorities to keep track, and it was best not to invite introspection into business. Leave that to the scholars, who were notoriously slow to come to a point.

Stone's company did what they all do, at their core: exchanging promises for coins. A boutique start-up with a promising pedigree, Cry-O-Less, had gone bankrupt, as such fledglings were wont to do, and *his* company purchased their remaining inventory to resell to whoever wanted and could afford it. All business, as far as he was concerned, was a slimy mess, so there was no reason not to be honest about the grime. Only, he didn't sell literature, or art, or even foreclosures.

Stone moved bodies.

Legally, at least, they were bodies. And bodies, legally, were property. That was what the court had ruled in a 327 page document so thick it could have been a dissertation, and was read in full only by the same number of folk who usually dive into such things. Minimal. The argument against, cried out by writers with opinions and a flagrant use of fancy vocabulary (and one particularly virulent performance artist who stood nude outside of the courthouse and covered herself in pig's blood until she was dragged away by the police; some fancy if confusing way of saying people weren't meat, he supposed) was that these bodies were technically still alive; just suspended from living.

It was unfortunate they had signed all of their legal rights over to Cry-O-Less when they went into the big freeze.

For a relatively affordable price, Grandma and Grandpa, your aunt with the bad kidney, your lover with the brittle hair and sagging skin, had been able to suspend time in a glass coffin. Time enough, perhaps, to find a cure, if that was what one was looking for. Some had wanted to die with their grandchildren, to see the final seed of their line all grown up and withered before they went into the ground.

The Cry-o-less marketing campaign had been phenomenal: commercials and billboards of beautiful young women with coiffed hair and vibrant lipstick, staying fresh as the world around them rotted. It was said that the founder was the great, great, greatest grandchild of a famous glass-making family from the depths of the Black Forest, so he knew a thing or two about women trapped in coffins staving off decay. What was magic from an ancient age was now technology, a lovely mix of old time whimsy and contemporary anxiety about the unknown. Stone's company borrowed these tricks in their own marketing now.

Cry-O-Less' ideals had been just that: ideal. And not financially viable with the rising cost of electricity and anti-freeze. When one administration decided anti-freeze was bad enough for the environment to tax it, Cry-O-Less operated at a loss for a few quarters too many. Then they went belly-up, boo hoo, and needed to sell their assets.

Which is when Stone had swooped in.

"I know what you're thinking." He'd tired of watching Volk wiggle back and forth. The man was sweating; it was a race against the clock before odor set in. "What an unusual interview, eh? Not something you can prepare for. This is the nature of the job, you see. Unusual. If you catch my meaning."

Volk nodded, face blank.

"Tell me," Stone asked, leaning back in his chair. "Why do you want this job?"

Volk perked up. "I want to expand my skillset," he said, over-articulating the "k" and "t" as one does when they learn a new word. "And gain new opportunities." Clearly an answer he'd practiced. "And meet new people."

"Oh, you'll be meeting people, that's for sure," Stone chuckled. "But I don't want your half-baked ready answer, son. Tell me the truth or get out."

This question clearly made Volk uncomfortable, as it had many of the other applicants who'd applied for the role. Those who insisted their first answer was the truth were sent packing with less than a goodbye for their trouble.

"I . . ." Volk swallowed, and tried again. "I need the money."

"Bingo." Stone smiled with all his teeth. "And you'll always need dosh, won't you?" Ah, the good old root of all sins, and all progress.

He didn't bother to wait for Volk's answer. Stone had a meeting in ten minutes about spreadsheet design and he'd already wasted too much time explaining the moves of a box waltz. If they didn't cover the actual job duties, conveniently left out of the advertisement, the man would have no idea what he was to do.

It was the inherent tragedy of the whole scheme, really. Stone needed a man who didn't think too much, but it meant more work on his end. *He* had to do all the thinking. Ah, well. The trouble with being the smack-dab-in-the-middle man. Thankfully, Stone was a whiz at memorization and could list off the job duties almost as rote as he could his National Health Service number.

"Think of them as products," Stone finished, whipping out his usual line, eyeing the clock. "Products bring joy, do they not? And what better thing can anyone hope to be than the person who brings joy to others? It's a wonderful journey you're embarking on, my good man. Think of yourself less of a mover than as Father Christmas. The greatest mover of gifts all across the world."

With that, Dale Volk left the office an employee. And Harvard Stone opened a thrilling spreadsheet template, on which he had many opinions.

THE WORK OF A MAN HAVING A CRISIS HE DOES NOT KNOW HOW TO NAME

The dreamers screamed real loud when they woke up. The sound being one of many Dale took home with him to the bed-sit flat he rented for four hundred and fifty pounds, fully furnished, with unreliable broadband internet included. The tired bloke assigned to his case at the Jobcentre Plus office had once lectured him about creating boundaries between work and life, as though they were two separate states.

"Don't take it home with you, mate," he'd said, as though those six words were a great truth only he knew. "Once you're at the doorway, just breathe it all out."

How could he take it off, as though a job was a t-shirt to pull away from his flesh in a nightly transformation? He'd always worked with his hands, feet, and torso. There was no way to remove the scars, the flattened veins flowing across his forearms like tributaries, those calluses on each finger.

How could he possibly take *her* off?

She was like him, a body to be moved there and back again.

Most of what he did was relocating the inventory, as they were clinically called, once a month. Sometimes twice. Protesters, a few of whom were family of the dreamers, had a habit of showing up at the warehouse parking lot with signs, bullhorns and, worst of all, cameras. They called the operation the "bazaar of the lost." Dale had seen his own face on a few of the websites which tracked them, and read every comment decrying his culpability, often accompanied with a few sniggering remarks about his face. According to a handful of anonymous handles, he resembled a skinned potato more than a human being.

These comments didn't bother him, not really. After all, she didn't care what he looked like. None of the dreamers did.

The buyers were far worse, anyway. They could see his name-tag, could stand close enough to shake his hand, but rarely did either. To them, he was mere decoration. They did not ask his opinion, even though he'd read and memorized all the charts. He made notes on his lunch and bathroom breaks. Dale could have told them which man had lungs blackened with years of self-medicating tobacco. Which woman had lost too many pregnancies, and wanted to be frozen until she could be fixed. He knew who had been forgotten.

Buyers didn't care about that. They asked him to move the tarps away from the bodies. Most of the time, they asked for them to be removed entirely, so they might see what the dreamer looked like from crown to toe.

Sometimes Mr. Stone accompanied them, but only the very rich ones. He'd glance at Dale when he was removing a tarp and pull at the side of his lip, as though wondering, *Where do I know this bloke from?*

"This one," the guv said, as he yanked the tarp off a Mr. Toomsy, slumbering in his coffin with a breathing tube down his throat, "has excellent lungs."

"What's wrong with him?" the woman asked, lightly resting her fingers on the surface, as if she believed herself a patron at a zoo.

"Bad heart, I'm afraid." Mr. Stone flipped through laminated papers chained to the side of the glass box. "On the list for a transplant."

"A shame," the man said, in the tone one would use to comment upon finding a fly on their bowl of sliced melon. "Do you like him, darling?"

"Oh yes." The woman smiled with all her white teeth. "I like him very much. But my mother always said, never take the first horse they show you. It may be a winner, but you're looking for a champion."

"Your mother never had horses," her husband muttered. But he offered his hand to her with all indulgence, and Mr. Stone moved them to the next body.

Leaving Dale to cover Mr. Toomsy. He made himself look busy, as he always did when buyers were present. It paid a two-fold reward. The buyers were less likely to notice him if he was moving in the background. They were also less likely to notice that, as he was moving bodies around—some had to be packed for shipping, the international market was hefty—he made sure *her* coffin was never one they looked into.

Aurora. The error.

He often wondered what she sounded like. Some of the dreamers had made vids for their loved ones to watch when they visited, but Aurora had chosen not to leave one. Dale thought she must be one of those looking-to-the-future types, full of lightness, who wanted to leave nothing behind and jump into the unknown. A brave lass.

Mr. Stone approached him, the grin of a salesman who clinched the deal cutting into his face. "Friday, at nine P.M. Be there a little early. They appreciate punctuality." He handed Dale a piece of paper with an address, and a dress code.

The couple had returned to Mr. Toomsy and were taking turns running their fingers over the lid of his glass coffin, discussing how valuable good lungs were.

A shame. Mr. Toomsy still had a family. Grandchildren. Maybe great grandchildren by now.

At least Dale had saved her again. But he didn't feel like a shining knight. He only felt relief, an emptiness to replace the worry in his lungs, and averted his gaze to the floor.

On his days off, which were random each week depending on buyer interest, he spent his time at the library. It was only a thirty-minute walk from his flat, and best of all, it was free. He spent hours at a lonely row of computers, almost antiques. After a kind old librarian showed him how to refine searches, he read about and began to catalog the dreamers and their families.

All had little autobiographies chained to the side of their coffins, alongside the reasons for the freeze. Long lists of medical records. Some, like Grandma Evans, listed every member of her family, as though she could keep them close by having their written names next to her. She had fifteen grandchildren now, the oldest of whom was beginning high school. Captain Peters, an Army veteran who had suffered brain damage when he tripped and fell down his basement stairs, had no children, but his partner, Thomas, had written a eulogy in the local newspaper a year ago. He'd given up hope. Dale copied it word for word in a notebook. He tried to memorize it. Captain Peters had been shipped off to Germany three weeks ago with an American flag strapped around the glass.

Aurora was trickier to find information about. Under her personal story, the only thing written was *error*. Under reasons for freeze: *error*. Like she was not even supposed to be there. There was little published about her in the newspapers. Obituaries for her parents, who'd died when she was eight. She'd played basketball in high school, and her team won a small championship, but she was not the star player. Her name was listed along with the team, but no specifics. She disappeared from the internet after that, with no accolades, no poorly written poems published in small literary magazines, no marriage announcement. The only other clue was her enrollment in a graduate program in literature. The librarian taught him how to track down copies of her university's student newspaper.

There were Op-Eds from angry sociology majors. The university had accepted a grant, an award which came with an astronomical amount of zeroes, to study the effects of temporary cryogenic freezing on one of the graduate students. The name of the volunteer was not public record, but the students thought the process was inhumane. A dangerous business. There were demonstrations on the quad. Local news coverage that threatened to tip into the national level. One economics professor and an archivist threatened to look into the larger financial story of the college from inception to present day.

It was clearly a bollixed mess.

The last story he could find was of the president of the college, pale as a sheet of paper, standing on the steps of the administration building beside a beautiful young woman. The graduate student, the volunteer, seemingly awoken from slumber. She smiled prettily in the photos.

It was not the same woman who lay in the coffin.

Dale finally figured out the truth, though he had no one to tell. The woman on the steps was not the real volunteer. No, that one still slept and dreamt in a dark warehouse, forgotten.

He didn't know why she chose to leave nothing behind, but when he went back home at night to his apartment, he felt he could understand. There was nothing anyone would write about him. He'd been born, and now he worked. No achievements. The only record of his name was his pay-stub, sent to him every two weeks.

He covered his walls with their stories, printed out or handwritten in his messy script when he ran out of free prints at the library.

◕ ◑ ◐ ◯ ◯ ◯ ◑ ◐ ◕

At 8:46 pm on Friday, Dale wheeled Mr. Toomsy's coffin through the back doors of a reception hall. He wore his nicest black shirt and pants, and had wiped the dirt from his boot soles.

The woman ran on four-inch heels to meet him. He almost didn't recognize her. She'd painted her face, arms and legs a greenish gray, wore a skin-tight silver dress with matching gloves, and must have used an entire can of spray gel to make her hair stick out at such odd angles. Her lips were dark, bright red. Like dried blood. She'd dumped red glitter over her hair. When she caught the light, she looked like a monster out of a unimaginative child's nightmare.

"Did you get the note about the dress code?" she asked, eyeing his simple black outfit.

"This is what I have," he told her.

She shook her head and muttered something under her breath. "Set him up over there," she said, pointing to the centre of the room. "We'll find something for you. Don't worry. Does he need anything? An outlet?"

"There's a battery," Dale started to explain, but the woman only nodded and walked to a nearby table where men in silver suits were setting up a table of hors d'oeuvres.

He wheeled 81170323-113 into the centre of the room and checked occupant vitals. All normal. The coffins were designed for durability. He watched the slow rise of Mr. Toomsy's chest. Before leaving the warehouse, he'd started the unfreezing process. Toomsy was doomed to awaken at 10:36 pm.

Without anything left to do but wait, Dale moved to an unoccupied table and sat. The room was decorated with the tastefulness of the truly garish. The walls had banners written in a nonsense language; maybe wingdings. On each table was a large rocket surrounded by silver and red balloons. The lighting was dim; confetti littered the wooden floor.

The guests finally arrived, and Dale was asked to move to the corner with the rest of the staff to await further instructions. Each guest was announced, and a cheer rose from the growing crowd as each new attendee stepped inside. Friends embraced. They nibbled on hard bread with raw salmon laid over the top. They popped mounds of capers into their mouths like grapes. All had their faces painted; some had even opted for a prosthetic. A wide array of pudgy cheeks, long noses, jutting chins, plus one particularly effusive man with a wobbly horn at the centre of his forehead.

"I'm a unicorn!" he kept saying, which caused a few people to laugh.

The hostess frowned. Unicorns were not on theme.

Dale imagined Aurora, awake, standing next to him in this room of silver and red. They wouldn't say anything to one another—errors only spoke when spoken to, of course—but there would be a swift glance between them. A private joke. A hidden agony.

"Here," the hostess said to him, now wearing contacts that made even the whites of her eyes pitch black. She passed him a rubber mask and a pair of black gloves. "Wear these."

It was one of those cheap ugly masks sold in bulk at Halloween superstores. A long gray alien face with deep black oval eyes. A little too small for his head, and it itched.

"Now, everyone," the hostess said, spreading her arms over Mr. Toomsy's coffin. "Let us raise our glasses in a toast for our guest of honor."

They poured entire flutes of champagne down their delicate throats and immediately asked for refills. A solemn hush fell over the crowd. It was about to begin.

Dale went to work. He entered a code on the touch-pad of the coffin to shut down life support. A small amount of electricity surged into Mr. Toomsy. His body jolted. A few people gasped and were immediately shushed. The machine hummed and crackled. The lid began to move.

Someone giggled nervously. Others clamped their hands over their mouths.

The coffin whizzed and beeped. The clear glass slowly slid open. Mr. Toomsy's eyelids fluttered, his chest rose and fell. Dale entered a code—a simple one, even he couldn't forget 1-2-3-4-5—on the console. With a practiced flick of the wrist, he disengaged the thick, long tube from the old man's throat, and dropped it to the floor. There was no need to follow sanitary practices now. Mr. Toomsy coughed, a wretched noise, the sound of reanimation. Rebirth.

Dale stepped back and tried to blur into the background. Make himself invisible. If he wasn't being paid to witness, he would've closed his eyes and pressed his hands over his ears.

Mr. Toomsy opened his eyes. Brown and blurry. He blinked rapidly and tried to flex his fingers. The manual from Cry-O-Less described this awakening process. The client would be confused, as one feels when jolted awake from a deep dream. The skin would prickle and sting. Muscles, kept just intact with electric massages, would be jelly. After so much time in stasis, his body would take a while to adjust.

Unfortunately, Mr. Toomsy was nothing more than a broken clock. He opened his mouth. Closed it. Opened it and tried to form a word, but only managed a gurgle.

The audience breathed in one big gulp and then descended upon him.

They surrounded him, aliens of silver and red, face-paint and glitter. They chattered in nonsense words, disguised their voices in falsettos and a series of clicks from the back of their tongues.

The hostess, as shiny as the surface of a new credit card, put her thumbs on his temple. "Welcome to Jupiter," she said. "We do so hope you enjoy your stay."

Those brown eyes went wide. Toomsy opened and closed his mouth, straining to summon moisture to his tongue. He only managed a low, desperate keen.

They touched him, then. Ran their painted fingers and rubber claws over his nudity. No bit of him escaped their pinching, or their spitting. One overenthusiastic guest put Mr. Toomsy's big toe in his mouth. They flicked his nipples. Pressed their teeth into his neck. Covered him in sparkles. Collected the tears that crept down his face in their champagne glasses, to taste. All the while, they laughed, giving away their game. Only a human finds joy in suffering.

When the old man pissed himself, the cheering was deafening, like plates breaking on cement.

Though Mr. Toomsy had a bad heart, he had good lungs. He screamed, inarticulate and raw. He gathered enough oxygen to let out one loud, gargled syllable. "Cat!" he cried. "Cat!" He repeated this word, slurring and bawling, until the water stopped leaking from his eyes, until the twitches in his fingers stilled. Until he died.

Dale turned away, no longer needed until the end of the party.

The festivities continued for several more hours. A band played national anthems while Dale nursed the glass of water a frowning waitress had handed him. She looked as though she wanted to say something, but what words could articulate what they'd just witnessed? She didn't seem to know either, and went back to filling trays of Bellini and caviar.

He closed his eyes and thought about the woman in the glass coffin.

Aurora was different than the others. There was nothing wrong with her. Good lungs, a steady heart and excellent bone marrow. She was a volunteer, a graduate student in literature and debt. An *error.*

He felt that deep in the back of his head.

The hostess approached him at the end, handing him twenty quid. A tip. "Please tell your bosses we were very pleased with the product," she said. "We'll certainly be return customers. We're thinking of getting a woman next."

She watched as he carefully tucked Mr. Toomsy's arms and legs back into the glass box. Rigor mortis had set in as the party-goers arranged his limbs this way and that way for photos. Dale pushed the old man's eyelids closed, and entered the code to seal him back up.

"What he said. Do you know," the customer asked, pressing the tip of one red nail on his shoulder, "what that means? Cat. Did he have a pet?"

So she hadn't read Toomsy's personal statement.

"Cathy," Dale said. "A pet name. His wife."

Her face broke open. She had painted her teeth black. "Oh, marvelous," she whispered. "Honey!" she called to her man. "It was his wife!"

"Good show!" he said, raising a glass in her direction.

◉◑◐○○◑○◑◑◉

When Dale stepped through the door of his single-room apartment, he could not take off Mr. Toomsy. He lay on his bed with his arms at his sides, like the dreamers in their coffins. In one hand was a fifth of gin and a pack of filterless cigarettes, purchased with the twenty-quid tip. In the other, the alien mask. He'd been told to keep it. It contained his sweat.

He thought of Cathy, a woman who'd died five years ago. She'd left a note for her husband in an envelope sealed with pink lipstick. It was one of the first things Dale had been told to throw out when he started. The product that mattered was inside the glass. All those personal artifacts were garbage, Stone had said.

The envelope was taped to one of his kitchen cabinets, along with all the other trash, all those other memories.

Dale was not one to fantasize, but he did think, sometimes, about swords and dragons and princesses who needed saving. Sometimes, he imagined himself as the princess, locked in a long sleep, waiting for anything to change. What would it look like, that awakening? He did not know. His imagination was as rusty as the bathroom pipes in his flat.

He could imagine what she would look like, when she finally woke. Her eyes filled with imaginary numbers, minus and plus signs, errors upon errors. And how she would not scream when she saw him. She would laugh, wouldn't she? Because she'd see him as just another error, like her. A human-shaped mistake. And burst into hiccups of joy.

Because you have to laugh, don't you?

He rolled off the bed and moved to the closet. He pulled down cheap shirts and thick pants and lay down again, atop them. A nest for his body to mold around as he struggled to breathe.

The Dream of a Woman Stuck on the Minute Hand of a Broken Clock

It was the last thing she'd looked at. Household objects should come with a warning: if the dirty spoon in the sink is the last thing you see when your life pauses, every spoon will remind you what fear tasted like, years later. A day. When you least expect it. How will you ever safely eat soup again?

In this way, she considered herself lucky. How often did you come across a clock with two hands? One not reduced to numbers on a screen. Analog. Prone to error.

Not often, really. Well, once before, in her dissertation chair's man-cave of a basement, a private moment just between the two of them, away from the laughter of his annual Fall term potluck. The room had been almost barren, but there was a clock on his wall. Frozen hands.

She listened to him talk, but only heard the big words. The articles fell away. *Worried. Proposal. Late. Scholarship. Loss.*

It was coincidence. A bad alignment of the stars. Vegas odds astronomical.

His face had scrunched, a really bad look for those wrinkles, as he continued to talk over her short huffs of breath, which soon turned deep. She did remember nodding.

"People as commodities has been done before," he'd said, nodding at her one-page dissertation plan, nine pages too short. "No new angle. You're just regurgitating what's been said in the past. Nobody wants to read that anymore."

"Those who don't learn history are doomed to repeat it," she whispered. The wrong thing to say. Unscholarly. Uncouth.

The disappointment was great enough to form a new wrinkle near his mouth. "You must decide," he told her, with the same gentleness the executioner feels for his ax, "whether this is the right path for you. Your scholarship cannot be grounded in personal experience."

That's the funny thing about paths. They're only right in retrospect.

She saw the worry on his mouth. He wanted her to move forward, push herself in her research. He'd sent hundreds of emails, all with funny timestamps, about jobs she could do. Ones that didn't require she finish her degree. Something to get her moving forward. It was all up to her, of course. Her choice.

She'd wished he would choose for her, push her forward so she didn't have to move of her own volition. She didn't know how to do that by herself.

He spoke about her most recent seminar paper, a Ritalin-induced nightmare of twenty five pages started the week before, whose thesis was too broad for its eerily specific evidence. All of which went down too many rabbit holes on what might've happened to Walt Disney's antisemitic head, but whose conclusion hinted the author truly believed it may be frozen somewhere, in a vault, awaiting some awakening. It had earned a B- mark, a grad school slap on the wrist. He moved on to her dissertation proposal, a study of people whose bodies slowed down, fell asleep, became objects. Caught in timelessness. She wanted to argue that these were the only true tales ever told.

"Time always moves forward," he'd said to her. "Whether we like it or not."

She saw his mouth move, but the words didn't mean anything. She was somehow eight years old again, standing in front of the grandfather clock in the foyer, a piece of junk her parents once rescued from a neighbor's curb. They'd fixed it with every tax refund from HM Revenue & Customs, and for a few months it would chug away—tick, tock—until it stopped at 10:36 am.

If the clock was stuck, then so was time. She stood in front of it, mesmerized at the stillness, and believed everyone else was stuck there, too. It was always still 10:36 am.

"You've been here seven years," he said. "Most people finish in five."

Her professor's clock read 11:23. In twenty-two years, time had barely moved an hour.

"Your clock is broken," she'd told him, because she didn't know what else to say.

◐ ◑ ◐ ○ ○ ○ ◐ ◑ ◐

She signed up for the cryo-sleep study the next day on a whim born of panic. They couldn't kick her out if she was in the middle of researching, if she wasn't even conscious. She changed her proposal and emailed it to her professor. Remember the tale of the young woman who pricked her finger on a spinning wheel? The other one with snowy skin and black hair who ate a poisoned apple? They'd slept for a long time, and when they woke, they woke to a bright, new world. The restorative power of comas, she argued.

Secretly, she thought it would awaken a magic in her. Her parents had named her Aurora and then died—poof!—like magicians far too good at their craft. They took time away with them when they left her standing in front of that grandfather clock.

It was cruel of them, even if it wasn't their fault. They left her a little girl with dirt under her fingernails, staring up at a face covered in numbers. When she went to the grocery store and tapped on watermelons to check their ripeness? She was really in front of the clock. When Stephen Murphy invited her into his bed during a blizzard that shut off power in the dorms? Dirt under her nails, a chewed thumb in her mouth. When she drove to Niagara Falls because she wanted to see running water? Every sign on the highway contained a minute and hour hand.

Her parents should have taught her their tricks before they left. Then she might know what incantation to say to make time move forward again.

◐ ◑ ◐ ○ ○ ○ ◐ ◑ ◐

The study's paperwork was as invasive as a doctor's exam. Height, weight, menstruation cycle, the nature and size of her defecation. Fingers and objects inside every hole of her body. Did she have dreams often? Were they nightmares? Describe in detail. She wrote down dreams of flying and nightmares of falling. It wasn't true. She didn't want to explain time to people who only experienced it moving forward.

"Do I have to fill this out?" she'd asked the assistant. His Cry-O-Less lab coat was brand new. Shiny and white.

He came over and glanced down at the question. "It's helpful for our data. But no, not if you don't want to. You'll only be under for a month."

"I've read sometimes people come out of comas with memory loss," she said, casually. "Like, they're different altogether."

"Oh," he said, cheeks going pink. "Well, I don't think that's likely."

Unfortunate, but these technicians had never frozen the daughter of magicians before. She might wake up a new person, like the caterpillar whose body turned into goo in the chrysalis, and then burst out of its shell with crystalline wings as thin as paper.

On the white form she wrote down honest words. She wrote *loss* over and over. She drew the face of a frozen clock, and detailed everything she was afraid of: how time would never move forward for her again, how her body changed but she was stuck like a nail hammered into a piece of wood. That she didn't know what to do. She wrote down her hope: that when she woke up, everything would look different.

The assistant read it, frowning. "This is too long. I don't know if we can do drawings? It'll trigger an error in the computer." He handed it back. "Are you sure you don't want to… change this? Make it sound a little more palatable?"

"No," she said. "Put it in like that."

If it triggered an error. . . well, that might be an answer, too.

●◑◐○○○◑◐●

It was a prick, sharp as a spindle. But unlike her fingertip, the vein in her arm took several tries. *Count down from one-hundred, OK?* Voices in the air. Fairies.

"Ninety-nine," she said. "Ninety-eight."

She imagined how the old story would've gone, had Sleeping Beauty pricked her veins instead of her finger. Would the witch have rushed to save her, if only to extend the game? Would the prince, one hundred years too early, pop into being on a horse, in the room, sword in hand, and put pressure on the wound of a stranger who'd been clumsy at spinning? Wasn't that how true love worked?

Nah. She probably would've been ace at it.

"Thirteen o'clock."

A musical snort from the fairies, and then she only knew dreams.

●◑◐○○○◑◐●

Clocks have faces, don't you know? The number are eyes, the dot in the centre the nose, and the mouth, well. The two arrows spun around. It blinked all twelve eyes at her.

"You have to wake up," those arrows said over and over as they twisted around. "I've got things to do and places to be!"

Not until the magic worked.

"No magic," the clock laughed. "There is only me."

What an awful story.

● ◑ ◐ ○ ◯ ○ ◑ ◑ ●

When she did wake, she felt time in the stiffness of her joints, the fog in her head, the soreness in her throat where the tube had been yanked out. She blinked at a stranger who looked as bewildered as she felt. This was not the room she'd gone to sleep in.

"What time is it?" she croaked, then giggled. Her voice had changed. She'd turned into a frog.

"I don't know," he said. "Morning?"

She asked to see his phone. He pulled it from his back pocket and held it out before her. She watched the numbers move from 10:02 to 10:03.

A Master of Paper Performs His Greatest Trick

On a Thursday afternoon, Harvard Stone sat with a pile of resumes on his desk. He scribbled his signature on a termination slip for a man whose name he kept forgetting. No matter, his secretary would dig it up and fill in the details.

The problem with people was, the hungry were always ungrateful when you gave them scraps. Beggars could, in his opinion, be quite choosy. It was why most people never moved up in the world. Those idiotic, stagnant lumps.

Stone was in his element. If he pulled this off, he was on track to an upper office. Some of those had real wool carpets and were cleaned every night. The thrill.

There was a missing worker and a missing piece of inventory. With a few taps of the delete key, he disappeared them both from the files. Poof! Like they'd never been there in the first place. In another sort of work, this would be a scandal, but Stone knew how to make lines on paper tell all sorts of stories. Did the original listing say seventy three bodies? Oh, a simple miscount. Human error! There were only seventy two. The worker, so and so, who'd had no idea how to add sequentially? Fired for this carelessness. Only the best people worked for Stone, and anything less than best was cut off, like a skin tag.

This was the story written down, and it was the one he told the stockholders and government regulators. His numbers covered all sorts of neat little fibs. They could write people right out of time. And then replace them.

So now, there was the little matter of hiring a new employee. Someone who could be trusted to do exactly as he was told. Someone who could actually count.

Stone pressed the intercom. "Send him in."

The proprietress of The Queen's Raven always stocks a plethora of rare finds and historical oddities, all purveyed from this lovely striped Elizabethan-style tent. She keeps her ornate goods in excellent repair and shined to an impressive glow. All, that is, save for this exquisitely-engraved, though tarnished, round silver looking-glass. One so small it may be taken for an innocuous trinket. Though it's for sale to the right client, like all the other items here, this hand-mirror alone remains unpolished, and secured in a locked glass display box. Due to—as I recall—some previous incidents that were quite upsetting to the browsers involved; resulting in a ruckus that in the end required my direct intervention. But never mind all that; come along and I'll show you just what all the kerfluffle was about . . .

What You Seek is Seeking You

by Lenore Hart

LONDON, 1536

Outside the window, a May morning buds. Temperate breezes waft through the casements of the Queen's Lodgings. But Anne Boleyn has slept little the last few nights, in the luxurious Tower apartment built only three years earlier for her coronation. Bluish shadows darken the delicate skin beneath her eyes. She stands at the open window in a plain black gown, unwrapping a cloth bundle delivered by one of the Yeoman Warders. Inside is a small, round silver-framed mirror, and a terse note.

Liebe *Queen,*

Gaze into this side by side with another Lady. Tap the glass, and you will be Transposed. Thus retaining your true Fate.

The signature is a large scrawled "K".

"*Herr* Kratzer," she whispers. "You have taken your time, indeed. But now I shall be saved, body *and* soul."

Nicholas Kratzer, Oxford-educated astronomer and devisor of horologes—sundials, clocks, polyhedral dials—is the court astrologer. He's often cast Anne's horoscope. Three weeks ago he'd requested an audience.

"Highness, I've had a troubling . . . reading."

"What did you see in my future?" she'd asked, with both hope and dread.

He'd shaken his head, unable to speak. Then whispered, "Should the worst come to pass, I shall send a means of reprieve."

"A reprieve. But . . . how?"

"You shall be marvelously changed, Your Grace. And thus in disguise, leave and board a ship to Calais, and thence to France." He'd kissed her hand, then fled the chamber.

Two days later she'd been summoned before the privy council at Greenwich Palace, charged with adultery, and imprisoned. Until then she'd refused to believe Henry would send her—England's queen!—to pyre or block. After the sham trial, though, she'd understood he *was* capable of any cruelty imaginable.

But now, a magical reprieve . . . how it will amuse her old friend the Dauphin to give her sanctuary from his enemy. And, in hiding, she needn't grant Henry the divorce he craves, and surrender baby Elizabeth's claim to England's throne.

A key scrapes in the lock. Her ladies in waiting, who've been embroidering or reading Scripture, look up. Nan Zouche rises to greet the visitor. Anne sets the mirror on the window ledge and turns to see who's come.

The Constable of the Tower.

"Master Kingston," Anne says, "Have you news? As I professed yester morn, I do not wish to die, but I . . . feel myself ready to face death, if—"

Sweating in the red wool Beefeater uniform, Kingston bites his lip. He doesn't meet her gaze. "Your Grace, I am come . . . that is, I regret to inform you the hour is close at hand."

The ladies gasp, wringing their hands. Even Mrs. Kingston, the constable's wife, who was placed among her ladies to spy on everything Anne says and does.

Anne merely nods. "Acquit yourself of your charge, good sir, for I've long been prepared. When?"

Kingston's shoulders slump. His expression is that of a man just spared a roomful of hysterical women. "Early on the morrow, your Grace." He bows to her, to the others, then backs out.

Her ladies gather round. "Ambassador Chapuys was right." Bess Holland clasps Anne's small hands. "You are truly braver than a lion."

The queen smiles a little. "Our world is ruled by men like Wolsey, Cromwell, and my father. Thus, we women needs must find other ways to live. Or die, come to that." She sighs. "Now, I beg you all leave me for a nonce, so I may compose myself, and pray—all but you, dear Nan."

Mrs. Kingston hesitates, but at last files out with the rest.

Anne says to the woman remaining, "You are still willing?"

Nan nods. "It is . . . a temporary state, is it not? That I become . . . you?"

"In soothe, for a short span only. By the time I sail for Calais tonight, you will have regained your own visage. And I, mine."

Nan looks around. "Where is the mirror?"

"On the sill."

But just as Anne turns to point it out, the open casement fills with a dark flurry of wings. One of the Tower's great black ravens lands to perch on the stone sill. It cocks its head, greedily eyeing the gleamy bauble there.

"No!" cries Anne. "Stop!"

The bird croaks if mocking her and snaps the mirror up.

They both run to the window, but the bird's already taken flight. They hang there at the sill, helplessly following its progress, until the great corvid descends into a stand of rowan oaks.

"Oh, God! I am undone," groans Anne, tearing at her hair, ripping the bodice of her gown. "And dead, indeed. Evil bird! I curse thee and thy kin and progeny forever."

She collapses onto the stone floor. Nan sobs and kneels to cradle her, as one would a small, weeping child.

London, 1880

The gentleman in the bowler hat is the one to follow. I can tell right off. He's wearing a grey cutaway jacket, silk cravat, fresh-polished boots . . . and smells enticingly of a recent purchase at the meat-pie stand. Probably the one just outside the moat. I fall in behind as he tramps around Tower Green. Not a tourist, but local. He's been here before. And soon I'll relieve him of the newspaper-wrapped parcel tucked under his arm.

But as my old mum used to say, slow and steady wins the race. Don't crowd your mark, or hurry him. Just keep the bugger in your sights.

Hunching to make myself small, I dart from tree to bush to tree. He's headed to an empty bench away from the Tower, and the yeoman warders who guard it. That's good. Less chance of the Beefeaters noticing when I take my prize.

My mark drops onto the wood-slatted seat of a bench. Takes out a flask, unwraps his parcel.

Now for the tricky part. I sidle around behind the bench, hugging the ground, and slowly, slowly, creep up until I can duck underneath it.

He sets the delicious, unwrapped pie on the seat next to hm. Quick as a bird's wink I reach up through a gap between slats and seize it. Victory is mine! I can't help voicing one derisive croak as I scarper off.

Behind me the outraged visitor squawks, "Thief! *Thief!*"

A warder dashes across the Green, calling, "What's the kerfluffle, sir?"

Alas for Mr. Pie-less, too late. But more Beefeaters are pelting after me in hot pursuit. Not to worry. I simply fly up into a plane tree and savor my pork pasty in peace.

Let's be clear, though: I'm no common thief. My name is Magnhild, a raven of the Tower of London. My family has worked here for ages. First in, well . . . corpse disposal . . . and more recently as an official attraction at Her Majesty's ancient, bloody prison. Eight other ravens live at the Tower as well, all looked after by the blue-and-red-uniformed yeoman warders the public calls Beefeaters. Because everyone in England knows that if we ravens ever desert the Tower, both ruler and country will fall.

Finally, every tasty crumb of pie consumed, I hop branch to branch and fly down, evading capture. The day is yet young.

●◑◐○◐○◑●

Unfortunately it's slim pickings all afternoon. As the last new punter enters the gates, though, my hopes rise. A well-off lady, carrying a tapestry bag heavy with who knows what. When she joins a touring party of visitors, I tag along behind. She sets it down when they pause to hear a warder's spiel about the Tower's history.

"Her Majesty's jewels are no longer kept here, though we still guard. . . "

Blah, blah, Caw, I think, leaning in to rummage through the bag. Let's see . . . a hunk of lavender soap? No. A small, stinky cheese? No. Some leeks and a bunch of radishes?

Damn. What a tragic assortment.

I'm so bored it's a relief when the warders come for us before sunset, scooping up the more reluctant corvids. We all troop to the Tower and the safety of our night cages, since Her Majesty's foxes also lurk about the Green. A vixen or dog fox is always fond of a raven dinner, and we are particularly sleek specimens.

"Well, Maggie," says my regular attendant; good-natured, bearded Kit. "Had your fun today, old girl, haven't you."

I'm in a good mood so I shake out my feathers and amble inside. Though not too quickly, lest he get the wrong idea about who's really in charge. He

· 148 ·

closes the cage door behind me. From the back, next to an archer's slit, I've a nice view of the Green and surrounding outbuildings. A bird is never bored for long here, one can say that.

◕ ◑ ◐ ◯ ◯ ◯ ◑ ◐ ●

I wake sometime later at a loud noise. All seems well. I yawn, stretching my wings. A rumble sounds again: thunder, then bright flashes of lightning. A storm's headed toward the Thames.

Looking out, I detect movement. A pale woman in a black, high-waisted gown glides from the old royal lodgings to pace the walk, as she often does 'round midnight. Dark-haired Anne. The Queen of the Thousand Days, we call her. She keeps her right hand tucked into a black fur muff as she wanders off the bricks and crosses the grassy Green.

I sit up straighter when she halts before my oak, and the hidey-hole that conceals my treasure. She stares down at the roots and trunk as if she knows what's inside. For a moment, her pale moon of a dead face turns my way. But she draws back and departs, on to another tree, and then another. Pausing at each as if seeking something in particular. Finally she wanders out of sight; I assume to make her usual rounds. Some nights she likes to appear suddenly, scaring the pantaloons off whatever warder's on night duty.

I fall asleep again, and dream an odd dream: I'm no longer Magnhild, the most attractive and accomplished raven dwelling at the Tower, but a human living in West London. How it's changed! Still gloriously dirty. Even more crowded. But everyone seems only half-dressed, and the carriages somehow roll about without any horses.

In the background of my dream a storm rages, so loudly it might be just outside my window.

I wake the next morning to a nice, still-warm mouse served up on a China dish by my ever-thoughtful Kit. As I feast, though, I recall my dream, and think: *Strange. Strange, indeed.*

London, 1966

Fiona Byrd departs her cheap one-room flat, taking the stairs down from the fourth floor two at a time. It's one of twenty bed-sitters carved out of a former mansion in Chepstow Villas, on the old Portobello Road. Out on the street she blinks against that rare occurrence in London: a sunny morning. The bright light illuminates a tea-stain on her new orange minidress. She frowns down, *tsks*, and rubs at it briskly. No bloody use. Giving up, she sets out for her job at the Lady Jane Boutique in Carnaby Street.

Henry, the shop's owner, has hired aspiring models to dress and undress in the shop's front window. "Draws a crowd, don't y'see," he'd explained, when he hired Fiona. "Makes 'em want to come in and browse." The papers call it scandalous, but Henry was right: lately sales have been smashing.

Fiona never expected to work in fashion. After acing her O-levels she'd left London to read history at St. Hugh's women's college at Oxford, on scholarship. In her fourth year she began the seven-month process of mapping out and writing her undergraduate dissertation, a study of early feminism in the Elizabethan era.

But near the end of Semester One, a telegram arrived:

Da dead. Heart attack. Pls come. Mum.

She'd rushed back to London for the funeral. Her father had always worked long hours at the greengrocer's; too many, it seemed. Her chronically-ill mother had never been strong; she proved this once and for all by following her husband to the grave just two weeks later. After that, at her parents' solicitor's office, a reeling Fiona discovered they'd mortgaged the house to help with her school costs. She returned to Oxford in a blue daze, staring blankly at her methodology notes, hand too limp to even lift a pencil.

When she missed the turn-in deadline for research proposals, the dissertation supervisor called her in. "Only one in a hundred students admitted here is *female*, Miss Byrd. Have we made a mistake with you?"

Fiona had numbly shrugged. Life no longer made sense. There was no one left to be proud of her great accomplishment. The house? Taken by the bank. How could she explain her paralyzing sorrow to a robed Oxford don who sat frowning at her like God behind a huge mahogany desk? She'd simply risen and left. Packed her few belongings and returned to London.

Now she works for a pittance, publicly putting on and taking off skimpy new outfits, while passersby pause to stare, whistle, and catcall.

It's temporary, she keeps telling herself. She spends weekends browsing the Portobello flea markets and junk shops for interesting old books and affordable 16th century artifacts. The closest she gets to English history, these days.

Now, crossing Portobello Road against the light, she hurries along, trying to not care that the Mary Jane platform heels are killing her feet. It's a three-mile walk from Notting Hill to SoHo, but she's too skint for bus fare. She passes a street magician at a drinks-crate booth. He's switching three small cups around while a credulous-looking young woman, already too lost to choose properly, gapes at the man's flying hands.

Fiona rolls her eyes. Well, if that isn't just a perfect metaphor for life.

Near the corner of Great Marlborough and Carnaby a huge crowd's gathering. "What in bleeding hell?" she mutters. Has Henry now got the models stripping starkers?

Weaving through gawkers, slowly getting closer, she glimpses a handsome dark-haired man and . . . isn't that a film actress beside him? They're walking a big spotted cat—a bloody *cheetah*, no less—on a jeweled leash, up and down Carnaby Street. It's hard to say which of the three is prettiest.

Around her women of all ages scream, swoon, even claw at their faces. "Tom!" shouts a spotty teenager beside her. "It's Tom *Jones*!"

Now Fiona recognizes the curvy blonde walking arm-in-arm with the Welsh pop star; she's on a poster for the new James Bond film.

Traffic backs up as drivers brake to gape at the beautiful trio, and Fiona's trapped in the growing, roiling crowd. With elbows and knees she fights her way through. But slowly, far too slowly . . . and look at the bloody *time*.

Bollocks. She is late. So very, very late.

When she finally reaches the façade of Lady Jane, Henry's standing in the doorway puffing on a ciggie, staring balefully at a new shop directly across called TOM CAT. A red *Grand Opening* banner is draped across its display window. A loudspeaker blasts Tom Jones' song "What's New, Pussycat?" at top volume, all but drowning out the folksy Donovan tune playing from inside Lady Jane.

"Bloody publicity stunt," Henry mutters, as if *he* is above such things. He finally notices Fiona standing before him, gasping and sweaty. "And you, stroppy cow. Fifteen minutes late. You're fired!"

Henry never minces words.

Fiona's eyes widen. "Criminy, wait a mo, I just—"

"Save it for the effing punters." He makes a disgusted face and flicks his fag-end into the gutter. Then turns abruptly and goes inside, slamming the door behind him.

"Tom! Tom! I love you!" cries a stout, teary, middle-aged woman, arms outstretched towards the grinning pop star. The blond actress pouts, striking a sultry pose. The cheetah yawns.

Someone in the crowd flings a skimpy pair of knickers toward Jones. The lacy scrap lands at Fiona's feet. She's trapped on the sidewalk, stunned, jostled by the pushing, shoving, celebrity-mad crowd.

London, 1880

After a delicious mouse breakfast I preen my feathers, then toddle off to check on my hoard. What a sight greets me! The storm has uprooted a different rowan oak than mine, leaving it lying on the grass as if the venerable tree's fallen asleep. I follow my beak to the outthrust, soil-clotted roots and poke around beneath them. At first it's just rocks, clods of dirt, frantically-wriggling earthworms. But then, at the farthest, most difficult reach, a dull gleam! I poke my head deeper and, with an awkward twist of the beak, jerk out a small, hard thing.

Tarnished silver frames a round glass caked with dirt. A real prize, far superior to the paltry scraps of metal, raveled red mitten-yarn, pink baby boot, and colourful sweetie wrappers currently tucked into my hidey-hole. This tree was surely the cache of some venerable old raven of the Tower, hidden uncounted decades, even centuries.

And now it's mine!

But before I can draw my head out and hustle the prize to my hiding place for leisurely gloating, something brushes my tail feathers. I croak in alarm and shoot backward.

Hurtling right *through* someone.

I look up and see the pale wraith of Anne Boleyn towering over me. She's tapping a black-velvet-slippered foot, and frowning.

Lady Raven, thou needs must serve me now. Her voice is the whisper of desiccated fall leaves blown lifelessly along a sidewalk. The dead queen almost never appears in the light of day. She looks even less substantial; more ghostly now than in her midnight perambulations.

I shiver, ruffling my neck feathers. *Serve you how, er . . . Your Grace?*

Yon silver mirror 'twas once mine, a gift devised to disguise and deliver me from the axe. But 'twas stolen from my chamber. By a large black raven, she adds pointedly, *sent no doubt by mine enemies. Now, 'tis once more found, and I mean to use it so.*

This sounds ominous, even to me. *Use it . . . so?*

I weary of life-in-death, and long to feel warm flesh clothe my bones again. For I was cheated . . . " She stops, teeth clenched, as if all these years later she can barely stand to recall it. "Cheated *of my youth, my dreams, my fated four-score of years. I fain would borrow a comely female form and walk amongst the living, enjoying the pleasures of life."*

I spread my wings to their four-foot span. *I do not understand.*

She rolls her eyes. *Herr Kratzer's mirror will marvelously permit me to change places with a living woman. For a time, at least.*

I hop sideways, then back again, in agitation. We ravens do help ourselves to trinkets. To food. Eat mice and frogs. But . . . don a human body like an overcoat? It's just not canny.

As if she's read my mind, Anne smiles thinly. *Only for a nonce, onyx-feathered fowl. Then 'twill be returned to its soul no worse for wear.*

Yet something in the twitch of her grim smile belies the words.

And if I refuse?

O, but you will not! Or 'twill go the worse for you and all your cursed kind. She sneers, as if seeing a place, or a time, beyond this one. *What care I if Henry's poxy kingdom falls!*

I could point out that it's Victoria's kingdom now, not Henry's. But prudence clamps my beak. Anne was known to be clever. Even a witch herself, of sorts. I would not endanger my own kind. And if some harm came to dear Kit . . .

Very well. I can't suppress a little distressed cough. *I will not fail you.*

You shall accompany me on a short journey, says Anne. *Carrying the mirror. For I have lately received a most intriguing invitation. And 'tis only upon the invitation of a great wizard or necromancer that I may cross the boundaries of these grounds.*

◑ ◕ ◐ ◯ ◑ ◯ ◐ ● ◕

An hour later I'm balanced atop the roof of a milk wagon, headed into the West End, clutching the mirror in my beak, a ghost sitting beside me.

We hop off at a market street of shuttered shops and booths and tents. I follow Anne toward a stall beside a narrow alley, at the end of which stands some sort of gate or turnstile. Or does it? The outline seems to . . . *waver* in the dim light. As I step in to peer closer, a fidgety punter clutching a square of parchment sidles past. He reaches the shimmering gate, holds out the paper square, and just . . . vanishes.

I start, nearly dropping the mirror. Blinking, I look again.

No punter.

I turn back uneasily to catch up with Anne. She's stopped at a wooden booth fronting a canvas tent painted with strange markings. A woman crouches nearby, unpacking crates and boxes.

As we approach, she rises. "Highness. I've been expecting you." The vendor is tall, slim, with brick-red hair done up in complicated braids. Her old-fashioned gown is high-waisted, of bright green velvet.

Anne inclines her head regally. *Then you surely know, madam, why I am come.* She holds out a slip like the one the vanished punter was clutching.

· 153 ·

Alarming, yet curious! How unfortunate I cannot read human scribbles.

The red-haired woman takes it, nodding. "You've waited for your wish a long time," she murmurs. "But need do so no longer. I've chosen the perfect specimen for your purposes. And for hers."

Anne's face lights up. She almost looks alive again. *Indeed? Who is it? Some noblewoman? Or one of royal birth?*

"Neither. She's a commoner. Who hasn't yet been born."

Not yet born! Anne clenches her fists. *Think you to gull me? Kratzer instructed I must stand* beside *the other, and—*

"No trickery, Your Grace," says the stall's proprietor pleasantly. "Unlike your previous, er, guide, I'm not constrained by the bonds of time. The craft has advanced a good deal since your unfortunate . . . experience. I'll arrange everything on my end. It's a good match, for both of you. And the actual wait *here* won't be long. Only one night."

Anne's tight expression smooths. *Very well. You shall not fail me, then.*

The red-haired woman turns to me. "Noble Magnhild, forgive my rudeness. I didn't mean to ignore you. Just drop the mirror in there." She points to a flimsy-looking box made of some very thick brown paper. It holds a mess of colourful goods. Interesting!

The two women turn away, talking again.

I carry the looking-glass over to the box. It is hard, so hard to let this lovely treasure go. But at last I open my beak and it falls within, mirror-side up. I gaze at myself reflected there: such a lovely bird! Then lean in and tap the glass three times with my beak, a formal farewell.

Something odd happens then: the glass shivers. Faintly glows. Momentarily giving off a faint blue fire behind the curved surface. And then, suddenly, it's gone.

It would be wise to say nothing of this strangeness, I decide.

The women at last say farewell. Anne and I walk to the next street corner.

Fly up onto that butcher's wagon, she orders, pointing to a boxy horse-van painted with convincing portraits of fat hams and thick sides of beef. My beak waters.

Now keep a sharp lookout, and again hop off at the right moment, she adds.

I obey, and perch on the roof, croaking a greeting to the carthorse, who whickers back a puzzled welcome.

Anne clambers up the opposite side, somehow managing to look regal while doing so.

Soon a stocky fellow with thick moustaches, wearing a blood-stained apron, climbs onto the front bench and flicks the reins. The horse tosses its head; the wagon jolts off. I cling to my perch, a wooden cross-piece, with difficulty, stretching my wings for balance whenever we hit a loose cobblestone or pothole.

Anne sits with slippers dangling, and an expression I've never seen on her face before. I peer closer . . . yes, she does seem to be, indeed.

Happy, that is.

LONDON, 1966

Biting the inside of her cheek to fight back angry tears, Fiona turns from Lady Jane's door and struggles through the crowd again. Muttering, "Bleeding stupid job, anyhow." And, "Henry's a cunt!"

A matron in a county-estate tweed suit huffs at the epithet, shooting Fiona a scowl daunting enough to make a royal nanny proud.

"Oh, bugger off," snaps Fiona.

She feels no better though. And the blister on her heel is killing her.

She limps onward to Portobello Road. The Saturday markets are open, the street packed with stalls, tents, and booths. Also antique, bath, jewelry, and clothing shops with front doors flung invitingly wide. From the next block delicious scents waft. Curries. Roasting meats. Yeasty baking bread. Lovely, greasy, salty just-fried chips.

We had no breakfast, her stomach grumbles.

Fiona ignores it. She grimly passes by Alice's, and The Good Fairy. Even Arbra's.

Eventually her steps slow. And, though she really shouldn't, she begins browsing the booths and sidewalk tables.

Near an alley on the stretch between Golburne Road and Westway she spots a new stall—or at least one she's never noticed before. Its freshly-painted sign reads THE QUEEN'S RAVEN. A very grand name for a tattered striped tent, a wooden stall, and some rickety tables. Still, it looks inexpensive. Why not suss it out?

A little girl with braided red hair sits cross-legged under one table, beside a dented cardboard Pear's Soap box. She eyes Fiona with an oddly mature air. The child holds a ratty-haired Barbie in a black gown.

"Hello, little luv," Fiona ventures.

The child doesn't answer. So mum and dad taught her not to speak to strangers, and rightly so. She has lovely, luminous skin, and wears some old pantomime costume; a moth-eaten high-waisted green dress with embroidered bodice. Too big; it keeps slipping off one shoulder.

"Playing dress-up, I see."

The girl smiles a little. She inclines her head at the box.

"Ah. Something good in there, then?"

Fiona kneels to look, pulling out a dented thimble, a fuzzy skein of red yarn, a folded length of hideous sulfur-yellow brocade, and two chipped green teacups. At the bottom she spots a tiny, round silver mirror. Of course she shouldn't spend a penny—she just lost her position at the shop! But it's a fab find. Looks quite old, possibly 16th or 17th century judging by the glass. And the whole box is marked just half a pound.

"So posh," she breathes, turning it over, admiring the incised Tudor roses. She could clean it up. Even sell it for a tidy sum, if need be.

Then she remembers the girl. "Say, this lot isn't yours, is—"

Fiona looks up as she speaks. But the child, who'd been mere inches away, has vanished without a sound or even a flicker of movement.

Fiona looks around, but only sees a woman unpacking crates at the front of the tent. At last she picks up the box and calls, "I'll take this lot. It's marked half a pound."

The woman has the same brick-coloured hair as the child; a long braid hangs to the middle of her back like a thick red rope. She waves over one shoulder. "Just leave ten shillings on the table, there's a dear."

Fiona takes out her change purse and does so, but hesitates. "Did your little girl go into the back?"

The woman finally turns around. "Girl? I've only two great lugs of sons. They're at a footballer match."

"Oh . . . well, never mind. Ta."

She heads down Portobello toward Chepstow Villas and her flat. Stopping only once, to spend ten pence at a food stall. She takes the hot chips, wrapped in a newsprint cone fashioned from *The Times*, tucks that into the box, and walks on.

Panting after carrying the lot up four flights, she sets it down on the lino next to the small red dinette where she eats and reads, evenings. After wolfing the salty chips she gets to work polishing the mirror's tarnished silver frame. The shine comes up so nice and rich it's clearly sterling, not plate. The glass has a bit of a curve to it. She gazes into it. So small, she can only see her chin and lips.

"Not very practical," she muses. "Just big enough for a lip-gloss touch-up."

But what excellent condition, She taps the glass once, experimentally, then frowns. What's that greyish stain spreading in the middle?

She holds it closer, peering in, and taps twice more.

Slowly the gray blot grows darker, larger. Then both dark and light. For, as Fiona stares, the reflection of her own lips and chin vanishes. Replaced by the faint impression of a deathly-pale face framed by a cascade of ink-black hair. But suddenly that too is gone. And now Fiona's staring into the beady-eyed, long-beaked visage of . . .

A *raven?*

"What the bloody hell!" she shouts.

Before she can let go or even pull her own startled gaze away, the room spins. It feels like she's being folded up and turned inside out. There's a hoarse, croaking cry. And then, Fiona hears nothing at all as she's dragged down a tunnel with walls of swirling black.

London, 1966

I wake with a squawk, and ruffle my neck. Or try to, but something feels amiss. There's no answering flutter of feathers.

Last thing I recall is strolling across Tower Green, trailing a family with a loaded picnic hamper. But now . . . I'm in . . . my cage?

No. This space is bigger, darker, full of strange objects. I leap up, stagger, and nearly fall. Am I ill? Perhaps. For when I look down, instead of my own feet with three dark-grey toes, I gawk at something out of a bird's fever-dream: long, pale . . . limbs. Human *legs and feet.*

And, attached to my shoulders? Human *arms.*

I use one to explore behind me and discover it's true . . . *no wings.* How can this abomination be?

Across the room is a spotted glass, like a reflecting pond stuck on a wall. I stumble over. A young woman stares back. With one clumsy, naked not-wing I touch the glass she's trapped behind. She does the same, only in reverse, as if trying to touch me, too. She blinks when I blink, and frowns at the same time, too. And, finally, gapes in horror, as do I.

Which can only mean one thing:

I am her, and she is me. We are *transposed.*

Magnhild, the Tower's most beautiful and intelligent raven, is no more. For it appears I've been . . . changelinged? Or cursed. Transformed like an unlucky bird in the old tales our mam used to tell us hatchlings. Ensorcelled from hunter into punter.

Oh, the sorrow.

I never knew human beings could force so much water from their eyes, or scream so very loudly.

London, 1880

Someone is laughing. At her?

Fiona whimpers. What a head; it's bloody *killing* her. She has a hazy impression of green grass, a stone wall, a circle of trousered legs and long sweeping skirts hemming her in.

What in the bleeding . . . *where* is *she?*

It feels as if she's been dragged through a knothole backwards—or maybe gone a pint too far at The Earl of Lonsdale? *Oh please god, let me not have buggered off with some overaged Teddy Boy.* Except . . . she shakes her head and falls over sideways. *But I didn't go out last night at all. Did I?*

"Silly bird," shouts a cracking adolescent male voice. "She's blotto, mate!"

Fiona grimaces. She hates it when men refer to women as "birds."

A little girl's voice pipes, "Mummy, is the poor birdie hurt?"

Ugh. Et tu, kiddie? The haze before Fiona's eyes clears. She's . . . lying down? No, but somehow far too close to the ground. The individual blades of grass look ridiculously large. Psychedelically so. She squawks in distress, and the people standing around her point, chuckle, and elbow each other.

The girl-child comes over and crouches a few feet away. "Do you got an ouchie? Or a bad tummy? Me mummy says—"

Just then a man in a red and blue tunic pushes through the crowd. "What's the trouble here?" He's dressed like an extra from The Old Vic Theatre, and seems enormous. When he spots Fiona he gasps, "Maggie, old thing! You look knackered."

Who's Maggie? she asks. But all that comes out is a hoarse, gurgling *"Kraa, Kraa?"* Fiona tumbles backward in surprise and throws out her arms . . .

Which are not arms anymore, but feathered black wings.

All the gawkers applaud, as if she's just nailed an *a capella* song on *Top of the Pops.*

This is a bloody nightmare. It *has* to be.

"Come along, my love," says the man in antiquated dress. Now she recognizes that, at least; it's a Beefeater's uniform. Before Fiona can protest he scoops her up, presses her close to his chest, and carries her away from the crowd. A chorus of disappointed *Awwww*s trail them like a swarm of bees.

Let go of me, Fiona shouts, though only hoarse caws and croaks emerge. Struggling to break free, she flails her . . . wings.

Surely not really wings? No! Impossible. And where's this bloody pillock taking her?

She screams again and again. Hoarse croaks, like a terminal case of croup.

"Shush, Maggie," her abductor croons. "Steady on, old thing. I know you hate crowds . . . let's get you over on the other side of the Tower. Everything'll be tickety-boo."

Remarkably, he keeps his word. So maybe he isn't a murderer or a pervert. For Fiona's (oh, bleeding hell) grey, three-toed feet do hit the grass, as promised. She shoots from his grasp and gallumps awkwardly away, around the corner of a tall stone building.

Straight into, or rather *through*, one very angry lady in fancy dress.

Halt where thou standest, poxy raven, snaps the see-through person. *I, Queen Anne, do order it.*

A well-bred Briton, Fiona instantly complies and stumbles to a stop. She turns and tilts her head to peer up at the, uh . . . the . . . wait a bloody minute. She recalls, from one of her history texts, a colour plate she'd really liked: an oil painting of Anne Boleyn, doomed second wife of Henry the Eighth.

So . . . that Queen Anne? Surely not.

Herr Kratzer's enchanted mirror has failed me yet again! the ghost cries, shaking her fists.

It's creepy how Anne's lips don't move, yet Fiona can hear her voice quite plainly. And shouldn't Anne Boleyn be headless? Though Fiona is glad at the moment that's not the case.

Anne slumps to the grass, ghostly gown puddling around her. *I remain naught but a spirit. No change has come!*

Fiona awkwardly spreads her new wings. *Really, no change? How bloody nice for you. Look at this! I blacked out as a woman and woke as a bloody raven. It must be a nightmare!* And then, *How are we talking without moving our lips?*

Anne frowns. *That matters not. How came you to change bodies with a bird?*

Fiona tries to think back. *Well, I . . . pfft. No bloody clue. Last thing I recall is polishing a little silver mirror, and suddenly—*

God's body! cries Anne. *Kratzer's spell has gone awry. Did you tap upon the glass?*

Fiona frowns. Yes? I mean, I suppose—

Anne grinds her teeth; the gritty screech makes Fiona shudder. *Then the girl's body, that is,* your *body, now houses the soul of a raven of the Tower. While you now inhabit . . . well, this. That same bird's carcase.*

She waves her right hand at Fiona, who blinks; it seems to have too many fingers.

Oh, but this is most wonderfully vexing to me, mutters Anne.

To you? Fiona tries to roll her side-mounted eyes, but the motion makes her dizzy. *Wait a tick . . . are you saying this dream is actually happening?*

If only 'twere a dream. Anne wrings her hands. *I fear I shall never live again, at all.*

Fiona shrugs a small, feathered shoulder. *Sorry, but I've my own problems, as you can see.* Though surely she'll be waking up any minute now, and then—

"Ah, there you are!" says a jovial voice.

Suddenly Fiona is airborne again, carried along in the same sure, male arms. She thinks about struggling, then gives it up as useless.

"Tea time, Maggie. Your favorite," the Beefeater bloke adds.

The yeoman warder is wearing the blue everyday uniform, not the dress one, which is the famous Tudor-era red tunic with gold trim, white stockings, and bearskin hat tourists love to take snaps of. That one's only for special occasions.

Fiona cranes her head around his arm and looks back. Anne Boleyn is nowhere to be seen. Fiona wonders if England's current queen knows one of her predecessors is still living at the Tower. Sort of.

The warder carries her to a side door in the tall, forbidding grey-stone building. Inside there are cages; all contain ravens except one.

"H'lo, Kit," says another bloke in the same uniform, nodding.

Her warder grunts, sets Fiona down before the empty cage, and opens its door.

Oh, bugger off. She has no intention of entering *that.* But her bird-body, as if it has another mind secreted somewhere, automatically works her grey, scaly feet, which carry her inside.

Kit—that must be his name—lifts a dish from a ledge and sets it inside the cage. On it, to her astonishment, lies a recently deceased mouse, framed by an artful circle of broken bits of dog biscuit. She should feel sick, but her stomach growls. Suddenly she lunges for the mouse. It's clutched in her beak before she thinks, *No! Ugh. Nasty!*

And spits it out, gagging.

She's absolutely starving, though. After a moment, she leans over to nibble at the bits of biscuit farthest from the grey-furred corpse.

I don't want *to be a raven,* she thinks bleakly. But if this isn't a dream, can I ever become myself again? And what was that raving madwoman—mad *ghost*—on about, anyhow?

Kit comes back down the row of cages, checking their latches. Before he reaches hers, a little dark-haired girl dashes in through the Tower entrance, giggling.

"Halt there, young miss," says Kit. "It's after hours. Where's your mum and dad? You'd better—"

The girl ignores him. She snatches up a brimmed, bearskin hat from a hook on the wall, and runs away with it.

Was that little girl . . . also Anne? Fiona pushes her head through the bars of her cage for a better look, but the child is already out the door.

"Bloody hell," mutters Kit, letting go of her cage's latch. He dashes off in pursuit.

When he doesn't come back, Fiona starts exploring her cage. And discovers it's surprising how well a beak can work a latch.

London, 1966

Magnhild, lying down again on the cloth-covered platform, has made another discovery: When water leaks from human eyes long enough, it backs up, and the ugly red knobs they call 'noses' can no longer pull air in and out. She wipes her face on the rumpled cloth twisted beneath her, then snorts into it.

"Ack!" she croaks, looking at the result. How disgusting humanity is.

She's also famished, having missed her morning mouse. And Kit will be wondering where his Maggie's gotten to. She almost cries anew, thinking of him. But sniffling won't feed a bird. So she sits, then carefully stands. Walks around the big cluttered cage, and finds a greasy wad of newspaper. It smells faintly of potato. But there's no food in here, as far as she can see.

On her next circuit she spots a familiar object: a small round mirror.

My thing! From my hoard. But why did it come here too?

Next to the mirror sits a shiny, equally-enticing silver bangle. She lifts it, but then sighs and drops it. So hungry . . .

When there's no food in your cage, a bird must go out there—wherever 'there' is—and find some. Perhaps she can also manage to get up somewhere high, spot the Tower, and find her way home.

But where's this new cage's exit? Magnhild lurches over to the single window, which is pushed up, and open a bit at the bottom. She's very high up.

To get down from high up requires wings. She sighs and backs away. Then she sees there's a *door*. People use doors to keep ravens either in or out. "Shut the cage door," Kit sometimes tells new yeoman warders. "The birds will open the latch if it's not properly fastened." They also open and shut the bigger doors set into the Tower's walls. How this trick is done is, the human grips a small round knob, turns it, then pushes and walks through.

She looks down. Maybe these pale paws at the ends of her not-wings will be good for something, after all. She hesitates, looking at the chest where several shiny treasures lie, then snatches up the silver mirror. There's a handy pouch in the cloth wrapped around her body; she tucks it into that.

Making the door behave is easy. Even the long line of stairs down isn't so difficult once you learn not to step too far over their edges.

Out on the street, Maghhild thinks: *Food. Food. Food.* She turns in a circle but sees nothing edible. No woods hiding fat mice. No broken biscuits softened with beef blood. Because . . . no Kit.

There comes just then the tantalizing aroma of meat braised in flames. A familiar smell that wafts every day from the big-wheeled food carts set about outside the Tower moat.

And—can it be? *Yes.* The delicious crisp-crusty spoor of pork pies.

Magnhild's new nose twitches as she follows it down the street. Gradually the walkway grows more crowded. She's never seen so many people all at once. She dislikes crowds, especially when they press close. But the lovely scent of roasting beef and hot pastry crust and herbed gravy . . . she hugs her arms close to her body, trying not to brush anyone as she plows ahead. Sometimes her gaze snags on a shiny trinket on a stall table, or a bright scarf on a hook, fluttering enticingly in the morning breeze.

But—breakfast first.

She pushes on, weaving around badly dressed children, women, and men. And many nasty dogs on leather leads. Jumped-up foxes to whom she gives a wide berth. Some people have carry-bags laden with . . . well, who knows what. Magnhild would like to see inside all of them.

After she eats.

At last she spots a brightly-painted food cart. A white-aproned man is handing over a steaming meat pastry. The nearly-grown boy reaching for it digs into his pocket, pulls out a shiny coin, and drops it into the pieman's palm. Then walks away, bobbing his head to an inner beat.

Magnhild's mouth floods with saliva; her chest tingles. A tourist. A pork pie. She knows this game.

She hangs back, leaving some punters between them for cover. A few steps farther and her mark stops to talk with another boy. They laugh and gesticulate; the hand with the wrapped pie hanging loosely by his side.

Magnhild strolls up behind, yanks the pie from his grip, then melts into the crowd.

Outraged cries rise behind her. "Oi!" and "Bloody thief!"

She grins and keeps walking. A few steps on, she runs. Darts into an alley and crouches, back pressed to a cool, rough brick wall, wolfing warm, heavenly crust and tender meat, sucking up gravy filling. Humming in ecstasy.

A girl in pink shorts pauses at the neck of the alley, staring in. Just then Magnhild also sees a mouse creeping out from under a broken crate, nose twitching toward some fallen crumbs. Her hand swoops down automatically, scoops up the mouse, and stuffs it into her mouth. She bites down on its futile writhing—crunch! And savors the tiny spurt of blood.

Heavenly.

The child staring at her screams like the boiling teakettle in the yeoman warder's kitchen.

Magnhild flinches and shouts, *"Kraaank! Kraaank!"*

The child's face crumples and she runs off, crying, "Mummy! Mummy! A *monster!*"

Magnhild grins. Yes! I'm a very big monster. After licking clean her greasy fingers, she strolls boldly out the other side of the alley, eager to partake of more good things.

Down the street is a place much like Tower Green, with grass and plants and trees. It's locked behind an iron fence, but scaling it proves dead easy. Then, just climb the tallest oak within . . .

But she's so much bigger now, the branches bow alarmingly under her weight as she goes higher. The very top, which she desires, is out of reach. Still, she can see far over the rooftops, and—there! A familiar sight: the spires and conical roofs of the Tower's tallest turrets. Not close, but not too far, either, as the raven flies. Without wings, though, she'll simply have to find it on foot.

As she leaps down on the outside of the fence, an elderly lady with a shiny purse and net bag of groceries stops to glare. "Shameful!" she mutters, tsking.

Magnhild merely eyes the bulging shopping tote.

But a large group of people are coming their way, led by a bossy young man who points to everything around, talking about "history." She's seen their kind before. These people like to look and look at everything. Probably they'll be going, sooner or later, to the Tower.

She leans forward and whispers, *"Kraaa,"* at the old woman. Who looks alarmed and hurries away, muttering something about 'hoodlums' and 'bobbies'.

Magnhild falls in behind the tourists, following them casually down the sidewalk.

●◐◑○○◐◐●

In the shadows cast by dusk Fiona stalks around on her stumpy new bird legs, looking for Queen Anne. How does one summon a ghost? Especially with no spell book. Or fingers. Or thumbs. If she makes a racket she'll probably only annoy the warders, and get stuffed back into that sodding cage.

As she walks past a bench she notices some pale white things scattered across the grass. A sprinkling of seashells, some of them broken, as if dropped from a child's pocket and accidentally trodden on. A beach-jaunt souvenir.

Shells. A shell game.

She recalls the street magician she'd glimpsed on the way to Lady Jane that morning. His shell game con. The old switcheroo . . .

Is that what's happened to her and the raven Anne spoke of? But when a thing is switched, sometimes it can be switched back. Maybe they need everything to be in one place, though? Mirror, ghost, raven, Fiona.

Where can she find that bloody ghost again? Her history course covered Anne's imprisonment in what was then called The Queen's Lodgings, an apartment in the southwest corner of The Tower. Not much to go on, but all she has at the moment.

As she turns the northwest corner, huddled close to the stone wall, Fiona glances back. And sees not one but two shadows there. Only one is her own. Someone is stealthily following her. Someone short, four-legged, and bushy-tailed.

She's always thought foxes quite lovely. Fuzzy-tailed and cute. But now the red-coated predator is over twice her size, and it doesn't seem very cuddly.

She speeds her pace.

As does the fox. Canny, but cautious, it's patiently closing the gap. By the time she reaches the southeast corner it's only a few yards behind.

Here's the royal lodgings, thinks Fiona, looking up anxiously at the wall looming above her. And there's an open window. Without another moment's hesitation, she launches herself into the air. Thrashing awkwardly as if swimming upward, she crashes onto a stone sill.

Hopping inside, she crosses a Turkish carpet. From the next room come muffled voices. First, a woman's. Then a man's. "Ah, beans on toast. Now that's what I call a proper tea, love."

Fiona freezes, horrified. It's *Kit*. The warders *live* in the Casemates.

Panicked, she scurries back toward the sill, hops up, and looks down. A red fox sits at the base of the Tower, tongue lolling, grinning up at her. As she stares, though, it wavers. Stretches. And grows, until she's looking at . . . the ghost of Anne Boleyn.

Fiona stifles a croaked curse and glides back down to the grass. *What sort of bloody effing joke was that?*

To ensure you kept on until you found me. I dwell in yon royal lodgings, forced to share it now with several commoners. Anne sniffs with disdain.

Well, I'm here. Fiona ruffles her neck feathers. *So all we need do, perhaps, is find me—my body, that is—and the mirror, and switch everyone back? If I return to my flat in the Portobello Road, then I . . she . . . it is bound to turn up eventually. I left the cursed mirror on my dresser.*

And what of me? says Anne. *In sooth, how will all of that benefit your queen?*

You're not my—I'm not responsible for your problems! croaks Fiona.

Anne looks sly. *And yet, should I raise an alarum now, I would be responsible for yours.* Then her face crumples. *I only wished to live a wee bit more. But the foibles of weak yet powerful men condemned me.*

Fiona sighs; her wings droop. *I get it, believe me. I should be graduating Oxford in British history right now. But then the don . . . and now, instead, in either body. . . well, I'm just a bloody* bird.

Anne brightens. *Why not join forces? I ken a good deal about the past, from the inner circles. Things so-called historians have yet to dream of.*

Join them how? Asks Fiona, who nevertheless feels a thrill of interest. Oral history! In-person research! Though she's no longer enrolled at St. Hugh's, of course. Still . . .

How would that work?

You share your comely form with me. Perhaps . . . one day of each week?

Fiona narrows her beady eyes. *For how long?*

Anne looks thoughtful. *A thousand days in total?* she says at last. *It has a poetical symmetry.*

Can a ghost be trusted? Really, what choice does she have? *So, it's over the wall for us?*

Anne nods. *We shall ride into London town on some common conveyance, and—*

"Oi! I know both 'a you," says a familiar voice. Familiar to Fiona because it's her own. "So, any mice left over from tea?"

It's her body as well, but different now. Confident, cocky. Swaggering about the Green as if possessed by a swashbuckling pirate, or . . .

Or a raven.

She and Anne exchange glances.

You've got a deal, says Fiona.

●◑◐○○○◑◑●

A long convo results. Magnhild explains how initially she followed some tourists back to The Tower. "But it was the wrong world, or day, or . . . something. You weren't here."

Then how did you return here, to our time? asked Anne, frowning.

"Found the dodgy red-haired witch again, didn't I. She said some mumbles and sent me back down the street and—hey, presto—here I be!"

Anne the ghost and Fiona the bird exchange glances.

Makes sense, says Anne briskly. *Very well then, here is what needs must be done next, to rectify the transmutation.*

In the end, they have to promise Magnhild an order of fish and chips, to be paid in full after they reach the mirror. Only then does she agree to go along.

Anne and Magnhild clamber aboard the roof of a late-running hackney cab; Fiona wings her way up. The cab jolts off.

Fiona stares at her own body, sitting a few feet away, inhabited by someone . . . something else. *Do you . . . like being human?*

Magnhild tilts her head, her affect still birdlike. "Food, yes. And scaring the punters. But . . . I miss my cage. My hoard. I miss my own dear Kit." She pouts a moment. "And breakfast mice!"

On Portobello Road they hop off; their destination the market stall where Anne and the raven first left the mirror.

You're sure she'll still be here? Fiona asks.

From within her fur muff Anne pulls out a shimmering note. It looks like a fancy invitation to a ball. *Yea, for the red-haired sorceress promised especially to heed my pleas, should we require more assistance,* she says.

Well, there you go, Fiona thinks dryly. The supreme confidence of the very rich. *So we'd better get it right,* she mutters.

Fortunately the stall's proprietor is still there. She nods a greeting as they approach. "Just doing a little inventory."

Fiona eyes the crates, wooden boxes, burlap sacks. One brass-banded chest gives off a muffled thump, as if something inside is alive. Probably best not to ask. *We needs must proceed forward in time for a nonce, to this maiden's lodgings,* says Anne.

Then she explains about the promise of fish and chips.

And the raven wants to return afterward. Back to 1880, adds Fiona.

"Is that all?" The vendor stifles a yawn. "Pardon. Up late last night. Fine; just return here again after the swap," she tells Magnhild. "So. First off to the year, er . . . ?"

1966, Fiona croaks.

The sorceress, or whatever she is, nods once and smiles. "Done."

Then Fiona disappears, a feeling like the flame on a pinched candle wick winking out.

There comes a brief spin, as if they're standing on a record turntable at 78 RPM. Then a cacophony of noise: car horns, shouts of vendors, several pop songs playing loudly from various shop doorways.

A truck rumbles by and Anne shrieks, *What devilish sorcery is this?*

Try to be cool, Your Majesty, says Fiona. *Only a horseless carriage. Science, not magic.*

Science. What is science? Anne looks dubious, but follows Fiona and Magnhild to the Chepstow Villas. They pant up the four flights, Fiona riding Magnhild's shoulder for the last two.

Anne skips ahead. *Far more steps in a castle,* she taunts.

Inside the flat, the small silver mirror still lies on the dresser-top.

We must get it right this time, says Fiona. *So I assume that, first, Magnhild and I should change back to our proper, er, places? And then—*

"When does I get fish and chips?" Magnhild complains.

Later, Anne and Fiona tell her, simultaneously.

Human and raven stand at the dresser, gazing down at the glass. One human chin and one raven's beak reflected there.

Ready? says Fiona. Magnhild nods; her stomach grumbles.

Now! croaks Fiona, poking the glass three times with her beak. Magnhild's index finger taps the curved surface.

Nothing happens.

Fiona groans, "Bloody He—"

Then, as if a gale wind is blasting through the flat, bird and human fly backward. Fiona's body lands on the bed, the raven sprawled atop her chest. Fiona groans and sits up. "Ugh. All the pain of too much porter, and none of the fun." She clutches her head.

With hands. Not wings. It worked!

Behind her a groggy croak sounds like, *Chips?*

"Soon." Fiona flexes her fingers, reveling in their lack of feathers. "Now, your Highness—shall we?"

Anne nods. They stand before the mirror, looking down into the glass. Impulsively, Fiona takes Anne's right hand. The queen squeezes back, not even trying to hide the sixth finger. Fiona decides she actually finds it attractive; like the extra digits on a six-toed cat. Only sexier.

◑◐◑◯◑◐◐●

Properly a raven again, I, Magnhild, return to the witch's stall. After another quick spin through time, I slip back over the Tower wall and into my unlocked cage.

Next morning a welcome voice says, "Morning, my darling."

Kit sets a plate on the ledge, then opens my cage door. "Bollocks. It's unlocked." He frowns and looks around, then laughs. "Well, I was the silly beggar who put you to bed. Can't blame someone else, and no harm done. Our secret, eh, Mags?"

How I long to tell him of my adventures! And about all the fantastic things I didn't actually get to steal. The crowds of half-dressed punters and stinking horseless carriages. Of being a pirate bird set down amongst them all.

"By the by," Kit adds, looking quizzical. "Someone's arranged a delivery of fish and chips for you, once a week, every week. Anonymous donation."

Ecstasy! But the why of that, too, I cannot tell him. Close as we've been for many years, we speak different tongues. Still I love Kit all the same.

He sets the plate before my open door: a plump grey mouse haloed with broken biscuits softened in beef juice. Beautiful; a big mousey daisy on a plate.

I bob my head in approval. Ah, but it's good to be home. And so well taken care of! With a hearty 'thank-you' croak, I tuck in.

LONDON, 1966

Unlike Magnhild, Anne does not return to the market stall to be sent back to 1880.

Whatever for? she says, when Fiona asks why. *Being a ghost, I would've lived in your time, anyhow, eventually. And I quite prefer this era. It's so much more . . .*

Fiona smiles. "Groovy?"

Exactly.

The queen is also modernizing her vocabulary, and has taken to wearing (somehow, mysteriously, acquired from who knows where) miniskirts, halter-tops, and bellbottoms. Her posh model's figure would be a smash hit at Lady Jane, were she not mostly invisible.

One morning Fiona says, "Know what I'd like? To do, well, my own show. About the 16th century. It was my dissertation topic—women back then, and the bloody horrible way they were treated. *You* know. By kings, nobles, fathers . . . and, well, almost everyone."

Indeed? Anne leans across the table as Fiona sips her morning Typhoo with milk and sugar. The queen's eyes sparkle. *Tell me more.*

So Fiona does. And then she sighs. " . . . but I suppose I'd have to graduate and finish the bloody dissertation first."

They sit at the table and write all afternoon. Anne has great stories of court life, and what really happened behind the scenes of Henry's palace. What's more, once Fiona explains how students must show their research, Anne tells her where to go for the best original sources, to list on her bibliography.

"I know where all the bodies are buried," she says casually.

Fiona assumes she means that quite literally.

They knock out a plan and a first-draft chapter in two weeks. Fiona needs an appointment to see a new advisor at St. Hugh's—certainly not the old one. She decides to risk everything and approach historical scholar Dr. Edwina Morley, the first woman to be made a full British History professor at Oxford—surely no stranger to controversy and paternalism herself.

A week later, on the campus of St. Hugh's, Fiona's ushered into a wood-paneled office. A woman with a greying blond chignon, wearing a tweed jacket and white blouse, is sitting behind a modest oak desk. She still looks formidable, though—until Fiona sees she's stroking a black cat snuggled in her lap.

Fiona takes one of the two chairs across; Anne slips into the other. Today she's wearing lime-green tights, a Mary Qant babydoll dress, and white patent-leather boots.

Go on, then. You'll be smashing, she tells Fiona, and winks.

Fiona clears her throat and explains what happened the previous semester: her parents' deaths, the bank foreclosure, the shock of losing literally everything in just two terrible weeks. "And so, I . . . well, I went to explain it all to my advisor, but everything seemed to be . . . to be so . . . " She's horrified to feel hot tears pressing behind her eyes.

"Overwhelming?" says Dr. Morley. "Devastating?"

"Paralyzing."

Morley nods. "A kind of trauma not much recognized yet. Still, what a shame a man that educated in history was so lacking in compassion." She scratches the cat's chin; it purrs loudly.

"And . . . you received my revised dissertation plan?" Fiona asks anxiously.

"Yes. Rather amazing! Reads almost as if you lived the times. Your theories on rudimentary underground feminist networks and their links to magic, astrology, and invention were refreshing. I *was* skeptical about some sections until I checked your sources." For the first time, Morley smiles. "Just so you know, you may well be excoriated, even vilified for your novel approach to the period. But you'll survive."

Fiona's trying to contain her excitement, but she can't help bouncing in her chair. "So that means—"

"You're readmitted to St. Hugh's. I've no doubt you'll astonish us, Miss Byrd."

Told you, says Anne, swinging one booted foot.

On their way out, she adds, "Don't forget, tomorrow's my day with the body."

LONDON, 1968

After Fiona's graduation, an academic press picks up her dissertation. She and Anne work up a one-woman show called "The Anne Boleyn Hour." Just a local production at first, playing town halls and country theatres. Sometimes it's Fiona in period garb, Anne hovering nearby in case she needs help fielding questions afterward. Sometimes it's both of them up there, as one, Anne inside Fiona, cutting loose with wild historical tales.

Those nights always garner even more applause.

After a smashing review in *The Sunday Times*, the BBC offers her a regular weekly spot. Of course she accepts.

These days, Fiona and Anne have an option on a nice semi-detached in Notting Hill, convenient to everything, especially the club scene. They're currently dating a drummer in a band. A nice polyamorous bloke originally from Glasgow who appreciates history, and both of them, very much indeed.

This purple velvet tent contains a most intriguing item whose backstory involves a delicate topic. I can't recommend staring into it or into certain other mirrors for long, though, lest one find oneself . . . well . . . changed. What do I mean? Come closer. Consider this fine antique looking-glass. When the silver backing on a mirror's glass ages badly, it can create a sort of mist or dark, clouded patches that experts call "foxing." A perfectly natural aging process, ordinarily. But look a bit closer. There! Did you see it? That subtle movement, as if something had just shifted beneath the glass. And now . . . oh dear. I fear we both look a bit ghastly, reflected in those darkly-spotted depths. Let's move on quickly to the next story . . .

The Foxing Effect

by Aphrodite Anagnost

Creaking open the hospital's basement door, I traversed the dark corridor that led to the main autopsy chamber. A small corpse lay on a metal table in the centre of the room. I shivered, throat clenching automatically at the stench of decaying flesh, which always holds an unsettling, musky sweetness. A scent one never forgets.

No diener waited in the cold, dark morgue to assist, which was just as well. The air here seemed insufficient for two living people. I drew in a breath and coughed. Reached for an apron and tied it over my skirts, then pulled a pair of gumboots from a low shelf and slipped them on to protect my new white-canvas plimsolls.

I examined every inch of the child first, before lifting my blade to make a Y-shaped cut from the corner of each shoulder and down to meet at mid-chest, the stem of the incision ending just beneath the belly button. I removed the lung and heart block, examining each organ separately. After settling them back inside the body cavity, I neatly sewed the skin flaps together again. Only then did I allow myself to take a step back and gaze upon the corpse with grief and pity.

"Poor girl," I said aloud, voice echoing faintly in the large, near-empty chamber.

I sighed and went to sit at the mahogany desk in a far corner, lifting a steel-nib pen to make notes and complete my report.

The body is that of a well-developed, well-nourished Caucasian female infant who appears the stated age of four months. An odor of rotting flesh with fruity undertones exists; normal for this early state of decay. The body weighs ten pounds and measures twenty-two inches from crown to sole. Head circumference, sixteen inches. Brown hair. The anterior fontanel is patent at eight tenths of an inch. The irises blue; pupils fixed and dilated. The sclerae and conjunctivae are unremarkable. No evidence of petechial hemorrhage. Upper gingiva is edentulous but the deciduous left central incisor of the lower jaw has erupted. No evidence of injury to cheeks, lips or gums. No corrosive injuries; no peculiar odor given off by the mouth.

There is a half inch by one inch raised Mongolian blue spot in the left axilla, one inch below the final rib in the midaxillary line; a mark colloquially referred to as "witch's tit." Pallor mortis and algor mortis are present. Livor mortis, fixed. Rigor mortis is trace, putting death at approximately twenty hours prior to this examination, consistent with the report of the child's mother. No malformations, deformations or dysplasias. The infant is non-syndromic in appearance. No evidence of trauma. There is frothy sputum in the oral cavity; a mouth sweep and manual investigation of the upper larynx reveals no foreign body. No foreign substances are present in any of the natural apertures.

Internal examination was limited to the chest cavity, per parental request and order of Chief Inspector Donald Swanson. Therefore, no analysis of stomach contents or brain is available. Chest organs were removed en block via the Rokitansky method. Bones are intact. Heart, great vessels and lungs reveal no malformation. Small pleural effusions are present bilaterally.

Histopathologic examination of all tissues reveal no abnormality save atrophic thymus. Significant early apoptosis of thymic cells are present. Manner of death was natural. Mode of death is determined to be "cot death"

—Rose Montressor, MD, Medical Examiner.

By the time I finally left the morgue, the Abbey bells had been royally pulsating for three hours, chiming their patch of Cambridge Quarters in celebration of Queen Victoria's sixty-first birthday. The moon bathed the streets in cool light while the gas lamps cast a warm glow. I stood at the corner of Absolution Alley and Sanctuary Snicket inhaling the aroma of beef pies with gravy wafting from a nearby cart. I'd not yet supped, so the mingled scents of rosemary and meat juices set my stomach growling. But the silk-clad Turkish vendor also sold suspicious-looking sheep trotters, so it was easy to say no. I decided to shop first. Autopsy supplies and tools for antisepsis—those cornerstone of modern medicine—were my primary goal, though I was not averse to a little browsing as well.

Though perhaps "modern" wasn't the best descriptor to apply to the medical profession in London. For half a decade I'd been denied access to St. George's University of London, and subsequently resorted to studying anatomy in Italy—where I'd excelled. Back home a dozen years later, after a long campaign I gained an appointment as the first female deiner at Scotland Yard. Carrying on in this capacity after finally "being *permitted*, despite your sex"—as I was so often told—to complete my medical degree at New London School of Medicine for Women. My reward for enduring this lengthy process, though, was to be well-known as a peerless surgeon with an irreproachable record.

I headed for the shops on Regent Street. Before I could reach them, a boy stepped in front of me, cradling a stack of newspapers. He was oddly dressed all in black, even his squat newsboy cap.

"Dr. Montressor!" He looked me up and down, flashing a grin. "You're front page in the evenin' news! Only a ha'penny. "The Whitechapel Butcher Strikes Again . . . aw, but you a'ready knew that."

● ◑ ◐ ○ ○ ○ ◐ ◑ ●

Of course I knew. Sir Wynne Edwin Baxter might be the officially-appointed coroner for East London, but *I* was the doctor who'd examined the uterus expertly dissected from the most recent murder victim's pelvis by the infamous though still unidentified killer. I'd placed the organ in a glass bowl. There it had floated, staining the water pink with blood, surrounded by small bubbles. Some, risen to the surface, emitted the musty odor of indoles, reminiscent of freshly turned soil. The endometrium had been oddly marbled in black, as if recently injected with India ink, or soot. I'd described this on the gross pathology report using a new term coined for the purpose: "Black Uterus." A condition which I suspected might have an adverse influence on female health, though I was still researching it.

Also, based on my examination of the young woman's body, I'd stated that a killer this meticulous and obsessed would undoubtedly strike again. When I'd suggested the murderer may have had medical training, though, Chief Inspector Donald Swanson had rejected my theory and taken me off the case. I'd been assigned to a new project: autopsying dead infants to investigate a pattern of mortality without apparent cause.

The death of a small child is a grievous event; the disposition of such small bodies even more fraught, perhaps, than in the case of an adult. Autopsying corpses had only recently become a respectable practice, since its dark, earlier days when the infamous murderers Burke and Hare killed for profit, selling their victims to less scrupulous hospitals, claiming they'd died of "natural causes." Some Londoners still considered dissection abhorrent and unnatural, rather than a useful scientific learning tool, or a means of gaining evidence to solve a crime.

But I'd never flinched in my responsibility to fully investigate all cases, even unpopular ones. Beginning with the first infant autopsy I'd conducted five months earlier on a twelve-week-old child. Apparently in perfect health, she'd been put down for a nap three hours prior to being found dead in her cot by her mother, Mrs. Mara Asphodel, a local purveyor of herbs.

Like the child I'd just examined, the Asphodel infant's mouth had contained a frothy discharge, the thymus was more atrophied than expected, and a small effusion of both lungs was present. I'd ruled that death unexplainable, idiopathic. Another new term had occurred to me then, and I'd written it for the first time on the certificate: *Cot Death*.

●◐◑○◐○◑◐●

"Only seven pence," the newsboy was still cajoling. "It's all about you, Doctor!" He tapped the headline of the front-page article: *Dr. Rose Montressor's Strange New Findings at Autopsy in the Horror of Whitechapel.* "See? Ever'body in London knows you now."

"Thank you, young man." I paid, then dropped an extra shilling into his cupped hand. "That's for you."

I admit to vanity, for my heart skipped with pride as I read and then reread the article. And of course, to see my name there in print! This was *The Times*—not some scandal rag or penny dreadful. I looked up and down the festive, boisterous street for, to be honest, I somewhat relished being recognized by strangers. But I hoped Mrs. Asphodel, the grief-stricken, unhappy young woman who'd been dogging me would not turn up again tonight.

The mother of the first cot-death babe had been following me, you see, as if she were a moth, and I the moon. She also frequently sent letters on parchment in violet ink, accusing me of infant mutilation in the autopsy suite. Calling me "a profane dissectionist and butcher." When I did not write back, she addressed even more virulent missives to me, using such labels such as "grave robber," "foul practitioner," and finally, "ghoulish resurrectionist."

I'd consulted my mentors, who advised me to remain aloof and ignore the letters. Which I had done, scrupulously. *No answer is also an answer.* This had been the general wisdom of my role model and former professor, Dr. Lizzie Garrett Anderson, and I stuck to this wise practice.

As soon as Victoria's bells fell silent, a marching band commenced, playing "God Save the Queen." Clearly this would be a night of revelry and profligacy. But then London was overdue for some fun.

As I traversed the street, gaslights flared and flickered. The cobbles seemed to present fewer islands of horse droppings, and were possibly less coated with coal dust—perhaps in honor of Her Majesty. Lights in all the buildings glowed, and shutters had been flung wide. Shopkeepers' doors were hung with fragrant, verdant wreaths and garlands made with twisted cuttings of spring flowers, ivy, and boxwood. The raucous marching band was just then passing a line of carriages, which had stopped to allow the procession to safely proceed.

I was not completely surprised to spot young Mrs. Asphodel out of the corner of one eye. She'd wedged herself between two corpulent masked dignitaries with a look of the East India company about them.

The wretched woman was still trailing me, relentless as a Gypsy's curse.

Just then looked directly at me, her expression one of deep sadness. Her face a pale palette upon which rosy cheeks, dark hair, and green eyes seemed merely painted on. She was somewhat stout, yet firm. Nature had blessed her with height, while a good corset provided a fashionably narrow waist.

I decided to evade her by entering the rows of tables flanking the sidewalks, featuring delicacies from across the world. Platters of marrow toast and cauldrons of Brown Windsor soup sat on the highest table set across cobbled Markham Street, connecting the opposing sidewalks of percussive stone.

I strolled past the cheers and laughter of celebrating Londoners, catching a perfumed whiff of peonies from a walled front garden. Thank goodness for my rubber-bottomed plimsolls. Not very fashionable, perhaps, and low-soled enough to make my skirts into real street-sweepers. But they were silent, sure-footed, and comfortable. I touched my reticule to ensure no pickpocket had yet nabbed it. Then—hoping to throw off Mrs. Asphodel's pursuit—stepped inside the first shop door I came upon. Its front window display featured several lovely framed mirrors; a small card inked with *Room to Let* was posted there as well. A tiny bell tinkled merrily overhead as I closed the oak-paneled door behind me. Inside, the air was thick and cloying with some sort of ecclesiastical incense; it caused me to sneeze half a dozen times. What burned in those unseen censors? And why was incense needed in a mirror store, at all?

The mix of strong musky oils and sweetish flowering herbs took me back to my time spent studying in southern Italy. I'd encountered a few practicing *stregas* there. Those robust, unapologetic witches had been fascinating, yet also annoying. For chaos had reigned in Puglia, where I'd interned in a small medical clinic and had to deal from time to time with the odd rain of toads or hand of glory sent by a territorial Italian witch.

The shop's dark-brown velvet-covered walls to my left and right were hung with gilt-framed pier mirrors facing each other, a trick which made the long, narrow space feel broader, almost immense. A pair of women were gossiping somewhere in the back; I heard whispers but could not see them. Wall shelves were draped in the same brown velvet, and on these were displayed more mirrors; some lying flat, some propped upright on gilded easels. My reflection was multiplied infinitely by their sheer numbers.

One in particular caught my eye: The largest and tallest looking-glass I'd ever seen, its warm gold-leafed frame glowing enticingly in the light of many candles. No new-fangled gaslighting for this shop . . . two large candelabra burned upon a round central table and two more upon both mantelpieces. Still, why keep a showroom so unnaturally dim, in this day and age? For hadn't Mozart's requiem told us, Out of darkness, light?

Just then a woman stepped out from behind a wall-like display of mirrors set up in the middle of the shop. Her pale face appeared placid, save for almost alarmingly protuberant brown eyes. Tight grey ringlets cascading over her temples; a few locks had escaped their prisoning combs at the crown of her head.

"Dr. Montressor," she greeted me. "I'm Mrs. Specchio. We've been expecting you."

"Indeed?"

How odd. For I'd made no appointment. Perhaps she'd just read of my work in the evening paper. In any case, I made a polite bow. "A pleasure to make your acquaintance, Mrs. Specchio." I pointed at the front window and its hand-printed sign. "Is your accommodation to let meant for tired shoppers to rent by the hour, or are you seeking a regular lodger?"

She laughed. "Oh, I'm open to all offers. Plenty of back-row hoppers need a nap after nipping into the pub! Life isn't all beer and skittles, is it? There's the morning's aftermath . . . come, I shall help you find a mirror to your liking." She looked me up and down. "You're a very beautiful woman, Doctor. I like your gigglemug!"

"Thank you. That's most kind. You do possess a fine collection here." My cheeks forced my often too-stiff upper lip into a smile. Might as well be pleasant—and a new mirror would look well in my flat. "And I admire your fine sense of humor, Mrs. Specchio. We ought to cultivate such spritely banter in today's girls. For tomorrow's women will have far more to laugh at, I am sure. Besides, indulging in humor makes one smarter."

"Aye, indeed." The purveyor winked. "Still, the mirror is a woman's truest friend. Reflections of reflections…"

"Do you really think so?" I caught sight of my face multiplied thrice in a triptych. "I'm not always so sure of that. But I do believe a regular occupation, eight hours sleep, plenty of chlorophyll, and a meatless diet do have a positive effect on one's countenance."

She tsked. "But the life of a lady doctor, ma'am," she mused, tapping her lips with one finger, "surely can't be an easy one."

"Far easier than the life of a female medical student." I examined multiple angles of my face, taking full advantage of the well-crafted triptych. The tuft of silver hair I'd acquired before medical school graduation, from so much intense studying, had finally been restored to its dark, shiny state—all through healthy living.

I glided my index finger around one of the triptych's beveled edges. "Oh my, so smooth."

"That piece, my dear, was hand-rubbed with a fine pumice stone. Then rinsed and re-rinsed for a year, like a river rock, to attain that soft bevel."

"It's awfully smoky, though." I frowned at my face, seeing it as if through a dark veil. "I look, well . . . like a ghost."

"Ah. It's a venerable piece; that's merely foxing. But we have many others which will surely suit your taste." Mrs. Specchio invited me to explore with one grandiose wave that took in the entire shop.

It had been arranged in rows and columns, like graphed data. A window left open a crack allowed a gentle breeze to waft in and rustle the linen curtains. I wandered up and down the aisles, sampling reflections. Mrs. Specchio followed in my wake like a museum docent, commenting on carving and beveling techniques, and the various finishes of stained wood or metal with silver foil and gold leaf.

I paused before a very tall oval mirror feeling as though I could fall right into that sea of glass in its heavy silver-blue frame. It was roofed by a pair of carved sea dragons facing each other. Never before had I been surrounded by so many likenesses, the irregularities of glass changing how I saw myself. "Tell me about this one."

Mrs. Specchio pulled a long silver pin from her hair, and one gray lock tumbled forward. She pressed the pin's sharp tip to the glass. "See how the actual point is nowhere near the pin-point's reflection? This mirror is made of mercury; a substance with special powers." She smiled at her reflection. "Created probably about fifty years ago. My age exactly."

"You certainly remain lovely at five decades," I said. "But I have a discordant relationship with my reflection. My sister and I were raised by our father and uncle, after our mother died of a mysterious illness. Her irises developed a gold ring. Her fingernails became black and pitted. From youth we were determined to discover what disease had consumed her from the inside out." I sighed. "Alas, it remains a mystery."

Mrs. Specchio nodded. "Indeed. As with much of life, and death."

"My sister became a nurse, currently serving in South Africa. I fear there may be war there soon." I shivered, already fearing for my intrepid Harriet's safety. "We women do make the best healers, you know. Every girl should be exposed to all areas of study, to determine aptitudes. Or else, upon reaching womanhood, their focus so often sadly shifts to trivialities, and merely finding a husband. Thus are many otherwise bright resources wasted, every day."

The proprietor smiled at this but made no response.

We resumed meandering through the aisles, stopping now and then to glance at ourselves and take in the various distortions offered. I was happy enough to wander in this strange little shop, for at least I'd managed to lose Mara Asphodel, my stealthy, aggrieved shadow.

"When my daughter was a child, I taught her how to slip into houses, just to explore and sit in the various rooms," Mrs. Specchio said, still at my elbow.

"I was a master at locksmithing, having learned from my father. I'd take my girl along to find the libraries and make note of any books in them we'd never heard of . . . you know, *forbidden* topics. Alchemy, astrology, magic. Then I'd look for those titles later in bookstalls. We found other rarities, too: herbs from the Far East, and once pieces of a meteor. We even cleaned a baronet's closed-up summer cottage after spending every day in its library for a week."

"That was most polite of you!" I jested. Thinking, *What an odd hobby*.

"We were ladylike house-prowlers, of course."

I imagined a young Mrs. Specchio and daughter entering private homes and snooping through the occupants' things like a pair of rude Goldilocks. Why had she shared this odd confidence with me? Underneath it all, I felt sure she was conveying something else: perhaps a story of desperation, of actions betraying a deep yearning to *learn*.

"There is more to our gender's destiny than serving others." I picked up a small mirror. Its round velvet back felt soft in my hand. I gazed at myself. Somewhat appealing by modern standards, yet I wanted to throw what I saw away. "There's a gap between real life and the image. Due to our society's obsession with pale, limp, almost lifeless beauty. . . seen obsessively in our paintings and sculpture. And now Daguerrean portraits are all the rage. Really, just another false measure of woman's true value. I myself am not immune. It makes me angry."

She regarded me thoughtfully. "I see."

"Of course you do. The promotion of vanity and subservience as the lifelong goal for girls makes any intelligent lady angry, and well it should."

"Although . . . I *am* a purveyor of mirrors." She chuckled. "A collector of all manner of baubles. This is not my only shop, you see. But the mirror business does bring in quite a bit of trade. And women are not the sole possessors of vanity, Doctor. Gentlemen too are preoccupied with image. Gentility, status . . . even fashion. *They*, in fact, are my best customers for these beauties. "

"Indeed, they are lovely. I hate and yet love them, and what they show me. Seldom do we see ourselves in full this way. As a physician, I like to take in the whole image at once. And such large mirrors are so rare."

I was about to remark on how sound carried in this wind-tunnel corner of London. Each tinkle of the bell over the door, or flap of curtain, or stray creak of hinge seemed louder than it should. But I was just then startled by the reflection of another woman in the mirror with me. I turned, astonished, to see Mrs. Mara Asphodel poised between two full length pier glasses at the back of the shop. Suddenly I felt caged. No doubt she'd just overheard, possibly even witnessed, our entire conversation. Mrs. Asphodel had a careful gait made for sneaking around. Softly, softly, as if she constantly worried about waking the dead. And for the love of God, what did she want this time?

I hived off by reflex, turning down another row of large floor mirrors, and stood there holding my breath.

She did not follow. I leaned out to peer between two Louis XV vanity mirrors and spotted her, just removing a carven ebony hand-mirror from a shelf. She carried it over to Mrs. Specchio and said, in a husky *sotto vocce*, "This is an important one. It will do the trick. Can you put it aside? Show it to her before she leaves."

Young Mrs. Asphodel paused to blot her shiny forehead with the back of one hand, then came down each aisle until she found mine. Oh, why had I lingered? Now my escape route through the only visible door had been cut off.

She approached me almost fawningly. "Dr. Montressor, it *is* you! I've heard some incredible stories about your medical abilities. The ladies at the Sheffield Political Association claim you've much experience in treating maladies of the clapper."

Mrs. Specchio raised a prudish eyebrow at that rather coarse term, and marched away to the back of the store. She laid the hand mirror Mara had given her on a small desk, then sat and busied herself making ledger entries.

"Mrs. Asphodel," I began, ready to chastise her for this dogged hounding of me. But just then I noticed a trail of dark blood beneath her hem, seeping into the cuff of one kid boot. That and the flushed face, the feverish stare . . . no normal monthlies would flow so far, even if the cloths needed changing. This woman was clearly unwell. I could infer a great deal about her diagnostically, without a formal examination. She stood slightly bent at the hips, as if in chronic abdominal pain. Her hair was thick and dark with a high widow's peak, a bit like Mrs. Specchio's, but thinning in spots. Acne spotted the jawline, amid a few unplucked hairs. Her pale complexion was sheeny, her brown eyes exophthalmic.

I was used to gaining trust by always being more eager to help than my male colleagues. Who generally demanded and were granted automatic respect for their station, however fresh the ink on their medical diplomas. So, instead of asking the lady why she continued to harass me, I said, "May I assist you with something related to your health, Mrs. Asphodel?"

"Oh! Well, Dr. Montressor, I . . . it's rather embarrassing." She looked away and wiped her greasy forehead again. Perhaps she thought I judged her, but I was merely evaluating, and it was clear she had an imbalance of humors.

"Please, go on," I urged.

She blushed. "Since the passing of my baby daughter, much as you described with that woman in the newspaper . . . I, too, have been afflicted with distressing symptoms. And the *Times* described your discovery and naming of, well, a . . . certain female condition."

"Ah. You refer to black uterus." My interest was piqued. Could she suffer from the condition, named by me, about which I had not yet published in any medical journals? Its only mention to date had been in the London papers, though possibly it had been discussed in local tea rooms as well. "What makes you think so?"

"I too am a healer, like my mother and grandmother. Leeches, herbs, root infusions, opium." She began to cry. "I'd so longed to pass the gift on to my poor little daughter."

As if on cue, the door creaked and the bell jangled as another customer entered the store.

Mara wiped her forehead with the back of one hand again, such a frequent gesture it appeared to be a tic. She pressed a hand to her chest. "I tended a woman who also lost a baby. She had spots like mine." She stroked the small red bumps on her jaw. "Also infertility, rapid aging, and finally madness. Nothing worked. I brewed yarrow tea, burned dried mugwort, and cinnamon too." Mara's lips trembled. "I've been unable to cure myself either, Dr. Montressor. Will I go mad as well?"

"Not necessarily, Mrs. Asphodel. In fact—"

"Please. Call me Mara."

"For you, Mara, I shall proffer my medical services free of charge. But my dear, you *must* stop following me. And cease the poison-pen correspondence as well."

She nodded. "Oh, I will! Yes, of course."

"You've been in serious distress, so I will overlook your, er . . . misplaced devotion. The black uterus is likely caused by an imbalance of certain substances in the body. Cease consuming all sweets and wines at once. Take a brisk walk by the river, morning and evening. Find some pleurisy root, boil it several hours into an infusion, and drink that every night until the bleeding stops. But I should also examine you now, to rule out a cancer of the womb. That's a dangerous condition, yet some women do not seek help."

"Because of normally praiseworthy modesty, most consult too late?" She nodded and sighed deeply. "Yes, thank you."

"And then you will shadow me no more?"

"You've my word, Dr. Montressor," Mara said. And then she called out, "Mrs. Specchio, may we have use of your spare room?"

"You may." The proprietor peered over demilune spectacles and blew a stray, curling lock off her forehead. "One hour minimum. It's been freshly lime-washed. Well worth the price of a shilling an hour for the perfume alone."

She led us to the back, and down a short hallway, opening the door to a well-appointed chamber. Then she held out a hand.

Mara dropped a worn shilling into the waiting palm. "That special mirror I asked to you put aside. Be sure to let Dr. Montressor have a look."

"As you wish." Still hovering in the doorway, Mrs. Specchio bowed to Mara. Then she stood eyeing me with the blinking simplicity of a small child. Really, her agreeableness seemed excessive, even for an ambitious shopkeeper.

"I'll leave you ladies alone now," she said at last, and marched off. She returned a few moments later carrying a rattan basket filled with scraps of cotton fabric of varied fineness, which I assumed was normally used for polishing metal and glass. Setting this next to a cot in the corner, she said, "Just in case." Then exited again, this time pulling the door shut until the latch clicked firmly into place.

Mara laid her reticule on a deal table in one corner of the room, sat on the edge of the bed, and lifted her skirts quite readily. I helped her scoot back on the ticking, and tucked several of the linen squares beneath her.

She stared up at me. "Thank you for doing this, Dr. Montressor."

"I haven't a speculum with me. Still, I should be able to tell if your uterus has grown out of the pelvis and into the abdominal cavity. Which would be ominous. But we'll see."

Mara sniffled. "I've just not been myself lately."

I nodded, wondering, *Then who have you been?* Her savage mood swings concerned me, and I was determined to discover a physical cause.

I begin every examination at my first glimpse of a patient. Noting the way they breathe. Whether they blush. Their gait and posture, the pupillary dilation. Are some words oddly repeated? Also, detectable body odors of various regions, pleasant and otherwise, can be quite informative.

Mara Asphodel wore a fret on her face so chronic, the knurling muscles twitched from fatigue; the inscribed frown of a neurotic. I'd assumed until just minutes ago that she'd been contemplating some sort of revenge for the autopsy on her child, if that had been her reason for following me. Now I wondered, could she have agreed to the exam for that purpose? Certainly she'd suggested as much in her letters. But I hoped we could part ways on better terms, and for good, after this.

"Now lie back and relax." I patted her shoulder, trying to reassure. Reminding myself, as I tugged off my second-best kid gloves, that this young woman was suffering. I must keep professional objectivity, lest I lapse into acts of punitive medicine, even unconsciously—quite an easy feat, especially during a gynecological examination.

A particular risk with a patient within whom a physician detects *Lex Telionis.* Literally, the law of such a vengeful nature; the old eye for an eye principle.

But if I discovered and helped her stop the cause of her excessive bleeding, surely she'd leave me alone. That she clearly hated me for cutting up her baby's corpse was not an unusual reaction. People fear and therefore hate autopsies, or find them sacrilegious, or both. Yet they are the rational process through which we learn the most about the science of medicine.

I grabbed a stool from under a table in the corner and positioned it at the foot of the bed. "Now, bend your knees and let your legs fall to either side, with the soles of your feet together." I helped guide her. "That's right, dear. As if they were butterfly wings."

"You mean like frog legs." Mara cackled rather witchily.

The skin of her inner thighs had the darkened, velvety appearance of acanthosis nigricans. I'd noticed the same texture on the back of her neck. The thigh muscles were well defined, rounded as beef shank. Feet certainly presentable but much walking had callused and caused them to spread. Clearly Mara was no slave to the tight, narrow fashion in ladies' boots. I'd studied the relationship of footwear to the health of the individual for an entire week of my podiatry rotation, after dissecting and labeling a right foot, then a left, in just two days. Concluding at the finish that, as the foot goes, so goes the body.

Mara had the hands of a gardener, thickened and muscular. The thin, delicate ankles of a dancer. A polite manner and the vocabulary of an educated woman, along with the deportment of a farm wife: a double standard unto herself. Grief and worry had imbalanced her bodily chemicals further.

"Let's take a moment and breathe together, three deep inhalations." I kept pace with her inspirations, one hand on her belly. I noted her diamond escutcheon, then felt her organs: the liver slightly fatty, as I'd suspected, as is often seen in one who loves sweets too well.

She squirmed in discomfort when I palpated the smooth edges of the soft, spongey spleen. I repositioned myself on the stool and rolled my sleeves up. "Now we shall inspect below. And finally I will examine the vaginal canal, while together with my other hand atop your belly I shall size your uterus and ovaries. Don't fear, I will be gentle."

When I pushed aside the menstrual diaper, her clitoral hood appeared red and swollen. I felt for marbly growths along the edges of the groin. "No enlarged lymph nodes. That's a good sign." No ulcers or apparent chancres either.

I carefully slid two fingers into the vagina, then palpated deeply to be sure of my diagnosis. As expected, the uterus was boggy. Smooth, but not enlarged and seated within the pelvic rim. By then, though, my knowledge of Pasteur's germ theory was giving me a strong desire to get the examination over with so I could wash my hands. I never brought a medical bag along to go shopping, of course. But what had I been thinking. leaving home without any phenol?

I reached for the basket of rags and rubbed as much blood off my hands as possible, swallowing the sputum pooling under my tongue. Someone should invent gloves to be used strictly for such physical examinations . . . I would call my friend Louis Pasteur after this, and get right on that task.

"A healthful diet will rebalance your cycle, Mara. So, as I said, no pastries, no sugared tea, no sweeties. I also recommend regular sexual intercourse, once a week on the same day, in addition to a standardized bedtime to aid in sleeping straight through the night."

"My husband enjoys relations in the middle of the night." Mara murmured and smiled. I realized this memory was meant for her, not me.

"I see. Well, he just needs retraining."

Mara looked startled, as if only just then realizing she'd spoken aloud. Then she laughed, giggles shaking the bed like the faint, final rumblings of a distant earthquake.

I pulled the stool back a foot or so to give her space to reposition herself. The flow had increased, thanks to my thorough examination; now her menstrual diaper was saturated with wine-dark blood. It smelled of rust, like the rest of her Lady Jane.

"We'll use Mrs. Specchio's linens to fashion some new padding." I tried hard to sound pleasant and optimistic as she frowned. I unsnapped two safety pins, let the saturated cotton diaper fall to the floor, and rolled it inside one of the larger rags provided. "Do you have a good deal of pain?"

"No," she said, rather sullenly. "When I was younger the bleeding stained the cloth only in drops. It was steady after accouchement. But now it overflows and even bleeds through. And is of an evil colour, not according to nature. Sometimes strange clumps gush forth from my womb."

One of those was just then poised to drop onto the floor. Preferring not to root around another's flesh with my bare hands any more than absolutely required, I reached up and pulled it out with my fingertips. Then wrapped it in clean cotton and pushed the balled-up square into one pocket. I would examine it further under the microscope—if it didn't disintegrate before I got back to the laboratory.

"Now I'll show you a method much more absorptive and comfortable than these clumsy menstrual diapers. Those things have really got to go." I took a fresh sheet of muslin from the basket. "Wrap clean cotton cloth around a small stick into a tube-shaped bundle, and you can insert it straight into the birth canal. Look, I'll show you how to roll it around your finger, in situations when you can find no sticks." I twirled the cotton into a tight, layered wad and handed it over. "Here, you can do it."

Mara stared at me as if horrified. Her face was red; her neck veins were bulging.

"Now, now. Let's breathe together again, Mara. No reason to get excited."

She exhaled a long, voluminous breath which, when it reached my skin, smelled a touch sweet. Then she sputtered, "My symptoms over the past months, were, in order, the spotting, the dark blood smelling of iron, the surges of bleeding, the spotting, the weight gain, the insomnia."

She went on to list what she called the 'hag hairs' on her chin, a deepening voice, an increased desire to pleasure herself, plus the prominent clitoris and oozing pimples.

I nodded. "Yes, I see."

She laughed so hard the bed creaked. "Oh, but do you?" Then she cried silent tears that ran down her face like rain.

"Mara, is there something else I should know?"

But now she fell mute, her eyes wide and bloodshot. Finally she made a sort of warding-off gesture and cried, "But I *can't* put what you're making there up inside of me! What if it wanders and finds its way into my lungs or heart?"

"Oh, Mara," I said. "The wandering uterus has long ago been disproven in the autopsy suite. The dead tell no lies."

"All right, then I guess we must suppose that's true," she said reluctantly. "You're the doctor, after all." And yet the heat of her unrelenting glare was all but palpable.

"Shall I show you how to do it again?" I stood and demonstrated rolling the device in my palm. "See? Like furling croissant dough. Whatever fabric you choose, make sure it's very clean."

She blinked rapidly several times, as if confused. Was she merely acting? The woman was an herbalist, with experience midwifing. How could she not understand?

"What if it never stops?" she suddenly blurted out. "I thought this sort of everlasting bloodbath would lead to madness."

"Pasteur and Lister have definitely disproved this sort of gross misinformation. It's not apoplexy, my dear. All will be well. We are rational women and must not let society deceive us into thinking moonbeams can drive us insane."

"No?" Mara sniffled and finally stopped crying. "What *must* I do, then?" Her eyes gleamed like amber in the dimly lit room.

"As I said, healthy moderation in all things is indicated."

The celebrated renaissance surgeon and obstetrician Ambroise Pare had observed, *Many women, when their flowers or terms be stopped, degenerate after a manner into a certain manly nature, whence they are called Viragines; that is to say stout, or manly women; therefore their voice is loud and big, like unto a man's, and they become bearded.* I quoted this to Mara, and then added, "In modern terms, black uterus."

Mara frowned. "But . . . you are saying this . . . *condition* . . . is normal?"

"Not so much normal as . . . a natural progression. If you desire the cascade of events to cease, and for your fertility to return, heed my advice." I rolled up the rusty-smelling, stained fabric squares and dropped them into the basket. They, and my hands, now badly needed soap and water. "Be sure to only push the clean plug in halfway to the neck of the womb," I said. "You've given birth. It will easily fit, and cause no discomfort. I promise."

Mara sat up and turned the roll over in one palm. Sniffed at it, and finally inserted it with one finger.

"Well done. Now perhaps you can find a bowl of soap and hot water. And some alcohol," I said.

Mara glared. "Are you suggesting I'm unclean?"

"No! It's for washing my hands…and to get the blood off your legs. Now, do you have any further questions?"

She got up from the bed and briskly smoothed her skirts. "No, I understand the diagnosis. My problem is sanguinary, influenced by diet. I must stop sweets at once, drink no wines, and eat, sleep, work, and fuck at regular intervals. Then my problem will resolve."

Yet she still scowled, clenching and unclenching her fists. Patients could become angry when a physician attempted to educate them, though, and such reeducation is always part of a medical intervention. There is a unity in plurality which occurs when like-minded people meet. A kind of synchronous concordance. But with Mara I felt only discord; a combination of musical notes that strike the ear harshly.

A knock came at the door. "Yoo-hoo! It is I, Mrs. Specchio. Your hour is up!"

Mara opened it. "May we have a bowl of water, soap, and some alcohol for the doctor's hands?" she said grimly.

"Of course. Anything else you require, Doctor? I hope you'll resume browsing through my mirrors? I've sold several just in the past hour. Annual income one hundred twenty pounds, annual expenditure one-nineteen and six, result happiness." Mrs. Specchio's eyes glistened at me over her glasses. "Have another gander, please. You will find no such place as this elsewhere on earth."

"Certainly, after a wash. I cannot walk around in public like this lest I frighten your customers." I held out my redly-besmirched hands. "I shall sit at this desk and wait for the basin and towel."

"Very well," said the shopkeeper. "Would you come along, Mrs. Asphodel, to assist?"

As I sat trying to avoid looking at the gore besmirching my hands, my gaze was drawn to a tattered copy of a novel on the small bedside table. Mary Shelley's *Frankenstein: A Modern Prometheus* lay on the table's scratched deal top. The corner of a folded paper peeked out from between its pages.

I flipped open the book, unfolded the missive, and gasped. Violet ink, in the same swooping hand so often studied on the threatening letters I'd received. But how had Mara slipped it into the book without my noticing?

To glean some understanding of the madwoman who, it seemed, would perennially hound my footsteps, I read quickly. For Mara and Mrs. Specchio were both fleet of foot and full of surprises, and would no doubt return soon.

The salutation was "Dearest Mother." It was signed "Your Mara."

Gods! Mara and Specchio were mother and daughter. No wonder this missive was secreted here. Though she'd mentioned a husband, perhaps this room was Mara's own lodgings, at times.

The opening lines referenced my name, calling me "the tainted resurrectionist." I recognized the baby's name a few lines later: "She wickedly defiled our precious Ruby."

I froze at a muffled tapping; footsteps headed this way. I quickly folded the paper and reinserted it between the pages, blood thrumming in my ears. I had to escape this den of . . . whatever it was. But what if the diabolical duo had laid some trap for me out in the shop? Above all, I must maintain at least a semblance of self-control and a confident demeanor, to prevent them realizing I was onto their game.

Mother and daughter entered with a basin of water, more clean rags, and a bottle of gin. Now their kinship was apparent as they stood side by side gazing at me. The twin widow's peaks, the protuberant eyes . . . as I washed up thoroughly I wondered, Why the elaborate charade? What fate did they have planned for me?

The liquor burned my trembling hands as I rinsed them.

I *would* be leaving, though. After all, frail grandmothers had been known to go up against wolves, and prevail.

I pulled on my kid gloves. Then lifted my reticle, hands trembling, clutching it to my chest to still the tremors. "I'll be going now," I announced, and started for the door.

Just before I reached it, Mara stepped in front of me. She smirked and pointed at my face. "Wait. There's a smudge on your cheek, Dr. Montressor." She thrust a mirror into my free hand.

I gripped it fiercely, lest it slip from my sweaty palm. I would not scruple to use it as a weapon, if need be.

They both stared, leaning in as I reluctantly peered into the hand mirror. What spot still marred my cheek?

As I looked, the glass began to change. A bloody thumbprint on one beveled edge shivered, then spread like a film of red lace across the surface. My reflection was first made hazy, then blotted out.

I gasped and rushed out the door, into the main shop. Toward another mirror, the tall one I'd admired earlier.

When I paused before it, panting, there wasn't any reflection.

"No," I breathed and looked again, stepping ever closer. Still I could not discern my own figure there. This large glass also was smeared with dark blood along its beveled edges. What had the two witches done?

I scrubbed at the centre with one sleeve, but still . . . nothing. Only a reflection of the aisles of mirrors behind me. I thought bitterly of Narcissus, the young man who had stared endlessly into a tranquil pool, admiring himself, mesmerized. But there was nothing here to hold *my* gaze. I'd been erased.

Trickery, surely! Merely cheap hedge-magic. Or possibly a form of mesmerism? Freud and Breuer had already been demonstrating the great power of the hypnosis they used with their patients. How very effective it could be . . .

My terror turned to outrage. The pair of them thought this parlor trick would break me—a woman of science! They assumed my image meant more to me than my work, or my soul. But *I* was not my reflection. Their pitiful dark magic could be given, yes. But I would not accept it.

I turned back toward the back of the shop, and the doorway leading to the room I'd just fled. There they stood, huddled together, gloating like an incomplete set of Weird Sisters wandered in from a Shakespeare drama.

But I had learned a thing or two about how to deal with witches during my medical studies in Italy. In fact, it had been part of the second year curriculum.

"I reject this curse!" I cried. And then, lifting the hand mirror foxed by Mara's blood, I flung it at the tall mirror before me, shouting, "*Sublata causa tollitur effectus!*"

The tall frame groaned; it warped and twisted. And then the silvered glass shattered, shards exploding outward to fall in a crystalline rain around me. I caught a daggerlike sliver in one gloved hand, and held it out like a glinting scalpel as I traversed the centre aisle of mirrors, headed for the front door, and my escape.

I was grateful to step out onto the sidewalk and be swallowed by the crowd of celebrants still reveling in the Queen's natal day. A group of Yorkshire farmers marched past, carrying ribbon- and flower-bedecked pitchforks and scythes at port arms. It was twilight now, the time of deep shadows. As I left behind the dark echoes of that macabre chamber of mirrors I heard cannons booming over the Thames, like the roaring of some mythical beast. A few droplets of cool rain landed upon my upturned face. Still holding the crystal shard, I fell in behind the farmers and followed them into a nearby pub.

Being a lady, I should normally have sat in back, inside the closeted snuggery reserved for female clientele. But this was no ordinary day. I boldly approached a table between the farmers and a well-dressed pair of bankers or barristers and—perhaps only because of the days celebratory nature—they smiled and made room, all nodding pleasantly my way. One of them pulled out my chair.

I considered ordering a sherry, that oh-so-respectable ladies' drink. But when the publican came round, one eyebrow raised, I said, "A half-pint of stout, if you please."

He nodded, draped the bar cloth he'd been holding over one shoulder, and ambled off to fetch it.

Finally I felt ready to let go of my makeshift dagger. I laid it on the table and gazed down at myself in the triangular bit of silvered glass. It was a very good thing I had known beforehand the efficacy of that powerful Latin phrase, *Sublata causa tollitur effectus.* Which translated to: *The effect shall depart when the cause is removed.* Not so much a medical "spell" as a profound dictum for life. One strong enough, yes, even to shatter a maleficent curse.

My foaming mug of molasses-dark stout arrived. I paid the publican and took a sip. Now that I could catch my breath and ponder the afternoon's events,

I felt it was a shame that magic and science so often seemed opposed. I was on the side of the latter, of course, but could still appreciate the art of a well-phrased spell or a finely-crafted herbal remedy. Maybe one day this difference would lessen, until it finally became meaningless.

I drank more stout, feeling the drumming of my heart finally slowing to a regular beat. Still staring down at myself reflected in the triangular shard. It would be some time yet, I decided, before it felt safe to look away and still feel certain that, when I looked again, I would still be there, gazing back.

What is that matched set of books, you ask—the ones sitting alone on the farthest shelf at the book stall called Illusory Incunabula? It's a complete set of ledgers, bound in fine Morocco leather, which altogether contains the whole of a most unusual project. A lengthy accounting, assigned by me, and undertaken and completed by a retired university librarian over in the States. This widower sought an answer to one of the greatest mysteries in the universe: the hidden life and secret desires of another soul's heart. Ah, but the dead so rarely give up such secrets! At least not willingly, nor directly. As one will discover upon reading the contents therein of one man's diligent work, entitled—

An Inventory of Ghosts

by Jim Scheers

So many souls and yet still no closer to my goal. I have searched this town, from the somber lecture halls and manicured grounds of the university to the wealthy estates to the west, withdrawn and silent beneath the shade of tall elms. From the cramped clapboard houses to the north to the tidy churches and chapels to the east. I've walked these streets in the hush of dawn and the bustle and clatter of the mid-day market. In the resigned quiet of dusk and the gaslit loneliness before dawn. But I have not found my wife, and the narrow lines of these notebooks have not revealed any clues to lead me to her.

I doubt I can continue the inventory much longer. They are eager to speak—exiles that they are—seeking someone who will listen, someone who may offer some comfort in their isolation. I fulfill the former, as I am bound to do, but the latter is beyond my abilities. Such is my character, as my wife had lamented in times past.

●◐○◯○◐○◐●

I was once a well-respected, if not necessarily well-known or well-liked, member of my profession: a librarian at the College of New Jersey for forty years, until my recent retirement. But I have since become, I'm afraid to admit, that mainstay of our times, a figure glimpsed and then quickly dismissed: a solitary old man, in a rumpled but still presentable topcoat and suit, walking about and talking, so it would seem, to no one.

Princeton is more town than city, despite its pretensions and the scholars and diplomats that pass through here. So I still encounter some of my former colleagues on those occasions when I make my rounds in the daylight hours. A few deign to nod or touch their hat brims. Some are accompanied by their wives, who glance quickly downward in embarrassment or sympathy. I cannot recognize which.

At Vivienne's funeral, they all had been solicitous and kind—even though we were never what one would call convivial at the library—offering condolences, aid, prayers. But my wife had been the one blessed with social graces. Without her, I floundered, mumbling muffled thanks, grasping at stray platitudes. Finally surrendering and submerging into silence, head bowed, staring at the intricate weave of the funeral parlor's Persian rug. Gradually, one by one, the mourners withdrew, leaving me alone beside the casket and a towering bouquet of white lilies sent by the university, accompanied by a polite, if not somewhat vague, note of condolence.

I talk all the time now, and listen even more. An actuality my wife would find impossible to credit.

Tuesday, February 7, 1871 (morning)

I wake up wheezing and coughing. My shoulders ache. Downstairs in the dining room everything is unchanged: the wine bottle unopened, the glasses empty.

She never appeared. Last night I'd thought I heard her footsteps on the creaking floorboards outside our bedroom door, but I was too numbed by sleep to rouse myself from bed. I thought perhaps she would leave some sign, but the table I had set—plates, placemats, forks, knives, wine bottle and glasses— remains as I'd left it the evening before.

As I stack the plates in the cupboard (I dismissed our maid some time ago) I recall the handfuls of dust I'd swept off the tabletop the night before. The dining room had fallen into disuse years before I lost her. The custom we grew into in our later years was to eat in silence at the small, warped table in the kitchen. My lavish orchestration of last night—a romantic dinner for two!— was clearly a mistake. Even if she had appeared, she would've seen it for the ruse that it was. She was—is—not a woman fooled by a well-intentioned but ostentatious gesture.

Perhaps it is too late to mend the rift I have wrought, but I must keep trying.

I do not leave the house until 8:30. A late start. Colder today, with a few gray smudges of clouds. The walk loosens the stiffness in my bones, but a weariness still weighs upon me, set just between my shoulder blades. The shops swarm with people. Through the fogged glass I see the colors of their coats and day gowns and hear muffled chatter. I watch them pass in and out, men in hats and wool coats, collars turned up, shoulders pitched forward against the wind. Women shivering in long coats or shawls, grasping at fluttering scarves. An unbearable stream of people, moving too quickly, too intently, too noisily. Too much alive.

I quickly turn away and continue on to the quieter, residential locales.

My first encounter occurs at 9:10 on Greenview, a narrow and serene side street flanked by a few tall, bare elms. A skinny lad of about ten years, barefoot, dressed in baggy short trousers and a loose, white cotton shirt in the style of the colonists. He trails a small girl walking with her mother. I follow at a discreet distance. The girl makes a game of throwing her red mittens into the wind, then chasing after them. The boy chases after the mittens at first too, but grows angry when the girl does not appear to notice him. He yells, waves his arms and stomps his feet to no avail.

Finally, the mother, looking annoyed at the game, shoves the mittens into her coat pocket and, with a mild reproach, takes the girl by the hand to hurry her on her way.

I approach the boy. "Hello, what is your name?"

"Robert, sir," he replies, somewhat defiantly. "Robert Oliver."

"Robert, I'm afraid you are under a misapprehension I've witnessed often in my wanderings."

He stares up at me, gaping.

In an even voice, and with simple words, I explain who I am and what has happened to him. I watch the stunned fear transform his face as he contemplates an emptiness beyond the limits of his youthful understanding. And then slowly there appears a sort of resolve, an urgent frown. A steely acceptance, I assume. This boy will weather his exile.

But then he clenches his fists and meets my gaze, eyes bright with anger.

"I don't believe you," he says, and marches off, unbowed by the sudden gale that has kicked up dust from the road.

I wonder if I should've said nothing, but no: better the truth then an eternity spent in delusion.

I sit on a bench and record the encounter in the leatherbound notebook: Name, Date, Location, Description, Commentary. I drag a line with my pencil stub across the next three rows, in case I should encounter him again. Most likely I will not. Children do not usually linger here the way adults do. But there has been, I recall, at least three I've met repeatedly, flitting about, simultaneously hiding but also watching me with eager curiosity once they realize I've seen them. All of the mediums I've consulted in the past said these wandering souls persist because they have left something unfinished. If so, how does that explain the children? What great mission or act of contrition would a child have possibly left undone?

At 12:40 I encounter the farmer Isaiah again, his slender, bent-backed form almost fading into the shadows of the looming Gas Works building. Rivulets of sweat gleam along his neck and darken the blue kerchief he has tucked into the collar of his cotton shirt, never to dry. His search for his family continues in vain.

He laments, "People move about so quickly, it is impossible to keep up with them."

I listen to his reminiscences, as I've done thrice before, then nod and wish him well. He motions towards the blank, brick face of the building. "This was a sawmill once. I'd collect the wood shavings for my mother. She'd stuff pillows with 'em."

I do not ask him about my wife. I learned long ago over the course of my inquiries that they cannot perceive any other souls who might cross their path. They are consumed solely by their own plight.

●◐◑○○○◑◐●

A week or so after the funeral (my sense of time back then was muddled: hours passed both too fast and with interminable slowness), I sat in the cramped yet sparsely furnished parlor of a widow of Perth Amboy; Mrs. Cavendish, a medium and spiritualist. The other people, seated on wooden chairs that creaked at every movement, clutched mementoes of their lost ones: a framed daguerreotype, a knitted scarf, neatly folded, a cloth doll with yellow silk ribbons for hair. I had brought nothing—I didn't know to do so—and, seeing there were no empty seats remaining, positioned myself near the doorway and didn't even remove my topcoat. I felt embarrassed, ashamed to be there, an educated man who should know better. But my wife's absence happened so suddenly—

such an intractable silence had descended on me—that I was desperate for any word, any sign from her.

We were escorted to another, slightly larger room, and gathered around an oval table, inlaid with marble, with one lit candle flickering in a silver holder in the center.

We shared brief reminiscences and Mrs. Cavendish nodded and quietly repeated everything we said, as if memorizing, but gradually, her eyelids drooped, her shoulders slumped forward. Suddenly, with a sharp, drastic inhalation she straightened, eyes wide, staring at the ceiling. We all gazed upwards, too. This, I learned, would become the pattern at every salon I attended, from Trenton to Raritan to Manhattan. Each evening ending the same way: heads cast back, staring at shadows wavering across the molding.

Seeing nothing.

Finally, in the cramped but well-appointed parlor of another widow, Mrs. Galindo of West Windsor, I gave up on ever hearing from Vivienne. As everyone stared upwards, gasping and tearful, I instead watched the steam from our teacups dissipate.

But Mrs. Galindo had pity on me. After everyone else had departed, she said, "You aren't looking for reassurance like the others. Comforting visions, and all that. You truly want to speak to her."

I nodded. "Yes."

She pursed her lips and shook her head. "No one here in the States can do that for you." She wrote a name, an address and a date on a slip of paper and slid it across the table to me.

I pulled a few folded bills from the pocket of my waistcoat.

"I can't take your money," she said. "You'll be helping me as much as yourself if you can do this. I owe this woman for the great talent she passed on to me." She gestured with a broad sweep of her hand, indicating the tribute her clients had left on the table: folded bills, pearl necklaces, silver pocket watches. "You may be what she needs and, more importantly, she can help you. Can you arrive in London, at this address, on this date?"

I glanced at the paper again. Nothing was preventing me from travelling there, or anywhere else. "Yes, I can."

"Look for me there and I will introduce you. But you must be present on this exact day and no other."

With little recourse left, I booked passage. Two weeks later, in a labyrinth of booths and tents sagging beneath the pelting London rain, I was granted this gift, such as it is. And thus my servitude began.

Tuesday, February 7, 1871 (later that day)

Late afternoon and I am already very tired, my knees quite stiff, but I endeavor to make one last visit. I sit on a bench in the center of the campus of the College of New Jersey, overlooking a brick courtyard encircled by squat, dour buildings of gray fieldstone. And simply wait.

My wife used to come to the campus often by herself: lectures in the afternoon, the student theater in the evenings. Sometimes, train trips with a ladies' auxiliary group to Pennsylvania or New York. She seemed to derive great joy from these outings. But I have yet to see her, despite the many hours I've spent here.

At home I collapse into my armchair and fall asleep, coat and scarf still on, until startled out of a disturbing dream by the sound of scuffling feet on my porch step. A multitude of hands had been reaching for me, grasping at me, but passing through me as if through mist. Befuddled, still mired in the dream, it takes me some time to reach the door.

No one is there. Squirrels, most likely. I remove my rumpled coat; my scarf is damp with sweat.

I put on the kettle and light the stove, then ponder for a moment. I return to the foyer and open the door so it's slightly ajar. Then I prepare two cups of tea, take them to the tiny kitchen table and sit and wait.

Nothing happens. Silent, empty moments pass. I pretend to have a conversation—as if she is there—but my voice sounds strange in the empty house. Not my own. I have difficulty now remembering what we used to talk about.

I close the front door and go my desk to record today's encounters. My final entry for the day—a supplemental note about Isaiah and his roving search for his family—fills the last line on the last page of the ledger. I close it and take it to the study.

The woman who Mrs. Galindo brought me to, in London, was the proprietress of some strange bazaar.

Go back home to America, she had said, *back to your university. Perform this inventory and you will find your wife.*

In times past, my study was a reliquary of solitude and comfort. I would sit in the armchair by the window and read Chaucer or Dickens by the lamplight. But no longer. I do not even glance inside the open doorway as I pass down the hall. My inventory fills an entire bookcase.

I complete this and she will appear to me? I had asked.

If not this one, she'd said, then the next. Or the next. Mrs. Galindo will fetch the inventory when you are done.

Now I slide the latest ledger into place and return to the kitchen, knowing a new blank one will be waiting there on the table for me.

Wednesday, February 8

I spotted her at last! On Witherspoon Street near the jewelry store. She was following a gray-haired man with a cane. This is a sight I have witnessed often: they frequently trail behind one person for hours at a time, not speaking or otherwise attempting to make themselves known, but gazing intently. I am certain it is Vivienne, even though she is already at the far end of the block. My eyes are still good, even if all else is failing me.

I take off after them at a quick trot, but this damned cough! I double over in the middle of the sidewalk, phlegm rattling in my throat, hands cupped over my mouth. Once it subsides, I steady myself against a lamppost, body shaking with each painful exhalation. People passing by glance at me, then hurry on.

A young woman in a green apron—from one of the shops presumably— approaches me.

"Sir? Are you well? Do you need to sit down?" She touches my arm.

At the soft press of her fingers through the thick wool of my coat, I turn away and wipe my mouth with one gloved hand. I have no handkerchief; each day when I leave the house, I seem to forget something new.

The young lady watches me, eyes wide with concern. Her solicitude feels like an affront. I am sure there is something I should say, some mild, self-deprecating joke.

"No, thank you," I mumble. "I am quite well." I escape her gaze, rushing down the street as best I can, but my wife is already gone.

● ◐ ◑ ○ ○ ◐ ◑ ◐ ●

In the evening I return and wait on the corner where I'd seen Vivienne. After two hours, my face is numb from the cold, and my breath rises in misty clouds beneath the streetlights.

A patter of quick, light footsteps approaches behind me. A little brown-haired girl, alone, draped in a red winter coat fastened at the collar by a gold stick pin. She looks like a Christmas ornament being blown down the street.

I turn my back to her and head home, her soft footsteps following at a short distance. She knows I've seen her, that I am capable of that, but I've had enough for one day and want only to take off my shoes and sit in my armchair with a cup of ginger tea.

I close the front door behind me without glancing back at her.

As I put the kettle on the stove, light tapping sounds on the front door. I dim the gas lamp and stand in the kitchen in darkness. After a few minutes, the tapping ceases. Faint muttering comes from behind the door, as though she is talking to herself. This is followed by long sniffling sobs, finally building to that high, piercing, anguished cry only a child can muster. It sounds as if she were suffering some unendurable physical pain.

Her cries are like daggers to my ears. Why must I be the only person to hear such things? Why must their suffering always fall on me?

I press my palms against the door panels as if that would stifle her. Short breathless gasps precede each cry. Small, booted feet stamp on the porch landing; a tiny, muted rhythm. I thought here at least, in my home, I could be free of them. I am weary and my bed and heavy wool blanket beckon, and yet, this encounter should be recorded.

I open the door a crack. The crying quickly subsides to whimpering. I hear a rustle of clothing. I open the door wide.

She has curled up on the bricks with her back to me, head cradled on her hands.

I crouch, joints popping, and ask, "What is your name?" No answer. Her face is hidden beneath a shock of brown curls.

Puzzled, I go back inside and put on my coat. When I return, she quickly buries her head in her arms again. While my back was to her, she'd obviously been watching me out of the corner of one eye.

With no idea of what else to say, I proceed to tell her a story from many years ago, about the day my wife and I took a surrey down to the Delaware River for a picnic. "We passed a field filled with so many flowers one could hear the bees buzzing from the roadside."

Presently, the girl sits up, yawns heartily, then curls up again and pretends to sleep. I cannot restrain a slight smile. This is merely an affectation, but an endearing one. For they do not sleep; that is a habit of the living. I rise and peer up and down the block, but the sidewalks are empty.

So they come all the way to my door now: this is a new development.

Thursday, February 9

The next morning I take a hansom cab to the train station at Princeton Junction and wait, ledger in hand. Vivienne perished near there, a mile north up the tracks, where an incoming train going much too fast caught up with the outgoing one—my wife's train—which was running far too slowly.

I have only gone to the site once and will never go back.

The policeman who had come to fetch me said she had been thrown from the train. "She didn't suffer, sir," he'd assured me, his hard stare beneath the brim of his cap fracturing with pity and discomfort. "It was quick."

Two other passengers had died as well, but the remaining ones survived— including a colleague of mine, a mild-mannered but pleasant professor of Greek and Roman history—albeit with various degrees of injury.

It was a mistake to come to the station now. Too many people, in seemingly perpetual and hurried transit.

Isaiah from the former sawmill was right. People move too quickly. Especially women. They are like sparrows, flitting nervously about. Their eyes casting to and fro but never fixing on one thing; their hands always moving, brushing loose strands of hair behind their ears, adjusting necklaces, gloves; fingers lightly touching temple, lips, throat. They look perpetually distracted, ready to fly off at a moment's notice.

Those souls I encounter are beyond the petty worries that dog the living. Their eyes are steady. They are easy to converse with. No secret words are required to hold their attention. Their hearts are open. I know if I could see my wife now—rather, *when* I see her—I would at last know how to talk to her. I cannot bring her back, but I cannot leave things as they have been, both of us mired in our singular miseries.

At the least, I will endeavor to grant her enough peace to move on.

Sunday, February 12

I stay in again today, unable to rouse myself except to transit from bedroom to kitchen and then my armchair. Hours pass unmarked. Finally, around mid-afternoon, I set down the newspaper and rise from my armchair, intrigued by an intermittent rustling from upstairs. A loose gutter, perhaps. I part the curtains to peer out the front window. No wind at all. The bare branches as still as if captured in a tintype. And beneath the elm trees that line the street, a dozen gray upturned faces. I'd not made my rounds in three days. I did not realize that they would seek me out.

Once more, the noise from upstairs. A rustling, then two light taps, followed by a thump. I climb the creaking staircase, pausing at the landing to let out a fit of coughing. Then I wait and listen. The entire upstairs is too silent. Someone is *trying* to be quiet. There are only three rooms on this floor. The washroom is empty, my bedroom as well. The third room I have not entered in years.

The iron hinges squeal when I open the door.

Over the lone window hang thin drapes, once white and sheer, now yellow and brittle. The room itself is nearly empty. At one time it was meant to be a nursery, but the only vestige of that ambition is the dust-shrouded wooden cradle pushed up against the far wall. The quilt is long gone and, in its place, stacks of old books. I step in and a familiar feeling comes over me, a sense of void. Much like the sense of absence one feels at the moment a strong winter wind that had been buffeting you suddenly ceases.

Out of habit, I announce myself in the usual manner. "Hello? I only want to speak with you for a brief moment. I mean you no harm."

The dust that coated the oak floorboards has not been disturbed, but of course that indicates nothing. Although they can affect some slight influence on the physical world, they rarely leave any sign of their transit. I cough again and wipe my mouth, recalling the tapping I'd heard from downstairs. I have heard that rhythm before, years past, along the sidewalks outside my window. From a children's game . . .

Oh, yes. Hopscotch.

I bend low—not an easy feat given the ramrod stiffness of my spine—to peer beneath the crib. "Hello, little one."

It is the girl from days ago, the one who'd appeared on my porch steps. She does not respond to my greeting. Only stares.

"You're not in any trouble. I'm not angry. But I must say I don't know how you gained entrance to my house."

"Your door was open," she whispers, after a while.

This is most likely true. I had been preoccupied and forgetful of late. I ask her name, her town of origin. I inquire about her kin. Grasping, I even ask what is her favorite color, favorite dessert, favorite animal.

She again falls silent and does not respond.

"You are even less of a companion than the ones outside," I sigh.

I return downstairs, feeling, I must admit, some unexpected disappointment that the child does not wish to speak with me. Surely one such as she, who must've perished, I would estimate, more than a century ago, would be eager to converse with anyone.

Eventually she comes down the stairs, gaze fixed on me. I ignore her and go about making dinner for myself, moving from counter to ice box to stove, a glimpse of red always moving out of the corner of my eye. After dinner, and all through the evening, there comes the whisper of small feet across the wooden floorboards, a sound never before heard in this house, though fervently wished for, once, a long time ago.

◑◑◐◯◯◯◑◑●

At that market in London years ago, in a tent reeking of spices and smoky oolong tea, as rain pattered on the canvas above our heads, the proprietress had handed me the first ledger. Madame Vera was a woman of unknown provenance; even Mrs. Galindo, our interlocutor, confessed herself unsure of her origins.

The ledger's title was embossed in gold on the brown leather cover. I'd immediately set it back down on the pile of books on the table from which she'd selected it.

"You don't believe this will suffice?" she asked, head cocked. I suspect she was far older than her appearance suggested; tall and thin, her skin smooth but drawn, face all sharp angles. Yet she had the grace and poise—the arched spine and elegant, flowing gestures—of an equestrienne or ballerina. A vestige, perhaps, of former days.

"Indeed, I believe you. I'm a rational man but I've seen enough at this place alone to realize there is more to the world than mere rationality. But if you, or someone else here, has the ability I'm seeking, why can't one of you simply come back to America and show her to me?"

She sighed and smiled patiently. "It doesn't work like that. And perhaps we aren't as talented as you believe."

"I have money, that's—"

"What you have is more valuable."

I frowned. "Absent money, I have nothing."

"I require something else. Your compassion."

An unexpected laugh escaped me, bitter and rattling, harsh as a sudden cough. "And yet, I have none. Except for my wife, but I fear she never knew.

· 201 ·

I could never quite summon the proper form of expression—That is to say, I didn't know how . . ."

She spoke over my equivocations. "Compassion for one person isn't compassion. It's merely self-grasping." She picked up the ledger and held it out again.

I looked at the title once more. *An Inventory of Ghosts.* "But I am only seeking one."

"There are many who could benefit from this undertaking, besides yourself."

"My wife is alone and needs my help. In spite of your misapprehension about me, I only care about her. Please put your book away."

"No one's ever really alone." Madame Vera flicked some invisible dust from the cover and presented the ledger to me again. "But everybody believes they are." Then she added, with an ageless and weary smirk. "Until it's far too late, of course."

Monday, February 13

The next morning the little girl has gone. I return alone to Witherspoon Street and sit for an hour and a half on a bench, shivering in the chill breeze. Then I see the man with the cane again, wearing a baggy camel-hair coat. And behind him, in her pale blue overcoat, following with a deliberate, measured gait, is my wife. Vivienne's gaze is fixed on him; she neither looks right nor left. Her shoulders are pitched forward slightly, as if she were about to fall into him.

I can only stare, open-mouthed. I have seen a father haunting his children from outside their bedroom windows. I have a seen a woman, the drops of bathwater from the tub in which she'd drowned herself perpetually streaming down her naked limbs, curled up on the steps of her former lover's new house. But no sight I've witnessed seemed as intimate as the manner in which my wife stares at this man. With such longing. I cannot even bring myself to call out to her.

They disappear around the corner.

I rise, knees popping, and follow them down a wooded side street of small apartments. The man struggles along with a tortured faltering stride, body pitching side to side, lame leg swinging. He wields his cane like a weapon, as if trying to keep the ground at bay.

He stops at last in front of a set of narrow steps, gripping the wrought-iron railing with his free hand. His fingers curl into hooks and he pulls himself up the steps. He unlocks the door and pauses at the threshold, head bowed. Fatigue, perhaps. His shoulders lift in a resigned sigh, and he vanishes into the shadows of the building. My wife, unnoticed, walking closely beside him. The door closes behind them; the lock clicks like a tiny bell.

I approach the steps. There are three brass mailboxes set in the wall beside the door, the tenants' names written in ink on slips of paper. One name faded, almost entirely. I lean forward and squint. I know this name, from years ago. My colleague from the university; the former professor of Greek and Roman history.

The man who had been in the same rail car, the same accident, as my wife. Of course.

●◑◐○○◐◑●

I walk without direction, head bowed, not stopping for any inquiries, even though their shadows tarry just outside my range of vision, attempting to make themselves seen. Some even call after me, their voices like a gale hissing across the tops of very tall trees. After a long while, I arrive at the campus. The grounds are quiet; classes are in session. A few students rush by, hands in pockets.

I find a small courtyard and sit on the granite bench there. A quiet spot, bordered on three sides by gray field-stone facades laced with ivy and interrupted by shutters of dark wood. Between the spires of the buildings, swollen gray clouds roll across the sky. A lone tree stands in the corner of the courtyard. With each passing breeze its branches claw at the window of the adjacent building.

An older couple strolls through the courtyard. I keep my head down until they pass. I think about my wife following the man in the camel-hair coat. The cold creeps beneath my overcoat but I do not stir, stunned by my miscalculation, my complete and utter ignorance.

A rustle of quick footsteps in gravel. The little girl in the red coat runs up to the bench and stops just to my right. She looks at me with that bold clear-eyed stare only children possess.

I look away and rub the weariness from my eyes. "Will you tell me your name today?" I finally ask.

She makes a game of hopping up and down over the gravel while bracing her hands on the edge of the bench.

I lean forward on my elbows and bury my face in my hands. The weight of lost sleep tugs on my eyelids. From beyond the courtyard comes the faint hum of the market on Nassau Street. When I open my eyes, the girl is kneeling at my feet and looking into my face. Her eyes are as gray and vacant as a puff of smoke. Then, assured that she has my attention, she crosses the courtyard, pausing once to look back and wave for me to follow.

I watch without moving. She waves again, somewhat impatiently. I rise and follow her out of the campus and towards a row of old stone buildings across the street. She climbs the steps of one house. At the top of the landing a heavy oak door stands ajar. She slips inside.

I push the door open onto a dark and narrow stairwell. The only light comes from beneath a closed door at the top of the stairs. As my eyes become accustomed to the dimness, I can make out the stairwell's peeling plaster walls, its steep stone steps.

She points at the stairs.

Oh. "You fell?" I ask.

She bites her lower lip and gazes about.

"You fell down the steps?"

She shrugs. Finally, she says, "My room doesn't look like my room anymore."

"I suppose it wouldn't. But what happened on these steps here?"

She lowers her chin to her chest, her face lost beneath the brown curls. "I was a horrid little girl."

"Who told you that?"

"My ma."

"Your mother was angry with you?"

"She didn't mean to do it."

For the first time since I began these inquiries for the inventory, I struggle for what to say. "I am sure she didn't," I say finally, though not sure at all.

"I was a horrid little girl." She kicks at the lowest step.

"What is your name?" I ask. "Please, I would like to know."

She looks up again and blinks at me. "Isobel."

"Do you want to go home, Isobel?"

She continues kicking at the lowest step, but with less vigor.

"Do you?"

"I am home."

"This has not been your home for a long time, I'm afraid. You understand that, don't you?"

I wait for as long as I think necessary, then descend the steps and push open the heavy oak door again. I have never had one of them as a companion, nor cared to. *Truly, you seem to have never cared for anyone*, my wife said on more than one occasion.

I turn and beckon with a wave of my hand. "Will you come with me now?"

The girl follows me out of the dark hallway and into the sunlight, looking directly up at it without blinking. She pauses once and looks back up at the steps, then down at the ground.

"I understand," I say. "I know I'm not very good company."

I leave, cross busy Nassau Street, then hobble down the quiet side street that leads to my house. Away from the jangle of carriages and the sing-song cries of the hawkers, taking care never to glance back.

I slow my stride until, finally, I hear her footsteps, skipping along the sidewalk behind me.

Once back at my house, Isobel heads directly upstairs to what she has now apparently claimed as her room.

I step cautiously down the narrow stairs that lead to the dark, damp cellar and poke around. I open musty boxes stuffed with children's books and wooden dolls and striped balls and blue blankets and pink blankets. We had never known if it would have been a boy or a girl and so purchased items in both colors.

Upstairs, in Isobel's room, I clear the long cradle of my books and spread out a small quilt. "There you are," I say, still trying to catch my breath.

She climbs in and lies on her back, folding her hands over her chest. I wince at the funereal pose.

"I'm going to sleep until the sun comes up," she says, closing her eyes. "And then tomorrow I will play with my new toys."

A few moments pass, then she opens one eye and peers up at me.

"Not sleepy yet?" I ask.

She shakes her head.

"Would you like to hear a story?"

She smiles. I select a book at random from the box I'd brought up. Something about young elephants in a circus. The delight in her eyes as I read catches me off guard, so I keep my gaze fixed on the page.

"I can really see it," she whispers.

When I finish, she stares at me patiently, waiting. I rub my chest and wince. I've never spoken aloud for such a sustained an amount of time. It is exhausting.

"Can you please read another?" she says at last.

"I'm very tired."

"Oh, please. Just one more."

I rise and pick through the box of books, and find *Cinderella*. As I read, I cannot refrain from peering over the pages to watch the emotions pass across Isobel's face: the wrinkle of concern on her brow for Cinderella's plight, the puzzled wonder at the fairy godmother and pumpkin carriage, and then, at the ending, a contented smile and a soft sigh.

I turn the last page, reach down and place the book on the floor. Something has changed; the silence altered. I glance upwards.

Isobel is gone. Not one wrinkle on the bed sheet.

I sit for a while in the empty room, then rise and shut the door behind me.

Any words I may say to my wife now would do no good. My chance passed a long time ago, when I could have wiped away the tears that streamed down her face but did not. "Why are you crying?" I asked, but she only bowed her head and pressed her hands over her mouth to stifle her sobbing. And I sat beside her, motionless, mystified. Hands lying uselessly on my lap.

Whatever she wanted from me was beyond my ken. I could not provide it because I could not understand it: the relentless void that want creates.

But I know it now. Want is what binds these seekers that fill my inventory. Want is what imprisons them in the empty and ever-tighter circles they haunt. Want is what draws them to me, as want drove me to search for them, through the neglected alleys, past looming factories that were once sawmills, down the narrow side streets crouching beneath the shadows of overhanging trees.

From downstairs, the slightest creak of the old floorboards. I've left the door open again.

The inventory is now complete. My wife wants nothing from me any longer. I will turn to the next blank page and sign my name, adding, *Service rendered and completed on the 13th of February, 1871.*

Then I will close this final ledger, climb down the steps and out into the wind and warmthless sunshine, and seek out those souls like me, who wander without knowing and want without end. And I will listen, and I will comfort them.

A Fox in the Rookery

by Naia Poyer

Marko's gaze followed the skinny grey cat as it scaled a dilapidated tenement across the alley. It flowed like a sooty cloud from window to rotting window. At each sill, the moggy paused to peer past torn lace or filthy rag curtains, examining each squalid interior. A wonder, the way that slight feline frame could counterbalance with violent tail-lashing, keeping itself aloft. Alternatingly graceful and awkward, and clearly searching for someone or something concealed from view on this disreputable London street.

"Oi, gyppo!"

Knuckles rapped the top of Marko's head, and he jumped.

"Make me repeat myself once feckin' more," said Finnegan, "and ye'll play a legless sheep, with no lines to overtax that rotten cabbage yer ma calls a brain."

Marko cowered theatrically, shielding his head with both hands. "Sara Kali! One more insult from your potato trap, bogtrotter, and you'll earn another Gypsy curse."

The tall, blond Irishman smirked down as the rest of the troupe chuckled. The Romany and Irish players indulged in such mutual volleying of affectionate insults as a small, private rebellion; a way to make light of the epithets and spitting that followed them through pubs, town squares, and lodgings. Anywhere their motley crew—who'd dubbed themselves simply 'The Wayfairers'—were doubly unwelcome.

"Now then," Finnegan continued, feigning aggrievement, "where *was* I? Ah, yes— blocking Scene Two. In my opinion we ought t' stage a scene from the monologue by Ishmael, King of the Gypsies—"

Patrin, an eighteen-year-old Rom six years Marko's senior, smirked in his direction, and began rattling off lines as if to prove he'd been paying attention.

"*Once more I return to this village where darkness befell our people. On this very spot, in years gone by, we pitched our gay tents. My daughter, Zella, was the sunshine of our—*"

"*Kushti*, Patrin," Marko's mother, who stood next to the young man, covered one ear and winced. Her English was fluent, though her unusual accent—a blend of flowing Romanes and strident Irish—tended to turn heads. "Yer projection's improving, at least. Finnegan, I understand fine city *gadjos* always require a quaint Gypsy or two in their melodrama, Saint Sara help us. But I'll cackle and paint my teeth with pitch no more. It's embarrassing nonsense, and the stuff tastes of shite."

Finnegan smiled and shook his head. "Nah, we'll forego the crone this time—winsome as yer crazed cackle is, Magda. This show's already replete with tinkers. The only role ye'll be takin' is Maria's bereaved mam. Though ye'll need to lighten up yer face with powder, and put on that curly blonde rug."

He ignored the sour twist this information brought to Magda's mouth.

"The Murder of Maria Marten" seemed a curiously low and out-of-fashion sort of play to be commissioned by an aristocratic lady. Though one thing was certain: they'd never had something so grand as a *patron* before.

Marko shot a glance back at the building across the alley. The cat was gone, having either climbed to the roof or breached an open window.

Turning back, his gaze crossed with that of Saoirse, Finnegan's sixteen-year-old daughter. She gave him a small smile, then looked back to her father. Marko's mind tended to wander when he had to sit still overlong. Saoirse helped him fill in the gaps later. He retreated back into thought, knowing he could rely on her.

Three days ago the Wayfairers had shunted their two dilapidated caravan wagons—one a rundown rattletrap of a Romany vardo—down London's spacious, modern New Oxford Road. The thoroughfare bisected the seething slum locals called the Rookery of St. Giles. They'd planned to spend the winter days busking for ha'pennies in the West End, and shelter in the Seven Dials by night. The location was strategic; pitching camp at the heart of central London would allow them to go wherever the money was.

But Marko hadn't anticipated what a rotten, stinking husk of a heart the City would show them.

That first night, the Irishmen had cleared a grimy alley of drunks and coiners, and made fast the valuables. Then the troupe gathered around a small cookfire to raise their spirits with music and dancing; the Irish and Romany players all agreed that nothing was better for the spirits than a song and a caper. When their new neighbors began to scream out of windows for them to shut up and shove off, they'd only laughed and played faster and louder, drowning out the complaints.

Afterward, a light snow had fallen, and Marko sat for a while on the wagon tongue, watching as thick pale flakes obscured the shambly slum and muffled its music of cries, moans, and drunken shouts. He'd caught a single icy crystal and watched it melt into the lighter skin of his palm. The cuff of his loose, cream-coloured sleeve was already attracting smut from the stinking London air. His sprightly blue vest had also dulled. Pondering the lean season ahead in this joyless midden, he'd taken comfort in watching pure whiteness limn the cobblestones like lather atop a tub of dirty laundry.

Until he'd spotted a tall, feminine shadow moving closer across the dully glowing snow.

As she'd neared their encampment his right hand strayed towards the little knife, hilted with carved antler, tucked into his vest's inner pocket. In the country, folk were often openly hostile toward outsiders. But that was preferable to the London custom of quietly slitting throats in back alleys.

She'd smiled as she drew near, bright teeth glinting against lips of dusky rose. Half her olive-skinned face was cast in shadow by the cowl of a black woolen manteau and Inverness cape. A long snake of thick black braid with reddish glints lay against her neck. He'd have thought her a Romni, a striking *chi shugra*, if her fine green-velvet gown hadn't denoted a fashionable lady of means. A few moments passed as she regarded him, unblinking. He'd stared back with not the slightest idea of what to say or do. The snowflakes crowding his lashes made the sight of her sparkle all the more.

"Good evening, dear boy." She said at last, her voice unexpectedly sonorous. "I wonder, might I impose—just briefly—upon the proprietor of your theatrical ensemble?"

"Er—no. I mean, yes! Yes, marm. That is, we've no boss as such, but Mam and Finnegan'll be the ones you're wanting to—" he'd blushed hot, icemelt trickling down his cheek like nervous sweat. Why did he feel like an idiot child in her presence?

"Splendid." She'd patted his shoulder with a kid-gloved hand, and swept past to knock on the vardo's painted red door. Abelard, the *vanna* usually hitched to Mam's caravan, knickered softly from their canopied shelter nearby. Next to him, the Irish cart-horse, Emmeline, had blown and stamped the cobbles. The restive beasts both craning their necks out into the snow to spy the visitor.

The Lady's meeting in the caravan with Magda and Finnegan had been brief and hushed, so Marko's attempts to eavesdrop failed. All the rest of the troupe had been told afterward was that a Madame Wolfe was arranging some sort of holiday festival in three weeks' time, and she'd commissioned a particular play. The price offered was so generous the Wayfairers could leave the city afterward, and live in well-fed idle luxury 'til springtime—and beyond! This news was met with few questions and much enthusiasm by all, save for Marko.

For, curious down to his bones, he'd stepped up to question the Lady as she emerged alone from the caravan and gently closed its flimsy door. Her dark gaze met his and she'd smiled, drawing from a pocket of her Inverness cape a small package wrapped in a black handkerchief.

"Ah, you're still here. Good. I trust this will prove edifying for you, Marko."

Then, before he could speak, she'd handed it to him and rejoined the darkness beyond the curtain of falling snow. Which seemed to have been obligingly waiting for her.

He'd closed his mouth, and removed the wrapping. A small red clothbound *Book of Common Prayer,* worn in spots from much handling, bookmarked by a strip of black-and-yellow cloth dyed in bold geometric patterns.

Marko's insides had gone suddenly cold as his numbed fingers. So: a wealthy, proselytizing do-gooder. Perhaps come to divert them from vagrancy and theatrics into a life in this slum as tithe-paying *gadjos.* To turn them into good English citizens, with walls to chain them and erode their *Romanipen* . . . or worse, she'd tried to buy the children. Assuming shiftless Gyppo parents would surrender them to a workhouse or factory for the right amount of British pounds.

His fingers had tightened on the faded red cloth. *My life, my freedom, can't be had at any price!*

He threw the book at the alley wall. The crack of binding on brick had given him the savage satisfaction of a cat biting through the neck-bones of a rat. Then he'd dashed for the warmth of the caravan.

Learning the Lady had requested "The Murder of Maria Marten, or The Dream of the Red Barn" hadn't eased his anxiety much. Nor had Magda's assurances that Madame Wolfe had mentioned neither the virtues of the Anglican Church, nor those of circumscribed city life.

"Then why does she want *us*?" he'd protested. "We're not Ebleys. We're nobodies. Our troupe can't possibly please the likes of her!"

The only answer he'd gotten was a stern look and a slap on the rear from Mam. And, in truth, he couldn't blame the adults for refusing to look deeper. Dangers abounded everywhere they traveled, sure enough, but this city was a dense thicket of thorns and prowling wolves. The extra coin could buy them a quick exit, banishing so many worries: illness, theft, violence, unpredictable neighbors.

So he'd held his tongue ever since.

It was Marko's job to carry the nightsoil buckets to dump in the gutters, mornings. That was when he saw the grey cat again, and nearly slopped the mess over his shoes. For the scruffy moggy was in the alley, crouched over the battered Book of Common Prayer Marko had chucked away the night before. Sniffing the dirtied binding and making guttural moans of distress.

"Shoo, puss!" Marko hissed, glancing around.

If Mam spotted the creature this close to the vardo she'd come waving a broom. For all that she'd learned to read against her husband's wishes, been shunned by their community, and now scorned most of the superstitions of her upbringing, she still recoiled from cats. "They're *mahrime*," she insisted. Unclean. She'd put her foot down when Finnegan proposed a cat to guard their flour and grain stores against vermin. "I'll not have a dirty beast inside the home!" had been her response. What she did not say then, but most likely thought, was that cats could also signal impending death.

This was not the only lingering superstition. She was preoccupied, too, with shame regarding her lower body. Marko noticed the whiteness of her knuckles when she clutched her skirts and swept them away from men who brushed carelessly by on the street. She'd only glared Marko down, though, any time he pointed out all the other 'impurities' they freely committed during their daily lives. Such as sharing possessions with the *gadje* members of the Wayfairers.

"Whisht, *chauv*," she'd scoff. "That's only being practical."

Marko loved animals too much to worry about a little impurity. He liked to feed and brush the cart-horses, Emmeline and Abelard. He only avoided petting cats or dogs within Mam's sight, to avoid her scrubbing his hands raw.

But this cat sounded distressed, possibly in pain.

Setting the bucket down, Marko glanced around once more, then slowly approached. The animal hissed and scrabbled back, then stood its ground pressed against the alley wall, hackles erect. Its orangey-yellow eyes flicked from Marko to the book, then back again.

"Sorry I frightened you, puss. Here, now. I'm a friend." He extended a hand, rubbing the fingers together, clicking his tongue invitingly. Most strays wouldn't respond, but perhaps a city cat was used to being fed scraps. Although, given the neighborhood, more likely it was accustomed to being chased for the stew-pot.

The cat shot him a disdainful glare. *Yes, you've ten fingers and can make noises. Well done, idiot,* it seemed to be thinking.

Giving up on making friends, Marko grabbed the abused tome and brushed off the cover guiltily. Books deserved gentleness just as much as did animals, be they dirty or pure.

A torrent of furious noise, part hiss and part yowl, erupted from the cat.

"Whoa there!" Marko yelped, taking a cautious step back. "What's the damage, moggy?"

Its gaze flicked again between him and the book. The patchy ears, which revealed a delicate tracery of veins, were notched all over from old battles. They trembled in agitation.

"What's a tatty old book to a mangy cat?" Marko wondered aloud.

The creature spat and gave an aggravated growl. And then, in strangely-accented human tones, it snapped, "Mine—insolent guttersnipe!"

Marko gaped. "What the . . . did you just . . . ."

The cat froze, pupils reduced to mortified pinpricks. It whirled away and bounded out of sight.

● ◑ ◐ ○ ○ ○ ◑ ◐ ●

Marko had more trouble than usual focusing on rehearsal that afternoon. He missed three cues and endured a lecture from Finnegan on the importance of learning his sides. Later, to feel useful, he joined Saoirse and Kezia, Patrin's younger sister, in touching up an old canvas backdrop of quaint country scenery. Saoirse was skillfully re-sketching the requisite red barn onto a distant hill with red chalk, while Kezia filled in faded patches of colour. No artist himself, Marko set about filling in the grassy fields. But his gaze kept drifting past where Lugan and Emmett sat tuning their instruments, to the windowsills of the tenement next door. Or toward the corner where alley met street. He couldn't decide if he hoped or feared to spot the flick of a grey tail.

"Marko!"

He flinched.

A shriek of laughter from Kezia. "You've plowed under a whole cow, *dinlow*."

Siaorse frowned, licked her index finger and rubbed at the smear of green paint covering the cow's haunches. "What's going on in that vazey head? Stop helping 'til ye've at least woken up."

He considered confiding in them about book and cat, but didn't think he could bear to hear Saoirse laugh and call him mad. And Kezia . . . she always made him feel like a child. Besides, what if he'd daydreamed the whole thing?

He certainly couldn't go to Mam. Magda would think he was mocking her superstitions.

Marko sighed. "Sorry. Need some air, and . . . to study my sides."

But the streets of St. Giles were so grimy and stinking he felt he was choking on that same air, as many of the locals with hacking coughs seemed to be doing. He doubted a single soul in the parish could boast a clean bill of health, judging from the broken windows, turds, and horse-droppings in the streets. Not to mention fog and a persistent rising damp.

To live in "The Rookery" of Seven Dials meant scuttling termite-like through a honeycomb of dead-end streets, filthy courts, and narrow, covered alleys with barely any view of the sky. It must've felt claustrophobic even for lifelong city-dwellers. Marko had been horrified to learn from a vendor totting rags that, prior to the cutting of the nearby New Oxford Street through the one-time heart of St. Giles, there'd been only one way in or out of this rabbit-warren. The inhabitants, snidely called 'rooks,' lived like a neglected flock shut up in the mews, left among their droppings to starve and fight and die.

Wealthy toffs, the rag-and-bone man claimed, preferred to think the slum a thing of the past. But chopping the parish in two had only crowded the poor closer together at its outer edges.

Since the Wayfairers now had a performance to prepare, they'd no time to escape to the nicer parts of London and busk. Instead, they rehearsed in the same dank alley most of each day, taking it in turns to run errands—in pairs, whenever possible—for a change of scenery. Marko had learned to watch out not just for pickpockets and belligerent doxies with rotten teeth and aggressive cleavage, but for near-collisions with staggering rumdums.

"Mind the grease," bellowed a jaundiced man with a toothless strumpet tucked under one arm. Marko hugged the nearest wall to avoid them. They staggered past, the doxy's hysterical laughter quickly fading into the general din of shouting, singing, fucking, coughing, and the hawking of goods.

Even at noon he walked in shadow; the dilapidated tenement houses leaned inward to form an ugly bower blocking the sun. Some had been carelessly constructed of cheap flaking brick. Others, defunct townhouses, still flaunted traces of wealth through a century's grime and coal dust. Above a door to the left was a bas-relief carving of fruit-laden cornucopiae; across the street a curtain of rags draped a fancy mullioned window long denuded of panes. Abruptly a woman leaned out, loose shift hanging nearly to her waist, and vomited thin yellow bile down the building's cracked façade.

Marko had more than once imagined getting his first glimpse of bare breasts, but this wasn't quite what he'd pictured. Little wonder the English liked to say the Great Plague had started here.

If he could only get up a little higher, perhaps he'd catch a cleaner breeze.

He spotted a crumbling brick wall that must've once been part of a great house, and scrambled up to perch on the lowest spot. Here, a rare slice of sunlight draped his shoulders like a friendly arm. Sucking down a breath of less-fetid air, he pulled a set of rolled pages from his pocket. Then settled in to study the play, idly swinging his leather-soled boots.

Skimming for his cues and lines, Marko huffed in annoyance. Even setting aside the absurdity of gangly, spotty Patrin playing a wise and respected 'Gypsy king,' his Ishmael character went on interminably. Whereas Marko's role, the Ghost of Ishmael's daughter Zella, said nothing save "Beware, beware," and "Maria . . . Maria . . ."

Still, he grew absorbed in the story. It had a bit of everything: seduction, murder, intrigues, prophetic dreams—and of course, the mystical Gypsy nonsense that gave his mother headaches. Unsurprisingly, not until a *gadji*— the titular Maria, a beautiful white girl—was killed did the villain come to justice. The Gypsy King's unfortunate daughter Zella had been despoiled and murdered before the play even began.

But Marko found neither Maria's family nor the Gypsy clan terribly sympathetic. The *gadje* Martens were ignorant and passive, while Ishmael and the Gypsies were willing to let innocents die in order to expose Zella's killer. Blazes, Ishmael actually sold Corder poison, then watched the man administer it to his own infant daughter!

Ishmael reasoned, *She is not one of our people. And what mercy has the white race ever shown us? Have they not driven us from their villages, spat on, chained, and imprisoned us?*

While true, it left a bad taste in Marko's mouth. There was little nobility of spirit to be found in depictions of his people—only a great many offenses taken, revenges plotted, and curses given.

An ash-coloured streak drew his gaze. Now, on the corner of the same crumbling wall, not three meters away, sat a skinny grey moggy. Watching him.

Marko held his breath. Could this be the talking feline he was half-convinced he'd dreamed? Plenty of strays in every shade hunted these rat-infested alleys.

"Here, puss." His hand shook slightly as he held out a strip of dried rabbit, still warm from riding in his vest pocket. The perfect orange globes of the cat's eyes remained fixed on his face. Its posture erect and expectant. Certainly looked like the same cat. Same notched ears, same black lips with the yellow tips of canine teeth peeking out.

He set the meat on a single loose brick, as far as possible from himself. The creature's gaze flicked down, pink tongue darting out. It half-rose from its haunches, as if about to take the bait. Then gave an abrupt, sharp shake of the head and sat back down.

"Do you . . . truly speak, then?" Marko asked, feeling a complete nump.

The cat only lashed its tail, sending up a small cloud of brick dust.

Remembering the *Book of Common Prayer*, Marko drew it from the satchel. The tail-lashing grew fiercer. The creature emitted a growl like the rumble of cart wheels on cobblestones.

Was the object of its displeasure something about the book, or his maltreatment of it? Cat fixed in his peripheral vision, he gingerly opened to the spot marked by the colourful scrap of cloth. The pages were fragile, translucent, and made a dry whisper as they turned. Their elusive odor, something like beeswax and old furniture polish, tickled his nose. Clearing his throat, Marko chose a passage that had hand-inked annotations, and read just loudly enough for himself and his companion to hear.

"For the poor and the oppressed, for the lonely and the destitute, for <u>prisoners and captives</u>, and for all who remember and care for them, let us pray to the Lord. For deliverance from violence, oppression, and deg—degradation, let us pray to the Lord. For <u>our missing sisters,</u> let us pray to the Lord. That we may end our lives in faith and hope, without suffering and without reproach, let us pray to the Lord."

Marko paused. The cat's tail was still, but now its eyelids were closed, chin tucked to chest as if . . . yes, praying.

A moment later it opened them; its fiery gaze met his. "It is good to be read to, since these damned animal eyes seem to grudge me that pleasure. That prayer you read . . . it was mine, on the last day of my life."

The cat ignored the plummeting of Marko's jaw. Gazing upward, it began to unspool a story. As the creature spoke, its dainty pink tongue struck an odd contrast to the deep musical voice with its staccato rhythm.

Marko held his breath and listened.

"There was once a man. Named Sukuba Koroma. A man of God, and of the Limba people. Hailing from Sierra Leone." At a quizzical look from Marko, he added, "On the west coast of Africa."

"His mother's bestowing of a name meaning 'my one and only hope' left him . . . a burden of responsibility she could not have foreseen. He grew up in a small village in the Wara Wara mountains, yearning to save the world. At maturity he moved to the port city of Freetown and became a preacher in the Methodist faith. Full as it was of liberated slaves from England, Freetown taught him a certain disdain for the old ways of his village. In time, he returned to it, meaning to exert a . . . civilizing influence. He thought to bring a gift, yet calamity dogged his steps.

"Back home, his evangelizing was rejected by the matriarchs of the Bondo society, who were entrusted with initiating the village girls into womanhood. Their rites, conducted in utmost secrecy, included unspeakable mutilations to 'purify' females. To make them docile for future husbands. When driven from his birthplace by those matriarchs, he absconded with four girls on the cusp of womanhood—scheming to get them an education and a better life in Freetown. Sukuba viewed himself as a noble savior, and they believed in him. But he failed them."

The cat's voice rose higher with emotion. Marko shot a nervous glance toward the street below. But the passersby appeared either drunk, immersed in phlegmy fits of coughing, or busy watching the muddy ground for broken glass and excrement. Each insulated in a personal bubble of misery.

"He intended to send them to school," the cat added, self-contempt in his voice. "Get them placed in good homes, when they'd reached Freetown. Instead he kept them with him because they reminded him of home. But a church is not a fortress, and one day he returned to find the girls missing.

"They'd been lured away by an Englishman named Liam Foxcroft. His ship, a merchant vessel carrying palm oil, sat in port for a week with those young women trapped in its belly while Sukuba fruitlessly searched. By the time he learned the truth, it had sailed for England.

"He found passage on another ship, and followed their trail to London, excoriating himself for being careless with their lives. Why had he not tried harder to reason with the elders, to change their culture from within? His playing at God had taken these innocents from a grim situation into one of abject horror . . . for with slave-owning abolished in England, their passage would be secret. Their fate doubly sinister."

Si-ni-stah, his accent made it, which for some reason sent an extra chill down Marko's spine.

"And . . . what fate was that?" Marko ventured.

The cat's gaze of molten gold burned into his. "Foxcroft means to profit by selling their bodies to English men seeking the exotic."

Marko nodded, feeling his face heat. "And this . . . Sukuba Koroma?"

"I am he. Or rather, I was."

"But . . . how?"

The cat's narrow chest heaved in a sigh. "If only I knew. Perhaps this changed form was a curse set upon me by the Bondo matriarchs. But the *cause* of the transformation—my death—was not at their hands."

Marko gaped. "Your *death*?"

The cat tilted his head. "Oh, yes, dear boy. I was murdered. But how rude of me—I haven't even asked your name."

After introductions, the creature seemed hesitant to continue. He regarded the street, then jerked his head up to watch a dove fly past; movements both dignified and feral.

Marco said gently, "Are you all right . . . Reverend? Is that what I should call you?"

"No!" the cat replied sharply. "Rather . . . call me Preacher," he added in a softer tone. "For I have preached much, yet understood little."

Had the cat prepared that self-abasing retort during his long hours alone? They sat in awkward silence a few moments. Preacher's eyes seemed never to be still, gaze flicking from person to person on the crowded street.

"You're looking for someone, then?"

"I am."

"The Englishman—Foxcroft?"

"Yes. Around here, I've learned, he's seen quite often. They call him the Dogfox."

Marko had never heard the name. "Erm, why?"

"For his cunning."

"Oh. Right." After another moment, he added, "D'you want this jerky then?"

Preacher gnawed the tough strips of rabbit, crouched low to the brick, tilting his head to chew with one side of his mouth, then the other. Morsels of meat dropped to the bricks along with strings of the hungry beast's saliva.

"I s'pose you told me all this because you want my help, some way or other."

Preacher glanced up and quirked thin lips. "Smart boy."

Marko picked at the hem of his vest where a frayed spot needed mending. "I'd like to help, but dunno what I can do. The watchmen're like as not to cuff me 'round the head and spit on me as listen to a word I've got to say."

Preacher convulsed, making a choking sound Marko first took to signal a hairball. "Pin my hopes on sending you to those body snatchers?" The cat guffawed again. "No. Even were you respectable—beg pardon—there's no use going to a constable. Perhaps I neglected to mention it, but the man I'm seeking is Police Constable Liam Foxcroft."

Marko's stomach flipped. If that were true, this cat—no, man—was well and truly up the flue. He suddenly regretted making its—his—acquaintance. Moreover, just as disbelief had yielded to the reality of the cat's existence, acceptance was now turning to suspicion. Imagine what Mam would say to all this! Visions of demons and trickster spirits seeped into his thoughts like muck through cracked old shoes. Plainly the talking part was real. But that didn't prove him *not* a liar. After all, bloodsucking striga could shapeshift into animals, and they could also be those who'd died of curses. What demon was he sitting here breaking bread with? Perhaps Mam'd been wise to warn him away from cats, after all.

As if Preacher sensed he was losing Marko, he said all in a rush, "Certainly it would be a risk, but I've located the girls, learned the Englishman's comings and goings. I need only a clever set of hands to help me set them free."

Yes, my brave lad—follow me into this dark cellar. There's pretty damsels to rescue and honor to be won. I certainly shan't be gnawing on your bones in the dark tonight.

Marko began to rise, brushing brick dust from his backside and avoiding his companion's eyes. Never mind that it was a crowded street in broad daylight. Surely a creature of darkness could hunt in St. Giles, day or night.

He must get back to Mam and Finnegan and the Wayfairers, the safety of their commingled wisdom that guarded against the gamut of evils. And hope with all his might he hadn't just supped with the Devil.

"Wait!" Preacher bolted up too. "Time is wasting, and the Dogfox nearby. You don't know what they endure."

"I don't," Marko grunted as he clambered down and onto the street. "And I'd like to keep it that way, Old Scratch!"

The cat hit the cobbles behind him with a thump. But Marko was already off and running, dodging drunks and beggars, a frustrated yowl following at his heels. He turned into a narrow alley, glancing back to see if he'd lost the beast, and fetched up hard against an unyielding body. He fell backwards, bruising his tailbone on slimy cobbles.

"Piss off, you little ratbag," snarled the man.

Blond and good-looking, he almost resembled David, one of the Wayfairers' Irish chavs. But well-groomed and robust, with a neatly-trimmed beard and stylish waxed moustache, he looked supremely out of place in the Rookery. Especially with that blue coat, with its polished copper buttons. . . .

A constable! Marko's heart sank as cold green eyes pinned him to the ground. A dirty old cove struggled in the copper's grip, spitting blood. Flecks hit Marko's face as he scrabbled backwards. In the dimness, the two were framed before a heavy door painted with flaking red.

Forgetting Marko already, the man turned back to his prey. "You'd never've touched that door if you'd a scrap of sense," he heard the Bobby snarl.

The thud of the officer's billy club drowned the man's feeble cries. "I'll put your lights out for good!" was the last Marko heard as he fled.

It was the first time he'd ever seen a copper in Seven Dials. The constable must be green to bother over a trivial breaking and entering on Gin Lane. Either that . . . or he'd just encountered the Dogfox in the flesh.

Two weeks later, on the evening of their final rehearsal, Marko took a deep breath and opened his throat as the band played Zella's warning song. His voice, still clear and high enough to pass as a girl's, echoed from the close alley walls.

Do not trust him, gentle lady
Though his voice be low and sweet
Heed not him who kneels before thee
Sweetly pleading at thy feet
Now thy life is in its morning
Cloud not this thy happy lot
Listen to this Gypsy's warning
Gentle lady, trust him not!
Heed the girl who fell before thee
Gentle lady, trust him not!

Letting the echoes linger a moment, he glanced at Emmett, the musical lead, for approval. The middle-aged harpist winked, freckles reflecting in the polished arch of his cláirseach. Marko had finally stopped substituting "praying" for "pleading" in the fourth line. "She ain't the bleeding Virgin Mary, ye pikey dunce!" Emmett'd needled him last time. To which Marko replied, hands clasped in mock rapture: "As you'd know, being an eternal virgin yourself."

The troupe had fallen about in laughter for some minutes.

But, Sara Kali be praised, he'd finally gotten it down on the eve of their final rehearsal, a fortnight since his run-in with the demon cat and the hard-eyed constable. And the performance at their patron's mysterious fête would be tomorrow. At least Marko hadn't been the only one crutching along 'til the last moment. David, the chav playing William Corder, had spent so much time in the gin shops in St. Giles, he'd been no further along with his lines.

Marko had felt too knackered with rehearsals to dwell on the Lady's strange gift, her true intentions, or even the chatty moggy with its tales of murderous mutton shunters and exotic damsels in distress. Truth be told, when he did think of it, Marko patted himself on the back for twigging the supernatural danger. Even if he'd initially been captivated by the yarn.

As the players packed props in the wagons, a rough voice slurred with drink turned their heads toward the mouth of the alley.

"Oi, you lot!" A man swayed there, bottle of gin hanging loosely at his side. He propped one shoulder against the brick wall as he took a long pull.

"Ya, ya's, erm. . . ." He frowned from the freckled faces of the Irish to the dark ones of the Roma, clearly groping for an epithet that would cover such mixed company. Outsiders abounded in St. Giles, but that hardly seemed to dissuade the English rooks from asserting their one claim to superiority.

". . . ya *bumpkins*," the man concluded weakly. "Didja 'ear? Someone did for one of you darkies. Gutted like a pig she were, an' dumped naked in the gutter by Little S'nt Andrew's. Saw the entrails. C'ndolences," he slurred, drawing out the word with a nasty leer. "Used t'be a pretty thing, judgin' from what was left."

The man took a long pull from the bottle. The Wayfairers exchanged uneasy glances. They steered clear of the rooks when possible, the men taking turns at night to guard the wagons against would-be robbers and rapists. But there were always those who couldn't leave well enough alone.

"What's he on about?" Mam whispered to Emmett. "A dark girl, just now killed? *Dordi,* but Kezia's been out to the butcher—"

Emmett glanced uneasily around and lowered his voice, though Marko could still hear. "It's not Kezia, Magda. I heard the craic outside that lushery on

Church Street. Some lass was killed and dumped in the street. Maybe last night. But word is, she was an African."

Marko's stomach lurched. Death was not uncommon here, even murder. But a young African woman, murdered so soon after Preacher's plea for help?

So the story was true, he thought. *And I ran away from him.*

"Are ya deaf-mutes too, ya paddies and crows?" shouted the tippler. "Buck up! Dogfox's cleanin' up the neighborhood for us, and givin' you lot one less worthless mouth to feed."

Finnegan leapt up, kicking his stool over. "Is that right, rusty guts? I wager your Mam'd buck up too if I did her the favor of smashing your head in. Feck off, ye living miscarriage." The big Irishman's face was scarlet with rage.

The giggling drunk swayed back toward the street. He chucked the empty bottle over one shoulder, and glittering green shards skittered towards the players' feet. Magda wrapped her arms around Finnegan's waist—to hold him back or comfort him, it was unclear which. Marko caught Siaorse's eye, and they quickly looked away from their parents' vulnerability.

Dogfox, the drunk said. Corroborating Foxcroft's reputation among the rooks. It had been a terrible mistake to dismiss Preacher's story.

"I'm—I'm going to fetch home Kezia." Marko fled without bothering to change out of Zella's costume, with its long black wig and ghostly white skirts.

The fabric caught at his ankles as he dashed towards New Oxford Street, dodging elbows and jumping the dirty feet of tramps dozing on muddy cobbles. The foul, smoky air tore at his throat. Most likely Kezia was alive and well, but if the murdering brothel-bully was out there, a girl of fourteen shouldn't be walking alone.

A creature of darkness could hunt in St. Giles, day or night.

It was true, Marko realized grimly. Just not how he'd thought.

He stumbled to a stop then. For across the narrow street walked Kezia, head held high, haughtily watchful. One hand rested on her hip, near the *chiv* concealed in her sash. The other gripped the necks of two plucked geese, fresh from the butcher. As Marko watched, a ragged youth approached her, raking girl and birds with a hunger-bright gaze. Kezia halted, fixing him with a hard glare. Touching the pendant at her throat, she stage-muttered some nonsense, as if casting a spell. The boy stepped back, staring into those dark, kohl-rimmed eyes under the scarlet headscarf . . . then hurried away.

The held breath left Marko in a tide of relief. Of course Kezia was fine; her life before joining the troupe had been a harsh lesson in self-reliance. Suddenly embarrassed he'd run here without changing, Marko ducked into the nearest blind alley before she spotted him. It was that or endure merciless ribbing for it the rest of his days.

He recognized this spot: the alley where he'd seen the copper beating a ragged beggar. And the red door, now hanging open. Its brass knob and latch—saleable metal that'd likely attracted the old cadger—were now missing. Had Marko encountered Liam Foxcroft that day, guarding his secret brothel? If so, where were the girls now—save, of course, the one found disemboweled in the gutter that morning?

You'll keep away if you've got any sense. . . .

He turned from the unsettling memory, hurrying away, back toward the bustle of Church Street. But his foot came down on something soft. The high-pitched scream that followed nearly made him piss his trousers.

"You've trod on my bloody hand, boy!"

He looked down at a cat, tail puffed out, one forepaw held in the air.

"It's you!" Marko gasped. The grey moggy must've dashed out from the open door.

"Thought I recognized you under that preposterous getup," the cat huffed. "Listen, you may still think me a liar, but I've brought you proof." Preacher scrabbled at his front leg, where a strip of cloth was crudely tied. After the cat struggled a moment, Marko hiked his skirts and bent to help. The scrap was of some exotic fabric: blue, white, and rusty red, with a design of fan-shaped leaves.

But on closer inspection, the red was not part of the original pattern.

It was a large bloodstain. Startled, Marko dropped the fabric.

"Foxcroft has done all I feared, and worse . . . slaughtered Thakande like an ox and humiliated her in death."

"I heard," Marko gasped. "What happened?"

"When I discovered the girls imprisoned behind this door, I smuggled in a knife. A little thing nicked from the butcher. Foxcroft must've found it and . . . all I know is, I tried to help and now she's dead. I've again made everything worse! He moved the others, and now I've lost them."

Preacher shook his head violently. "I've done all I can alone, at least in this useless form. Please, there is no more time!"

If cats could cry, surely the dirty tracks at the corners of those feline eyes were made by bitter tears.

"I—I'm so sorry for your loss," Marko murmured. "But why me, for pity's sake? I ran away, calling you the Devil."

Preacher huffed, "Do not mistake me. I mostly need you simply for your opposable thumbs. But out of every wretched soul in this rookery, I chanced speaking because you seemed decent. Perhaps I foolishly took it as a sign, you holding my *Book of Common Prayer*. Regardless, every other wretch I've encountered has either kicked me, thrown bottles, or tried to have me for Sunday dinner!

"But I know—oh, indeed how I know—I'd have even worse luck with the swells outside our walls. Not only would they spit on me, call the dog-catchers, or lay down poison—they'd never believe a constable, their protector and defender, capable of such evil."

Marko compressed his lips. It *did* make sense. A rook would've scorned whatever wasn't edible or shiny, and never've given Preacher an opening. The prayer book would've been pawned at the earliest opportunity, and quickly forgotten.

He thanked his stars to have been born on the Road. The comforting rocking of the vardo; the smell of wildflowers in different seasons; swirling patterns made by colourful skirts as women kicked their heels to fast-paced fiddling 'round a big fire; the warm glow of embers, escaping to become stars in the wide, cold sky . . . these luxuries created in one's head a quiet space. A haven reserved for thoughts beyond mere survival.

All at once he felt ashamed of his disdain for the benighted of St. Giles. And of his dismissal of Preacher's tale as fiction devised to ensnare. Though he'd never seen a shapeshifting, bloodsucking monster for real, he'd glimpsed human ones and the damage they did . . . in real life and on the stage. He thought again of Ishmael, the closest example he'd seen to a heroic Gypsy character—who nevertheless would watch an infant murdered because it was not of his own.

In truth, Zella was the more heroic. Only a wraith, dead before the curtains parted, but the only one who tries to warn Maria. Committed not to revenge, but to preventing more bloodshed. *See, Maria, my name and his carved together on this tree. A timely warning for maidens such as thee. . . . Maria, do you see?*

But not one other character sees. Her efforts come to naught, in the end, for she remains invisible all.

This must be just how Koroma felt. Stripped of all power, fighting to save lives that, seemingly, he alone cared for. Worse, he placed the blame on his own skinny shoulders.

"*Please.*" Preacher pawed at Marko's muddied skirt. "We can still catch him up now, and follow him."

Marko started. "Foxcroft's nearby?"

"*Yes*, the matter is urgent! He's been tailing some girl who looks not unlike yourself. I—why *are* you wearing a frock, by the way? And surely your hair wasn't always that long?"

Marko ignored the heat rising in his cheeks and rose from his squat, shaking mud from his hem. "Oh, *dordi*. So he *is* following Kezia. Let's go!"

"That's what I—never mind, *let's*."

●◑◐○◐○◑◒●●

The copper's uniform of smart blue wool wasn't hard to spot in the throng. The buttons he must polish daily, for they flashed at the wrists as if his hands could wield fire. Kezia, ahead by a block, seemed unaware of him.

Bystanders sober enough to notice hung back, darting fearful glances while pretending not to see the predator in their midst. Two pockmarked girls, who'd been offering to bare their breasts for a ha'penny, abruptly threw on shawls and tried to look virtuous.

They needn't have worried. Foxcroft's attention was fixed on Kezia.

"We've got to draw his attention away," Marko mumbled.

"But," Preacher hissed, "If he loses his quarry, he may not lead us to his safe-house!"

Marko chewed on his lower lip, uncertain. He wanted to help Preacher, but wasn't about to use Kezia as bait. Impatiently, he batted away strands from the long black wig that kept falling into his face.

Then he paused, as a new idea took hold.

"We mustn't lose him!" Preacher hissed.

"We won't." Marko broke into a run. "I'll serve well enough for bait."

●◑◐○○○◐●●

"Excuse me, Sir?" Marko's voice shook as he strove to maintain an innocent, feminine tone.

The constable wheeled at the tug on his sleeve and snapped, "What in blazes do you want?" His clean-shaven cheeks were pink from the brisk walk, the heavy brow furrowed in irritation. His green eyes shone feverishly. The moment he took in Marko, however, his features assumed a placid, friendly expression.

The shocking facility of the change sent acid creeping up Marko's throat. "I—got separated from my brother, Constable. Might you help me find him?"

"Why not simply return home and wait?"

"I can't, Sir." Marko bit his lip and looked away, twisting fear into theatrical sadness. "We've no home *dandi* . . . Mam and Da have gone to God." He tucked a strand from the wig, a tangled mess by now, back into the white kerchief.

With the state of his clothes and hair, he must appear indeed a wretched immigrant orphan. A wounded rabbit-kit to the cunning Dogfox. He only hoped he didn't seem too childlike to arouse interest.

"Sorry to hear it. What's your name, pet?" The bobby rummaged in his breast pocket, then crouched down a bit to offer his handkerchief.

Bloody ridiculous overacting. Only the naivest bumpkin would credit such kindness between constable and dirty urchin. But Marko must play exactly that—easy victim. Letting a bit more Romanes slip into his accent, he said, "M-Maria. You will help a friendless Romni, Sir?"

A wide smile spread across Foxcroft's face, exposing slightly pointed eye-teeth. Marko needn't have worried over his age. The Dogfox was practically slavering.

"Why, of course I will, Maria! A pretty name for a pretty child. First let's get you to a safe lodging-house, where you can rest while I locate your brother."

"Bless you, Sir!"

"It's merely what I'm here for." Foxcroft smirked down as he took Marko's arm.

As they walked, the constable attempted to make light conversation. But Marko barely answered, bogged down in anxious thoughts. Fortunately, Foxcroft seemed to take silence for acquiescence. They headed north, toward New Oxford Street and the British Museum, making turns more frequently than seemed necessary.

He tried to commit each street to memory. He'd expected to be steered to another decaying rowhouse in Seven Dials. Instead, his throat constricted as their surroundings grew cleaner, the streets wider, their cobbles in better repair. He'd been glancing back every so often to make sure Preacher was still tailing them, but for some blocks now he'd not seen a whisker.

Foxcroft cut off his tumbling thoughts. "So then, Maria. You are a Gypsy?"

"I—yes. We come from Românja."

"Fascinating. And would you say you possess what the Gypsies call the 'pure, black blood'?"

Marko stared, unable to make sense of this question.

Around them, the elegant townhouse facades began to sprout ornate urns of roses. Foxcroft kept going. "D'you know, there's great interest in you people among the learned of London. The traditions, the lore. That unique, peripatetic way of life. It fascinates men of letters and culture, tickles their fancy for the exotic."

"Is not an easy life, sir, begging your pardon. Perhaps they should look to their own blessings."

"Oh, I agree. I'd take the life of an idle gentleman over pissing in the woods and rutting in horse-carts any day—pardon my vulgarity." But he didn't look contrite. A brittle smile twitched the corners of his mouth. His eyes kept flicking over to gauge the reaction to his words.

Marko fixed a look of polite discomfort on his face and kept walking.

"We did have that, for a while. My family," Foxcroft continued. "Not that I was grown in time to enjoy it, though I've dreamed of restoring our wealth and lands . . . But I digress. There are many well-heeled gents who enjoy slumming it, so to speak."

"Sir, this boarding house is much farther? It is cold, I have no coat."

Foxcroft offered neither answer nor assistance, but took firmer hold of Marko's arm as if to support him.

"Here's a titillating fact. In order to join the Gypsy Lore Society—a gathering of open-minded gentlemen—one must, as a prerequisite, make a conquest of a pure Gypsy woman." The pad of Foxcroft's thumb pressed into Marko's wrist, where he must've felt the frenzied drumbeat pulse.

Marko swallowed hard, fighting the urge to flee. He'd knowingly entered this trap, but as its jaws closed his marrow buzzed with fear. Foxcroft seemed to sense this; from his grin he was enjoying it immensely.

"Here we are. The Magpie Inn!" The constable gripped Marko's shoulder, turning him to face a stately white townhouse, with a bird in flight graven in pink marble above the lintel. It bore no other sign, as would a proper inn.

Marko flinched away, scanning the street for Preacher. He saw only well-dressed ladies and gents, their servants and coachmen. Most ignored Marko and the constable, though a couple of older matrons smiled and nodded. Whether they saw one of Her Majesty's finest bestowing charity or meting out justice, he couldn't tell. He and the constable were perhaps only part of the pleasant scenery, much like the primroses lining a wrought-iron fence. After all, the blue coat with its shiny copper buttons signified all was as it should be.

"Shall we?" Foxcroft guided him towards the steps.

"I—I—I feel unwell!" Marko burst out. "I need air." Now was the moment to break Foxcroft's feverish grip and sprint as fast as his skirts would allow. He'd give the location to that thrice-damned cat and never lift another finger for him.

But as he turned, his leather-slippered foot was blocked by the bobby's steel-toed boot, sending him tumbling. Foxcroft caught Marko's arms with bruising force and hoisted him back to his feet, laughing merrily. As if he hadn't just intentionally tripped a girl-child.

"Whoa there, little miss! Let's get you inside. You seem near to swooning." He stepped between Marko and the open street, then, shielded from view, delivered a hard, precise jab between his shoulders.

As the boy's nerves raged with fiery pain, he was vaguely aware of being carried up the steps like a bride across a threshold. Then, all was black.

◗◑◐○◐○◐◑◗

When he came to, Sara Kali's visage floated above him. The saint's red-brown eyes glowed like embers in a round face framed with black curls. Her kind expression flooded him with relief. Somehow or other, he'd been saved.

He instinctively began to whisper a prayer: "Holy Sara, Mother and Queen of the Gypsies, remove all evil and storms. . . ."

He trailed off as the saint's forehead wrinkled in confusion. She spoke, but her words were unintelligible. "What did you say?" he whispered weakly.

She tapped an ear and shook her head. Clearly she couldn't understand him, either.

Marko levered up onto his elbows, hissing as pain shot up his spine. His numbed fingertips were still buzzing.

Other faces gazed back. All young, female, and darker than his own. So, this wasn't divine intervention; he'd found the missing women. Or rather, joined their ranks. They were girls, really. No older than Kezia, brown eyes wide with concern for their new fellow.

Through pantomime and broken English they made introductions. He'd dropped the affected Zella voice; his own youthful timbre seemed to pass well enough. The three girls spoke only a little English learned between Freetown and Foxcroft. Mabela, Tenneh, and Fatou wore fine English day-gowns in feminine pastels, but each retained a boldly colourful head scarf that jarred with her frock. All were taller than Marko's twelve or so hand-spans, but Mabela was shorter by a few knuckle-lengths than Tenneh, and Fatou a bit shorter than that. Tenneh was angular as well as tall, with a taut build suited to running. Mabela was the prettiest, he thought; slender, with bright almond-shaped eyes, vigorous curls springing free here and there from her deep-red headscarf. Dainty Fatou, who seemed at once anxious and dreamy, kept both hands in her lap where they twisted slowly about like sea-swells.

"Thakande?" he asked, remembering the name of the girl found dead.

They exchanged sorrowful glances. Mabela haltingly conveyed that Thakande had been brave, too brave. Attempting to stab Foxcroft with the paring knife Preacher had smuggled. Mabela seemed brave, too, answering most of his questions and occasionally laying a protective hand on her companions' shoulders. Though she also had a thoughtful, calculating air. Marko didn't think she'd ever make Thakande's mistake, attacking their captor without a plan.

The small sitting room was dim but well-appointed: a couple of couches upholstered in velvet, a stiff-looking armchair, a low table and sideboard, a riotous red Oriental rug. Stylish cream-and blue floral wallpaper made the space seem dizzily cluttered. The walls also boasted a large gilt mirror and a massive framed watercolour of a country meadow. The room held a damp chill, though, and the brocade draperies and cushions smelled of mildew.

Glancing through a crack in the blue curtains behind where Tenneh sat, Marko realized the lack of natural light did not denote the waning of day. The window panes were painted onto the wall, their frames no more than ornate wood strips nailed directly into the wall-planks. No clatter of hooves, rattling carriages, or babbling voices filtered through.

Marko glanced sharply at Tenneh, pointing to the false window. "A cellar? We are underground?"

She nodded glumly. "Mm. We . . . missing sun." She passed her hands over face and collarbone, as if basking in the memory of warmth and light.

Marko was growing increasingly uncomfortable with the pretense of being a girl. But he couldn't think how to explain his disguise in simple language. Besides, their tenuous trust might dissolve with the revelation. Who knew what they'd experienced at the hands of men in this place.

Anger twisted his guts. Justice never came in life the way it did in plays. Life followed no script, unobliged to poetry or tragedy.

"Preach—err, Koroma?" Marko mewed like a cat, used the back of his hand to groom his face. Mabela cracked a smile, nodding in recognition. "Yes. Know him."

"He told me of you all. And . . . the knife he brought?"

"Yes, back in . . . dirty village." Her eyes squeezed shut, no doubt recalling what that risk had cost them.

Marko nodded. "Then Foxcroft hurt Thakande."

"He hide gun." She tapped her left breast.

Marko sucked a breath through his teeth. So overpowering the copper would be tricky. He could shoot any or all of them at the first sign of resistance.

"So we can't break out." He nodded toward the false window. "And Koroma can't reach us to help."

This strange false sitting-room had probably been built in the centre of the cellar, away from outer stone or brick walls, so no-one outside would hear a thing. He imagined Foxcroft constructing the little box of false dignity and warmth, like a stage set. Only these players couldn't take their bows and leave. The unreality was heightened by a lack of visible beds or a piss-pot.

Although . . . on a set, scaffolding and backdrops were made with disassembly in mind. He shot up, startling the others, and began pacing, pushing here and knocking there. But everything felt depressingly sturdy. Mabela caught his eye and shook her head. They'd tried the same already, of course.

Only when she laid a gentle hand on his shoulder did Marko realize he'd begun to breathe harshly, raggedly. Trapped in a stationary box—a Traveler's worst nightmare. The cold mustiness of the cellar mixed with the musk of warm bodies, a whiff of urine, and the fumes of two oil lamps. Not nearly as rancid as the stench of Seven Dials. But with no means of escape, it choked him even more.

The women began arguing in low voices, perhaps rehashing old escape plans.

Marko eyed the flickering lamps—one on the low table before the settee and another on a sideboard beneath the mirror. Light the walls ablaze? No, that would simply roast the four of them like chestnuts.

"Where sleep?" Marko asked, praying they'd be moved at some point from this eerie room.

"Sleep?" Fatou wrinkled her brow. Marko put his hands together and leaned his head against them like a pillow, closing his eyes.

"Oh. Here." She reached beneath the couch where she sat, showing him the corner of a tightly-furled sleeping mat. Bending, Marko also saw a painted metal chamber pot concealed there.

"You . . . sleep Thakande bed," Fatou added gently.

As if he could nod off even for a moment inside this ornate coffin. "No," he replied. The steel in his voice surprised even him. "No, we won't . . . stay here. Leave tonight."

He'd no idea how, but would surely suffocate or go mad by morning otherwise.

"You know him. Can we trick him? Confuse?" Marko asked.

"I . . . pretend sick?" Fatou proposed, without conviction.

Tenneh snorted. "Tch. He don' care."

Mabela nodded, regarding Marko thoughtfully. "For clever man, need a big show. So he can' look away."

"Yes!" Marko clapped, and Fatou jumped. "Sorry. A show, exactly. I know about acting. We'll need props." But then he looked around the room, and his shoulders slumped.

"Not many thing here," Mabela agreed glumly.

Marko pored over all he knew of stage effects and mechanical wizardry. Granted, the Wayfairers were small-time, but had basic props to work with: ropes and pulleys, trick knives, a double-chambered rain box of dried peas, a trunk with a false bottom. Nothing of the sort here, though.

Yet sometimes the most unlikely piece of junk could serve. When Finnegan happened on such finds, he saw their potential, and found an ingenious way to incorporate them into a show. Once the Irishman rigged up a thunder cart in the two hours before a performance by filling a listing old wheelbarrow with stones and scrap-metal, fastening it to a support beam, and setting it spinning in a crazed maypole dance.

Marko straightened, staring at the wall. From humble materials came ingenious trickery. If he broke things down to their basic parts, there had to be some useful material in this boxy prison. A lamp was a glass tube, oil, wick, smoke, ash, flame. A table was a wood flat, legs, nails. A framed picture. . . .

Mabela laid a hand on his knee. "Maria, idea?"

He blushed and surreptitiously checked his wig was straight. "Yes. Think so." He climbed onto the velvet fainting couch to take down the mediocre watercolour, and began to disassemble it.

Fatou tugged her high collar nervously as he lifted free the pane of glass.

"Glass break? For. . . ." She mimed a stabbing motion.

Dismayed glances were exchanged among the girls; they clearly pictured losing another of their number who'd brought only a makeshift knife to a gun fight.

"No." He lifted the glass intact from its frame, holding the pane up before his face and grinning through it. "Magic."

He'd try the technique the troupe had considered using to manifest Maria's spectre onstage during a dramatic dream sequence. "Who looks most like Thakande?"

Tenneh squeezed her eyes shut to trap sudden tears. "Sister," she whispered, thumping her breast with a fist.

Wanting to comfort her, but constrained by the language barrier, he only nodded empathetically before doling out instructions. How odd, to suddenly be in command of his own motley troupe.

"Here, Tenneh, my scarf. Fatou, burn this and collect the ash." He waved the big sheaf of watercolour paper over one of the oil lamps.

"Mabela, help me move this."

Miming and exaggerated gestures helped bridge the language gaps. A slight Irish brogue flavored Marko's instructions as his confidence rose. I sound like Finnegan, he thought. His heart squeezed, and he sent a prayer to Sara Kali: *Please, let me live to receive another of that big Irish lout's lectures. To be scolded by Mam for stroking a stray cat. To be teased by Siaorse and Kezia and bruise my arse on the vardo's hard benches.*

With enough luck and cleverness, maybe they'd all live—and be free.

The trick called 'Pepper's Ghost' had hit London theatres in 1862, brainchild of two academics named Pepper and Dirck. A fiendishly simple method of producing translucent 'spectres' onstage, it required only a strong light in a dark room and a large pane of glass, angled just so, to reflect a well-lit actor hidden out of the audience's view. Even the ragtag Wayfairers occasionally trotted it out, given the right venue. They'd run through the steps recently, on the off-chance their paid appearance at the Lady's Bazaar would accommodate it.

Since the two oil lamps were not terribly bright, Marko gave Tenneh both to hold up to her ash-daubed face, leaving the rest of the room in darkness. Clutched in one hand and shielded by the other, the lights illuminated only her head and shoulders as she stood concealed in the alcove left of the door.

The other two girls had panicked when they first saw her ghastly reflection across the room. Thinking, no doubt, the stranger had drawn their friend's spirit from her body. But Mabela had approached, and turned the glass to make the image come and go, then explained the trick in their own tongue. Then she'd sat Tenneh down and used the twisted tip of a handkerchief to etch a line of soot between her front teeth: Thakande's distinctive gap.

Tenneh had practiced contorting her ashen face into various grisly expressions while the others took turns standing at the door to assess the effect. The *coup de grace* would come when a concealed Marko let out his most theatrical wail, which would seem to emanate from the ghostly apparition.

● ◑ ◐ ○ ○ ◐ ◑ ●

He'd just finished directing a dummy run when the street-level door above slammed. The floor over their heads shuddered with heavy booted steps. Foxcroft, returning for the night. Well, so be it. Mabela had proved a quick study at stage trickery, and the thing would go down fast. They needn't be perfect—only work with the skill of seasoned players. And a language barrier. All after knowing each other for mere hours.

Marko shook his head. No use wishing for Siaorse's quick wits. He recalled the day she'd played Juliet, but forgot her stage knife for the suicide scene. Instead of freezing or panicking she'd skillfully, heartbreakingly ad-libbed a farmer in the audience into handing over his pocket knife. By the end of her monologue the man had been bloody blubbering. Begorrah, that girl could improvise.

"Places," he whispered. The others rushed to their spots. Marko crawled behind the mirror they'd pried from its golden frame and propped at an angle behind a low tea-table. From the doorway, it would reflect only the riotous pattern of the carpet, suggesting at a glance there was nothing beneath. Holding the others' gazes, he raised and lowered his palms while taking deep, exaggerated breaths. The three girls followed suit as though warming up for a performance.

He grinned, and they tentatively smiled back.

Then came a creaking on the cellar stairs. More than just one pair of feet.

Mabela froze on the fainting couch, eyes wide with horror. Then she pressed her lips into a resolute line and shrugged as if to say, *we must see it through.*

Fatou let out a strangled sob. Mabela grasped her hand in an almost cruel-looking grip that clearly meant, *get hold of yourself.*

A key rattled in the basement door's lock. Foxcroft's muffled voice was drawling, ". . . a real cherry of a Gypsy, and young to boot." Heavy steps descended the stairs and entered the cellar. Marko counted footfalls, estimating the distance to the cellar steps. Finally, another rattling of keys and the door to their prison swung open.

Chancing a peek around the obscuring mirror, Marko glimpsed the constable, still in uniform. A tall, gaunt gent stood at his side. The stranger swept the room with an avid, pale blue gaze, like a cat invited into the fishmonger's.

"Bugger, why so dark? Stupid whores've let the light—" Foxcroft halted as his gaze locked on the opposite wall, where a ghostly visage hovered.

"What the bleeding devil," he whispered. With a shuffle and thump, he retreated, backing into his guest, who grunted and staggered back, too.

The translucent face might've been easily missed had Tenneh not been so animated, cycling from soundless muttering to silent screams and violent head-shaking. Not to mention that this spectre sported deathly grey skin, wild, unbound hair, and a white cloth hanging over its eyes like a shroud. When its mouth stretched in a silent scream, the distinctive gap between the front teeth identified her as none other than the murdered Thakande.

As the men backed away, staggering deeper into the dim cellar, Mabela jumped from her seat. The cue for Marko, hidden beneath the apparition, to begin shrilly screaming.

And then, all hell broke loose.

Foxcroft dropped his lantern, which smashed on the floor. Tenneh quickly doused her lights as well, plunging the room into darkness. Cursing and fumbling, the copper drew his revolver.

Bang!

Glass exploded above Marko's head. He threw his hands up to protect his eyes, and a long shard bit deep into one forearm. Goaded by the pain, he hissed a stage-whisper into the brief, ringing silence and darkness:

"May you end in agony, and your bones lie forgotten. Bear my curse and die!" The clipped but musical Limba accent rolled off his tongue with ease, thanks to the hours spent straining to understand the girls.

A second shot rang out in the dark. The mirror shattered too, the bullet punching through the wall next to Marko's head. He lurched from concealment, crunching glass into powder underfoot. Only two shots so far; there'd be three or four left in the cylinder. Each wasted round improved their chances.

Foxcroft cursed. His heavy boots crunched around in the dark cellar beyond, as he stumbled over something, likely bits of smashed lantern.

Marko held his breath, listening for the others' movements. Likely there was only one egress from the cellar. If they'd any sense, the men would move to block the stairs rather than grope after them randomly in the dark. So he must try and lure them away.

Feeling his way past broken furniture, trunks, and casks to what he judged the remotest corner of the cellar, Marko began chattering to himself hysterically in several different voices, all Limba-accented. Though no accomplished biloquist, he even managed to throw his voice a time or two. Calling out:

"Where is he?"

"Here, Maria—here!"

"Door, door this way?"

Foxcroft took the bait, growling curses as he thrashed toward the back cellar wall. By now Mabela, Fatou, and Tenneh should be creeping along the front one toward the stairs.

As soon as he judged the bobby about a wagon's-length away, Marko went silent and began to pick his way up towards the exit as well. Using the toe of each kid slipper to probe the floor ahead, he avoided bumping anything that might give away his location. The soles were soft and pliable enough to soundlessly embrace the dirt floor.

The angry, ragged breaths of their captor grew distant as he struggled deeper into the maze of abandoned furnishings. Finally, Marko's fingers touched the cold stone of the real cellar wall. At that exact moment a crack of light shone ahead and above.

The cellar door was opening.

Rushing towards the light, Marko collided with another outstretched arm. A lean, strong one, clad in fine, soft wool.

The wig was knocked from his head as a hand shot out and grabbed at his neck. It slammed him back against the wall, so crushingly hard all the breath wheezed out of him. A tiny flame sprang to life before his face, close enough to singe stray hairs: a silver pocket lighter.

"Ah," rasped the gentleman, his pale eyes glinting like some cave-dwelling carnivore's. "Lucky me, it's the pikey tart." He took in Marko's snarling face and shortened hair, and those thin lips twisted into a sneer.

"But he's not even tart enough for sport." The man leaned into the hand crushing Marko's neck, and the boy's ears filled with a shrieking ring, his eyes saw only a spray of red stars.

. . . no, not stars at all.

The pressure on his throat eased. His face was sprayed with pulses of hot liquid. He tasted copper as it dripped into his gasping mouth.

Blood.

Before his attacker dropped the lighter, Marko saw the tableau illuminated. The gent's mouth working like a fish's. His rolled-back eyes showing only whites. Mabela, arms thrown about his shoulders from behind, like an affectionate daughter. Gripping the shard of glass embedded in his neck. Then, her eyes never leaving Marko's, she jerked the glass sideways, opening up the stranger's throat.

● ◑ ◐ ○ ◑ ○ ◑ ◐ ●

Fatou stood at the cellar door, flapping her hands wildly for them to run through. Mabela vaulted up the steps, dropping the bloody shard as she cleared the threshold. Down the landing hallway, Tenneh scrabbled to open the door to the main house. Marko was just reaching for its frame when a wild shout rose from the murkiness below.

"One more bleeding inch, and I'll blow her—I'll blow *his* brains out!"

Marko turned to look. Halfway up the cellar stairs, Foxcroft was stepping over his guest's inconvenient corpse. Heavy breaths rasped from his throat like animal snarls. The dead black eye of the revolver's barrel stared Marko down. Mabela froze behind him, her tense posture radiating indecision. Fatou turned and dashed down the hall, toward freedom.

The copper was only steps away from Marko. He wouldn't miss.

"Go ahead and run, darkie cunts. I'll keep this one. Ash my evening cigar into the hole in his head." He brought his spare palm up to steady his gun hand. There came a resounding *thunk* as Tenneh wrestled the back door open; tantalizing street sounds wafted inside.

"On the other hand," Foxcroft drawled, squeezing one eye shut to sight along the barrel, "Why not take the both of you with one bullet? I'm a crack shot, you know. Comes of serving at Her Majesty's pleasure."

The strength fled Marko's limbs. He didn't want to die. Maybe if he didn't put up any more fight, Foxcroft would let him live. After all, who in the constabulary would believe a Rom if he tried to peach on one of their own? And if the Dogfox recaptured Mabela as well—at least the other two would be free. Maybe they'd come back for them.

His foot hovered above the first step down.

"Good," said Foxcroft. "Nice and slow."

A pattering, similar to the sound of heavy rain, was growing louder out in the hallway.

Mabela grabbed for Marko's hand, hissing, "*No.*"

The pattering ceased. A small grey missile shot past Marko's shoulder, hurtling directly for Foxcroft's face. The copper fired a wild shot, nicking the lintel and showering splinters onto their heads.

Preacher hit the copper's face and neck with all four paws outstretched, claws extended. The man shrieked and flailed at empty air, falling backward over the crumpled corpse and then down into the dark. The thud of his head striking packed earth rang hollow.

Mabela's hand closed around Marko's wrist and dragged him through the doorway. She reached back to slam it shut, but Marko yelled, "Koroma!" They all stopped, staring into the quiet void.

"Could he have been . . . hurt, in the fall?" Marko said.

Mabela swallowed, shaking as she glared down the darkness. She emanated an earthy odor of sweat, but the hand squeezing Marko's wrist was clammy.

Twin points of fire appeared down in the gloom. Light reflecting from the cat's orange eyes as he bounded up the steps.

"Not dead," his deep voice announced.

How Marko had missed the melody of it, despite his anger at Preacher's disappearance!

"There is much blood," Preacher said, "Soon he will pass. Now, must be on our way!"

Mabela cast a glance back that suggested she'd prefer to stay, tear Foxcroft's heart out, and serve it on toast for tea. But Preacher yowled and batted her ankles, breaking her reverie.

They ran.

Through the hallway to an empty kitchen, where a massive cast-iron oven crouched cold in one corner. Past that, the great-room, sparse as the cellar sitting-room. Foxcroft must've sold off all he had to keep this place. Finally they sighted the servant's exit; a smaller door ajar and creaking in the breeze.

Mabela paused then to coolly look Marko and his short locks up and down. The palm that'd wielded the glass dagger dripped blood onto the floorboards.

"Telling real name now, *Maria?*"

◗ ◗ ◑ ◯ ◯ ◯ ◐ ◐ ●

Unlike in the Rookery, plentiful gaslights dispelled the gloom in these affluent streets. The illumination drew Marko's heart into his throat. They should not, could not be seen here all bedraggled and bloody. Though they drew a few odd looks, he kept them to side streets as much as possible as they weaved south toward Seven Dials. Both girls and cat would come home with him, of course. Where else could they go?

After a while they slowed, breath ragged and wheezing. Preacher collided with Fatou's heels. The women stared glassy-eyed at the bustle of Tottenham Court Road. As Marko led them across the street, a cabriolet nearly flattened them. He hoped the girls didn't understand the torrent of slurs from its irate driver.

At St. Andrew's Street, a wave of relief washed over him. Here were the gin shops, their walls propped up by gimlet-eyed whores. The narrow storefronts stacked with cages of shrilling birds; well-dressed card-sharpers; ragged nail-gropers scouring gutters for bits of iron. He breathed deep the mingled stench of booze, offal, and dung both human and animal. For the first time, he felt affection for the place.

He didn't, though, care for the looks coming their way—a *chavo* in a frock and three foreign girls in smart gowns all but screamed, "Easy pickings!" Perhaps it was the blood on him and Mabela that kept the rooks at bay.

Finally they turned onto Shiller's Lane, which led to the Wayfairers' alley. Kezia saw them first, stumbling to her feet, then turning to shriek toward the wagons, "Magda! Marko's back!"

Mam swept him up in a crushing embrace as his companions hung back. Reluctantly, he at last disentangled himself. "Invite the girls in, Mam."

Magda seemed too relieved to protest, or perhaps even to care, when he carried Preacher inside, too.

No-one objected to taking in the three young women, or even the cat. What was hotly debated was how to avoid the retribution that would follow. A few insisted the troupe must leave London at once. But Magda and Finnegan were firm in their resolve to put on the play.

"We can't feckin' afford not to!" Finnegan insisted.

"I trust the Lady," said his mother firmly. "She'll find us somewhere safe to kip, for the last night before we perform."

So much trust, after only meeting her once? Marko itched to be jounced and shaken about as the vardo put miles between him and this city. But the show, it seemed, must go on.

So they'd rattled out of Seven Dials, taking a winding route northeast at Marko's insistence to give Foxcroft's neighborhood a wide berth. And that night the troupe parked its wagons in the central courtyard of a grand mansion on Eaton Square in Islington.

Finnegan alighted from the Irish wagon to seek the servant's door, looking anxious. And no wonder. The Lady's sprawling estate sat behind wrought-iron gates crawling with intertwining moons and stars, left invitingly open yet still intimidating at nearly seven feet tall. The well-tended grassy grounds sloped gradually up to a breathtakingly elegant, strangely un-English-looking palazzo. Its stucco walls were painted a rich cobalt blue, the double-doored entrance flanked by towering columns of smooth pink-veined marble. These supported a triangular frieze carved from the same material: some Greek or Roman-looking gods or Muses draped in flowing cloth and playing instruments, dancing, singing. The manor house also boasted a great many tall, slim windows, wearing them as proudly as a lady bedecked with jewels. Each one, lidded with deep-blue velvet curtains, seemed to observe them languorously.

To the right of the house stood a low, whitewashed building; probably the kitchens. To the left a tall port-cochère with matching marble columns connected the house and, farther on, what must be the stables. Overall, the place looked as if it had been prized from the earth of some more exotic locale and dropped abruptly onto this decorous London street, without seeking anyone's approval.

The troupe waited in anxious silence. A country-fresh breeze, tinged with—was that jasmine, in winter?—wafted through the vardo's open door. Mabela, Fatou, and Tenneh sat across from Marko on a narrow bench, the cat draped protectively across all three laps. Occasionally one of them scratched

Preacher's cheek, and he'd purr. Then both would freeze as if realizing the strangeness of the interaction.

Marko'd expected Finnegan to bring back directions to some modest boarding house. Instead, the Irishman returned with brows knitted. "I spoke to a porter—tight-arsed fella in blue-velvet togs. Said the Lady was out. 'E also said she left him instructions to accommodate our wagons when we arrived, for she presumed we'd prefer our own digs."

Disconcerting as this bit of prescience seemed, they couldn't look a gift horse in the mouth. Especially since, at that moment, a cadre of servants— men and women whose loose, simple clothing was dyed in opulent reds and blues—were already arranging oaken tables around them in the courtyard.

Oysters, vegetable stew, and a strange but delicious dish of meat, tomatoes, and long, thin noodles soaked in wine arrived first, followed by a fresh green salad. Then came creamy almond candies, custard-filled cakes, and sugared orange slices of a blood-red hue. Also, baskets laden with twists of golden bread dipped in brandy and sugar. The players had never tasted such fine comestibles before. They ate slowly, tentatively, sharing the occasional baffled glance. The Lady's domestic staff were polite, but refused to answer any questions regarding 'Madame.' After dinner, they brought out metal bathing tubs and kettle upon kettle of hot water. Well-fitting new outfits were presented to every guest, including the three Limba women. But how could she possibly have known?

Restless in a new, stiffly-pressed white cotton shirt and checked woolen breeches, he passed the night without closing his eyes. Mabela, Tenneh, and Fatou had accepted a guest-room inside the manor. He didn't begrudge them this extra protection, but felt he'd have slept easier with them nearby. Instead, he lay on his side on the vardo's bench, a worn quilt thrown cowl-like over his head. He feared that without that familiar cotton pressing against his lids, he'd still see Foxcroft's blazing eyes receding into the gloom, and hear the crack of his skull on packed earth.

The nighttime quiet of the walled courtyard surpassed even that of the cursed cellar. The silence buzzed deafeningly in his ears, which had grown accustomed to the Rookery's squalid lullabies.

◗ ◗ ◑ ◐ ○ ◑ ○ ◐ ◑ ●

The next morning was spent in frenzied preparation for the evening's entertainment. Finnegan balked when, late that afternoon, a footman instructed them to drive their wagons directly into a garden square down the street.

"What! Drag the traps through there in broad daylight? Begorrah, think of the fine we'll get slapped with when some Islington toff sees us mucking through Charterhouse Close!"

The footman smiled. "No worries, *signore*. The neighbors will not be troubled. And rest assured, the residents of the garden won't mind, either."

Finnegan barked an incredulous laugh. "What d'ye mean, *residents*? En't nobody residing in a public park, save for the old bones."

Another inscrutable smile was the only response.

So Finnegan hitched up Emmeline and Abelard, muttering darkly about silly rich buggers. Sure enough, though there were folk enough about on errands or promenades, no-one seemed to take any notice when their cavalcade passed through the wrought-iron gates, grooving deep tracks into the muddy green.

Charterhouse Square was a large, lopsided pentagon, skewered by two long, perpendicular promenades. As Finnegan alluded, the land had once served as a plague-pit, but those bodies had lain for centuries beneath this two-acre park. Neat regiments of trees lined the giant X formed by walking paths. Brilliant spot for a summer market or fall fair. But it was hard to imagine wealthy folks wanting to attend such an event in chilly early winter. Marko pictured corseted ladies clutching fur stoles, dead grass and muck adhering to their white calfskin boots as they clung to the arms of cross-looking husbands for support. A well-heeled crowd shivering miserably through a Punch and Judy show as its curtained facade slowly sank into the mud. Surely such outdoors entertainments would hold no appeal to those who could afford better?

They quickly located a round platform off the path near the border fence, set up upon the crunchy dead grass there. Lugan and Emmett went about staking vertical poles into the earth and wrapping the canvas backdrop around them, so the painted scenery could be easily rotated. Discreet slits were aligned to form entrance and exit flaps for the actors. The canvas cut the circular stage in half, creating a backstage section where props and players could avoid any mucky ground. The setup suited them so well, Marko wondered if it had been stipulated in the agreement. Or whether the Lady had again simply anticipated their needs without having to be told.

The sun was sinking beyond the grandest houses of Islington as Marko helped Kezia and Siaorse lay out the props and costumes. Sara Kali be praised, they had a spare black wig and a clean white skirt he could use for his Zella costume. He again wished Mabela, Tenneh, and Fatou could be there, though he understood their preference to remain cloistered. As darkness fell, lights moved up and down the promenade.

Others arrived and began erecting stalls, shanties, even velvet tents. A wagon not unlike theirs rumbled in and staked its claim under an ancient oak. On the caravan's sides, *Mister Peculiar's Misfits and Monsters* was painted in crimson over a portrait of a dignified gentleman with voluminous whiskers. The head of an ostrich protruded from his open mouth, and its beak in turn disgorged a flock of electric-blue butterflies. Exotic animals and human handlers began spilling out of the caravan, more than should've fit inside. A lady sparsely dressed in spangled red clasped bare knees around the flanks of her steed, a huge tiger. As he stared in amazement she waved cheerily. Another person—man or woman, he couldn't say—was all over swarming with weasels or ferrets, like a live fur coat. An overpowering smell of mingled animal musks and dung wafted from that wagon.

As Marko leaned farther, trying to catch a glimpse inside, Kezia smacked his arm. He started and resumed spreading straw over the spot where the musicians would play. The older girl was all business, studiously ignoring all the strangeness surrounding them. Emmet, though, caught Marko's eye, tilted his head toward the tiger lady, and mimed picking his jaw up off the ground.

Even when he didn't look, that strangeness continued to filter in. Rising babble in a myriad of tongues echoed through the trees. Caviling squawks resounded; the mingled noise of unfamiliar instruments being tuned.

A cold breeze ruffled the costumes Marko was smoothing and shaking out. He shivered. What kind of audience would be staring up at them tonight? The fun of performing, of course, was seeing how different people reacted to the same tale you'd told a hundred times. But he'd never played a crowd like this before.

Coming round to light the down-stage lamps, he stopped dead. In the half-hour he'd toiled behind the backdrop, the Square had become unrecognizable. Will-o-the-wisp lights glowed and shimmered high in bare branches. Tents in a multitude of colours and patterns flew streamers that rippled and danced on a chilly breeze. Cook-fires and torches sent white smoke winding into a black sky in which the stars were gloriously visible. The omnipresent London haze had somehow cleared . . . though only in a sharply-delineated, pentagonal patch just above Charterhouse Square.

A cacophony of sounds and smells laced the night, clamouring for attention: smoke, meat, laughter, incense, perfume, sweat, snatches of song, the musky smell and plaintive cries of strange animals. It was as chaotic as Seven Dials, but absent the stinking sewage and gin-soaked caterwauling. Illumined by torches, a group of harlequin tumblers flipped and cartwheeled. Those lights, he belatedly realized, were also in motion—torches juggled by a stilt-walking jester with a huge, lolling head. Applause erupted elsewhere as an accordion concluded its wheezing serenade.

Seeking the source of a delicious meaty smell, he was drawn to the glimmer of blood on a silver blade. A man with torn shirtsleeves stood butchering carcasses before a giant iron cauldron. The flex of his sweat-polished shoulders was hypnotic. His long jawline and fangs evoked a pale, hairless wolf. An unsettling mask, perhaps, made of blanched leather?

Marko glanced at the butchered carcass . . . with a head that somewhat resembled that of a human being. He lost his appetite, turning away, cold sweat prickling under his arms.

The bulk of the crowd stuck to the well-lit paths lined with vendors and buskers. The corner occupied by the Wayfairers was as yet largely unexplored, though not entirely unpeopled. As Marko layered white grease paint on his face a group of middle-aged women dashed past. They wore only chemises and white underskirts knotted and tied between their legs, having abandoned both gowns and corsets. Pale calves gleaming in the starlight, they whooped and tumbled to the grass. Loping behind, a loinclothed man in a saturnine mask caught at their pinned-up, greying hair with muscular arms, unraveling the elaborate updos.

Another movement drew his gaze. In the shadows beneath a nearby tree two figures stood entwined. A middle-aged gent in black silk fit for a grand soiree, pressed against the bark by a bedraggled youth of the sort often seen grubbing for nails among the Rookery's cobblestones. The man's beaver top hat was knocked from his head by the violence of the other's kisses and bites. Their love play flickered between desire and joyful brutality. Then suddenly a knife was in the ragamuffin's fist, pressed to the other's throat. His free hand dipped swiftly into the silken coat's breast pocket, and he was gone. The older man didn't follow. Only wiped blood from his lower lip and stared as if fascinated by the red stain on his fingers.

Marko looked away, suddenly glad he wasn't free to wander the Bazaar.

Marko's first scene was brief: appearing as Zella to shout "William Corder!" and clutch her breast, then die. Beyond the foot-lamps, a crush of bodies jostled against the stage. On his next appearance, there seemed fewer, but by the third, even more were gathered than at the first. The fickle Bazaar-goers ebbed and flowed, wandering from spectacle to spectacle, it seemed, until they found something they couldn't bear to look away from. Those who arrived together quickly separated, their unique fascinations drawing them into peculiar intimacies with strangers.

He nearly lost count of the times he popped onto the stage to fruitlessly scold Corder or utter unheard warnings. Unlike in rehearsal, though, he now *felt* Zella's frustration and helplessness. Something in the air was drawing his anger and despair from deep down, his pain pouring out over the uplifted faces below. And they stared, mesmerized, drinking it in like a shower of champagne.

He knew what it was like to go unheeded and invisible, even as a horrible crime was about to be committed. If Foxcroft had been able to follow them from the cellar, would they have had the slightest chance of escape? Or might not passersby, perhaps some of these same audience members, have closed in and handed them back to the proper authorities?

Once again he returned to the stage, addressing Maria and Corder as they buried their infant child, poisoned by its father. He began to sing, sweeping his gaze over the audience and meeting the occasional eye. Expressions ranged from rapt to idle lack of interest. Briefly, he spotted a lady with curly black hair like the Limba girls'. A hooded silvery cloak obscured her face as she weaved through the crowd—searching for a misplaced companion?

Do not trust him, gentle lady
Though his voice be low and sweet . . .

He met another pair of eyes, and another. And then, a bloodshot stare blazing with hate.

Standing in a circle of lantern light at stage front, flakes of crusted blood flecking his eyebrows, Foxcroft stared unblinkingly past the foot-lights. He wore a plain black oilcloth, and his blond moustache was disheveled above a bleeding lip. Claw-marks peppered his bloodless visage. The Dogfox leant hard against the stage, as if unable to bear his own weight. But the clenched jaw suggested he was conserving his strength for an act of violence.

Marko turned and fled through the canvas flap, unsure if he'd finished his song. Backstage, he bent double, one hand clutching his chest. His heart clattered inside his ribs like a caged chicken.

Siaorse and David bumped into him as they followed through the flap. "Oi! Keep it moving, ye pigeon," David grumbled.

Siaorse patted Marko's arm. "Nearly finished."

Behind them, the canvas hissed as it began rotating to the Red Barn backdrop. He couldn't meet Siaorse's eye lest she notice his terror. She must think him suffering from simple stage-fright. After a moment, she left.

When he'd calmed his breathing, Marko glanced about. The musicians played on the straw-covered ground beside the stage. Mam and Kezia sat amongst crates and trunks stacked to lend the backstage area privacy, hastily mending a costume. Patrin and David lounged against the boxes to his other side, quietly jawing. Those with no parts or later calls were likely hanging about the wagons or wandering the Bazaar. He should warn everyone—or find the Lady, or—

Onstage, Siaorse was declaiming, "Ah, the old Red Barn. Even in my childhood, its shadows cast a chill. Did the old Gypsy not warn me that here I should meet my fate. . . .? Well, I suppose he was right! For William soon arrives to bear me to London, and marry me this very night."

Groans of dismay and nervous titters rose from the crowd. They all must know how this infamous tale ended.

Before Marko could decide on a course of action, he spotted movement at the platform's edge, between the stacked crates. From out of the gloom, a man grunted as he heaved himself onto the boards. Flickering lamp-light swept the bowed head, revealing matted bloody hair at the back. The fall had indeed been bad. But not quite as bad as they'd hoped.

Foxcroft straightened, holding the revolver loosely at his thigh. No-one reacted; the crates to either side concealed him from the others. He lifted a trembling finger to his pale lips, grinning at Marko. One pupil looked grotesquely large, dilated in the manner of a cat tracking prey. From one nostril, a thin stream of clear liquid trickled into the man's open mouth. He didn't seem to notice, nor care.

His pointer finger curled inward: *Come here.* The faintest of clicks as he cocked the hammer.

Marko wouldn't obey this time. He shook his head, backing towards the canvas. Beyond it, Siaorse's silhouette stalked to and fro as she proclaimed her adoration for Corder.

Foxcroft snarled, raising the gun, then faltered and swayed. His fingers twitched and then clenched, as if itching to intimately choke the life out of Marko.

Must get him away, he thought desperately. Away from Mam and Kezia and all. Beyond that, he had no plan.

Foxcroft staggered forward, closing the gap between them. Even as players saw him and cried out, the constable's clammy fingers were around Marko's throat. Those mismatched pupils inches from his, as the chemical stink of the injured man's fluids and blood filled his nose. The cold steel of the gun's barrel dug into his temple.

Marko clenched his fist and struck the weapon away. It flew from the bobby's grip, and Magda dived for it immediately.

But already someone *else* was at Foxcroft's back. A flurry of black curls as Mabela threw herself onto his attacker's back. The silvery hood fell from her head as she plunged a blade into the taut muscle between Foxcroft's neck and shoulder. A re-enactment of her rescue in the cellar.

The bobby bellowed, jammed an elbow into Mabela's ribs. She dropped to the boards. Foxcroft yanked the blade free without a whimper. Could he even feel pain any more, or was his brain, mercifully, too damaged?

With a horrible cry, the man swung the blade wide, lunging toward Marko, who flung himself to the boards. . . .

●◐◐○○○◑◑●

As Siaorse would later relate, the audience at the Night Bazaar was treated to a performance of "The Murder of Maria Marten" unlike any other. It ended something like this.

"Hark, I hear my love approach!" Siaorse cried, secretly fuming at the offstage players for making such a frightful racket. Then a man, apparently her suitor, erupted from the scenery behind her—brandishing a dagger and all but foaming at the mouth.

Gasps and shrieks from the audience.

As Marko had noticed, and Siaorse agreed, the copper did *passingly* resemble David, the Irishman cast as Corder. So when he burst onstage, knife-wielding and frightfully disheveled, the audience seemed to take it as a costume-change.

Siaorse-Maria screamed and jumped aside. Foxcroft-Corder lowered the weapon, seeming puzzled by his surroundings.

Behind him, the ghostly Marko-Zella entered from backstage. Calmly, with great dignity, she plucked the blade from the villain's hand. The spectre locked gazes with Maria, who was frozen in genuine shock and fear.

"At last!" Zella intoned, "You see Corder for what he truly is." Widening her eyes as if to say, *play along*.

The man snarled and lurched toward the spectre, but she evaded him, and hesitated only a moment before plunging the knife into the base of his skull.

"O, Harrow!" cried Siaorse-Maria, as real, hot blood gouted onto the boards. And then she collapsed in an equally real faint.

Lugan and Emmett would report, after things had calmed, that the ladies and carnies lavishly praised the cosmetics and costuming. The skill with which a bit of grease paint and a change of clothing had transformed a dapper young actor into a haggard madman. Not to mention the stomach-churning gore!

In contrast, the gentlemen seemed disturbed, even personally offended.

"That kerfuffle at the end was butter upon bacon, eh what?" one grumbled. "Totally nonsensical. And did Corder even bloody *have* a moustache before?"

"A bunch of tommy-rot," agreed his friend. "We're supposed to credit that some ghost, this little sprig of a Gypsy, could overcome a hale and hearty man?"

"I found it much more gratifying than the original," protested their well-dressed female companion.

"No doubt!" boomed a voice behind them. "It were 'igh time someone gave them poor lasses a crack at that gobshite Corder!"

The trio turned to stare. A man in gold-and-purple tights trotted cheerfully by, tugging a rope lead attached to the neck of a hissing emu. The monumental bird's feathers quivered wrathfully as it tried to peck at their eyes.

"Mercy," cried the woman as her man sheltered behind her, "that monster nearly got me!"

The crowd dispersed, still debating the play. Wondering why not one player had emerged to take a bow during the standing ovation.

In truth, they hadn't the time. For they were too busy stowing the body.

●◑◑○◑○◑◑●

On the other side of the canvas the troupe stood in a circle, staring down into a massive oak trunk. They'd finally gotten the constable's corpse inside—cramming, bending, folding, and then re-cramming and re-folding—until it had finally been made to fit beneath the trunk's false bottom.

"Thank Sara we got the *kar* squared away afore he stiffened," muttered Magda. "Tight as a tin of kippers, but we managed."

"Thank Sara in general." Marko, still panting from the effort, shot a grateful look at Siaorse. Ever the improviser, she'd coped admirably when he and Foxcroft burst onstage.

Mabela glared at the corpse. She'd come alone, clad in a borrowed cloak and carrying a knife Marko didn't recognize. Which he'd had to bury in the back of Foxcroft's neck, up to its crescent-moon hilt, before an audience of hundreds. He wondered if Mabela was angry with him. But he'd had no choice; *she* couldn't have ad-libbed away a public murder. There'd been no satisfaction in it. He'd surely break down at some point, remembering the awful *crunch* as the spinal cord severed. But for the moment, he felt numb.

Suddenly, Preacher's ember eyes and grey nose poked out from the girl's tight black curls. He lay across her shoulders like a shawl, all but hidden by the hood.

"Psst." Marko jerked a thumb towards the weapon in its fleshy sheath. "Did you give that to her? Where d'you get all these bleedin' *chivs*?"

Quietly dignified, Preacher murmured, "A very reputable source this time. Here she comes now."

When Marko turned, the Lady was standing in the gap between the stacked crates. No woolen cape swathed her tonight; only a sleek gown of burgundy silk ruched and gathered at the back in a modest bustle. Her bare arms and collarbone shone a warm copper in the lamplight, framed by a plunging collar of black lace. At her ears and throat trembled glittering drops of onyx. Her luxurious hair—glinting reddish in the lamplight and piled atop her head—was scattered with rubies. Under the circumstances, these put Marko in mind of a spatter of gore.

She looked even more powerful than before. Truly in her element.

Then it hit him. She could've been standing there for ages, calmly watching them stomp the corpse's unruly limbs into the chest.

"You." His voice cracked.

The assembly whirled, closing ranks to obscure the evidence.

"I pray you do not trouble yourselves." A guileless smile crinkled the corners of her eyes. "I'm not unaware of the circumstances here."

She approached the chest and bent over the tangle of blood and oilcloth that had been Liam Foxcroft. "No-one of consequence, though he believed he could be—if only he got enough capital. By any means necessary, of course." She sighed. A head-shake set the onyx earrings dancing. "I knew his family when they made their fortune by selling human beings like cattle. Their star set long ago. It should never be allowed to rise again."

The Lady locked eyes with Mabela, and the young woman raised her chin to stare fearlessly back. "*Yseke*, Madame Wolfe."

"*Yseke*, Mabela."

What in the devil had gone on in that manor house last night, while Marko tossed and turned in the vardo?

The Lady gave Mabela a near-imperceptible wink, then dipped a slender hand into the trunk to pull the blade free. Dark blood oozed sluggishly from the wound. "I'll take this back now. Oh—and don't concern yourselves about the trunk. My staff will take it off your hands."

Madame Wolfe wiped the gory blade on her wine-coloured skirts, then disappeared it into the folds of silk. The deep-red fabric showed no stain. He wondered if she selected her wardrobe with situations like this in mind.

"You have my thanks for a diverting performance," she added. "I've never seen anything like it. And for me, that is saying something." She huffed a little laugh. "Oh, and the rest of your fee." Handing a thick vellum envelope to Magda, she turned to leave.

As if on cue, several of her queerly-dressed servants clambered onstage to close up the makeshift coffin.

"Wait!" Marko was surprised at the rage in his own voice.

She regarded him over one elegant shoulder. "Yes?"

"Did you know about . . . about everything? Why didn't you do something yourself, end it sooner?"

"Oh, I knew very little. I simply prodded things into motion with the book, which I found in a lot of secondhand goods. I pay well to have my choice of any interesting items that come to light."

"But why did you give it to *me*?"

"I believe the outcome speaks for itself. *May you end in agony, and your bones lie forgotten.* A good curse, and so efficiently realized."

Marco felt the hairs on the back of his neck rising. Those were the very words he'd spoken to Foxcroft, in Thakande's voice. "How did you—hold on, I have more questions!"

"I've no doubt." Her expression softened, though, before she turned away to exit the platform. "But I have many, many more engagements tonight."

Then she was gone, and four muscular men in the same loose, simple red and blue clothing worn by the staff at the Lady's palazzo were lifting the trunk to their shoulders. Before the troupe could do more than exchange looks, they too disappeared.

"Sure and it'll be me has to explain all this to Finnegan," Magda grumbled.

Weeks later, Marko and Mabela sat together on the *vardo's* wooden bench. Preacher sprawled, with an uncharacteristic lack of decorum, across their laps. As Marko read aloud, the cat's orange-gold gaze remained fixed on his face.

"I wander thr—thro' each charter'd street,
Near where the charter'd Thames does flow.
And mark in every face I meet
Marks of weakness, marks of woe."

Mabela's English was not yet quite ready for Blake, but she picked up words here and there by following along, running a finger across the page as he read aloud.

Marko looked down at the cat and laughed. "Must you goggle at me, Preacher? I'm not the best reader. You're making me nervous."

"I like to watch your brain work, grinding away behind your eyeballs," Preacher declared. Insults always sounded grand in his deep, dignified voice.

When they were in company, the cat kept silent, occasionally throwing out the odd *miaow*. He'd decided to accompany the Wayfairers for now. "I shall sample life as an idle, unprincipled animal for a change," he'd proclaimed. "Which means *no* mousing."

The one thing Magda had grudgingly agreed he'd be good for. Instead, he was growing round on table scraps and lying in the sun.

He wouldn't give up books, though he still swore reading was too taxing for feline eyes. The one text he never asked Marko to read was the well-worn *Book of Common Prayer*. Perhaps because the "afterlife" had thus far fallen short of his expectations. But this was one of a few topics the three of them either couldn't or wouldn't discuss.

Each of us has reason to resent the other, Marko mused, but we seem to have agreed not to, without saying a word.

Tenneh and Fatou had returned to Sierra Leone as soon as Madame Wolfe could book them passage. But Mabela stayed. Of course, she'd cried with the others when they parted ways. But she seemed to find strength in facing the unfamiliar. If she'd been a man, English, and wealthy, well . . . she'd like as not be in Egypt plundering pyramids and confidently dodging Pharaoh's curses.

A lot of 'if's.

She showed a talent for the technical side of theatre, taking especial interest in visual tricks like the one they'd used in the cellar. Siaorse and Kezia were teaching her to paint props and backdrops. The horses fascinated her too, so she and Marko often squabbled over who got to feed and groom Emmeline and Abelard. Marko hoped she would stay with them, but she hadn't shared her plans, if she had any.

Funnily, she was learning Romanes faster than English. She'd recently, haltingly, used it to relate the Limba folk tale for which she'd been named.

"In olden times, some were clever and others foolish. The cat was clever; the mice were mostly foolish. Except Mabela, who was a very clever mouse indeed."

She certainly lived up to her name, he thought. Meanwhile, his own efforts to pick up Hulimba from her were progressing like cooling molasses.

Catching him staring just then, she scrunched up her face and said in Romanes: *"Čitaj, dinlo."*

Read, idiot.

He snorted approvingly and turned back to the poem.

How the Chimney-sweepers cry
Every black'ning Church appalls,
And the hapless Soldier's sigh
Runs in blood down Pa—Palace walls.

"Certainly captures London," Preacher muttered. "Even if he wrote it nearly a century ago. Does not seem to have changed much."

"Well." Marko shrugged. "Some parts are nice. Like Madame Wolfe's mansion, and Charterhouse Square—"

"Not our parts." Mabela cut him off with a raised palm. "Not for us."

"No," Marko agreed. "Except for that one night in the Square. Then it was for everyone, I s'pose."

He paused, recalling the lamplit faces of the motliest audience ever. Some had looked like dowager empresses, some like consumptive guttersnipes; still others less human than wild creature. Some *were* wild creatures, he conceded, thinking of the masked butcher and the gigantic leashed bird.

"Still, I'll take what I have. Leave the rest to those as fancies it." He flicked open the latch on the rear windows, letting them flap wide.

A plume of dust trailed behind them, rising into the expanse of blue, cloud-dotted sky. A chilly breeze carried the scents of coming spring. Oh, how gloriously his backside ached from the hard bench and bumpy road! From the sleeping area, he heard Mam humming an old Irish tune, while Kezia clicked her tongue and tapped her foot as if at a Romany folk dance.

When he glanced back at Preacher and Mabela, though, they weren't appreciating the scenery. Instead, they were gazing at each other, sharing a moment of silent contentment.

There was forgiveness in that look. Also intimacy, and fierce loyalty. As he regarded them, they turned and enfolded him in it, too.

After The Bazaar . . .

Reader, by now you may be wondering: upon the Night Bazaar's arrival in London, did I anticipate being the target of a nefarious criminal scheme plotted and carried out by a murderous fanatic? And did I know I'd be disposing of a gigantic trunk containing the battered remains of a brutal serial killer? Or that I'd be helping a woman, a ghost, and a raven serial time-travel through various eras?

Well, should anyone routinely assume such odd occurrences are a possibility, really? The answer is, of course: Yes. Some of us simply must. Though even I do not normally start my day thinking: *This morning after tea I shall most likely be abducted by a madman, trussed like a Christmas goose, and strung up to be blast-incinerated at a gasworks outside town.* Otherwise, on my habitual morning constitutional I'd best be taking along a battle-axe and some chain mail from the Ye Olde Iron Mongers booth at the Bazaar. Or, like a film star of the future, only move within an entourage consisting of my largest and most daunting-looking staff, should such threats ever became commonplace in my line of work.

In fact, I live according to the belief anything *might* indeed happen, at literally any place or any time. And so, I maintain a bevy of faithful coworkers and international connections—in all eras—just in case.

Aside from my impromptu visit to the Gasworks, our weeklong sojourn in London went smashingly well. It was also quite a study in contrasts. We discovered Victorian Londoners were ever so concerned about status in all its permutations: titles, honors, lineages, fashion, finances, and business affairs. Yet at the same time, these privileged toffs happily drove about in posh carriages, living excessively luxurious lives within spitting distance of abject poverty, ravaging disease, crumbling tenements, starving orphans, and cruel workhouses. The more things change—eh, wot? Beware of nostalgia and the misty view offered by its rosy-hued spectacles, I always say.

Those Invited this time around discovered our Bazaar was in no ways like a county fair jumble sale or weekly town market. Many had their first taste of exotic foods, spices from afar, services to be had nowhere else on Earth—and sometimes were made an offer they simply could not refuse. The terminally bored were entertained. The desperate, offered solutions. The wicked shown the error of their ways. And the hopeful—sometimes—got their hearts' desire, without too many strings attached.

Ah yes . . . no doubt they'll all miss us when we're gone.

And so, once we've folded our tents and packed up the stalls and carts and merchandise, where shall our company appear next? In her floating crystal ball, the venerable Vadoma—previously encountered in the company of a Mr. Sherlock Holmes and a Dr. Watson—has foreseen a jaunt far eastward. Arriving in Japan's capital city at a certain point in the early Heisei Era. A time when salarymen escape offices thick with cigarette smoke and the clamor of fax machines to while away their lunch breaks in arcades and deafening pachinko parlors. While at night, the glittering lights of clubs, restaurants, and karaoke bars illuminate "drinking meetings" presided over by domineering bosses and glamorous hostesses. Cheeky Shibuya-Kei and a hundred other J-pop microgenres play everywhere—while on the flip side, underground clubs cater to musical and social misfits of every kind. Here, even amidst the deep recession of the Lost Decade, one can lose oneself entirely in the hedonism of Shinjuku, Shibuya, or Roppongi.

I will admit to a personal fondness for taking walks down ever-evolving Cat Street, and a great interest in partaking of the latest food cart trends while observing the outrageous fashions of the Harajuku District . . .

Perhaps we will see you there, as well? One fervently hopes so!

Until then, I shall remain—

Your Humble and Somewhat Obedient Servant,

Madame Vera.

CONTRIBUTORS

APHRODITE ANAGNOST is a country doctor, horse trainer, and equestrian-book editor at Xenophon Press. She's the author of two novels, *Memoir of a Death Angel* and *Passover*, a 2016 Chanticleer Award winner. Find more at xenophonpress.com or follow her on Instagram @aphroditeanagnostauthor.

● ◐ ○ ○ ○ ○ ◐ ● ●

A.A. BALASKOVITS is the author of the story collections *Strange Folk You'll Never Meet* and *Magic for Unlucky Girls*. An enthusiast of fairy tales and other dark stories, she is currently working on a novel. Find her on Twitter @aabalaskovits and at www.aabalaskovits.com

● ◐ ○ ○ ○ ○ ◐ ● ◐

D FERRARA has been a writer and ghostwriter for more years than she cares to admit. Short stories are her obsession. Inclusion in publications including *The Main Street Anthology, Sanskrit, Storytellers Magazine, The Broadkill Review, MacGuffin Press, Crack the Spine, Green Prints, Amarillo Bay, The Penmen Review, At the Inkwell,* etc. has fed this mania. As editor of the *American Writers Review*, she gets to see wonderful new work regularly. Her script, *Arvin Lindemeyer Takes Canarsie*, won the Oil Valley Film Festival, and was a finalist in both the Hollywood Blvd. Film Festival, and the ASU Screenwriting Contest. See more at www.americanwritersreview.com and www.facebook.com/Dferrarawriting.

Novelist and poet LENORE HART is the author of eight books of fiction, including *The Raven's Bride*, and series editor of the *Night Bazaar* fantastic fiction anthologies. A Shirley Jackson Award finalist, she's received prizes, grants, and fellowships from various arts organizations in the U.S., Ireland, and Germany. A writer for Kevin Anderson & Associates in NYC, she also teaches at the Ossabaw Island Writers Retreat. Find her at: www.lenorehart.com; Facebook @LenoreHartAuthor; Twitter (or 'X', if we must) @Elfair, or Instagram @lenore_hart_author.

REBECCA LANE was telling stories even before she could write. She went on to tell them in grad school, earning an MFA in Creative Writing from NYU. She's been published internationally, and has been active with the S.L.A.T.E. charity for over twenty years, supporting their work on behalf of writers and students. She lives in northeastern Pennsylvania with her family.

DANA MILLER graduated from Wilkes University with an MFA in fiction and screenwriting. Her debut novel, *Twisted Fate*, received a Starred Review from *Publishers Weekly*, and was an Award-Winning Finalist in the Fiction: Romance category of American Book Fest's 2019 Best Book Awards. She lives in Pennsylvania with her husband, son, and one Sphynx cat. She is currently working on her second novel. See more at www.danammiller.com.

Assistant Series Editor FAE TYLER MONTGOMERY is a high school teacher, fashion designer, and freelance editor. She graduated from Swarthmore College with a double major in Art and Fantasy Writing. Her original designs are inspired by myth, fantasy, and period clothing. A Renaissance woman, she prefers to wield pen, needle, and sword in equal measure. Find her fantastical creations at www.instagram.com/faetailor.

CORINNE ALICE NULTON is a teacher, scholar, and horror story writer. As the Writing Center Coordinator at University of Scranton, she helps students cultivate their skills. She's also the drama and poetry editor for *Door Is A Jar* magazine, and has contributed to *Critical Pedagogy in the Language and Writing Classroom*, and has crafted stories for each *Night Bazaar* anthology to date. Her play, *14 Symptoms*, was produced at the Brick Theater's Game Play Festival in 2014. She's currently pursuing a Ph.D. in Composition and Applied Linguistics at Indiana University of Pennsylvania. See more at www.doorisajarmagazine.net.

Nearly fifty of DAVID POYER's bestselling novels and nonfiction books are in print. His work has been published in Japanese, Dutch, Italian, Serbo-Croatian, and Hungarian. After a Navy career and many years teaching at the postgraduate level, he's dialed back to being core faculty at the Ossabaw Island Writer's Retreat and editing at Northampton House Press. His latest novel is *The Academy* (St. Martin's/ Macmillan) and his latest nonfiction book is *Writing in the Age of AI*. His play *Shadowland* has been produced in various venues, including the ZEST Theatre in Zurich; his latest, *Blood Moon*, was adapted from his novella in *The Night Bazaar London*. See more about him and his work at www.poyer.com and on Facebook @DavidPoyerBooks.

Originally from Virginia's Eastern Shore, NAIA POYER holds a BA in art from Swarthmore College and a Masters in East Asian Religions from Harvard University. Poyer currently works at Harvard with undergraduates focusing on East Asian Studies. Also a graphic and book designer, they created the covers for all three *Night Bazaar* anthologies to date, including the Shirley Jackson Award finalist/Ippy cover-design award winner *The Night Bazaar Venice*. "A Fox in the Rookery" is their third story published in the Night Bazaar series. Visit NaiadArtDesign.com, Instagram @NaiadArtDesign, or Facebook @Naiad Design.

●◐◑○○◐○◐●

JIM SCHEERS is the author of a novel about the suburban punk scene, *This Is What You Want, This Is What You Get*. His short story, "Weekly Pass," appeared in the first installment of *The Night Bazaar*. He lives in northeastern Pennsylvania. Find him at www.jimscheers.com or on Twitter @JimScheers.

About Northampton House Press

Established in 2011, Northampton House Press publishes selected fiction, non-fiction, memoir, and poetry. Check out our list at www.northampton-house.com, and Like us on Facebook—"Northampton House Press"—as we showcase more innovative works from brilliant new talents. We can also be found on Twitter @nhousepress and on Instagram at nhousepress.